Not In the Mood

Ariel Henwood

To heartbreak.
You suck, and I hate you, but I can't deny you gave me good material.

1
TRAUMA DUMPLING

"That's it. It's over. Relationship failed. Another one bites the dust." I exhaled hard into the phone like I was doing breathing exercises with a therapist and hauled myself up the front stoop to my apartment like the emotionally bedraggled, birthday-cursed creature I was.

The phone was cradled between my ear and shoulder as I swatted at the twisted strap of my purse, which was doing its best to strangle me on the way to my door. I jiggled it loose, pulled it around front, and did the ritualistic purse-shake to confirm that yes, I did in fact have my keys – because if this day had any more surprises in store for me, I was not above jumping into oncoming traffic.

"Are you sure? Like sure-sure? Like – it's done, done?" Eli's voice crackled through the line. His breathing was ragged, which meant he was probably climbing that giant hill near Sixth and Franklin again. He was a sucker for self-inflicted cardio.

I shoved my key into the lock and threw the door open with more force than intended. It bounced off the wall with a loud *thunk*.

"What do you mean 'am I sure'? Eli. He broke up with me. Through a group text." I stepped inside and kicked the door shut behind me. "On my birthday."

A pause. Then: "Oh. Happy birthday, by the way."

"You're not funny."

"It was a little funny."

I dropped my bag with a dramatic *thud* by the door, peeled off my jacket in the entryway, and stomped toward the kitchen like the whole apartment had personally offended me.

"I'm not going to this dinner tonight," I declared, grabbing the half-full bottle of chardonnay I'd corked last night and yanking it from the fridge. I didn't bother with a glass. Glasses were for people who weren't dumped via digital group humiliation.

"Romy," Eli said, in that way people say your name when they're about to pretend they know what's best for you.

"No. Don't 'Romy' me." I took a huge swig straight from the bottle. Classy. Efficient. Devastating.

I could hear him pause at the other end. He was probably reaching the top of the hill, finally, and leaning on someone's poorly maintained fence. I'd seen him do it a dozen times.

"Did I mention," I said, wiping my mouth with the back of my sleeve, "that the *new girl* – Kelsey or Kayla or whatever – was *in the group text*?"

Silence.

"You're joking," he said finally.

"Eli," I replied calmly, "you can't make this stuff up. My life is the rejected B-plot from a canceled nineties sitcom. This is my legacy. This is what I get for trying to be emotionally available."

"Okay, but like... what was the context of the text?"

"It was a multi-paragraph breakup... sent to a group of five people. Like I was being excommunicated from a friend group I didn't know I was in. It was me, *her*, and three of our mutuals. One of them just responded with 'yo wtf' and a single skull emoji."

I could hear Eli stifling a laugh. Not well, either.

"You're an asshole," I muttered.

"I'm sorry, it's just – *who does that?*"

"Apparently the man I'd been dating for five months. Who – might I add – said he didn't believe in labels but apparently believed in *group texts*." I slumped dramatically onto the couch like a silent film star in emotional ruin. The cushions swallowed me whole. I stared at the ceiling like it owed me something.

"Fine," Eli said after a beat. "Bail on dinner. Did you let Mia know?"

"Of course. I'm not a monster."

"You know how seriously she takes RSVPs."

"I'm pretty sure she keeps a spreadsheet of who's flaked on her and cross-references it with gift bags."

"She's still mad at me for that charity auction two years ago."

"You won the silent auction and didn't pay."

"I thought 'silent' meant it didn't count!"

I let the silence stretch between us for a moment. Then: "I wonder how long she'll not talk to me for not coming to my own birthday dinner."

"Ballpark? A week. Maybe two, if she already told her Instagram followers about the restaurant."

"That tracks."

There was a soft shuffle on the line as Eli's footsteps slowed.

"Chinese or Thai?" He asked casually.

I blinked at the ceiling. "Chinese."

"Be there in thirty," he said, and hung up.

Exactly thirty-four minutes later, a series of muffled thuds echoed through the front door – like someone trying to kick their way in with polite enthusiasm. I could already picture it: Eli, arms full, chin tucked, doing some awkward shoulder-knocking routine like a delivery guy on his first day.

I groaned, peeled myself off the couch like a post-breakup lasagna noodle, and stumbled barefoot to the door. I unlocked it and swung it open to reveal all five foot eleven inches of Eli Reed, carrying roughly three linear feet of brown paper takeout bags across his chest like a human buffet tray.

"How are you even holding those like that?" I asked, grabbing the middle bag and stepping aside to let him in.

"Not well," he grunted, shuffling past me into the kitchen like an exhausted caterer.

"Oh god, I am *so* hungry. Today sucked. This week sucked. Honestly, this month can kiss my ass."

"I know," Eli said, already unpacking with one hand and flicking on the kitchen light with the other. "I've heard all about it. In great detail."

"You know, for someone who claims to be my best friend, I'm not feeling *particularly* emotionally supported right now."

"Do you feel supported *now*?" he asked.

I turned to see him standing at the kitchen counter with something cradled gently in his hands. He pivoted slowly, presenting it to me like a contestant on *The Price is Right.*

A plain white grocery store cake.

In aggressively uneven blue icing, it read: MAYBE NEXT YEAR!

"You *did not*," I whispered, horrified.

"I absolutely did," he grinned.

I smacked his arm, and he immediately doubled over in a fit of unrepentant laughter, nearly dropping the cake.

"Oh my god, Reed, that is – first of all, how did you even get that written so fast? And second, you're a monster."

"I gave the woman behind the counter at Whole Foods fifty bucks to squeeze it in."

"*Fifty?*"

"It's Whole Foods."

"Okay, fair."

We moved the rest of the food to the coffee table in the living room. I plopped down on the floor cross-legged while Eli took his usual spot on the couch, stretching his legs out like he owned the place. Within seconds, the table was completely overtaken by steamy white cartons, each one promising a minor miracle. Chow mein. Potstickers. That weird garlicky broccoli I always pretend I don't like but then inhale.

We didn't speak for the first few minutes – just the soft rustle of cartons and the heavenly sound of lo mein being shoveled into mouths with no regard for dignity.

"I'm not Venmo-ing you for any of this," I said, slurping a noodle between my lips like a woman reborn.

"Wouldn't dream of asking," Eli replied. "I deserve to pay penance for the cake bit."

We ate in companionable silence for another beat, until Eli made a show of dramatically finishing his bite, wiping his mouth with a napkin like he was preparing for a board meeting.

"Okay," he said, serious now. "Show me the fucking text."

I blinked. "What?"

"The breakup text. I want to see it."

"You *want* to see it? Was the retelling of my digital shame not descriptive enough for you?"

"So, you *haven't* deleted it."

I hesitated just long enough.

He grinned. "I know you too well. C'mon. Let me see it. I promise not to laugh."

"You will absolutely laugh."

"I probably will. But only a little. And then I'll comfort you. With more noodles."

I sighed and reached for my phone, feeling both horrified and deeply comforted by the fact that this was our version of friendship. Trauma dumplings and cake-based sarcasm. I pulled up the text, my thumb hovering for a second longer than necessary. The glowing blue bubble of humiliation just *sat* there, like it knew it had power over me. I sighed and chucked my phone onto the couch beside Eli.

He scrambled for it immediately – because of course he did – nearly knocking over a carton of rice in the process.

"They really used the skull emoji," he said, already half-laughing through disbelief.

"They certainly did."

He tapped the screen a few times, eyes scanning.

"No, but seriously, Ro..." His voice softened. "I'm sure we'll laugh about this – hell, *we are* laughing about this, and we'll probably retell it dramatically over cocktails for years to come – but... you didn't deserve this. Especially not today."

I looked over at him. His eyes were serious now, a quiet flicker of warmth behind those vintage-ass glasses he wore like some kind of smug Clark Kent. It caught me off guard.

"Thanks, E," I said, swallowing past the knot in my throat. "It's nice to see you be human once in a while."

"Far and few between. Like a solar eclipse. Enjoy it while it lasts."

I snorted and set down my carton of broccoli beef. My appetite had already started to fade now that I'd spoken the words *group text breakup* aloud more than once.

"I just..." I leaned back until my head made contact with the rug on the living room floor. "I can't believe it happened again. Do men just seek women out to humiliate them? Is that a thing? Like, do they gather somewhere in a secret basement and assign humiliation targets? Because at this point, I swear to God, it's starting to feel like a conspiracy."

"You can't take it personally," Eli said gently.

"Okay, but after *how many* failed relationships do you start to think, 'Hmm... maybe *I'm* the problem?'"

He didn't respond right away. Just picked up my abandoned broccoli beef like it was his now and casually speared a stalk with his chopsticks like a therapist stalling before dropping a hard truth.

"Look who you're asking," he finally said.

"When's the last time *you* got laid?"

"Leave me alone."

I smirked, but it didn't last. The weight of it came rushing back.

"I've been dating since I was sixteen, Eli. *Sixteen.* I turned thirty-two today. That's – what, math? – sixteen years of trying and feeling and falling and... for what?" I jolted upright and threw my hands up, nearly knocking over a soy sauce packet. "To get a breakup birthday text?"

"*Group* text," he corrected, deadpan.

"Thank you."

"You're welcome."

I picked up the wine bottle, stared into it like it held secrets. "I'm too old for this, E. I can't do it anymore. My future children be damned. It's not worth it. I can't go through this again. The apps, the endless swiping, the God-awful bios – 'fluent in sarcasm' isn't a personality, Brad. Neither is 'dog dad.'"

"Preach."

"Then you finally meet in person – which is always a gamble–"

"Always," he echoed.

"–And then comes the awkward small talk, the second date, the third, the *sex*, and hoping their junk isn't
weird–"

"That's a universal fear, by the way."

"–And then thinking maybe, *just maybe*, this is it. The guy who doesn't mind a label. The guy who doesn't still live with his parents. The guy who – God help us – doesn't *hate the clitoris.*"

Eli laughed. Actually, full-on *laughed*. "That's still

your best worst-date story. Hands down."

"Thank you."

"You're welcome."

I stared at him for a moment, letting the silence stretch. He looked back at me like he was about to say something important, something grounding – but instead, he picked up another carton and opened it like we weren't unraveling my romantic history on his lap.

"I just don't have it in me anymore," I said, quieter now. "I give up. The universe wins. Romy Becker dies alone. End of story."

He didn't argue. Didn't roll his eyes or give me the stock "you'll find someone" pep talk everyone thinks they're contractually obligated to say to single women in their thirties. He just passed me an egg roll.

And then, casually, like we were discussing the weather instead of my personal apocalypse: "We should make a podcast about this."

I blinked. "What do you mean?"

"I mean," he said, popping a wonton into his mouth, "we should make a podcast about this."

I tilted my head. "You're not nearly as jaded as I am when it comes to love."

"Well," he shrugged, "nobody is."

"Exactly. You still have hope. You still, like, believe in the possibility and shit. You still have that dumb little twinkle in your eye that life hasn't beaten out of you yet."

"That twinkle came with the prescription." He tapped the corner of his glasses with his chopsticks.

Okay, fair. The man could sell used optimism if he tried.

"But my boat's not that different from yours," he added. "Remember Laurel?"

I made a face. "I'd successfully scrubbed that name from my memory."

"Wish I could. She's the reason I haven't had sex in so long."

"It's been two months, Eli. Calm down. Some of us *have hobbies*."

"Two months in dog years is a lot."

I snorted and jabbed at a sad-looking chunk of broccoli at the bottom of a random container. "I still can't believe she told you she was gay *while* you were inside her."

"My penis will never emotionally recover from that moment."

We both cackled, the sound a little too loud for the size of my living room. The walls practically vibrated with secondhand shame.

But then he leaned forward, elbows on knees, voice shifting just enough to make me look at him again.

"I'm serious, though. People need to hear this stuff. That love doesn't just suck *for them*. That their worth isn't measured by how many likes their profile gets or whether their mom's best friend's niece got married before them."

I paused, chewing slowly. The idea was outrageous. And yet... comforting.

"Yeah... true. I mean, it wouldn't be that hard. Just us. Talking. Like we always do."

"And think of the passive income," he added, with a grin that could sell me anything, including overpriced podcast microphones.

I nodded slowly, wiping my fingers on a napkin. "We record the conversations we already have. Which, let's be honest, are unhinged."

"Exactly."

I bit my lip, hesitating. The idea felt a little too big for my post-breakup haze. "I don't know, Eli. This isn't exactly a peak innovation moment for me. I'm staring down middle age while emotionally pancaked. I'm not in the mood."

He hesitated. Then broke into the kind of smile that made his dimples pop through his scruffy facial hair, the kind of smile that made it way too easy to forget what kind of mess I was in.

"What?" I asked, already suspicious. "Why do you look like you just solved a crossword in ink?"

"That's it," he said.

"What's it?"

"That's what we'll call it."

I blinked. "Call *what*?"

He grinned wider. "The podcast. *Not in the Mood.*"

And just like that, the worst birthday of my life got its own punchline.

2
WEAPONIZED OPTIMISM

I woke to the kind of headache that pulsed behind my eyes like a strobe light. A low-grade, chardonnay-induced hangover. Manageable. Familiar. The kind that whispered, *you made choices last night, didn't you?*

For a few merciful seconds, I was blissfully unaware. Just a body in a bed, cocooned in warmth and wrapped in a slightly damp comforter that still smelled vaguely of birthday candles and sugar.

Then, the memory returned.

My birthday.

I groaned, face-first into the pillow, and yanked the down blanket over my head like I could reverse time if I just wished hard enough. But it was no use. The highlight reel was already playing: the breakup group text. The cake. The mortifying toast I'd given to myself after three glasses of wine and half a Xanax. A solo standing ovation, no less.

I rolled onto my back and stared up at the ceiling, where a faint crack split across the plaster like the universe mocking me in the shape of a broken wishbone.

My romantic life was a garbage fire. And I was the idiot gleefully tossing in more kerosene.

Why was it so easy for other people?

My mind, ever the masochist, conjured Mia Milanova. My best friend (after Eli), whose name sounded like a luxury perfume line and whose life looked like the inside of an Anthropologie catalog. She'd followed the formula: college, casual flings, self-discovery, therapy, a brief stint identifying as a professional candle maker. One time, she *accidentally* went on a date with a guy she met at a silent meditation retreat and didn't realize he was celibate until date four. She stayed with him for three more weeks just to "see what the sex *would* have been like, energetically."

That's Mia for you.

Then she met Etienne. A French chef with a jawline so sharp you could slice a baguette on it. I remembered the first time I met him. He wore a scarf indoors and pronounced "croissant" correctly without irony. He once told a bartender he was "wounded by the lack of cognac." Mia had found that charming. I had found it grounds for violence.

They met when she was twenty-six. Married by twenty-nine. Now she was thirty-two, just like me, and trying for a baby.

And I...

I was peeling my face off a pillowcase, unsure if I'd taken off my mascara or if it had simply migrated to my cheekbones. I sat up slowly, clocked the crumpled tissue beside me, and decided the night before had ended in at least one cry. Possibly two.

I couldn't help but compare. Even though I hated myself for it.

I peeled myself out of bed and shuffled to the bathroom, turning the shower up to "scorch the sins off my skin" hot. I stepped in and tried to imagine I was being baptized – reborn as a woman who didn't cry at rom-com trailers or drunk-text her exes under the guise of "closure."

No more dating apps, I told myself. *No more algorithmically-approved disappointments.*

Let the universe do its thing. Let serendipity – or whatever smug force controlled this shit – find me when I was *not* actively begging for it. Wasn't that how it was supposed to work?

Twenty minutes later, freshly steamed like a lobster, I stood in front of the mirror brushing my teeth and wondering how I'd become the kind of person who owned three kinds of dry shampoo but couldn't remember to buy milk. I half-heartedly blow-dried my curls and thanked my mother for passing down model-tier cheekbones. It was genetic luck, not confidence. I was barely holding it together, emotionally or hairstylistically.

Outside, San Francisco was finally waking up from its September heat coma. October here meant soft breezes, fog creeping in like gossip, and that one magical week where you could wear a sweater without sweating through it. I pulled on my favorite oversized knit, black skinny jeans (which I will die in before I give them up), and my scratched-up Doc Martens.

I glanced out the window – just a sliver of Coit Tower peeking through the fog. I was a rare Bay Area native, which meant, yes, I worked in tech. At LumenLoop, a mental health start-up with kombucha on tap and enough buzzwords to make you black out from synergy.

I owned several Patagonia jackets. I would not

elaborate further.

I gave the comforter a dramatic fluff, declared the bed "made", and headed out to the living room, bracing for the remnants of last night.

Shockingly? Not a disaster. No cups balancing on corners. No soy sauce stains on the rug. No trail of rice leading to my shame.

Eli must've cleaned up before leaving.

He did that sometimes – when he felt guilty or just liked pretending to be the kind of person who folded blankets. Either way, I was grateful. My only contribution to tidiness was not dying in the middle of the floor.

I walked into the kitchen and there it was: the cake. Or what was left of it. A massacred wedge was missing. Fork stabbed into the side like a fallen soldier. I stood there, arms crossed and tried not to re-live it. But of course, I did.

The breakup group text. The pity party. The part where I cried mid-bite and Eli said, "You still look hot, just like...weird hot."

I groaned. My phone had hurt me too much in the last 24 hours. But I needed bagels. And bagels meant Eli.

I found my phone, miraculously not dead, abandoned on the coffee table like it too needed space from me.

I tapped out a message on my screen: *Need bagels to soak up the wine from last night.* I stared at the message, balancing on one foot like that would summon him faster. The dots appeared.

This time ur Venmoing me.

I hearted the message and unlocked the door. In the

kitchen, I poured orange juice into two mismatched glasses – because I knew better than to expect Eli to bring his own beverage. The man had a strict anti-paying-for-liquid stance.

"Why would I spend money on a beverage when water is free?" He'd once said while I watched him drink *tap water* with French toast.

"You've got to lighten up, Reed," I'd said through a mouthful of Denver omelet.

My stomach gurgled ominously. I paused at the sink, hand on my abdomen, trying to decide if I was going to throw up or just regret being alive for five minutes. A chardonnay burp escaped. I winced.

"Thirty-two," I muttered to myself, like a confession. I carried the juice to the coffee table, sat cross-legged, and took a long sip, trying to chase away the pit in my chest.

I hadn't expected to have my life together by thirty-two. But I'd hoped I'd at least be *closer*. Maybe dating someone who used a coaster. Maybe on the way to something permanent.

My dad never asked about my love life. We talked about articles he read, how Sacramento was too hot this year, whether I was getting enough sleep. When I visited, he and his partner would offer wine and let me exist without expectations. They were like a safe house for the emotionally sunburned.

My mom, on the other hand, cared. She didn't pressure me, exactly. But she always asked. Always wanted to know if there was anyone new. And when I told her no, every time, she'd do this sigh. This long, wistful breath that said, *well, maybe next time.*

Sometimes I wanted to scream: *I'm trying, okay?* Other times I wanted to throw my phone into the Bay.

The front door creaked.

"They had the good bagels," Eli called, pushing it open like he lived here.

"Asiago!?" I called back.

"Got the last two."

"You're my favorite person this week."

"I better be," he said, dropping the bag on the coffee table. "You cried on me last night."

"I was drunk," I muttered, unwrapping the bagel.

"You were wiping your mascara on my hoodie."

"Tomato, tomahto."

I loved Eli. Not in the write-it-in-my-journal kind of way, and certainly not in the way I loved *men* – which was typically messy and short-lived – but in the way you love someone who's always there, who always gets it, who makes life easier just by existing.

Not that I'd ever said that to him.

We had a rhythm. A shared language of side-eyes and sarcasm. I'd never felt more myself around someone than I did around Eli, which was both comforting and occasionally concerning. He was annoyingly thoughtful – the kind of person who remembered something I'd said once, offhandedly, while standing in line for ice cream three months ago and would bring it up in passing like it was natural to be so considerate.

He was also a catch. Objectively speaking. If Glen Powell had a nerdier younger brother with better taste in music and zero social media footprint, it'd be Eli. I had no idea why he wasn't in a relationship. Maybe he liked it that way. Maybe he was just better at being alone than the rest of us.

"So," Eli said as he plopped onto the couch, legs spread out like he'd invented leisure. "How are we feeling?"

I took my usual spot on the floor, cross-legged, bagel in hand. The crinkly deli paper crackled like firewood.

"Can you ask that without sounding like a condescending prig?"

"Oh. So, it's one of *those* mornings."

"I don't know," I muttered, staring down at the asiago swirl. "I just feel stuck. Like I'm doing something wrong. Like I'm the problem."

"I can't imagine you being the problem," he said with a full mouth, barely pausing before groaning into his next bite. "Jesus Christ. What do they put in their cream cheese? Ecstasy?"

"Really? That's the takeaway?" I lifted an eyebrow. "Because according to Smith, I was *definitely* the problem."

"God. I forgot his name was Smith. That's not even a name. That's a placeholder in a legal drama."

"That's not the point," I said, chewing slowly. The bagel was offensively good. Creamy, warm, a little too perfect for my fragile state. I managed not to make a sound about it. I had dignity. Barely.

"Wait a second," Eli said, dropping the bagel like it offended him and reaching into his hoodie pocket. "Continue."

"Continue what?"

"Speaking."

"What the hell are you doing?"

"We're recording," he announced, placing his phone

on the coffee table like it was a sacred object.

"You *can't* be serious. I'm baring my soul here and your first thought is *content*?"

"Your pain humors me," he said with a shrug. "Let's see what happens."

"Masochist."

"Come on," he said, taking a more composed bite. "You were saying you're the problem?"

"I think I might just be... sensitive. And mildly poisoned. I'm still kind of hungover."

"You were cradling the chardonnay like it was a dying child, Romy."

"Was not."

"I have photographic evidence."

"My point is," I said, sitting upright like that would somehow make me sound more credible – or at the very least distract Eli from scrolling through his camera roll, searching for what I could only assume was the photo of me holding a wine bottle like it was a wounded animal. "What if I *am* the problem, Eli? Like, what if I'm just... fundamentally unlovable. In a hot way."

He didn't even look up. "That's not a thing."

"It should be. I'm quirky and emotionally magnificent. It's basically my entire personality now."

He finally glanced over, chewing thoughtfully. "You're not unlovable, Romy. You're... preferentially aggressive."

I blinked. "Excuse me?"

"You don't dislike people. You disqualify them with Olympic-level precision."

"That's absurd." A beat. "I once unmatched a guy because he used 'lol' twice in a sentence."

Eli raised an eyebrow. "Was the sentence at least threatening?"

"No, it was like: 'Lol I had fun tonight lol.' I panicked. It was too much optimism."

"For argument's sake," Eli said, licking cream cheese off his thumb like a philosopher at brunch, "let's say you *are* the villain."

I pointed my index finger in warning. "Fine. But only if I can be the kind of villain with really good eyebrows."

"You already are."

"Thank you."

He set his bagel down with ceremony. "But doesn't the villain still deserve to find their person?"

I let out a groan and flopped backward onto the rug like I was auditioning to be a human spill. "That's the million-dollar question."

"No," he said, leaning back against the couch, "the million-dollar question is why you're bending over backwards to prove you're the issue. It's like you're compiling evidence for a trial that hasn't even happened yet."

"I'm not compiling evidence–"

"You're building a PowerPoint presentation for people called 'Why I Suck: A Memoir.'"

"I was just talking about men," I huffed. "And now you're dragging women into it too?! *People*? Really?"

"Oh, unclench. I'm saying *you* have to realize that sometimes – most of the time – you're not the problem."

"That feels like a cop-out."

"Fine," he said, shrugging. "Even if you *are* the problem, you're just the problem for *that person*. You might be the literal solution to someone else. Like, emotionally speaking."

I squinted at him. "You're being weirdly insightful."

"I am the Oracle," he said, touching his temples. "Bow before my wisdom."

"You're lucky I'm too hungover to throw this bagel at you."

We paused.

I exhaled. "Honestly, it wasn't even the breakup itself that wrecked me. It was the tone."

Eli sighed like a man settling into a familiar monologue. "And the rant continues."

"No, listen – it was disturbingly *hopeful*. Like, he tried to sound emotionally evolved while simultaneously stabbing me in the chest."

"Weaponized optimism."

"Exactly!" I shot a finger toward him. "It was all, 'I care about you so much and I hope you find the love you deserve,' and meanwhile he's sending this in a group text with the other girl included."

Eli recoiled. "He broke up with you in a group thread *with the next contestant* already in the room. That takes... something. Was he planning a live Q&A after?"

"It was less of a breakup and more of a TED Talk," I muttered. "Like, *we're all growing. Especially me. Away from you.*"

"That's not a breakup, that's brand management."

"THANK YOU!" I waved my arms. "Like I was supposed to slow clap and cry tears of personal growth while being publicly dumped in a chat with my replacement."

Eli shook his head, deadpan. "He should've just sent a Google Calendar invite titled *'Romy's Emotional Spiral*

Begins Here.'"

I wheezed out a laugh and sank further into the rug. The fibers scratched the side of my face. It felt oddly comforting. Like surrendering.

"At least if this podcast takes off," I murmured, "I can monetize my heartbreak. Maybe get a mattress sponsor out of it."

Eli raised his glass of orange juice. "To turning pain into passive income."

Eli left not long after our bagel therapy session, which was probably for the best. I needed time to spiral in solitude – proper solitude – the kind where you lie dramatically on your couch like a Victorian widow and whisper "why me" into a throw pillow. I needed space to overanalyze every romantic failure I'd ever had, mentally chart a timeline of all the red flags I'd ignored and convince myself that I was destined to be the fun, slightly bitter aunt at future dinner parties who brings a bottle of wine and unsolicited opinions.

Mia had texted me a few times, but I wasn't emotionally stable enough to handle someone whose life looked like an Instagram reel curated by the Gods. With my luck, she was texting to announce she was pregnant with her beautiful French husband's inevitably bilingual, model-faced baby.

Maybe Etienne has a tiny penis, I thought, and felt instantly, profoundly better.

I was shoulder-deep into my pity-party by the time the afternoon hit. Wrapped in a throw blanket, cradling a lukewarm mug of tea I wasn't drinking, I let season one of *Gilmore Girls* wash over me like a warm bath of other people's problems. It was comforting. Familiar. Slightly manic.

My phone pinged with a new text. I stared at it for a second, debating. If it was Mia, I was fully committed to ghosting her for the next four to six business days.

But it wasn't Mia. It was Eli.

Made the teaser trailer for the pod. Lmk what u think.

I opened the attachment and pressed play, fully prepared to cringe at the sound of my own voice. Instead, I laughed. It was sharp. It was chaotic. It was... actually kind of great.

It was us. Unfiltered. Unhinged. Weirdly magnetic.

I sat with it for a moment, then muttered, "Fuck it."

I tapped over to my home screen and opened TikTok.

3
DELUSIONAL PARTY

I could feel it was Monday before I even opened my eyes. Not because of some sixth sense or internal clock – just because Mondays have a vibe. The air gets heavier. Your bones revolt. You start bargaining your soul by 7:03 AM.

I'd figured it out around the time I turned thirty: the reason Mondays hit so hard was because I wasn't doing something I actually enjoyed for a living. Not even close. And worse, I wasn't sure that was even possible anymore.

How do you monetize what you love without turning it into something you eventually hate?

That's a question for people with trust funds and energy. I had neither.

I'd been working at LumenLoop – a mid-sized tech startup that wanted to "disrupt the emotional well-being space," whatever the hell that meant – for two years. My title fluctuated depending on who asked. Officially, I was the People Ops Director. Unofficially, I was a professional Slack babysitter. My days mostly consisted of rewriting PTO policies in a "gender-neutral, trauma-informed tone," fielding weirdly intense complaints about shared fridge etiquette, and occasionally sitting in on all-hands meetings to nod supportively.

I knew I was overqualified. I stayed for the health insurance. And the fact that I could leave at 3:58 PM every day and no one would stop me.

But it was never a job I *chose*. It was a job I kind of... slipped into. Let's be honest – no little girl grows up dreaming of a career in HR. Unless she's a sociopath.

I was still face-down in my pillow when I reached blindly for my phone and yanked it off the nightstand.

The lock screen was chaos. Dozens – no, *hundreds* – of notifications stacked on top of each other like a mini digital panic attack. I blinked. Sat up. Shoved the hair out of my eyes.

No. Fucking. Way.

I scrolled. And scrolled again. Then again, just to make sure I wasn't hallucinating or accidentally logged into someone else's phone.

The teaser Eli made had gone... *mildly viral*. Like, actual-not-made-up numbers. Overnight.

I didn't think. I just hit "Call."

"Eli! Eli Eli Eli!" I stage-whisper-screeched into the receiver, bouncing to the edge of the mattress like a caffeinated squirrel.

"What?" Came the reply, muffled and resentful. He sounded like he was speaking through six pillows.

"We went viral!" I whispered, except it came out as more of a hiss-scream hybrid. "Kind of!"

"What?"

"The clip! From the podcast – or, whatever we're calling it. It has over ten thousand views. In, like, *nine* hours. And there are comments. Real people. With opinions."

There was a pause at the other end. A long one. I could hear him blinking.

"Romy, it's six thirty in the morning."

"I know! Isn't that great?"

"That's not what I meant."

I flung the blanket off me like I was shedding my old life. "I know I shouldn't care this much, but people are actually responding. Like, people get it. They're commenting stuff like, 'Omg, it's like you pulled this out of my diary.' Someone said they sent it to their therapist! Eli. That means we're either geniuses or deeply unwell."

"You've always said those aren't mutually exclusive."

"I'm just saying – we struck a nerve. And we didn't even try. What if we *actually tried*?"

I heard him groan; the kind of groan that meant he'd sat up. "Are you going to do this all day?"

"Depends. Are we recording a real episode or what?"

"You're already spiraling, aren't you."

"Obviously."

"Please don't make merch."

"I already have a Canva tab open."

A few minutes later I'd opened TikTok again while brushing my teeth and was scrolling through the comments with foamy urgency:

LITERALLY SOBBING, WHO GAVE YOU THE RIGHT
is that girl okay
this is the first time i've felt seen since 2020

My brain did not know what to do with this. It was jarring. Disorienting. Deeply validating in a way that made me vaguely uncomfortable.

The clip wasn't even our best material. It was just me drunkenly ranting about being the villain in my own dating life while Eli deadpanned something about my "preferential aggression." But apparently, that hit a nerve.

Not to mention, it's weird as hell when people start relating to the worst parts of you. These weren't carefully crafted thinkpieces. These were ramblings about emotional dysfunction and unmatched trauma humor – and *they were resonating*.

Was this what connection felt like? Was this how influencers started?

Please, God, don't let me become an influencer, I thought as I screenshot a comment that said *"she's so unwell but in a fuckable way."* I smiled big – like actually *smiled*, mid-toothbrush – and realized I'd been brushing for nearly seven straight minutes.

I was on my second sad desk coffee of the morning, poking at a stale croissant with a sense of betrayal, when the full reality of it hit me: people were listening to my voice while I sat here trying to rephrase a sentence about bereavement leave.

The contrast was jarring.

One part of my brain was still in HR mode, drafting an email titled "Friendly Reminder: Please Don't Microwave Fish in the Breakroom." Another part – the part still buzzing from internet attention – was scrolling TikTok in a minimized window, watching the views climb.

14.2K.

14.7K.

15.1K.

I refreshed. Again.

A new comment: *I feel so seen. It's embarrassing. Pls make more.*

I stared at the comment like it had personally handed me a shot of espresso. That weirdly sharp, buzzy feeling surged in my chest again: the realization that strangers, actual people, had heard me say things I usually reserved for 2 AM vent sessions and post-breakup meltdowns. And they *understood.*

I texted Eli: *"Emotionally magnificent" on a hoodie. Just think about it.*

He replied after a beat: *i'm blocking u*

I grinned and set my phone down, ignoring the looming Slack message from a product manager asking if it was "appropriate" for a coworker to share astrological compatibility charts during meetings. (Short answer: no. Long answer: only if you're a Virgo).

By noon, I needed air. Not the kind from the AC vent above my desk, but the kind you breathe when you're contemplating mild career rebellion and the possibility of becoming a semi-ironic micro-celebrity on the internet.

I texted Mia: *Want to grab a drink tonight?*

She replied: *Girl. Always.* Her response came with three champagne emojis.

I leaned back in my chair, trying to focus on the spreadsheet open in front of me. But the screen blurred a little as my mind wandered.

People were listening. Not just out of boredom, but because something I said made them feel less alone. I didn't even *mean* to do that. I was just being my usual trainwreck self.

And now they wanted more.

The idea made my stomach twist in the best possible way.

That night, Mia and I met at a trendy bar in San Francisco's Financial District – the kind of place where the drinks came in mismatched vintage glassware and cost more than my weekly grocery budget. We both worked nearby, just a few blocks from each other, so it didn't take much effort to coordinate. A rare luxury in this city.

I got there first, slipping past a bachelorette party already one espresso martini too deep, and scoped out a corner table away from the worst of the happy hour crowd. You know the type: dudes in Allbirds talking about IPOs like foreplay, women laughing a little too loudly like they were auditioning to be cast as "chill coworker" in a workplace sitcom. It was like watching a mating ritual on fast-forward. No one looked like they wanted to be there, but everyone was pretending like it was the highlight of their week.

Mia arrived in a cloud of effortless elegance and passive judgment. A few heads turned as she walked through the bar – mostly tech bros in quarter-zips who instinctively straightened their Patagonia vests as she passed. She was the kind of woman who had presence. She didn't even have to try.

I stood to hug her. She smelled like citrus and generational wealth.

"For the millionth time, I'm so sorry about the dinner," I said as we pulled apart.

"Honestly, it's the only excuse that would've worked. A breakup via *group text*?" She shuddered as she slipped off her trench coat – Burberry, because of course it was – and draped it neatly over the back of her chair. The lining even had that distinctive plaid I'd only ever seen in Instagram ads and Vogue spreads. "I need something bubbly," she sighed, grabbing the drink menu and scanning it like she already knew what she wanted but was giving the menu a fair shot anyway.

I sipped my whiskey – on the rocks, naturally – letting the slow burn chase away the tension in my chest. I'd felt jittery all day, like my skin didn't fit quite right.

Mia and I had known each other for years. We met back when I had a fleeting but deeply committed idea to start a women-only social club in the city. It lasted all of six months, but it gave me Mia, and honestly, that alone made it worth the burnout and the poorly attended rooftop brunches.

She was stupid beautiful – like, offensively pretty in a way that made me question if God had favorites. She was one of those rare women who could pull off a chin-length bob without it making her look twelve. Winged eyeliner. A swipe of nude lipstick. That was it. Meanwhile I still hadn't figured out how to properly part my hair.

And of course, she was brilliant, too. She did something in data analytics at one of the bigger tech companies – one with a name that sounded like a made-up word and probably paid its interns six figures. I'd tried to understand her job once. Gave up halfway through her explanation. She was a quiet powerhouse, the kind of person who could destroy you with a look and then gently explain how your calendar invite could be "better optimized."

A server approached and Mia ordered champagne using the correct French pronunciation, like she'd been born in a vineyard and educated by sommeliers. She nailed the fake accent she'd perfected after several trips to France with Etienne. I rolled my eyes fondly.

"So," she said after the server left. "how's it been otherwise?"

I filled her in on the podcast. The clip. The TikTok explosion.

"Forty-two thousand views?!" she choked, nearly spitting out her water, before recovering with a smooth sip like it was all part of her process.

"I mean, should I hire a publicist or...?"

"Delusional party, table for one."

"We already have people making stitches of the clip."

"What's a stitch?"

"It's when someone takes part of your video and adds their own commentary. Like a remix, but for feelings."

She nodded like she cared, which I appreciated. I took another sip of my drink and let the warmth settle in my chest. I'd needed this. Not just the alcohol – the conversation. The normalcy.

"So, what's the end game here?"

"Honestly? No clue. I didn't really take it seriously when Eli suggested it. But now... people are responding. And it's not just bots or weird men with anime avatars. It's women. Women like me. Saying they feel seen."

Mia raised a perfectly groomed brow. "Oh, Eli."

"Don't start."

"You two just need to fuck and get it over with."

"Absolutely not." I nearly dropped my glass. "It'd be like fucking a brother."

"You don't have a brother."

"Yeah, well, he *feels* like one."

Mia wasn't convinced. She arched her eyebrow even higher, which I hadn't known was physically possible.

"It's not like that," I said, waving a hand. "I could give you a million reasons why it wouldn't work."

"Give me three. Go."

I sighed. "Easy. First of all, the timing has never been right. When we met, I was with Derek. Remember Derek?"

She grimaced. "Trainwreck in a leather jacket."

"Exactly. And Eli was with someone. Then the break-ups. Then I was with someone. We've basically never been single and on the prowl at the same time."

"Except now."

I ignored her and swirled the ice in my glass. "Second, we're comfortable. We have this rhythm. It works. He's not chaos. He's... the person I call when my life's falling apart. I don't want to make him the reason it *falls* apart."

"That's two. What's number three?"

I hesitated. "Because I think I'd ruin it."

Mia stared at me over the rim of her champagne flute.

"I mean it," I said. "We have something really rare. We're a constant for each other. No pressure, no expectations. If I caught feelings, that dynamic would shift, and I can't risk that. Eli is safe. He's my buoy in a storm."

"What about me?"

"You don't have a penis."

"You don't know that."

I snorted. "My point is, I'd rather have Eli as a forever friend than risk it all for a maybe."

Mia swirled her champagne, watching the bubbles rise like they might hold answers. "You can't tell me you haven't thought about how big it is, though."

"Mia!"

She grinned, unbothered. "Come on. You've wondered."

I opened my mouth to protest – and closed it again. I hadn't thought about Eli like *that*. Not really. I mean, sure, he had arms. And a voice. And sometimes said things that made me feel seen in a way that felt... dangerous. But that didn't mean I wanted to climb him like a rock wall. Right?

"God, you are *deranged*."

"I'm right."

And the worst part?

I *had* wondered.

But I wasn't about to admit that.

"Anyway," I said, gently steering the conversation away from my own spiral, "what's going on with you? How's Etienne?"

Mia's posture shifted, just enough to notice if you knew her well – and I did. Her eye contact dropped, her fingers traced the rim of her champagne flute like it was a worry stone, and I felt the mood dim like someone had drawn a curtain in the room.

"He's fine," she said, with a little too much brightness. "Work is crazy, but good. The restaurant got an amazing review in the *Chronicle* last week."

"I saw that!" I said, maybe too quickly, like I could drag the energy back into the light. "They said something about his duck confit being 'life-altering,' which feels dramatic, but also on brand for San Francisco food writers."

"Yeah. So... naturally, he's been on a high," she said, a little laugh catching in her throat.

Then she paused.

The silence between us felt like someone pressing the mute button on the whole bar.

"Talking about your husband always makes me want a baguette," I offered, in a weak attempt to resuscitate the conversation with a joke.

Mia gave me a flat look. "Is that racist?"

"I think it's more complimentary than racist."

She rolled her eyes, but the tension didn't ease. If anything, her smile was quieter now. Not real. Her attention returned to the bubbles rising in her glass like they were delivering stock market updates.

"I don't know," she murmured, voice suddenly fragile. "I've just been... mentally checked out the last week or two."

I leaned forward, the noise of the bar fading behind her voice. "Mia, what's up?"

She blinked hard, shook her head like she wanted to chase away the emotion, but I saw it – *that* look. Eyes slick with something unshed. She swiped the corner of her eye with her fingertip like she was dusting off something imaginary.

"Oh, it's – it's nothing," she said, but her voice cracked around the word. "I just... I thought I was pregnant. Again."

"Oh." I sat up straighter, suddenly off-balance. "Oh, Mia."

"I got my period four days ago," she added quietly, like that one sentence was a thunderclap. Like saying it out loud made it heavier.

"I am so, so sorry." My hand moved across the table, automatically finding hers. I gave it a gentle squeeze, and she held on for a second before pulling away and tucking her hands into her lap.

Part of me wanted to say, *why didn't you tell me sooner?* But I didn't. Because deep down I knew the answer: this was the kind of thing you kept quiet until it was real, or safe, or over.

"I didn't want to say anything until I was sure," she said, as if reading my thoughts. "And I don't know – I just can't believe it happened again."

"It's not your fault," I said, my voice soft. "it's not anyone's fault. Sometimes it just... takes time."

Mia nodded, but her expression didn't change. "I know. I *know*. But it's hard not to feel like something's wrong with me. Everyone else makes it look so easy. My phone's just a constant slideshow of bump updates and gender reveals, and first birthday cakes shaped like animals."

"Ugh. The fondant animal cakes." I wrinkled my nose. "Why are babies eating sculpted jungle scenes? It feels disrespectful to the bakery industry."

That got a small laugh out of her. Just a breath. But I'll take it.

"Except your baby," I added, pointing at her with mock severity. "Yours will be chic and tasteful and somehow wearing a cashmere beanie by the time it's three hours old."

"God willing." She sighed and looked back down at her champagne like maybe the bubbles would give her some kind of answer. "I just don't know what to do."

And just like that, I felt like an idiot.

I'd been consumed all day about a stupid TikTok clip and the imagined potential of a podcast – meanwhile, my best friend was quietly unraveling in her multi-million apartment in Pacific Heights, quietly carrying a hope she couldn't even speak out loud until it broke.

"Have you talked to a doctor?" I asked carefully.

"They said it's too early to start running tests. We haven't been trying for long enough. They want us to give it another three months."

"Well," I said, slowly, "that's something. That means there's still time. That they think it's possible."

"Yeah." She nodded, but it sounded like resignation, not hope.

There was a long, soft pause between us. I wanted to fix it. To say something comforting or clever or profound. But I wasn't equipped. Not for this.

So, I just sat with her.

Let the silence stretch.

Watched the candlelight flicker between us on the table, reflected in her glass.

We didn't need to fill the space. Not all moments were meant to be talked over.

Eventually, Mia sniffed once, cleared her throat, and set down her champagne.

"Okay," she said. "let's go split a brownie sundae the size of my head and pretend sugar is a healing agent."

I stood immediately. "You're speaking my love

language."

She smiled, just a little. "That and trauma-bonding."

"Honestly, it's how all my best friendships start."

We walked out into the cool San Francisco night, the fog curling at our ankles like a cat, and for a moment, the world felt quiet. Still. Like maybe we'd both be okay, in wildly different ways. Eventually.

As we reached the corner and waited for the light to change, Mia slipped her arm through mine.

"Just promise me you won't ignore it if the friendship between you and Eli ever starts to feel like something else."

I opened my mouth to protest – and didn't. Instead, I rolled my eyes so hard they nearly fell out of my head. "It won't."

"Sure, sure. And don't make me be the maid of honor when you inevitably marry your podcast co-host."

I groaned but didn't let go.

We crossed the street together – two women, two drinks in, quietly holding each other up.

4
DATING IS A MINEFIELD

"I think this setup works," Eli said, adjusting a cable with casual confidence. "Your apartment is way quieter than mine, so I doubt we'll pick up any background noise."

I glanced around. "Eli, we're literally sitting on the floor of my closet right now."

"Exactly." He raised an arm and gestured toward my hanging sweaters, a few of which were gently brushing the top of his head. "These bad boys are excellent for soundproofing. Textiles, Romy. Nature's acoustic paneling."

"If you say so," I muttered, crossing my legs under me and adjusting my posture like a kid at summer camp who just found out they're bunking with the counselor who brings their guitar everywhere.

"I'm an *actual* audio engineer," Eli said, side-eyeing me. "And yet you still don't trust me."

"It's not that I don't trust you, I just... this is weird. We're in my *closet*. There are probably scarves older than this laptop in here."

He smirked. "Would you feel better if we played seven minutes in heaven first?"

"Get away from me."

He chuckled and turned to his laptop, the screen

glowing softly in the small space between us. "Okay, so. Do we know what format we're doing? Slightly scripted? Totally off the cuff? I asked you to think about this, did you decide?"

And of course, when he asked me a week ago, I hadn't thought about it. I'd been too busy spiraling about the TikTok comments, doom-scrolling pregnancy announcements, and staring at my fridge like it owed me money.

"I think we should have a topic to start," I said, hoping I sounded like someone with a plan. "Just so we're not rambling in here for three hours and end up with eight usable minutes."

Eli grinned. "You're a natural."

He clicked a few keys with the ease of someone who actually knew what half of those buttons did. I leaned over to peek at the screen and instantly regretted it. The audio program looked like a spaceship control panel. Colorful sound waves bounced across it like digital heartbeats, and I immediately decided I'd never be able to touch it without causing an explosion.

Eli adjusted the microphone stand in front of me and gave it a quick tap. "Alright. We're live."

"*WAIT, WE'RE LIVE?*"

He laughed. "No, no. I mean we're recording."

"Jesus Christ, Eli. You can't say that! My cortisol just spiked."

"Relax. I can edit all of this in post."

"Post?"

"Post-production."

I paused. "I'm scared."

"Of what?"

NOT IN THE MOOD

"Of sounding stupid!" I flailed dramatically. "I already hate the sound of my own voice. What if I say something dumb and people make TikToks about it?"

"Too late. You're already the internet's emotionally magnificent queen."

I raised a hand like I was going to swat him. "Don't you dare. It's too easy."

He nudged my knee. "Just pretend like the mic's not even here. It's just us. Like always."

Which, to be fair, was true. We'd had this exact kind of conversation a hundred times. The only difference now was that there was a mic in front of my face and a growing crowd of strangers online who might actually hear it.

No pressure.

I exhaled, adjusted my posture, and said with as much fake confidence as I could muster:

"Welcome to *Not in the Mood* – the podcast where we overthink, overshare, and occasionally spiral into the void."

Eli picked it up, his voice smoother, steadier. "I'm Eli Reed. I'm here for emotional support and audio levels."

"I'm Romy Becker. I'm here because I'm not currently in therapy."

"Every week, we unpack modern dating, mental health, cringe-inducing text messages–"

"And why everyone who says, 'no drama' on their profile is absolutely, a hundred percent, the problem."

Eli smiled, trying not to laugh. "It's messy. It's mildly unhinged. But it's honest."

"We're definitely not experts," I added, "just emotionally self-aware enough to be dangerous."

A beat passed.

Then, together:

"Welcome to *Not in the Mood*."

I blinked. The silence stretched. Then I squeaked out a laugh. "Wait, what was that!? That sounded – *so good!*"

"It's because I know what I'm doing," Eli said smugly, leaning back.

"No, but like... wait. You actually know what you're doing?"

He blinked at me, stunned. "Did you not realize I get *paid* to help people with their podcasts?"

"I think I just never took you seriously," I said, doubling over with laughter.

Eli stared at me, mouth agape. "I cannot believe I helped you go viral. This is slander."

"To be fair," I said between wheezes, "I didn't even take myself seriously until yesterday."

He sighed like a man who'd seen too much. "We're doomed."

I grinned at him across a pile of jackets and half a dozen tangled headphone cords. "This episode," I said directly into the mic, locking eyes with Eli, "is on partners, and if we actually need them."

He raised a brow. "Interesting choice."

"Because I firmly believe that we don't."

"Says the girl who just got broken up with," he replied without missing a beat.

"*Eli!*" I scream-whispered, shoving his shoulder hard enough that he rocked sideways. "I cannot believe you just said that!"

"I can't believe you were going to lie to the people," he said, gesturing broadly toward the closet door, as if our listener base was standing just outside it.

"Break-up or not," I huffed, adjusting the mic like I was about to deliver a TED Talk from hell, "I genuinely don't think we need relationships. Romantic ones, anyway."

"Explain, please," he said in his usual soft tone, which only made me more determined to sound like a jaded oracle.

"Okay. Anybody who seeks out a romantic relationship is just asking to get hurt. Like, *willingly* walking into a haunted house with no shoes on. Think about it – first you have to find someone you're attracted to. That's already exhausting."

"Say it, sister," he said, leaning back against the couch cushions we'd brought in for optimal comfort like he was settling in for a sermon.

"You get carpal tunnel from swiping on apps, and maybe, *maybe*, you stumble on someone decent who doesn't look like a rejected cast member from 'Love Island.' You match, you message, you schedule a date... and then you have to meet them. *In person.* Like some kind of ancient ritual."

"Brutal," Eli muttered, nodding solemnly.

"And even *if* that goes well – which, statistically, it doesn't – you have to hope they're funny, and kind, and that they didn't lie about their height, and they don't say things like 'I'm not like other guys' or 'my last girlfriend was crazy.'"

"Or that they have one decorative sword in their apartment."

"Oh God, yes. And that's before we've even touched on the physical stuff."

"Go there."

"I'm just saying – what are the odds they're a good kisser? That they don't kiss like a golden retriever trying to resuscitate you?"

"I have heard horror stories," Eli said.

"We *all* have. So even *if* you get past that – and that's a big if – then you have to hope you're sexually compatible, that there's chemistry, that nobody says anything horrifying like 'I want to imprint on your soul.'"

"Is that a Twilight reference?"

"Always."

He laughed.

"And then!" I continued, getting increasingly animated. "You start catching feelings. That's the real danger zone. Because now you're vulnerable. You've opened up. You've let someone see your weird skincare drawer and the way you eat cheese directly out of the bag."

Eli raised his hand. "Guilty."

"My point is, it's a *minefield*. Like a real, emotional minefield. And every time, we act surprised when our legs get blown off."

"Good luck out there, troops."

I leaned back, exhaled dramatically. "I lost my legs decades ago."

Eli let the silence stretch just enough before he spoke, gently. "But doesn't part of you think it's worth it?"

I glanced at him. He didn't look smug this time, just curious.

And that was the problem with Eli. He always knew

exactly when to dial back the sarcasm and go soft. Which made it impossible for me to stay in defense mode.

I leaned toward the mic again, quieter this time. "I don't think it's worth it. Not right now."

Eli didn't say anything for a second. Just that soft, thoughtful pause he did sometimes, like he was trying to read between the lines of what I wasn't saying.

Then: "It doesn't have to be."

I exhaled slowly, almost embarrassed by how much those five words settled something in my chest.

But of course, Eli couldn't leave it there.

"But," he added, adjusting his mic like he was about to shift into philosopher mode, "for arguments sake, just because you're not in the mood right now doesn't mean love's a scam forever. You act like dating is a crime scene, and everyone who flirts with you is holding a knife."

"Well, statistically speaking–"

"Don't bring statistics into this. That's *my* department."

I rolled my eyes. "Fine. But am I wrong?"

Eli shrugged. "Not completely. Dating can be a nightmare. People lie, they flake, they ghost, they text 'k' and think that's normal human behavior – yes, I'm still triggered. But I don't think it's pointless."

"Tell that to my most recent group breakup text. GROUP. TEXT. Eli. With the other woman *in the thread.*"

"That guy was a literal war crime in khakis," Eli said. "But he doesn't get to define your entire belief system."

"He's not my belief system," I muttered, even though, okay, maybe he'd helped shape it a little.

"Romy," Eli said, gently now. "you're smart. Funny. Emotionally combative, but charmingly so."

"Thank you?"

"And just because something ends badly doesn't mean it wasn't real. You connect with people. Even when you say you don't want to. You're doing it right now – with me, with whoever's listening to this later on."

I paused. "That's different. You don't scare me."

"Why not?"

I blinked, shrugging slightly. "Because you're safe."

Eli leaned back against the wall of sweaters and wires, eyebrows raised. "Is that a compliment, or are you saying I have the sex appeal of a therapy dog?"

"Those golden retrievers get around," I said. "don't underestimate them."

We laughed, but underneath it, I knew what he was getting at. And I hated how he could sometimes see what I was trying so hard not to say.

Eli continued, more quietly now, "It's okay to not want love right now. But don't bury the part of you that still does. You're allowed to be angry and tired and heartbroken. That doesn't cancel out the hope."

"Hope is exhausting," I said. "Hope is the thing that gets you to send the text, to wait by the phone, to pretend you're okay when you're definitely *not* okay."

"Yeah," he said. "But it's also the thing that keeps people trying. It's why people get back up. Why they record podcasts in their closets and tell strangers about their heartbreak. It's why you're here."

I didn't respond. Couldn't, really. I just looked at him for a long moment.

Then I leaned back toward the mic.

"I think... I'm not in the mood to think it's worth it. Not right now."

This time, Eli didn't try to fix it. He just let the silence settle around us for a second.

"Should we cue the sad violin music?" he finally said.

I laughed. "Only if it's royalty free."

We both smiled – small, tired, real.

Then Eli sat up and clapped his hands together. "Okay. Great first episode. We were vulnerable, we were funny, we didn't cry on mic – which honestly, feels like a win."

"I almost cried," I admitted.

"You always almost cry."

"Because I'm in touch with my emotions."

"Because you drank an iced coffee on an empty stomach."

I rolled my eyes and watched Eli hit stop on the recorder. The little red light went out, and suddenly it felt like we were back in the real world – where things didn't always tie up in clean eleven-minute arcs.

But still, it felt like something.

Maybe not healing. But a start.

"Alright," I said, stretching my legs and blinking into the dark of the closet, "let's cut the trauma, add music, and see if we can get a Squarespace sponsorship by Thursday."

Eli stood up with a groan. "God bless capitalism."

I pushed open the door and stepped into the light, blinking like we'd just survived a war.

"Wait, what should we call this episode?" Eli asked. I turned and looked at him, sitting on the floor of my closet surrounded by all this recording equipment I had no idea how to use.

"Dating is a Minefield."

5
WHAT IF

Two weeks later, we uploaded the first full episode to TikTok.

We'd agreed on nighttime uploads – my idea. I told Eli it was a strategy, that the algorithm liked overnight engagement. The truth was simpler: I didn't trust myself not to obsessively check it every six minutes if we posted during daylight. This way, I could toss the phone on my nightstand, flip on some ambient rain sounds, and pretend to sleep like a normal person.

Spoiler: I did not sleep like a normal person.

My phone, facedown in Do Not Disturb mode beside me, taunted me like a glowing slab of doom. I lay there in the dark, anxiety swirling like static under my skin, the weight of what we'd done finally crashing into me.

Was it good? Was it even coherent?

I grabbed my phone, opened the files app, and – like the glutton for punishment I apparently was – listened to the episode again.

For the hundredth time.

My voice was somewhere between anxious squirrel and sentient chihuahua. Eli, meanwhile, sounded like a podcasting angel – calm, collected, charming without trying. The perfect sidekick. Was I annoying? Did I come off like I hated men? *Did* I actually hate men?

This was the worst kind of vulnerability: not the quiet, personal kind, but the kind where you willingly launch your emotional entrails into the public void and wait for strangers to dissect them.

It was like post-sex texting anxiety. You know the kind. When you're the first to send a "Had a nice time :)" message and sit there spiraling because you've shattered the fragile silence of emotional indifference.

Except this time, it was public. And permanent.

I could pop a Xanax. I considered it. But I didn't want to become *that* girl – the one who couldn't make a move without chemical backup. Besides, I did that enough already, if I was being honest.

This isn't even that big of a deal, I told myself. People post stuff online every day. It's just another voice lost in the cacophony of teenagers dancing and hot people selling face wash.

Unless it wasn't. Unless people kept paying attention.

And that's what scared me.

Because suddenly, this wasn't just a dumb little thing we recorded in my closet. It had my name on it. My face. My opinions about the romantic-industrial complex. What if a future employer Googled me and found a podcast about why men suck? What if this thing went from fun to something that actually derailed my life?

What if I'd just made a massive mistake?

I fell asleep somewhere between self-doubt and disaster fantasy.

I woke up the next morning with the reflexes of

someone disarming a bomb.

My hand shot out, grabbed the phone, and I blinked through sleep haze as the notifications exploded across my lock screen.

64,321 views.

9,832 likes.

487 comments.

Follower count: tripled.

I didn't breathe. Just scrolled through comments.

I feel attacked.

This is my Roman Empire.

Who else is now obsessed w/ them???

People were tagging their friends. Stitching the clip. Sharing it in group chats. We weren't just getting noticed – we were getting *quoted*.

My heart raced, a giddy kind of dread crawling up my spine. It was happening. We were going viral. *This was not a drill.*

I checked our account's inbox. One DM from a random guy asking me out (bold). A former situationship replying with a single nervous emoji (coward). A woman I didn't know with two kids and a soft smile in her profile pic: *Thank you for saying what I've never been able to put into words.*

That one got me.

I never wanted to be anyone's compass. That was kind of the whole point of my life – keep it light, keep it easy, keep it safe. I was the background person. The quick-witted friend. The one with the funny stories and extra hot sauce packets in her purse. I knew how to be likable without ever being essential. But now, somehow, I'd wandered into territory I wasn't built for

– where people looked to me for insight, for answers, for meaning. And I didn't know how to carry that without dropping something else.

I felt... pressure.

Buzz.

A text from Eli: *Morning. Ur being crazy already, aren't u?*

I typed back: *Absolutely not. Just wondering if we need to scrub the whole episode from the internet and move to Iceland.*

A pause. *I know u so well Becker.*

I laughed and replied: *Just because you're emotionally bulletproof.*

After a few moments: *Just because we've had 3 fake fights at IKEA doesn't mean u know me.*

I set the phone down and pressed my palms into my cheeks, grinning. I wasn't sure if I was spiraling or ascending. Both felt suspiciously similar.

Later that morning, I stood in the break room at work obsessively refreshing TikTok comments under the guise of making a cup of tea.

Grace Callahan breezed in like a beam of morning sunshine. She wore a ballet-pink wrap sweater and those sneakers that only tiny, perky women can pull off without looking orthopedic. Grace was the human embodiment of a Pinterest board: cheerful, functional, aesthetically pleasing. She was also absurdly thoughtful – the type who carried granola bars, extra tampons, and $5 bills "just in case" someone needed one.

When we first met, I couldn't stand her. It took

everything in me to not beat her to death with the HR benefits binder. But she'd won me over when she stayed late one night to help solve a missing PTO request that had caused a minor HR scandal. Now, she was my closest ally at LumenLoop. She made me do yoga in the park as penance for my bad decisions. I encouraged her to drink wine on weeknights and ghost her Bumble dates. It was a fair trade.

She held her phone up across the room like it was a police badge. "When were you going to tell me you dropped a podcast?"

I blinked. "What?"

"This." She spun the screen toward me. *Not in the Mood.* Our page. Our video. Our faces.

My stomach flipped. "How did you find it?"

"A friend sent it to me!"

"You're kidding."

"Why are you freaking out?" she asked, crossing to the counter to pour herself coffee.

"I'm not freaking out," I said, clearly lying. "I just... I didn't expect you to find out *organically*."

Grace grinned and took a sip from her World's Okayest Coworker mug. "Romy Becker, viral internet girl."

I groaned and leaned against the counter. "This is so weird. So, so weird."

She smirked. "Weird? Or amazing?"

I didn't have an answer yet.

"Who's this co-host guy?" she asked, eyes still on her phone.

"Oh, Eli? He's my best friend."

"Best friend, huh?" Grace raised a brow and zoomed

in on one of the photos from our podcast page that thankfully Eli ran entirely. I watched her analyze his face like it was a Zillow listing.

"Yes. Completely platonic. Completely manic."

"He's really cute."

"Is he?" I sipped my tea, noncommittal.

"Like, *really* cute. He looks like if a cardigan made a wish to be a real boy."

I burst out laughing. "I mean, if that's your thing."

"Is he single?"

"I'm pretty sure, yeah."

Grace looked at me like I'd just said I wasn't sure if the sky was blue. "What do you mean, *'pretty sure'*? How do you not know if your best friend that you have a love-hate podcast with is in a relationship?"

I got up and walked to the sink, suddenly feeling the need to do something with my hands. "I don't know, I don't ask him on the daily."

She hummed, scrolling. "Hm. Well, he's hot."

"I'll tell him you said so," I said, drying my hands with more effort than necessary. "he'll probably get all flustered and weird about it."

"Well, back to the grindstone," She sighed, refilling her coffee. "Here's hoping this actually does its job."

"If it doesn't, I have some blow in my bag."

"Romy, you're HR. Shut up." She laughed and disappeared back into the hallway.

The second she was gone; I sat back down and unlocked my phone like I hadn't just done that four minutes ago. The podcast comments were still rolling in, faster now. All positive. Like, *suspiciously* positive. One DM read: *You guys made me feel less alone in my breakup. Thank you.* Another said: *I needed this more than I realized. You get it. You really get it.*

I sat with that for a minute. Phone in hand. Fingers resting on the screen, not scrolling.

It was heavy reading these. There's this logical part of your brain that knows – *knows* – that other people are going through things. Maybe worse things. Probably worse things. But having them tell you directly? In your inbox? That's something else entirely.

I hadn't set out to help people. That wasn't the goal. I wanted a distraction. A joke. An outlet for all the things I didn't say in real life. But suddenly, this thing we made – this scrappy little podcast recorded in my closet – it was becoming meaningful. People were projecting themselves into our banter. Our stories. Our dumb bits.

And now I felt something like... responsibility.

I didn't want to be responsible for anyone's emotional awakening. Hell, I could barely remember to defrost my chicken breasts. Being a shoulder to cry on was never the goal – I just wanted to make fun of modern dating and maybe go semi-viral for a well-timed joke about ghosting. That was it.

But now we had followers.

Followers.

How the hell did we accidentally make something *important*?

I texted Eli: *People are responding like we saved their lives.*

A minute later, he replied: *Cool. When do we start charging them?*

I snuck out of work like I always do – ten, maybe fifteen minutes earlier than I was technically allowed to. A passive-aggressive rebellion I repeated daily. It was my way of flipping the bird to the system without actually doing anything brave. Nobody tells me when to leave my job. Not even my job. They could dock me fifteen minutes of pay and I'd still walk out with the smugness of a whistleblower.

The late afternoon air was cool in that indecisive San Francisco way – sunny, but shady, warm, but windy. The kind of weather that could turn on you if you dressed with too much confidence. I hugged my coat tighter around me and made the familiar walk home, earbuds tucked in but playing nothing. I just needed the illusion of distraction.

My brain, however, was staging a coup.

It started like a trickle. Just a few thoughts. Harmless. Then it turned into a full dam-bursting flood.

I could picture it too easily: one of us starts dating someone serious, and the vibe shifts. The late-night recording sessions become inconvenient. The honesty feels like betrayal. The conversations turn careful.

What if this whole thing is just a fluke? A lightning-in-a-bottle moment we can't recreate?

What if we're that kind of semi-funny podcast that people remember for a second, laugh at once, and then completely blank on when they try to recommend it to a friend?

What if I overshared? Like – *actually* overshared? What if no one ever dates me again because I said "hope is exhausting" like a walking Tumblr quote from 2014?

My dating life was already held together with dry

shampoo and blind optimism. And I'm picky. Too picky, apparently. I swipe left on men who use "u" instead of "you," or have fish in their profile pictures. Now I had to worry about some stranger recognizing my voice from TikTok while I'm trying to flirt over margaritas?

I pulled out my phone and voice-noted Mia as I walked. "Is this imposter syndrome or am I actually a fraud?"

Her reply came in a few minutes later, calm and brutal like a slap from someone who loves you. "Neither, bitch. Stop overthinking and go with it."

Fair enough.

When I got home, I dropped everything at the door. Literally. My bag, my coat, my existential dread. All of it landed in a heap by the entryway. I flopped onto the couch, curled into the throw blanket like a human cinnamon roll.

I played the episode. For what felt like the thousandth time.

I knew every pause now. Every inhale. Every moment where I talked too fast or too slow.

Eli, of course, sounded great. Calm. Charming. Like the human equivalent of a weighted blanket. His voice was meant for podcasting. Mine felt like it was meant for sending "I'm outside" texts and leaving voicemails no one listened to.

Still. There was something there. It wasn't perfect. It didn't need to be. It was real.

I let *Gilmore Girls* play in the background like ambiance, the warm buzz of Stars Hollow keeping my anxious thoughts from screaming too loud. I opened my dating apps more out of boredom than anything else and swiped with a mix of cynicism and habit. Most were left swipes. A few right swipes happened, and a couple matches followed. But I waited. I wasn't in the mood to say something witty or ironic or interesting enough to start a conversation. I was too full of static. I needed to be still.

Sometime before bed, a TikTok notification popped up. A new message.

Marissa. Chicago. Stranger: *I've never heard someone explain the "hope is exhausting" thing like that. I cried in my car. Thank you.*

I stared at it for a long time. Not just read it – *absorbed* it.

I took a screenshot and sent it to Eli without saying a word.

His reply came a minute later: *Told u.*

I set my phone down and stared at the ceiling, my insides buzzing like a broken vending machine trying to dispense a soda. I thought about how far I'd spiraled earlier. About how scared I was to be seen. To be known. To matter in ways that meant I could let someone down.

Because what if this is it?

Not *just* a thing we do.

But *the* thing.

The thing that finally feels like me. Like something I didn't fall into or fake my way through.

Something I chose. Something that chose me back.

And then the biggest What If of all settled in my chest like a weighted stone:

What if I'm finally doing something that matters – and I'm too scared to let myself enjoy it?

The sound of *Gilmore Girls* muttering in the background reminded me I was still here. Still me.

6
FEDORAS ARE A RED FLAG

By Wednesday, the walls started closing in.

Not literally. The LumenLoop office was a mid-century modern shrine to open floor plans and vague wellness. But metaphorically? Oh yeah. The walls were closing in.

It started small. A Slack message from someone in engineering I barely knew: *romy i just listened to your podcast and lmao'd in my car this morning. do ppl actually send group text breakups???*

I stared at the message for a full ten seconds before replying: *unfortunately, yes. and I was on the receiving end. thx for listening?*

Then came the side-eyes in the breakroom. The whispered "that's her" in the hallway. The HR department – which is to say, *me* – had become watercooler talk. I was both the memo-sender and the content.

By lunch, I had two more DMs from coworkers – one kind, one weirdly flirty – and someone had tagged our podcast on the company-wide #fun-finds Slack channel. My stomach flipped.

It was Grace who broke the news in person. She approached my desk looking deeply amused and only mildly apologetic.

"So, funny thing," she said, leaning in. "You're... famous."

I groaned. "What now?"

She pulled out her phone and showed me a screen grab of the podcast's TikTok comments – one where someone had clocked my employer from a LinkedIn screenshot I'd apparently posted *last year*. Rookie move.

"I can't breathe," I muttered.

"It's not that bad," Grace grinned. "You didn't name the company or say anything that'd get you fired."

"Yet," I replied. "I didn't say anything *yet.*"

Her expression softened. "Are you actually worried?"

I paused. Was I?

Yes. And no. And yes again.

"I mean," I sighed, swiveling in my chair, "I'm a People Ops Director, Grace. My job is to protect the company. The policies. The people. The image. And now half the office knows I've cried over a man who owns three fedora hats and can't spell 'their' correctly."

She blinked at me. "Okay, *first of all*, fedoras are a red flag. But second of all – so what?"

I looked down at my keyboard.

"So, what if people here think I'm unprofessional? Or unstable? Or not the image of 'HR' they want walking around rewriting their sexual harassment training modules?"

I could feel my heart thumping harder than I wanted to admit. Grace gently bumped her hip into my desk.

"You're human, Romy. If they didn't know that before, maybe it's good they do now."

I wanted to believe her. I really did.

But when I ducked into a meeting that afternoon and caught one of the product guys smirking at me across the table, something twisted in my gut. I wasn't *just* Romy anymore. I was "Romy from the podcast." Romy who didn't believe in relationships. Romy who talked about her exes in vivid, occasionally horrifying detail.

It made me wonder:

Where was the line between honesty and oversharing?

Between being real and being reckless?

And worse – had I already crossed it?

It had been six days since the first episode went live, and somehow, the world hadn't collapsed. Not yet. But it felt like it was getting close.

Every morning since, I'd woken up with the same low-grade panic that maybe I'd said something unforgivably stupid. That some internet sleuth would pull a thread and unravel my whole life with a TikTok exposing me as problematic, unqualified, or worse – cringe.

But the clip kept growing. And the episode kept climbing.

By now, we were hovering around 213,000 listens. Which wasn't, like, Dax Shepard levels. But for two people recording in a closet with zero marketing budget and a podcast title that sounded vaguely like a depression commercial, it was... something.

The numbers weren't what got me, though. It was the comments. Hundreds of them. From strangers. Strangers who somehow felt like they *knew* me. Who heard one ten-minute episode and decided I was someone worth listening to. Or worse – worth *relating* to.

That part messed me up a little. I felt that pressure again.

Eli texted me Thursday morning: *analytics look good. u alive?*

I stared at the message while I poured my second cup of coffee and stood barefoot in my kitchen like someone in a medication commercial who's *not quite* better yet. I didn't reply right away.

Instead, I walked in circles around my apartment like I was waiting for news from the front lines. I was itchy with nerves but didn't know where to place them.

I kept thinking:

What if people expect us to be this polished?

What if I already said too much?

What if Eli meets someone and suddenly, I'm just the girl from the thing he *used* to do?

Not because I was into him like that. I wasn't. Of course I wasn't.

But still, the thought of becoming a footnote in someone else's highlight reel? It stung in a place I hadn't let myself acknowledge yet.

When I finally texted him back, it was hours later: *technically breathing. spiraling softly.*

He replied with a meme of a raccoon holding a knife. It felt right.

We'd planned to work on episode two that evening. When he showed up, he brought three bags of kettle chips, a single protein bar, and a six-pack of some obscure craft beer that claimed to be "emotionally complex".

"You know we're not actually recording tonight, right?" I said as he dropped everything on my kitchen counter.

"Yeah, but we *could*." He looked at me with that dumb little crooked smirk that meant he was enjoying how much I hated his optimism.

I rolled my eyes and opened one of the beers anyway.

We didn't talk about the numbers. Not right away. We didn't talk about the DMs or the comments or the sudden trickle of emails from strangers asking if we did guest interviews or branded partnerships. We just sat on the couch, beers in hand, with YouTube lo-fi in the background and the soft glow of the city through my windows.

And for a second, it felt exactly the way it always had. Easy. Untouchable.

But then Eli looked over at me, and for the briefest moment, I had this stupid, fleeting thought: What if this is the beginning of something we can't come back from? What if this intrinsically affects our friendship in a way we can't change?

I shoved it down. Hard. Then I asked him if he wanted to order Thai and talk about episode two structure. "To be honest, I don't think we need to really hammer out details right now," Eli said, connecting some device to the charger port of his phone and setting it gently on the table between us. His fingers hovered for a moment, then he pointed to it casually.

He'd attached a weird looking microphone to his phone. He was recording.

"What? What was the point of coming over then?" I asked, raising an eyebrow.

He placed a hand over his heart like I'd personally offended his ancestors. "That *hurt*."

I laughed. "What do you mean?"

"We're only on the second episode," he said, shifting to sit cross-legged on the couch in his usual spot. "We can spit out a few more like the first before we start interviewing people or going full NPR. Clearly, we're onto something here. Why mess with it?"

His words caught me off guard – not because I disagreed, but because hearing him say *clearly, we're onto something* made it feel a little more real. "Yeah," I said slowly, "why change it, sidekick."

A notification buzzed on his phone, and he picked it up quickly, smiling at the screen in a way that wasn't his usual amused smirk. No – this one had a softness to it. It lingered.

He tapped out a reply and set his phone down gingerly like nothing had happened.

"What was that?" I asked, my tone teasing but my curiosity was sharp.

"What was what?" He didn't even try to feign innocence. Just smirked and ripped open a bag of kettle chips like we were on a commercial break.

"That smile." I tilted my head, watching him like a hawk. "You *smiled*. At your phone. Don't play dumb."

He shrugged, noncommittal. "Don't know what you could possibly be referring to."

I narrowed my eyes. "Is Eli Reed texting a woman?" I got up on my knees, leaning across the coffee table like I was cross-examining him.

"No," he said, too blunt to be believable.

"A man, then?"

He tossed a chip at me.

"This chick – I don't know, I don't even *know* who she is," he admitted, crunching loudly. "But she sent me a total thirst trap."

I froze, mid-eyeroll. "Eli Reed likes the thirst traps, huh?" I tried to keep it playful, but I could feel something odd twist in my stomach.

"We have a date tomorrow," he said, tone casual. "So hopefully I end up thirsting over a different kind of trap."

"Oh my *God*, Eli." I clapped my hands over my ears and slid dramatically to the floor. "Please, I don't need these visuals."

But the twist in my gut didn't ease. I tried to laugh it off, but it hung there, heavy.

"Wanna see her?" He reached for his phone, and I instinctively batted his hand away.

"Absolutely not. I don't want to see the poor woman about to endure a night of Eli Reed's charm offensive. No, thank you."

He laughed, but I caught the edge in it – the part that didn't quite reach his eyes. "She's the fifth date I've gotten from us taking this live."

"Wait, what?" I leaned back to my side of the coffee table. "How is that possible, it's only been a few days?"

"I can't explain it, but I am *not* complaining." He laughed and ran a hand through his hair. "It's amazing, honestly. I feel like they just kind of come to me now. No effort. No stress. I just pick the flavor I want and have a taste."

"Eli, that's the ickiest thing you've ever said to me."

"You prude."

I was desperate to change the direction of the conversation. I leaned forward, suddenly aware that this was all being recorded. "For the record, I'm proud to say I've never sent a thirst trap."

"Never? Not once?"

"I don't need to," I said, lifting my chin. "Look at this face."

"Yeah, I wouldn't rely on that alone," he shot back.

My mouth dropped open in mock offense and he burst into real, genuine laughter – the kind that made my stomach flutter. "I'm just saying," I said, brushing chip crumbs off my hoodie, "some of us don't need strategic lighting and sultry angles to be desirable."

Eli smirked and leaned closer to his phone. "Wow. The confidence on display."

"It's not confidence. It's delusion. It's completely different."

"That tracks."

I leaned into the mic with exaggerated drama. "Hi. I'm Romy Becker. I have imposter syndrome, a caffeine addiction, and a soft spot for men who will absolutely destroy me emotionally."

He choked on a laugh. "Hi, Romy."

"Hi, Eli."

He shifted off the couch and onto the carpet, re-crossing his legs like we were about to do a guided meditation. "So, what are we actually talking about today?"

"I thought we could keep pulling the thread from last time," I said. "You know – modern dating, self-sabotage, thirst traps. The usual."

"Should we title this episode *Thirst Traps and*

Emotional Booby Traps?"

I cackled. "That's brilliant. We'll never get sponsorships with that title, but it's brilliant."

He held up his hands. "We're not trying to sell protein powder. We're trying to tell the truth."

I paused, biting the inside of my cheek as I watched him adjust some setting on his phone like it was second nature. He made all this feel easy. He always did.

"Okay," I said, getting back on track. "here's a topic. Thirst traps, and why people send them."

Eli raised an eyebrow. "Do tell."

"First of all, let me just say, men have *no* idea how much effort goes into those photos. It's basically a full photo shoot. There are drafts. There's lighting. There's creative direction. There's mood."

"There's editing."

"There's prayer," I added.

He laughed. "And why do you send them?"

I hesitated, then leaned closer to the mic. "Validation. But like... curated validation. Controlled. We want to feel wanted without risking actual rejection."

"Interesting," Eli said, and his voice got a little softer. "So, it's not really about seduction. It's about safety."

I blinked, caught off guard. "Yeah," I said. "Exactly."

He looked at me for a long second, his expression unreadable. "Okay, your turn. Why do you think men send them?"

I snorted. "Because they have a pulse?"

"No, I'm serious. There's a reason."

I thought about it. "Ego. Or hope. Or boredom. Maybe all three. But I think sometimes it's also a test. Like, hey, will this girl engage with the version of me I've created? Can I be liked without being truly seen?"

Eli whistled low. "Damn. That's bleak."

"That's dating."

There was a beat of silence, not uncomfortable, just thoughtful. The kind of pause that would probably get edited down in post, but that meant something in real time.

I shifted again, sitting on my heels now. "Okay, so here's a question," I said. "Do you think we're addicted to the chase?"

"You mean humans or us personally?"

"Both."

Eli let out a breath. "I think... yeah. I think we all kind of are. We've gamified attention. Every app, every post, every swipe – it's just another way to see if we're still desirable. Still wanted. We're chasing proof that we matter. To be desired is an addiction."

I blinked. That one landed a little too well.

"I think that's why ghosting hurts so much," I said. "it's not just rejection. It's being made to feel like we never existed."

We let that one hang in the air. Eli leaned back against the couch, his head tilted, thinking. I watched him – the way his face got all contemplative, like he was unraveling a knot behind his eyes. It used to drive me crazy that he was so emotionally literate. Now it just scared me a little.

"You know what's weird?" He said, voice soft but still clear. "We sit here talking about how hard dating is. How it's a minefield. But sometimes I think it's hard because we don't actually believe we're worthy of the thing we're looking for."

My stomach twisted again, but not in that weird way this time. In the *he's right and I hate that he's right* way.

"Jesus," I muttered. "couldn't we have just stuck to thirst traps?"

"Sorry," he said, though he didn't sound sorry. "Too real?"

"No, just... honest."

He turned his head and smiled at me. A real smile. "That's the whole point, right?"

I leaned toward the phone again, voice low. "It's messy. It's mildly unhinged. But it's honest."

Eli mirrored me. "Welcome back to *Not in the Mood*."

We paused. The recording software on his phone blinked steadily.

"Do you think people are going to relate to this?" I asked quietly, after a beat.

He didn't even hesitate. "I think people are going to feel seen."

I didn't say anything. I just sat there for a second, watching him, wondering what the hell we were actually doing with this.

And then I hit 'stop recording'.

7

DEMON FRIENDS

Brunch was Mia's idea. It usually was.

She said we were overdue for "real friend time," which, in Mia-speak, meant soft lighting, overpriced carbs, and the kind of cross-table interrogation that made you both want to cry and Venmo her for therapy services.

So, that's how I found myself tucked into a window seat at Butter & Bloom the following Saturday – an aggressively aesthetic little café in the Inner Sunset where the chairs were all rattan, the playlist was exclusively Phoebe Bridgers, and the pancakes were shaped like flowers. I'd invited Grace to come along. Her and Mia had met twice before – once at a house party I hosted, another time for a casual coffee when we all happened to be free – and against all odds, they got along *weirdly* well.

Grace was bubbly, bright, and a little bit golden retriever-coded – she dressed like a preppy Gap ad and complimented strangers on their nail polish. Mia, on the other hand, was a born skeptic with an affinity for dark lipstick and emotionally scalding one-liners. But somehow, they clicked. Grace adored Mia's brutal honesty ("It's refreshing!" she once told me, like she'd just been slapped and offered a cookie), and Mia had a soft spot for Grace's enthusiasm, even if she pretended she didn't.

I liked seeing them together. It made me feel like maybe different versions of my life could exist in the same room without fighting.

We sat at a table just inside the restaurant's bay window. Grace had squealed when she saw the menu. Mia had judged the latte art. I had quietly hoped the food would be hot.

I should've known better. By the second mimosa, the conversation had pivoted – as it always did – to my love life, or more accurately, the cold, empty crater where my love life used to be.

And I was already regretting coming.

"So," Grace said, drawing out the word like a silk scarf. "Are you seeing anyone since Smith?"

I didn't look up from my fork. "You just saw me two days ago, Grace. Do you think I met the love of my life in the produce aisle and just haven't wanted to tell you yet?"

"I don't know!" she said with a shrug. "Things happen. You could've locked eyes with a stranger over a cantaloupe and suddenly found yourself in a slow-burn rom-com moment."

"She doesn't even like cantaloupe," Mia deadpanned.

"Thank you, Mia."

"But seriously," Grace pressed. "What about that one guy from that one app? The one who looked like a sad Chris Pine?"

"Ghosted."

Grace's face fell. "No!"

"Oh, yes," I said, stabbing a very delicate poached pear.

"Men are cowards," Mia said, sipping her mimosa like it was gospel.

"I've decided I'm okay being single," I said, possibly for the seventh time that week.

"You *say* that," Grace replied, "but every time I listen to the podcast, I feel like there's this secret romantic tension going on."

Mia's eyes narrowed, suddenly engaged. "With who?"

Grace blinked at me like it was obvious. "With Eli."

I nearly choked on my mimosa. "*What?*"

"Oh, come on," she said, laughing. "The way you guys talk to each other? There's a *vibe*. You're like the Ross and Rachel of Spotify."

"There's no vibe," I said, too quickly. "there's a format."

"He flirts with you *constantly*," Grace said.

"It's called *banter*. It's literally our job."

Mia raised a brow. "You do talk about him more than anyone else."

"That's because I see him more than anyone else. We record together every few days. We're co-hosts."

Grace grinned. "You're co-hosts with chemistry."

"I hate this brunch."

"Just admit it," Mia said, sipping. "You like him a little."

"I don't," I said, because it was easier than saying *I don't think I'm allowed to.*

They both looked at me, expressions somewhere between amused and suspicious.

I focused on slicing my pancake into perfect, symmetrical bites, like that would prove something.

Grace leaned in, resting her chin on her palm. "You'd tell us if something happened, right?"

I met her eyes. "Of course."

And I would. Probably. Eventually.

But the thing was – nothing *had* happened. And I didn't want anything to.

I think.

Grace, sensing blood in the water, twirled her spoon like she was stirring a potion. "Okay, but *hypothetically*, if something *did* happen between you and Eli, would that be a bad thing?"

"Yes," I said, then immediately: "no. I don't know."

Mia arched an eyebrow. "Solid answer."

I pointed my fork at her. "I just mean it would complicate things. The podcast is seriously getting traction, and we work really well together. Throw feelings into the mix and it all falls apart."

Grace made a noise like a game show buzzer. "That's a classic 'I like him, but I'm scared' response."

"I'm not scared. I'm realistic."

"You're preemptively self-sabotaging," Mia said, as if diagnosing a recurring rash.

"Can we not psychoanalyze me before I've had hashbrowns?"

Mia ignored me. "Do you trust him?"

I blinked. "What?"

"If something *did* happen," she said slowly, "do you trust him not to ruin it?"

That gave me pause. I stared down at my plate, my pancakes now lukewarm and floral in a way that felt disrespectful.

I thought about how Eli always remembered to carry a second pair of headphones just in case mine broke. How he let me monologue during edits when I didn't realize I needed to vent. How he always handed me my coat by the shoulders, not the sleeves, like he was offering it to me – not hurrying me out.

"Yeah," I said, quietly. "I trust him."

Grace practically squealed. "Then what's the problem?!"

"The problem is me," I said, too honestly. "I don't trust *me*."

That shut them both up for a second.

Mia leaned back, eyes narrowing just slightly, like she was reading between the lines and didn't like what she saw. Grace reached for her water glass.

"I just..." I said, trying to laugh it off. "I don't want to ruin a good thing. Not everything has to turn into a rom-com."

"No," Mia said. "But not everything has to turn into a tragedy, either."

That landed harder than I wanted it to.

We sat in silence for a beat, the clink of silverware and Phoebe Bridgers crooning softly in the background.

Then Grace said brightly, "Well. At least if it ends in disaster, you can turn it into content."

Mia snorted. "Episode title: *'Oops, I Slept with My Co-Host and Now I Can't Look Him in the Eye.'*"

I groaned. "You guys are demons."

They grinned at me in stereo.

I sighed, shoved the last bite of pancake in my mouth, and raised my mimosa. "To emotional repression and poor life choices."

They clinked their glasses against mine without missing a beat.

"To women."

Three more mimosas later and the trauma-lite detour that was *Let's Unpack Romy's Love Life*, Grace finally pivoted, bless her.

"Oh!" she said suddenly, reaching into her tote bag. "I almost forgot – I brought these for you."

She pulled out two little foil-wrapped bundles and slid them across the table.

Mia raised an eyebrow. "What is this, a drug deal?"

Grace rolled her eyes. "They're mini candles. I made them last weekend."

"You made candles?" I asked, turning the one in front of me over. A pale lilac label read *Soft Chaos.*

"Yup. I'm in my crafting era," she said proudly. "Mia's is called *Sharp Tongue,* because duh. Yours is – well, that one."

Mia popped the lid off hers and sniffed. "Smells like bergamot and passive aggression. Nailed it."

"Yours smells like violet, vanilla, and whatever self-control I imagine you have," Grace told me.

"I have plenty of self-control."

Mia raised her mimosa glass in salute. "Sure."

I rolled my eyes but smiled, tucking the candle into my purse. "Thank you. This is very cozy witch of you."

"I've been trying to do something tactile every

weekend," Grace said. "Screens are frying my brain."

We all nodded like we'd just agreed on a national truth.

"I tried pottery once," Mia said, sipping. "Hated it."

"You don't like anything."

"I like some things."

"Like what?"

Mia thought for a second. "Long drives. Bitter coffee. Silence. Revenge."

Grace grinned. "Oh, I'm making you a candle that smells like *vengeance* next."

"I'd wear it as perfume."

They bickered back and forth for another few minutes while I leaned into my chair and let myself soften for the first time all day. It was always like this with the three of us – conversation shifting like waves, teasing layered with tenderness, interruptions forgiven mid-sentence.

It made me feel known. Not in the *seen through* way that made your skin itch, but in the *held* way. Comfortable. Safe.

I wasn't good at letting people in. I knew that about myself. But these two had wedged themselves in and made space whether I liked it or not.

And, annoyingly, I did.

We gave each other hugs outside the restaurant and I turned down the street, walking aimlessly, sun-drunk and just a little more than mimosa-blurred.

It wasn't until I passed the same mural-covered trash can twice that I realized I'd been walking the wrong way for four whole blocks.

"Cool," I muttered, spinning around and retracing

my steps, already texting myself a note to never brunch without carbs again.

That's when I smacked into someone.

Full chest-to-chest, mid-turn collision. I stumbled back with an embarrassed yelp, clutching my purse like it was going to cushion the blow.

"Sorry – oh."

I froze.

Of course it was him.

Of *course*.

Smith.

Standing there in a navy t-shirt and sunglasses, he looked like just some guy on the street – like any regular Sunday dude on his way to overpriced coffee or a casual run he'd pretend wasn't for Hinge profile content.

His skin was a warm brown, the same golden undertone I used to trace with my eyes when I still thought he might be my person. His curls were shorter now, tighter at the sides, like he was trying out "grown and responsible" after a year of looking like he lived exclusively in music festival lineups. There was still that quiet, practiced confidence in how he stood – like the world had always made space for him and he'd just gotten used to it.

He was still handsome. That wasn't the issue.

The issue was that he looked like he hadn't thought about me at all.

He pulled off his sunglasses, startled. "Romy?" He said, the familiar edge of his British accent clipping my name like it still belonged to him.

I didn't move. Just stared.

My brain briefly considered running. It seemed

logical. Brunch → panic → sprint into traffic. Full circle.

"Hey," he said, with that same casual, affable voice I'd once found charming. "Wow. It's been a while."

A beat passed. Two.

"You broke up with me in a group chat," I said bluntly, swallowing the tiniest, brunch-induced burp like a professional.

He winced. "Yeah. That was... bad. I'm really sorry about that."

"Are you?" I asked, smiling just slightly – dangerously. "Because you never actually said anything after that. No follow-up. No apology. Just radio silence and then... poof."

He looked sheepish. "I didn't know what to say."

"Wild," I said. "Because you managed to say it to four other people at the same time."

His mouth opened, closed. "I didn't think you'd want to talk to me again."

"You were right."

I turned to walk away, picking up the pace swiftly.

"Wait – Romy," he said, following a step behind. "Can I just – can we talk for a second?"

I didn't slow down. "Why? So, you can crowdsource another breakup strategy?"

"That's fair," he said quickly. "I deserve that."

Another beat of silence passed as we walked. I should've told him to buzz off. I should've just kept walking.

But I was a little day-drunk and extremely nosy.

So, I said, "What do you want, Smith?"

He let out a breath like he'd been holding it. "I don't know. I didn't expect to see you."

"Clearly."

"I've just... I've actually been thinking about you, weirdly."

"'Weirdly' is right."

He laughed softly. "Kelsey broke up with me."

I stopped walking.

He said it like it was supposed to mean something. Like *that* was the twist. Like the woman he'd left me for leaving *him* was supposed to shift the energy.

It didn't.

"Right," I said. "I think that's what they call *karma*."

"Yeah," he said, rubbing the back of his neck. "I guess I thought we were good. But it turns out I was just the person she dated while figuring herself out."

I raised an eyebrow. "Huh. Sounds familiar."

Smith looked at me then – really looked – and for the first time, his expression shifted. Gone was the polished, smug detachment I remembered. He just looked... tired.

"I've made a lot of mistakes," he said quietly. "But breaking things off with you like that... that's probably the one I regret the most."

I folded my arms. "Because it was cruel? Or because it didn't work out the way you planned?"

He opened his mouth, then closed it. "Both?"

I gave a half-shrug. "Points for honesty, I guess."

He offered a faint smile. "I'd love to buy you a drink sometime. Just to – talk. Catch up. Make it up to you, if that's even possible."

I laughed. It wasn't mean. It wasn't kind either.

"Smith," I said, brushing a loose hair from my face, "I think you had your chance. And you spent it drafting a breakup text like a press release."

He opened his mouth again – maybe to defend himself, maybe to beg. I didn't stick around long enough to find out.

I took a step back, smiled just enough to be polite, and turned away when his voice caught me again – softer this time, and weirdly earnest.

"My number's still the same," he said. "If you change your mind."

I stopped mid-step, blinking like he'd just said something in a language I didn't speak anymore.

He didn't wait for a response. Just shoved his hands into his pockets, gave me a small, lopsided smile, and kept walking – his sneakers scuffing quietly against the pavement as he disappeared around the corner like a loose end I hadn't meant to revisit.

I stood there for a long moment on the sidewalk, the late afternoon light suddenly too bright, the air suddenly too thick.

His number was still the same.

As if that was supposed to mean something.

As if, after everything, *I* might want to reach *him.*

My stomach turned. Not in that dizzy, butterflies, maybe-this-could-mean-something way. No. This was the other kind. The *alcohol curdling, eggs-benedict-in-retreat* kind.

The kind of nausea that comes when your body catches up to a truth your brain already knew: you are so far beyond someone, you don't even recognize the version of yourself who wanted them.

I pressed my hand to my chest like I could slow my heart down by force and took a steady breath.

And then I did what any self-respecting woman would do after running into her group-text-ex in broad daylight:

I texted Mia and Grace in our group chat.

Just ran into Smith. He still has his British accent and the audacity. Said his number's still the same in case I change my mind. Going to lie down in traffic brb.

8
THE PEOPLE WANT BLOOD

Three days later, I was back at Eli's place. He'd texted me that morning insisting we record "spur of the moment" – because, according to him, you never know when a gem might slip out mid-ramble. Besides, he said, we could bank content and get ahead. I mean... fine. It wasn't the worst idea.

Eli's apartment in North Beach felt like the kind of place that reveals itself slowly – like him. At first glance, it's modest, a little scattered, with a layout that speaks more to functionality than design. But the longer you linger, the more personal details you start to notice – each one quietly intentional.

It was a rent-controlled one-bedroom in a weathered 1920's building with creaky hardwood floors and crown molding that's seen better days. The kind of apartment with quirks I'd picked up on over the years: a doorknob that sticks, a bathroom window that never quite closes, and a kitchen drawer that refuses to stay shut without a gentle hip check.

The living room is the heart of it – half studio, half sanctuary. One corner is completely devoted to Eli's recording setup: a simple desk, sound panels, mic stands, and a pair of high-quality headphones that look far too expensive for someone who swears he's "not that fancy." A whiteboard leans against the wall behind it, covered in scribbled podcast ideas, half-crossed-off to-do lists, and the occasional doodle I'd draw nearly every time I came over.

The rest of the room feels lived-in and layered: a slightly sagging olive-green couch piled with mismatched throw pillows, a coffee table cluttered with coasters, unread mail, and two mugs that he insists he'll wash later. The lighting is soft – mostly lamps, because the overhead light hums in a way that drives him nuts.

On the wall near the window, there's a framed print of a foggy Golden Gate Bridge, an old concert poster from a band he insists changed his life (I still hadn't listened to them), and a shelf lined with small objects that seem random until you ask about them: a ceramic cat from Tokyo, a miniature ampersand from a typography exhibit, a rock he once picked up on a hike with his dad.

Eli was, unsurprisingly, a total bookworm. His books are everywhere – stacked horizontally on the shelf, crammed vertically between bookends made of concrete, even in a milk crate by the couch. Mostly nonfiction. Audio production. Memoirs. A few well-worn paperbacks with cracked spines and Post-it notes sticking out.

The kitchen is small but efficient. Open shelving. A fridge covered in magnets from places he's been and notes to himself written in black Sharpie. One says: "Buy more oat milk" Another just says: "Breathe".

His bedroom is simpler – cleaner. A low platform bed, flannel sheets, one pillow that's clearly his favorite. A bedside table with a small stack of books, a half-melted candle, and an alarm clock he never uses. A guitar leans in the corner, dusty, maybe more decorative than functional at this point.

The windows overlook a side street that catches late afternoon light just right, and if you lean out far enough, you can see the Bay.

It's not fancy. Not curated. But it feels like him – quiet, thoughtful, and unexpectedly warm once you settle in.

We sat on opposite ends of his couch, facing each other across a tangle of gear. Between us, the mic arm stands jutted out like awkward limbs and made me increasingly anxious that I was going to knock them over. Eli's laptop was balanced on the coffee table – every few seconds the screen flickered with live waveforms, tiny mountains of our breath and words. A coil of cables trailed down the side like vines, half-hiding a box of Cheez-Its and a pair of tangled headphones.

The space was cramped, but familiar. Comfortably cluttered. We both sat cross-legged, knees almost brushing when we shifted the wrong way. Eli's mic stand leaned slightly to the left – he refused to get a new one out of principle – and he kept nudging it back upright like a parent correcting a misbehaving child.

The room was quiet except for the occasional hum of traffic from Stockton Street below and the soft buzz of his old space heater in the corner. The lamp next to the couch gave off a warm yellow light, casting a soft glow over the whole scene. It was the kind of light that made it easy to forget what time it was. The kind that made you say things you didn't mean to say out loud.

I hadn't told Eli about running into Smith. Not because it was a secret – not really – but because I didn't know how to say it without it sounding like it still mattered. Like *he* still mattered. And maybe part of me didn't want to see whatever look would flicker across Eli's face if I said his name out loud. Curiosity? Pity? Disappointment? I didn't want any of them. The whole interaction had left me feeling raw and weirdly nauseous, and Eli had this way of noticing when I wasn't at full emotional capacity, like some kind of walking mood ring. So, I said nothing. I sat on his couch, pretended I was focused on mic levels and topic outlines, and didn't mention the man who once shattered me with a group text now thought I might want a drink sometime.

Eli leaned in to adjust my mic, brushing a stray cable out of the way, eyes flicking up to meet mine for a beat longer than usual.

Then he spoke.

"Okay," he said, adjusting the mic arm so it stopped drooping for the third time. It gave a faint metallic creak as he tightened the hinge with more confidence than precision. "Episode... whatever. Let's talk about emotional detachment."

I groaned and flopped dramatically back onto the couch, one arm slung across my eyes. "God, finally. A topic I can thrive in."

"Which is exactly what someone emotionally detached would say." Eli deadpanned.

"You say that like it's a bad thing."

"I'm just saying," he replied, his voice low and warm in my headphones, "maybe some people are less detached and more scared."

I lifted my arm, peering at him from my reclined position. "Wow. Did you just try to psychoanalyze all of our listeners in the first minute?"

"Just the ones who've texted their ex under the guise of returning a hoodie."

I snorted. "That was one time, and it was a good hoodie."

We laughed. The banter was easy – always was – but tonight there was something a little different in the air. It wasn't quite tension. More like... friction. The kind that hummed under your skin when someone says something that sticks a little longer than it should.

Eli cleared his throat and leaned closer to the mic. "Okay, but seriously – how do we unlearn the idea that romantic love is the default setting? That if you don't find 'your person,' you've failed some kind of cosmic assignment?"

I hesitated, thrown by the shift in tone. Eli rarely got serious without warning. When he did, it always caught me off guard.

"That's kind of the whole point of this show," I said after a moment. "You don't need love to be whole."

"Sure," Eli said. "But it's easy to say that when you've never really had it. Or lost it."

That quieted me.

He kept talking, his voice slower now. Thoughtful. "I think people confuse loneliness with longing. Like, we're taught to crave a person instead of connection. But those aren't the same thing."

I sat up straighter, staring at him. Not in a *he's saying something profound* kind of way – though, he was. But in a *who are you right now* kind of way. Because this wasn't the Eli I felt like I'd grown accustomed to recording with. This Eli wasn't performing. He wasn't joking. He wasn't trying to make me laugh.

He was just... speaking.

And I was listening.

"I used to think I wanted love," he continued, not meeting my gaze, eyes fixed on the waveforms dancing across his laptop screen. "But I think what I really wanted was to feel safe. To feel seen. That's not the same thing. And it definitely doesn't have to come from a relationship. At least not from a relationship with someone who's emotionally detached."

My throat felt suddenly tight. I reached for my water and sipped just to give my hands something to do.

"That's good," I said, my voice too casual. "Put that on a tote bag."

"No, but seriously. When I was with my ex," Eli held my eye contact until he mentioned his ex. "I never felt safe or seen. Or supported, for that matter. Because she had these issues, this emotionally detached aura, if you will, that made it easier to keep me at arms length. What it took me a while to learn was that you can get everything you need emotionally from a romantic relationship through yourself, and through platonic connections."

"Okay, but what *is* emotional detachment, really?" I said, angling toward the mic. "Is it survival? A symptom? A party trick?"

Eli leaned back, rubbing the back of his neck. "Maybe it's all of the above."

I narrowed my eyes. "That's a cop-out answer. Come

on. Say something vulnerable. The people want blood."

He laughed – quiet, but genuine. "Alright. Fine."

A brief pause. He glanced at the waveforms on his laptop, then back at me.

"There was someone I was with for a long time," he said. "a few years ago."

I blinked. This wasn't where I thought the conversation was headed.

"She was intense," he continued. "Brilliant, funny. Completely unpredictable. Being with her was like living in a thunderstorm – you never knew when it would turn electric or when it would tear everything down."

My fingers froze on the edge of my mic. I didn't say anything. I wasn't sure I could.

"I think for a long time, I thought that's what love was supposed to feel like," he said. "Big. Loud. Shaky. Like if you weren't constantly on edge, you weren't *in* it."

He gave a small, almost apologetic shrug. "By the end of it, I didn't really recognize myself. I stopped trusting what I felt. I was always questioning – was I overreacting? Was I too sensitive? Was I too much?"

His voice stayed calm, but there was something frayed at the edges of it. Something quiet and unraveling.

"And when it ended," he added, "it didn't end with a bang. No screaming match. No dramatic goodbye. Just a text. Like she'd already made peace with it, and I was the last to know."

I swallowed.

He smiled, but it didn't reach his eyes. "Anyway.

After that, I think I stopped believing in capital-L love. Not because I don't want it. But because I don't know what version of me is allowed to have it. All because I was with someone who didn't really want to be with me."

The room was still.

Even the mic seemed to hold its breath.

I shifted in my seat, trying to cover the tightness in my chest with a forced chuckle. "Cool. So glad we chose a light topic today."

Eli let out a soft laugh. "You asked for blood."

"Yeah, well," I said, trying to sound casual, "you didn't have to bleed all over the carpet."

We moved on from the topic a few minutes later, back into safer terrain. But my mind kept circling that moment. That voice. That truth.

He hadn't said her name.

He didn't need to.

It was the first time I'd heard him talk about *her* like that – with ache. With a kind of softness I didn't know he had in him.

I knew very little about the details of their relationship, but of those details, I could write you a story.

Her name was Kat, and they were together for three years. Eli and her met through mutual friends in the local music scene, bonded over shared playlists and late-night coffee, and quickly fell into a kind of fast-burning, all-consuming love that felt like gravity.

I'd met Kat a few times. She was magnetic – sharp-tongued, wildly creative, deeply intense. She challenged Eli in ways no one ever had, made him feel like he was finally someone, like he mattered. But over time, what started as passion turned into volatility.

She was hot and cold. Affectionate one moment, emotionally withholding the next. Their fights were intense – never violent, but psychologically exhausting. Kat had a way of twisting words, making Eli feel like everything was his fault. If he voiced a need, he was being dramatic. If he asked for space, he was selfish. He stopped trusting his own instincts. Started apologizing for things he didn't understand.

There were breakups – two of them, technically – but she always pulled him back in with promises of change and those brief windows of tenderness that reminded him why he fell for her in the first place.

The final straw wasn't explosive. It was quiet.

She ghosted him after a fight about something stupid – some dinner plan she bailed on last-minute – and didn't return his calls for two days. When she finally responded, it was a text. Just a few words.

I think we're done. I need something else. I think you do too.

He didn't see her again.

What followed was the unraveling. Eli lost weight. Couldn't sleep. Deleted all the playlists they made together. He started recording voice notes late at night, trying to remember how to feel like himself again.

Although the breakup wrecked him, honestly, it was the catalyst for what helped us become so tight, so fast.

So, I knew why he was so "anti-love" now. Why its so easy for him to fall in line with the philosophy that, let's be honest, I created for this podcast. It's not that he doesn't want love. It's that he doesn't trust it anymore.

"So, you're telling me it's just not possible?" I asked. "To meet someone who's emotionally present and actually available?"

"No," Eli said, still staring at his laptop screen. His brow furrowed as he swallowed. "anything's possible. I just don't think romance has to be part of it."

"But we're supposed to meet all our emotional needs through ourselves and our friendships?"

"Exactly."

I leaned forward. "But – just for argument's sake – how do we fill that... romance cup?"

Eli smirked. "Romance cup. That's filthy."

I laughed. "You know what I mean. The need to be held. To have someone brush the hair from your face and say everything's going to be okay. To feel like maybe you won't die alone. Like there's someone who sees all your flaws and chooses to stay anyway. Don't we still want that? Even if we don't want to admit it?"

"I think it's possible to evolve past that."

"Really?"

"You did."

That caught me off guard. "I did?"

He glanced up, just for a second. "You go on dating apps like you're trying on shoes. You're not hunting for something to complete you. You're just curious – seeing if anything fits. You don't *need* it. You're already whole. You're a woman on her own, in the best possible way."

I didn't say anything right away.

Mostly because I wasn't sure what to say.

Something about the way he said it – so casually, like he hadn't just dropped a live wire into the middle of our conversation – made my chest tighten.

Not in a bad way.

In a *noticing* way.

The kind of tightness that sneaks up on you, warm and unfamiliar, like stepping into a room and realizing the temperature's changed and you didn't feel it happen.

Because I hadn't realized he knew me like that.

Not just the obvious stuff – my bad taste in exes, my allergy to vulnerability, the way I deflect with sarcasm like it's a sport. But deeper things. The quiet things. That I wasn't dating to be saved. That I wasn't afraid of being alone. That maybe, just maybe, I'd made peace with it. That I was trying to *want* connection without needing it. That I'd built something solid in myself, and I wasn't asking anyone to fill in the cracks.

He saw that.

And not in a performative, "I listen when women talk" kind of way. He simply paid attention. Like he'd been watching me rebuild myself piece by piece and respected the shape I'd chosen.

I never knew he was looking that closely.

And I think that's what caught me off guard.

The realization that Eli – goofy, patient, snack-hoarding Eli – might care more than I thought. Not in some dramatic, romantic way. But in the quiet way that matters more.

The way that lingers.

I cleared my throat and leaned back. "Wow. High praise coming from someone who still uses the same four photos on their dating profile."

He laughed, but his eyes stayed on mine a beat longer than usual.

I looked away first.

"Still," I added, trying to sound breezy, "maybe I wouldn't mind being someone's favorite pair of shoes. Someday."

And even though I said it like a joke, I didn't miss the way his smile softened – like he heard the part I didn't say out loud.

We wrapped the episode a few minutes later, a bit quieter than usual. Fewer jokes. Less interrupting. A kind of stillness hung between us, like the room hadn't caught up to what had just been said.

I unplugged my mic as I'd seen Eli do in the past and started winding the cord, hyper aware of how close we were sitting. Eli leaned back, arms stretched behind his head, the hem of his shirt lifting just slightly to reveal the edge of his waistband. I looked away fast.

What is happening here?

"Wanna stay for dinner?" he asked, casual.

"Can't. I have a date," I said automatically.

He looked over. "Oh, yeah?"

I nodded. "With leftovers and Netflix."

He laughed. "Sounds hot."

"Scorching."

I gathered my things, moving slower than I needed to. Part of me wanted to linger. Just a little. Just enough.

As I rose from the couch and stretched gently, Eli spoke again – quiet, almost like an afterthought.

"Hey, Ro?"

I turned.

He hesitated. "You're really good at this. The podcast. The honesty. All of it."

My heart did something stupid.

"Thanks," I said, holding his gaze just a second too long. "You're not bad yourself."

I slipped my shoes on and ducked out into the cool San Francisco night, closing the door behind me with more questions than answers.

9
EMOTIONAL RESIDUE

There are days when the city feels like background noise. And then there are days – like today – when it feels like a mirror. A little too reflective. A little too honest.

I sat in my apartment with a cup of tea I had no intention of drinking, watching the fog roll over the hill like it had somewhere better to be. The mug was warm in my hands. I hadn't showered. My hair was doing something chaotic that I didn't have the energy to negotiate with. I was wearing one of Eli's old sweaters – the one I'd "accidentally" taken home after a long night of drinking and laughing when he'd said I looked cold and I'd pretended not to hear him offer it twice.

I hadn't told him I still had it.

I hadn't told him a lot of things.

I kept replaying the run-in with Smith like it had an alternate ending I could choose. But no matter how many times I rewrote it in my head, it still ended with him walking away and me standing there like an idiot, flooded with nausea and group text heartbreak.

I didn't miss him. Let's be clear about that. It wasn't about *him*. It was about everything else. The fact that he still had the audacity to smile at me like we were old friends and not like he'd detonated our relationship in front of a digital audience. The fact that part of me still tensed up at the sight of him, still half-expected an apology that could never come in the right shape.

And the worst part – the part I hated admitting even to myself – was that it made me feel disposable. Again. Like there had been no emotional residue on *his* end. Like I'd been a brief chapter in his story while he'd been the cliffhanger in mine.

I didn't want to tell Eli. Not because I couldn't. But because something about it felt too personal. Not in the content, but in the weight of it. I didn't want him to hear Smith's name and offer that gentle look of concern he gave me sometimes. I didn't want softness. I didn't want to be *handled.* I didn't want anything that would remind me I wasn't okay.

And, if I'm being honest, part of me didn't want to see how he reacted. I wasn't sure what I was afraid of. Indifference? Mild curiosity? Something that might suggest I was the only one whose emotional tectonic plates were shifting?

Because lately, things with Eli had started to feel different.

Not dramatically. Not suddenly. More like a steady trickle. A shift in air pressure. Like something unspoken was quietly rearranging itself between us when we weren't looking. Or maybe when only *I* wasn't looking.

We'd always been close. We'd always had that rhythm, that banter, that *thing* people commented on without really knowing what they were pointing at. But lately, it felt less like a performance and more like a tell. Less like a script and more like a confession.

And I didn't know what to do with that.

Because the podcast was doing *well*. Like, surprisingly well. People were sharing it. Messaging us. Quoting our offhand jokes like they meant something. Suddenly, we had *listeners*. We had expectations. And the more people leaned in, the more pressure I felt to stay exactly who I'd promised to be at the start of this thing: detached, disillusioned, romantically irreverent. Not secretly yearning. Not freshly unraveling. Not someone who lay awake wondering what it would feel like to be held in the middle of the night by someone who didn't have to hold me, but wanted to.

I felt like I was being split down the middle: the person I performed on the mic, and the person I didn't know how to be off of it.

And somewhere between those two people, I was disappearing.

I knew I should call someone. Mia. Grace. Hell, the guy who always seemed to pick me up when I ordered an Uber. But I didn't want to talk. I didn't want advice. I didn't want to be told to go for a walk or drink water or make a list of things I'm grateful for.

I just wanted to be allowed to sit in it.

The loneliness.

Because it wasn't just about being single. It was the kind of loneliness that came from not knowing how to talk about what you were feeling without sounding ungrateful. I had friends. A platform. A growing audience. I was doing something *real* for the first time in years.

And I still felt like I was floating off the edge of something.

I didn't want to want for someone. I didn't want to need anyone. But I couldn't stop my mind from wandering to Eli, to keep thinking about the way his voice softened when he asked if I'd eaten that day. The way he always saved the audio files under dumb inside joke names just to make me smile. The way he *saw* me when I wasn't trying to be seen.

And then I thought about how I was still thinking about him.

And how terrifying that was.

I set the tea down, cold now. I pulled my knees to my chest and watched the fog bleed into the city like it was trying to erase everything.

For the first time in a long time, I didn't know what version of myself I was supposed to be.

And I hated how badly I wanted someone to tell me.

10
AFTER THE CREDITS

About once a month, Eli and I have a standing tradition: Movie Night. It's probably the longest tradition we've kept – outside of being each other's emergency contact and our shared blood oath to never, under any circumstance, go scuba diving (sharks. Obviously).

Movie Night has rules. Whoever picks the movie doesn't handle snacks. We alternate picks each month. No repeats. No vetoes. And the snack buyer must provide both savory and sweet or suffer a dramatic reading of one-star Letterboxd reviews.

This month was my turn.

Which meant cinema. Which meant heartbreak. Which meant *Twilight*.

"Romy," Eli groaned from His Side of the couch – an unspoken but fiercely defended territory. "You cannot be serious."

I flicked through the streaming apps on the TV with the focus of a surgeon.

"Dead serious," I said. "It has everything. Passion. Mystery. Brooding. Bloodlust. Teenage recklessness. Also, he literally calls her his own personal brand of heroin. That's poetry."

He let out a laugh that said he was trying not to enjoy

this. "Or a red flag."

The apartment was lit only by the TV glow and a couple of candles I'd set out for ambiance. Outside the window, the city hummed – streetlights flickering against bay windows, Victorians stacked like dollhouses, a hint of fog curling down the hill like it had somewhere to be. I never closed the curtains during Movie Night. I liked being able to see the city. It reminded me that life was happening, even when I was curled up in sweats with mystery stains on my shirt.

Eli had handled snacks, which meant a Mission-style burrito the size of a newborn, a bag of tortilla chips, and a container of salsa balancing on my shins like a ticking bomb.

He couldn't handle anything spicier than mild, but I gave him points for effort.

"This movie is for emotionally stunted adults who haven't moved on from their first fictional crush," Eli muttered, peeling back the burrito foil.

I flung a chip at him. "Say that again but sexier."

He smirked. "You're impossible."

I shifted my legs, so they stretched across the couch, my toes pressing lightly against his thigh. He didn't move. I wasn't sure when we started sitting like this – comfortably entangled – but it had long stopped feeling unusual.

Still. I couldn't help... noticing things now.

He was scruffier than usual. Messier. A little unshaven. Glasses slightly crooked like he'd pushed them up with the back of his hand while doing something else. I remembered what Grace had said – about him being cute – and I'd laughed at the time. But looking at him now...

Okay. So, he was cute.

Objectively.

His eyes crinkled when he smiled. He had that kind of face that didn't just wear emotion – it invited it. Warm, open, like a fireplace in winter. And his voice, when it got low, had this steady cadence that made you want to tell it all your secrets.

Not that I wanted to. Obviously.

Obviously.

He reached across me for a chip and his hand brushed my knee. I startled, just slightly, then swallowed it with a sip of soda.

"You're being weird," he said.

"I'm always weird."

"Yeah," he said, smiling into his drink. "But not like this."

"Explain, Reed."

He popped the chip in his mouth, and it cinematically crunched. After a few chews he spoke. "I touched you just now and you jumped." He wouldn't look at me, eyes focused on the TV although I'd stopped scrolling the second he said I was being weird.

"Jeez, let me live. I wasn't expecting you to graze my knee like that."

"*Like that*? Oh, Romy, you need a boyfriend."

My breath hitched – but I forced it out like a laugh, nudging his thigh with my foot and fixing my eyes on the TV with surgical focus. If I concentrated hard enough, maybe my heart would stop sprinting.

Thirty-some-odd minutes later, somewhere in the blue-green glow of the screen, I realized I wasn't watching the movie at all. Sure, our commentary was solid – Oscar-worthy, honestly – and Eli joked about pitching it as a director's cut companion, but my brain wasn't syncing up with my mouth anymore.

It wasn't far, though. Just a little left of the TV.

It was on Eli.

"It's the little things," he said suddenly.

I turned. "What is?"

He nodded at the screen, though I wasn't sure he was really looking at it. "The things people remember. The way someone looks at you. What they say when they think you're not listening. The way you feel around them, even if you can't explain why."

Something flickered – and it wasn't the candles.

He'd said something like that on the podcast once, early on, when we were still bumbling through our rhythm and accidentally revealing things neither of us was quite ready to share. I'd been editing that episode and paused when I heard him say:

"Sometimes I think it's hard because we don't believe we're worthy of the thing we're looking for."

At the time, I laughed when relistening, texting him that it was his "deep cut moment." But now, with the room dim and quiet and his words echoing in real time, I wasn't laughing.

I said nothing. Just watched him from the corner of my eye as he tore the burrito foil into a tight, perfect spiral and placed it carefully on the coffee table. Then another, even smaller, stacking it like it mattered. His tongue poked out in concentration.

And – God help me – I stared.

At the slope of his nose. The slight furrow between

his brows. The barely-there freckle beneath his left eye. His jaw flexed as he chewed. I suddenly, stupidly wondered what it might feel like to press my palm there. To just... know it.

Panic rose like steam in my chest.

Outwardly, I shifted on the couch like I had a leg cramp. Internally, I was sprinting laps.

"You okay?" he asked.

"Leg cramp," I lied, spectacularly unconvincing. "too much salt. Probably dehydrated."

"Want water?"

"No, I want to suffer."

He smirked. "Classic you."

I reached for the chips and promptly knocked the salsa onto the rug with a wet, traitorous *schlop*. We both froze.

"Don't move," Eli said, diving for paper towels.

"This is your fault," I muttered, frozen in horror, praying the salsa hadn't oozed onto the floorboards.

"My fault?"

"You were being distracting."

He raised an eyebrow. "With my foil sculptures?"

"Exactly."

I watched as he got down on all fours and gently scooped up what remained of the salsa, the way he gently blotted the floor with such care.

Romy, what the hell are you doing? I thought, sinking back into the couch and trying to fixate on the salsa stain I'd be scrubbing tomorrow instead of the sharp line of Eli's jaw – or the way he was so annoyingly gentle. I wished I could clean the moment out of my head as easily.

We sat back on the couch once the damage was done, and for a few minutes, the movie took over. Bella was dramatically sighing. Edward was being intense and weird. And I was trying not to think about the fact that I knew how Eli smelled when he was this close – clean laundry and cedarwood and the faintest whiff of lime shampoo.

Eventually, he shifted to face me, legs extended, his on the inside of the couch and mine on the outside, one arm draped casually across the back of the sofa.

"Can I ask you something?" he said.

I didn't look at him. I was too afraid of what my face might say. "Sure."

"Do you think we're doing this right?"

"The podcast?"

"Yeah. All of it. Sharing what we share. Being who we are. On mic."

I finally turned my head. "What brought that on?"

He hesitated. "I don't know. You've seemed kind of... off lately."

I looked back at the screen. "I'm just tired."

"Of me?"

The way he said it – half-joking, but not really – made my chest go tight. I turned to him fully then, my eyebrows drawn.

"No," I said. "Not of you. Just... of trying so hard to be understood."

He was quiet for a second. Then, softly, "I get that."

And I believed him. I really did. That was the terrifying part.

The foil sculptures glinted faintly on the table. Outside, the city hummed. Inside, something else was humming too. Something inside me. A buzz I couldn't name.

I looked over at him longer than I should've.

He looked back.

And for one strange, suspended moment, neither of us said a thing.

Then I cleared my throat and grabbed the remote. "Let's watch the baseball scene. It's objectively the best part."

"Is that the one with the vampire running like a cartoon?"

"You're about to be educated."

The moment passed. The movie played. The chips disappeared. But something felt... different. Our dynamic. I blamed the podcast. We were being more real with each other than we ever had before. Yeah, okay we joked a lot, we always had, but we were also being real. Being serious. I was seeing a side of him I didn't know existed.

And I feared I was starting to like it.

By now, it was well past midnight, and we were both – if my casual mental math was right – two beers deep. I felt loose-limbed, lightheaded in that soft, jelly-like way that only comes from just the right mix of buzz and burrito. I took a second to actually sit in it – to clock where I was, who I was, and how lucky I felt in that moment. I lived in my favorite city. I was watching one of my all-time favorite movies, next to my best friend – who I'd recently launched a podcast with that was somehow catching fire online – while eating something warm and ridiculously good. And for the first time in what felt like weeks, the weight had lifted. I didn't feel stressed or scared. I felt still. I felt happy. I must've sighed – too loud, too wistful – because Eli glanced over and gave me that look. The one he reserved for moments when he suspected I was spiraling and was trying to catch me before I fell all the way in.

I'd just managed to balance the last tortilla chip on my stomach like a tiny edible mountain peak when the opening notes of *Supermassive Black Hole* came on. Eli reached for the remote and turned up the volume.

"God-tier scene incoming," I said, grinning. "This is cinema."

"I still think the vampire sprinting looks like a Sims glitch."

"You're just afraid of beauty in motion."

He smiled at me, and I tried not to feel it.

Tried not to notice the way his knees were pressed against mine, or how the blanket was stretched loosely across our legs like a question we hadn't asked yet. The room smelled like lime shampoo and burrito, and the glow from the TV made everything feel just a little too close, like the world had pulled in around us.

That's when my phone buzzed.

Once.

Twice.

I ignored it at first. Eli was mid-rant about Jasper's pitch stance, and I wanted to laugh at how seriously he was taking it. But then the third buzz came, and I reached for my phone with the kind of dread you feel before reading a work email after 10PM.

It was from Smith.

Hey. I know I probably shouldn't be texting you. I just keep thinking about running into you. You looked good. Really good. I miss you. Hope that's not too weird to say.

I stared at the screen like it had betrayed me personally.

The ache was instant, low and familiar – like pressing a bruise just to feel something.

Because here's the thing: I didn't want him. I didn't *like* him. But the attention... it was *known*. It was solid in its own broken, backward way. He had hurt me. He had abandoned me. But I understood the shape of that hurt. I knew how to carry it. How to live with it.

With Eli, everything was uncertain. Too soft. Too real.

Smith was a paper cut I could control. Eli felt like falling into something I couldn't define.

"Everything okay?" Eli asked, mouth full of chips.

I locked my phone, too fast, like a kid caught cheating on a test. "Yeah. Just a spam text. I think I signed up for something accidentally."

He gave me a side-eye. "Spam that makes you go completely still for ten seconds?"

I didn't answer right away. The text was burning a hole in my hand. My fingers itched to read it again, to respond, to step back into the rhythm I knew – attention, apology, flattery, repeat.

"Do you ever miss someone just because they used to miss you back?" I asked suddenly.

Eli turned fully towards me. His brow furrowed, gentle but alert. "You're asking if the missing is real, or just reflex?"

"Both."

He didn't speak for a moment. Just stared at me in that quiet way he did sometimes, like he was trying to read between the lines I hadn't written yet. "Familiarity can be seductive," he said eventually. "Even when it's bad for you. Especially when it is."

I looked down at my hands in my lap, the blanket pulled taut over my knees. "I don't want him back."

"Okay," Eli said softly.

"But I liked being wanted. Even when it wasn't real. Even when it came with fine print."

"That's not a crime, Romy."

I nodded. But I didn't feel better.

Because I didn't want to want Smith's attention – but part of me did. I didn't want to be affected – but part of me was. And worst of all, I didn't want Eli to see it – but I was pretty sure he already had.

The silence between us stretched.

On screen, Edward was saving Bella from a van or a vampire or a tragic outfit – who could say – but I wasn't watching anymore. I was too busy spiraling. Because sitting next to Eli, I felt safer than I had in months. But safety felt dangerous when you didn't believe you deserved it.

I accidentally exhaled powerfully, meaningfully, as if I had all the troubles of the world on my shoulders.

"What was that?" he asked, nudging my foot with his knee.

I blinked. "What was what?"

"That noise. You just sighed like someone who found out their Hogwarts letter was fake."

I shrugged and fiddled with my discarded burrito foil, mimicking his earlier sculptures. "It's nothing. I don't know. I'm just terrified that something's about to go wrong." I couldn't put my finger on it, but when I summed up my emotions into one feeling, this was it.

He tilted his head like he was reading between the lines. "Why do you always think happiness comes with an expiration date?"

I didn't answer right away. I focused on folding the foil into a crinkled square, my fingers suddenly becoming stiff.

"I think," I said slowly, "it's because I've never really trusted it. Happiness. It's like this rare thing that shows up unannounced, makes itself comfortable on your couch, and just when you let your guard down, it slips out the window without a note."

Eli was quiet. Too quiet. When I looked up, his expression had softened into something unreadable.

"I hate that for you," he said, stifling a yawn.

I gave a weak smile. "Thanks. I hate it too."

He looked up at the ceiling for a beat; fingers laced behind his head. "You know, you're allowed to trust it a little. The happiness, I mean. Let it stay the night. Give it a toothbrush."

"That's the dumbest metaphor you've ever said."

We laughed.

There was a long pause between us, but it wasn't awkward. Just full. Like it was waiting for something.

"I think you're really good at this," he said suddenly.

I turned. "At what?"

He looked at me like it was obvious. "At making people feel seen. Heard. Like they're not alone."

I didn't know what to say. That was the kind of thing you write on birthday cards, not say on a random Friday night with salsa stains on your socks.

"I don't try to do that," I said softly.

"I know," he said. "that's why it works."

And there it was again – that quiet little gut punch of emotion that always came with Eli. The gentle kind. The kind that made you want to peel your ribcage open and let someone in.

I swallowed the lump in my throat.

"I think that's what scares me," I admitted. "Because if people really start seeing me... what if they don't like what they find?"

His gaze didn't waver. "Then they're idiots."

I laughed, shaky and short, blinking fast.

"You're gonna make me cry. Plus, I'm wearing Twilight-themed socks," I said. "This isn't how I want to be remembered."

"You'd be remembered as iconic."

A few beats of quiet passed. On screen, Bella was whispering something melodramatic. In my apartment, my heartbeat was louder than her voice.

"Hey," he said, gently bumping my foot with his hip. "you're doing enough. You don't have to hold it all up on your own."

I looked at him, really looked at him, and something in my chest softened. It felt like a truth I'd been holding too tightly, finally loosening in my hands.

"I know," I said.

But I didn't really. Not yet.

Still, it felt good to say.

The movie had finally pulled me in, and by the time we reached the ballet studio scene, I was fully locked in – at least until I caught a subtle movement from the other end of the couch. I glanced over, expecting a comment or a reaction, but Eli wasn't watching the screen anymore. He was stretched out on his back, no longer angled toward the TV. One arm was bent above his head, resting across his forehead, casting a faint shadow over his closed eyes. His face was soft in sleep, unguarded. I let my gaze drift lower, to where the blanket we'd been sharing rose and fell steadily over his chest, the slow rhythm of his breathing almost in time with the muted soundtrack of the film.

Was Eli asleep?

I blinked at him.

In all the time we'd known each other – two full years of work, of banter, of inside jokes and hungover brunches – he had never once fallen asleep here. Not during late-night drinks. Not during our impromptu movie marathons. Not even after the time we tried ranking every kind of Trader Joe's frozen meal and nearly slipped into a collective sodium coma.

It wasn't for lack of opportunity. I'd offered plenty of times. Told him he could crash on the couch, that I had extra blankets, that I wouldn't even make him help me clean the kitchen in the morning. He always smiled and thanked me and said something about preferring his own bed. His own shower. His own space.

I'd told myself it made sense. That it was normal. Some people were just like that. But deep down, I think I'd always wondered – maybe even feared – it wasn't about his things or his routine at all. Maybe he just didn't feel settled enough in my space. Maybe being with me, in my world, had never felt easy enough to let his guard down. Not fully.

And yet here he was.

Asleep.

In my apartment. On my couch. Blanket tangled around his legs.

I stared at him, searching my chest for what that meant. What *I* felt about it. I wasn't even sure. It felt significant. Small, but significant. Like a bird landing on your windowsill and making eye contact before it flies off. Blink and you'll miss it, but still – somehow, it matters.

I didn't want to wake him. He looked peaceful. Unbothered. I hadn't seen him like that in a long time, maybe ever. So, I turned back to the movie, what little was left of it, and let it play out in the background.

By the time the credits rolled, the room had gone quiet. That kind of deep, late-night quiet where every sound feels amplified and the shadows grow taller than they were during the day. The soft blue light of the screen dimmed to black, and the candle glow took over entirely – amber and flickering, casting distorted shapes onto the walls. It made the apartment feel older. Like a memory.

I stayed there for a minute, staring at the dark screen. I could've fallen asleep right there, just let myself slide sideways into the warmth of the couch, but something about that felt presumptuous. He was here first. It was his space now, in a weird, borrowed kind of way. And besides, my bed was twenty feet away.

I stood up slowly, trying not to disturb the blanket we'd shared. It took a bit of careful maneuvering – one leg out, then the other, then the slow, awkward pivot away from him – but eventually, I was free.

He shifted slightly, letting out a low exhale. His lips parted more.

I paused. Stared.

I'd never really looked at his lips before. I mean, I'd *seen* them, obviously. I'd made jokes about how much he talked, how he had the mouth of someone with Very Big Opinions about Star Wars, and how he always managed to eat burritos with disturbingly clean precision.

But right now, in the hush of my candlelit apartment, his lips looked... soft. Pink. A little puffy, like he'd been sleeping for hours instead of minutes. They were absurdly kissable, which was not a thought I was proud of having.

Time for bed, Ro, I thought, not trusting where my brain might go next.

I tiptoed into the kitchen and pulled open the cabinet under the sink, rummaging around for that weird miracle disinfectant I'd bought in Chinatown a few months back. It had a cartoon panda on the bottle and was labeled in three different languages, none of which I could read. But the last time I spilled something; it worked like magic. Better than anything Target had ever offered.

I grabbed it and made my way back into the living room, crouching beside the couch and spraying the spot where the salsa had landed earlier. The scent – sharp citrus and something vaguely herbal – cut through the soft sweetness of the room. I blotted slowly, deliberately, trying to be as quiet as possible.

And then I felt it.

A brush – barely there – along my back.

I looked up.

Eli's hand had slipped off the couch, limp and loose

from sleep, and it was now resting lightly against my spine. His fingers curled slightly, like even in dreams he wasn't used to letting go all the way.

My breath caught. Not in panic. Just stillness. A moment suspended.

Gently, I reached up and lifted his hand, placing it back on the couch cushion beside him. His fingers twitched once and then went still again.

I stared at him for a few more seconds. Closer now than I'd been before. The candlelight kissed the side of his face, casting one cheek in soft gold and the other in shadow. He looked different in sleep. Younger, somehow. Less guarded. Like someone I hadn't quite met yet.

I forced myself to look back down at the floor. The spot was nearly gone. Good as new. You'd never know what happened here.

But I did.

I stood slowly, knees cracking just a little, and started to tiptoe toward my bedroom.

Then he moved again.

"Ro..."

I stopped cold.

His voice was hoarse, low, tangled in the haze of sleep.

I turned.

He didn't open his eyes. But his brow furrowed, just faintly.

"Don't... leave..." he whispered.

I didn't move.

Not because he'd said my name, or because I was startled by the fact that he apparently talked in his sleep. I didn't move because something at that moment cracked open inside me.

It was quiet. It was small. But it ached.

Not in the way heartbreak aches. Not sharp or jagged or devastating.

This ache was gentler. A dull, persistent throb. The kind of ache that comes from realizing you're carrying something you haven't had the words for. That maybe you've been carrying it longer than you thought.

And now, there it was. Named without being named.

I stood there, still as stone, in the candlelit room that had suddenly become too full of feeling. I looked at Eli – soft, sleeping, completely unaware of the hurricane happening two feet away.

I didn't know what it meant.

But I knew it meant something.

And I wasn't sure I could un-feel it.

Not anymore.

11
LAUNCH PARTY

The next episode was uploaded and naturally, I slept like total shit that night.

There was no logical reason for it. We hadn't said anything scandalous. No slander. No embarrassing confessions (well, none that weren't intentional). But something about putting myself out there – again – made my skin feel itchy and my mind loop like a skipping record. The weight of it all pressed against my chest like a too-warm blanket I couldn't kick off.

Everything felt weird. And I didn't like it.

It wasn't just the exposure. It was *everything*. The speed of it. The attention. The vulnerability disguised as humor. The way my voice – my actual voice – was now being quoted in someone's comment section.

Everything was starting to feel like it was too much.

There was Eli – who, lately, had become this glowing source of confusion. I couldn't tell where the friendship ended and whatever *this* was began. It was subtle, maddening. I kept catching myself watching him in these stolen glances, catching feelings like a cold I didn't have the immune system for. And just when I started to untangle that thread, Smith had the audacity to slither back into my life. The texts were harmless on the surface, but they clung to me like static. Familiar, flattering, and dangerous in the way old habits always are. I knew better, but it still made something shift in me – like I'd just remembered I used to be what someone else wanted.

And then there was the podcast.

This stupid, brilliant, accidentally successful podcast.

It was supposed to be a joke. A coping mechanism. A way to shout into the void about how little we needed love while secretly hoping someone would shout back. But now? Now we had listeners. Expectations. Brand deals hovering in our inbox and strangers quoting my throwaway jokes like scripture. My voice – my actual voice – was floating in comment sections, being memed and dissected and laughed at. And sure, that should've felt validating. But instead, it felt like I was being hollowed out in real time.

Meanwhile, Eli was thriving. *Thriving.*

He was getting actual dates out of this. Girls sliding into his DMs, practically begging for the chance to "talk shop" over cocktails. And he? He just laughed about it. Like it was all a charming side effect of a thing we accidentally stumbled into – not something I was pouring my soul into. I was the one glued to our metrics. I was the one staying up to write outlines, responding to comments and emails. I was the one taking hits at work because my brain was chewed up by content planning and secondhand heartbreak.

I didn't realize how much more cautious I was about this whole thing than he was. Probably because he wasn't the one whose Slack DMs were suddenly full of

"Heyyy didn't know you had a podcast" messages from coworkers I actively avoided at the office kombucha tap. He didn't have coworkers making thinly veiled jokes about "oversharing" in the break room, or HR policy documents mysteriously landing on his desk with a sticky note that said "page 12 ;)".

Being in Human Resources meant I was supposed to be *neutral*. Safe. Approachable, but not too real. And I had just aired my dating hang-ups, sexual preferences, and abandonment issues in a 10-minute episode called *Thirst Traps & Emotional Booby Traps*. I felt like I'd taken my HR badge and lit it on fire with a match made of oversharing and sarcasm.

And sure, Eli and I had always talked about dating and relationships – but there was something about *this* format. Something that felt like holding a magnifying glass up to him and realizing there were angles I hadn't seen before. Or maybe just never let myself see. Not like this.

The worst part was I was terrified of the change that might bring.

Mia and I met up Saturday morning for one of our ritualistic Hot Girl Walks through Golden Gate Park. That was the joke, anyway. In reality, it was usually just the two of us in matching sunglasses, black leggings, and the kind of unspoken emotional baggage that clung to us like overpriced perfume.

We started near the Conservatory of Flowers and headed west.

We walked in sync past eucalyptus trees and joggers with golden retrievers that looked better moisturized than either of us. I sipped my iced coffee like it held answers. Mia adjusted her headphones around her neck and gave me a sideways glance, the kind that meant she was about to emotionally interrogate me under the guise of girl talk.

"So," she said casually, too casually. "Are we just not going to talk about the fact that *Smith* texted you?"

I exhaled through my nose. "Jesus. Do you have a tracker on my notifications?"

"No. You sent me a screenshot and then never followed up, so naturally, I've been spiraling on your behalf."

I rolled my eyes but felt my stomach twist. "There's nothing to follow up on. He said he missed me. I rolled my eyes so hard I saw my brain. The end."

Mia squinted at me like she didn't quite buy it. "And how did that make you feel, hm? Empowered? Enraged? Mildly aroused?"

"Mostly annoyed. And slightly tempted. But in the way you're tempted to stick your hand in a candle flame. It's not good for you, but part of you still wants to touch it."

She hummed. "Dangerous. Classic. We love a human red flag carnival."

"I'm not going to text him back," I said quickly, maybe too quickly. "I just... I don't know. It stirred something."

"Like what?"

"Like... the part of me that misses being wanted. Even by someone who never really saw me to begin with."

We walked in silence for a bit, the crunch of gravel under our sneakers filling in the space. Mia didn't push, which I appreciated. She just nodded like she understood in that deep, best friend way that didn't require fixing or analysis.

After a minute, she spoke. "You know you deserve better than *familiar*, right?"

"I'm trying to believe that." I said quietly.

I still hadn't told her about Eli. Not really. Which made sense, I guess – considering I wasn't even sure how I felt about him myself. There wasn't anything obvious or nameable yet. Just a flicker. A spark I kept trying to smother with logic and sarcasm. But it was there now, unmistakable. Quiet, but steady. And growing harder to ignore.

I settled into my silence again.

"Let me guess," she said without looking at me, "You're spiraling, in perfect Romy fashion."

"I don't spiral," I said flatly. "I unravel at an artistic pace."

"What's going on? Is it Smith?"

I took a long sip of my lukewarm iced coffee and exhaled like it could cure everything. "It's everything, Mia. It's the podcast, the attention, the pressure – it's not even that people are being mean," I said. "It's that they're not. Everyone's being *so* nice. It's making me nervous. I feel like I'm stressing so hard about everything and Eli's just doing the fun stuff, you know?"

Mia glanced at me over the rim of her sunglasses. "It's called imposter syndrome, babe. Welcome to the club."

I laughed a little, but it didn't quite reach my chest. "I didn't expect to feel this much about it. Like, this was supposed to be a fun little thing with Eli, and now it's snowballing. People are reacting. People are messaging us about their breakups and life stories. I got an email yesterday from someone in Toronto who said the last episode made them realize they're in a toxic relationship they need to end."

"That's amazing."

"It's a lot. I can't help but feel like I'm shouldering it all alone." I paused, then added, "Meanwhile, Eli's out here getting dates because of it while I'm fielding desperate texts from my birthday dumper."

Mia raised an eyebrow. "Wait, what?"

"Yeah," I said, picking at the edge of my sleeve. "Some girl slid into his DMs with a thirst trap. They're going out tomorrow."

"Oh."

"I mean, good for him, I guess. But he gets attention and dates and all this positive feedback, while I get vague side-eyes at work and an inbox full of emotionally wrecked strangers. It's like I'm the brains and the emotional sponge, and he's the charming face that gets the perks."

"You sound jealous."

I blinked at her. "I'm not jealous of the girls. It feels imbalanced. Like we're both standing on a stage, but I'm the one sweating through my shirt while he's just vibing under perfect lighting."

Mia smiled, but gently. "Then fix the lighting. Make it work for you too. And maybe remember that he's not the enemy. He's just not as in tune with the stakes as you are."

I exhaled hard, like the truth had hit something tender.

"I think you both need to realize that you started this for fun. You need a reminder of the good side to all this," she said, stopping short and turning to face me. "Which is exactly why you need to do a launch party."

I blinked. "A what now?"

"A launch party," she repeated, like I was a child who'd forgotten their own birthday. "You've dropped episodes, gained thousands of followers, people are obsessed with your dynamic – *and* you live in San Francisco, where literally anything with a free drink and a ring light gets called a media event."

"People throw parties for *podcasts*?"

"People throw parties for *anything*, Ro."

"I–" I began, but my brain short-circuited. "Mia, no. That's–"

"Exactly what you should be doing," she said, cutting me off. "It doesn't even have to be fancy. A bar buyout, a few cute decorations, QR codes to your latest episode. You can even have it at Etienne's restaurant! You invite friends, let them invite friends. Boom. You get social content *and* build hype."

"I don't know."

"You're not hiding anymore, Romy. That ship sailed when you said the words 'emotionally magnificent' into a microphone and uploaded it to the internet."

She had a point.

"What if it's too soon?"

"It's not. It's perfect timing. Strike while the algorithm's hot."

I groaned and covered my face with my hands. "I hate when you're right."

"No, you *love* when I'm right. You just hate that I'm

never wrong."

We resumed our walk, my head buzzing with the idea of throwing an event where I might have to wear something that wasn't a hoodie and speak to people who knew me from *online*.

Could I do that? Could *we*?

I didn't know. But I knew one thing: if we didn't start treating this podcast like something real, we'd miss the window where it could become something extraordinary.

I glanced at Mia as she adjusted her sunglasses and launched into a story about her mild barista crush.

And in that moment, I realized: she was right.

It was time to stop playing small.

It was time to throw a fucking party.

Mia managed to pull the entire thing together in under two weeks. She booked Etienne's restaurant, curated the menus, designed the invites, and even talked her cousin into doing balloon art. I shouldn't have been surprised – this was classic Mia efficiency – but I still was.

Meanwhile, life kept clicking along like nothing earth-shattering was happening. Work was still painful but manageable. I was just HR-ing my way through each day, dodging comments about the podcast like emotional landmines. Eli and I uploaded two more episodes – *I'm Not Toxic, You're Just Annoying* and *I Faked Liking Their Band and Now I'm In Too Deep* – to what could only be described as sudden, mildly chaotic acclaim.

Blogs were reviewing us now. *Blogs.* One even called us "invigorating," which felt dramatic, but I wasn't mad at it. Another said we were "the podcast equivalent of group therapy with someone who brings snacks". We printed that one out and stuck it to my fridge.

But what I hadn't expected – what no one had warned me about – was the pressure that seemingly had no outlet. The mounting weight of strangers expecting me to be interesting. To be wise. To be raw, but not too raw. Funny, but not trying too hard. The pressure to *not* ruin what was working with Eli. To not say something that pushed us off-balance. To keep the rhythm of the banter without noticing too much how easily we fell into it.

And maybe the scariest part: to keep letting people *in*. Because they were listening. Really listening.

But what's even worse is they were *shipping* us. Like, rooting for us, Eli and I, to get together.

The comments started as a trickle, then flooded in like a busted hydrant:

Like this if you think E & R are secretly dating

I'm sorry, but no way they haven't hooked up

They've got the kind of chemistry you only find in a laboratory

We laughed it off, sure. But neither of us could deny it – there was something there. There had always been something there, but it was platonic and casual, we knew that. But now it was like people were pointing directly at it, screaming "KISS!!!" like we were in a high school hallway.

The night of the launch, I actually tried. Heels. A fitted top that I hadn't worn since pre-COVID. Red lipstick. Blush that made me look like I was in love. Mascara applied with the patience of a surgeon. And honestly? I looked good. I felt like a new version of myself. One who had fans. One who might actually pull this off.

If you'd told me two months ago that I'd be attending a *launch party* for something *I made*, I would've told you to go touch grass.

In typical Eli fashion, he showed up at my place to pick me up. I was just about to shove my foot back into one of the godforsaken heels when the front door creaked open.

I looked up – and couldn't see him. He was hidden behind a massive bouquet of flowers. Like, wedding-proposal massive.

My cheeks flamed. "Eli, you did not."

"Oh, these?" He peeked around the edge of the bouquet. "These are for your neighbor, not – *wow*." he paused, and I felt it – that flicker. That pause that means someone sees you. Really sees you. "Romy..."

I immediately panicked. "Tell me I don't look stupid. Because if I take these shoes off again, they're staying off forever."

"*Romy*," he said, lowering the bouquet, "you look breathtaking."

My heart skidded. Like, literal hiccup in my chest. The room went still. My smile twitched and I dropped my gaze to the floor. "I think you need that glasses prescription updated, Reed."

He stepped forward, his voice low and in a kind of way that undid something in me. "No. Don't change a thing."

Then he hugged me.

And I froze.

We had some tender moments in the past, sure. Like that time he was in a car accident and I rushed to his bedside, thinking he was about to die, only to find out he had minor concussion and some bruising to his ribs, but I wouldn't let his hand go until the nurses threatened to get security because I wouldn't leave his room.

This wasn't comfort. This was *something else.* I wrapped my arms around him and felt the air shift between us. The ground recalibrating beneath my feet.

I pulled away first, needing to breathe. My eyes were traitorous, glistening, and I ducked my face into the bouquet to hide. "These are incredible. Thank you."

He cleared his throat, his eyes darting away. "We're celebrating, right? It's a celebration. Let's celebrate."

And just like that, it was gone. The spell broken.

I laughed, set the flowers gently on the counter, and looped my arm through his as we stepped out the door. But inside, my thoughts wouldn't stop spinning.

There are moments that quietly rearrange something in you – small, almost imperceptible shifts that change the way you see someone, even if you pretend they don't.

One of those had just happened.

And now I had a launch party to survive without letting it show.

The launch was at one of those bars you only ever end up in if someone cooler than you made the reservation. Thankfully, we had an in with the owner. Tucked along the waterfront near the Embarcadero, Etienne's restaurant with some French name glowed like a jewelry box cracked open – twinkling light spilling out from every windowpane. From the outside, it looked almost unassuming, save for the soft shimmer of pendant lights hovering in the fog-dampened air.

Inside, it was all gleam and mood. The kind of place where the host wears a blazer with rolled sleeves and a well-practiced smirk. A low, honeyed hum of conversation rose up from the crowd, cut through by the clink of glass and the occasional pop of laughter.

Chandeliers – sleek, modern ones, not gaudy – hung low from the ceiling, casting soft golden halos onto the polished concrete floor. The bar stretched long and lean across the back wall, crafted from some dark, expensive-looking wood that had likely been imported from a tree with a tragic backstory. Rows of bottles lined the mirrored shelves behind it, glowing amber and rose and emerald, like stained glass in a cathedral built for bad decisions.

Each table was a curated vignette: low, round marble tops with flickering tea lights in gold-rimmed holders, flanked by plush velvet chairs in deep jewel tones. Even the menus were heavy, like they wanted you to know they'd been printed on thick card stock and not just dashed off on somebody's work printer.

Stylish waitstaff – beautiful people in all black with the kind of posture that made you want to straighten your own – glided through the room like sharks with serving trays. Everything about this place whispered indulgence. Nothing screamed, nothing demanded. It didn't have to.

The music thumped low and steadily beneath it all. A DJ in the corner was spinning vinyl with the kind of nonchalant cool that made me feel like I didn't belong at my own party. A remix of something indie and sad played beneath the chatter, a moody soundtrack to the night unfolding.

When Eli and I walked in, I was acutely aware of every eye that flicked our way. Not because people knew who we were – though I hoped at least a few might – but because we didn't exactly blend in. We weren't San Francisco polished. Not quite tech-casual enough to be effortlessly cool, not quite curated enough to look like we belonged here on purpose.

Still, we looked good. I knew we did. Eli's button-up was crisp, tucked in just enough, sleeves rolled perfectly mid-forearm. I'd managed to pull off a red lipstick that hadn't smudged yet and heels that I was already regretting but looked damn good under the lighting.

"Holy shit," I whispered as we paused near the entrance, taking it all in.

Eli leaned close to my ear, grinning. "Yeah. Mia crushed it."

"Crushed it? She annihilated it. This is like GQ meets Vogue meets dynamite."

He laughed and offered me his arm again. "Shall we?"

We wove through the space slowly, soaking it all in – the chatter, the clinking glassware, the warmth of something we'd helped create. A woman near the bar – gorgeous, glossy-haired, very *San Francisco chic* – caught Eli's arm as we passed.

"Wait, you're Eli from *Not in the Mood*, right?"

He smiled, sheepish but unmistakably flattered. "That's me."

"I knew it," she beamed. "God, your voice? It's unreal.

I could listen to you talk about tax policy and still be into it."

Eli laughed, rubbing the back of his neck. "Well, we haven't hit that topic yet, but... maybe season two?"

They shared a quick grin, and I watched her touch his arm lightly before slipping away into the crowd.

I told myself it didn't matter. People flirt. It was harmless.

But something about the way she looked at him – like she already *knew* him – sent a weird jolt through my chest.

I shook it off. Laughed.

I wasn't going to be that girl. Not tonight.

People were already gathered near a small display table with branded podcast stickers and tiny take-home cocktail kits, courtesy of Mia's ridiculous attention to detail.

I caught a glimpse of a few coworkers from LumenLoop near the bar. My stomach twisted into something between dread and pride. One of them nodded at me with a slight raise of their martini glass. Was that approval? Judgment? I couldn't tell.

"I feel like I'm about to give a TED Talk," I muttered.

"You are," Eli said. "a TED Talk with alcohol and less eye contact."

I smiled, but my hands were sweating.

This was happening.

People were here for us.

And somewhere in this glittering mess of ocean views, ambient lighting, and too-loud laughter, I had to pretend I wasn't completely losing my mind.

"Eli! Ro!"

The voice cut through the bass-heavy playlist like a melody breaking through static – bright, clear, unmistakably Mia. We both turned, scanning the crowd, and there she was, gliding toward us like she owned the entire night.

Mia looked like she'd walked off the cover of *Vanity Fair* and directly into our story. Her pantsuit was a rich, dramatic crimson – the kind of color that made you look twice, then again just to appreciate the audacity of it. The blazer was tailored within an inch of its life, cinched at the waist and buttoned just below the sternum, revealing a delicate peek of black lace from the bralette underneath. The look was commanding without trying too hard, powerful and subtly provocative all at once. She wore it like armor made of silk and confidence.

Her lipstick matched the suit exactly – deep and wine-dark, the kind that left faint marks on glass and would absolutely survive the apocalypse. Her hair was swept up in a style that looked effortless but clearly wasn't, and her heels clicked like punctuation marks as she approached.

I barely had time to take it in before she reached us, arms open, radiating joy like a human sparkler.

"Mia, this is insane – you've outdone yourself." I grabbed her without thinking, pulling her into a hug that was half admiration, half desperate gratitude. She smelled like jasmine and something faintly spicy, the kind of perfume that lingered in the air long after she left a room.

She squeezed me back, then turned and embraced Eli too, who looked visibly stunned in the best way.

"Seriously," he said, pulling away and raising his

voice slightly to cut through the music. "You need to do this for a living. I mean it, this is unreal. Thank you."

"You two superstars deserve it," Mia beamed, placing a hand dramatically over her heart like a proud mom at a talent show. "But wait – we need drinks. This will not stand."

She scanned the room like a general issuing orders on a battlefield and locked eyes with a cater waiter gliding past with a silver tray of drinks. With the elegance of a socialite and the precision of a sniper, she flagged him down with a single motion – just a lift of her fingers, perfectly manicured and painted a glossy, dark blood-red to match her suit.

"Here we go," she cooed, plucking three champagne flutes from the tray. She handed one to me, one to Eli, and kept the third for herself. The glasses sparkled under the chandeliers like little vessels of liquid gold.

Mia lifted hers high. "To *Not in the Mood* – the podcast that launched a thousand overshares!"

We clinked flutes, the crystal chime nearly lost beneath the throbbing bass and laughter rippling through the room. The champagne was cold and slightly sweet, bubbles racing up my throat like adrenaline.

I looked over at Eli, who looked back at me with that easy, crooked smile that always made me feel like I was part of an inside joke.

And then Mia leaned in again, voice low, conspiratorial. "You have *no* idea how many people have asked about you two tonight. And by 'asked about you two,' I mean *assumed.*"

"Assumed what?" I asked, raising a brow.

She grinned with the delight of someone lighting a fuse. "That you're together. Romy, the chemistry? You could bottle it and sell it as a skincare line."

"Oh my God," I groaned into my glass. "I swear, if I have to clarify one more time that we are *just friends*–"

Eli raised his glass again. "To being just friends. May it never get weird."

I raised mine. "It's already weird."

I felt it before I saw it – something warm and certain settling around my waist, gentle but sure. My breath caught, just slightly, as I instinctively began to turn, but then I didn't need to. I already knew.

Eli's arm.

It wasn't performative. It wasn't a joke. It wasn't one of our usual friendly digs or dramatic reenactments of being a fake couple in line at IKEA. It was quiet and natural – like his body had made the decision before his mind did.

He pulled me closer, and I went, easily, like a magnet falling into place. I glanced down, toward where our sides now touched, where the soft fabric of his blazer brushed the curve of my hip.

I didn't know what to do with my hands. Or my heartbeat.

So, I lifted my glass and took another sip, letting the cool fizz of champagne distract me from the warmth blooming across my skin.

He didn't say anything. Neither did I.

I looked out toward the crowd – friends, coworkers, strangers, fans. All here because we had the audacity to talk into a microphone about how modern love sucked.

And now here we were.

Celebrated. Champagne in hand. Hearts full. Minds racing.

Tonight was going to be something. I could feel it.

"Romy! Romy!" A voice rang out behind me – bright, eager, unmistakably Grace.

I turned, instinctively stepping out of Eli's hold, his hand sliding away from my waist like silk pulled loose. My skin tingled where his touch had been, and I felt the shift, immediate and uncomfortable, like being pulled from a dream mid-sentence.

There she was – Grace Callahan – bounding toward me with the kind of radiant energy that could light up a funeral. She looked adorable, as always, like a Pinterest board come to life. A soft sage-green slip dress hugged her petite frame; her hair swept into a loose knot that somehow managed to be casual and elegant at the same time. She even had the nerve to pair the look with pristine white sneakers and still make it work. I kind of hated her. I mostly loved her.

"Grace!" I grinned, arms already wide open. She threw hers around me, squeezing me like we hadn't seen each other in years instead of this morning in the break room. She pulled back and gave me an excited kiss on the cheek, the gloss from her lips leaving a faint pink sheen that I didn't bother to wipe off. "I'm so happy you came!" I said, genuinely.

"I wouldn't miss it," she said, eyes sparkling. "You're like, famous now."

"Stop," I rolled my eyes, heat rising to my cheeks. "Barely. Infamous, maybe."

I turned toward Eli, positioning myself between them like a bridge I wasn't sure needed crossing. My voice lifted above the music as I introduced them. "Grace, this is the incomparable Eli Reed."

Eli smiled, stepping forward and offering his hand like the gentleman he occasionally remembered to be. "Hi," he said, warm but reserved, like he wasn't quite sure how much charm to deploy.

Grace took his hand with both of hers, eyes twinkling. "So, *you're* Eli," she said with faux gravity. "I've heard so much about you. And your voice."

"Oh, God," I muttered under my breath. "Here we go."

"You're even cuter in person," she said, unabashed, like she complimented strangers every day for sport.

Eli raised his brows and laughed lightly, clearly caught off guard. "That's probably the nicest way anyone's ever accused me of being the guy on the podcast."

I could feel something strange bloom in my chest – a flutter, or a sting.

I placed a hand on Grace's shoulder and forced an easy smile. "Grace is my work wife. Which means she knows all my secrets. So be careful."

"Noted," Eli said, glancing at me, then back at her. His smile lingered, eyes soft.

Grace giggled. "Well, I'm very invested in this podcast. And now, I guess, in you."

"Wow," I interjected, raising my brows. "Okay, I'm right here."

Eli chuckled. "I'll try not to let the fame go to my head."

Grace leaned in, conspiratorial. "Too late. I'm already thinking about who should play you in the movie version."

"God help us all," I muttered, reaching for another flute of champagne from a passing tray. I took a sip, but the bubbles couldn't drown the low hum in my ears.

Eli, Grace, Mia and I chatted as the room bloomed with light, laughter, and a pulse of music so rhythmic it felt like it had its own heartbeat. The bar shimmered under twinkling chandeliers, and the clink of glasses mingled with bursts of delighted conversation. The DJ tucked in the corner had finally swapped out moody lounge tracks for early 2000s bangers – music that made everyone nostalgic enough to let their guard down and dance like nobody was documenting it, even though every third person seemed to be filming something on their phone.

I found myself caught in the whirl of it all – champagne in one hand, other hand stolen every few seconds for photos. Someone from a local lifestyle blog wanted a shot of Eli and I posed with finger hearts. A group of girls near the back waved me over to say how much the podcast meant to them. Another person asked for a selfie and then whispered that their situationship ghosted them after the third date and they cried while listening to episode two.

"Therapy's expensive," I replied with a wry smile. "we're glad to offer the budget version."

And I meant it, even if it still didn't feel entirely real.

Everything felt golden. Eli had taken my hand at one point and spun me dramatically in the middle of the restaurant, both of us laughing so hard we nearly fell over. We clinked glasses, shouted lyrics over the music, and occasionally clutched each other's shoulders in disbelief that this was actually *our* party. That people came for *us*.

I couldn't remember the last time I felt so adored. So seen. Like I'd stepped into a version of myself I forgot I wanted to be.

But then – just as quickly as the night had lifted me, I found myself separated.

Someone had pulled Eli away to meet a couple from a podcast production agency – he'd mouthed "I'll be right back" over the music – and a friend of Mia's had grabbed me by the arm to introduce me to some San Francisco creatives who were 'desperate' to talk about a collab. From there it was a blur. Hands shaken. Names forgotten. Compliments fielded. Someone offered me a CBD mocktail. Someone else handed me a plate of mini sliders.

Still, I was having a good time. I let myself sway to the music, my cheeks glowing with exertion and champagne. The party was beautiful, and it was *mine*. It was working.

Then – mid-conversation with a woman in an architectural jumpsuit and very bold eyebrows – I looked across the room.

And I saw them.

Eli. And Grace.

They were standing at the bar, just slightly apart, angled in toward each other like magnets testing proximity. Grace was laughing, her head tilted back in that glossy, effortless way that made people lean closer. And Eli did. Torsos touching, obviously flirtatious – and definitely closer than he'd ever stood with me. Close enough that I could see the shift in his posture, the softening in his eyes. Grace rested a hand on his arm.

My stomach dipped. Cold. Suddenly.

I gripped my champagne glass tighter, the stem slick with sweat. I couldn't hear what they were saying, but I didn't need to. Blood rushed through my ears and made me feel off-balanced. I knew what was happening. I felt it in the tilt of her smile. The way he didn't pull back. A high-pitched ring pierced the music, or maybe it was just in my ears. My breath caught in my throat and stayed there, tight as a secret.

Someone beside me said my name, but it sounded like it was underwater. I blinked, smiled too wide, nodded at something I didn't hear. My heart was thudding too loud in my chest, matching the beat of the music but just slightly off. I couldn't seem to blink it away.

I told myself it was nothing. That I was overreacting. That I was tired.

But I wasn't tired.

I was breaking.

For the first time that night, I felt something unfamiliar creep in around the edges of my happiness.

Something sharp. Something quiet. Something that felt an awful lot like jealousy.

12
SUPPOSED TO BE

I woke up with mascara crusted beneath my eyes and the taste of stale champagne clinging to the back of my throat. My heels were still on – one dangling pathetically off my foot – and someone (me) had eaten half a sleeve of saltines in bed. Crumbs everywhere. Of course.

The sun leaked through my blinds like it was trying to punish me, and I rolled over with a groan, immediately reaching for my phone. 6:42 AM. Too early to be alive and far too early to be emotionally coherent.

I blinked at my screen, hoping for some clarity – or, at the very least, no new notifications. No such luck. Thirty-six texts, two missed calls, and the *Not in the Mood* Instagram account was blowing up with tags from people who'd attended the party. A dozen blurry selfies. A few aesthetic snaps of the venue. Someone caught a boomerang of Eli and me mid-laugh, mid-toast, and I don't know what it was about it – maybe the angle, maybe the way I was looking at him – but something in my chest tightened.

That's when I saw it.

I didn't quite register it at first. Just another blurry photo from someone's story – fragments from the launch party last night. A dark room. String lights. Faces I half-recognized. Arms slung around shoulders. The usual.

But then I saw them.

Eli.

Grace.

His head tilted, just slightly. One hand on her hip. Her arms curled up against his chest – one hand resting gently on the fabric of his shirt, the other cupping the side of his face.

And their mouths – pressed together.

Not a peck. Not some clumsy, caught-on-camera brush.

A kiss.

A real one.

I stared at it like it might change. Like the screen might blink and show me something else. A different angle. A misread moment.

But it didn't.

It was them.

Something inside me gave way. Not a dramatic collapse – just a quiet rupture. Like a seam I hadn't realized was holding everything together had suddenly split.

They looked good together.

That was the part I hated most.

They looked like they made sense.

And me? I was sitting alone in my bed, deeply hungover, half-scrolled through a story that hadn't even been posted with malice. It was just a moment. A blurry, stupid moment. But it was sharp enough to cut.

It wasn't like he was mine.

And it wasn't like she'd done anything wrong.

But the flicker I'd been trying to ignore?

Yeah. It was fire now.

And I couldn't un-feel the burn.

I closed the app and let my phone fall onto the pillow beside me.

What the hell happened last night?

Not the party – that was perfect. It sparkled. It danced. It buzzed. We were toasted and celebrated and photographed like we were something worth noticing. I should've been floating. Instead, I felt like I was sinking. Rapidly.

Because somewhere between the cheers and the confetti and the damn espresso martinis, something cracked open inside me. Something I hadn't planned for. Hadn't wanted to examine. Not when it involved him. Not when it involved Eli.

I pulled the blanket tighter around my shoulders and stared at the ceiling, that pit in my stomach swelling again.

I couldn't get the image out of my head. It seared itself into my retinas – bright and permanent – and every time I blinked, it was still there. Staring back at me. The more I tried to shake it, the more the tears welled up, hot and angry behind my eyes.

I kept seeing them at the bar, just moments before – or maybe just after – the kiss. Replaying it like a scene from a movie I never wanted to be cast in. Eli standing too close. Grace looking up at him. His body language giving him away.

He didn't lean back.

He didn't hesitate.

He looked comfortable.

He looked into her.

And I felt... disposable.

I pressed the heels of my hands to my eyes until all I saw were colors behind my lids.

This whole thing, the podcast, was supposed to be something fun. Something safe. A little lifeline to grab onto while everything else in life felt like it was floating out to sea. It was supposed to be ours. Mine and Eli's. Simple. Stable.

Now, I didn't know what it was anymore. I didn't know what anything was anymore.

I didn't sign up for any of this. The pressure. The responsibility. The heartbreak. That was never the goal. My whole life, I'd done everything I could to avoid all of it – relationships, work drama, even friendships that got too tangled. I liked being the funny one, the helpful one, the behind-the-scenes girl with quips and takeout recommendations. Not the person people looked to for answers. Or comfort. Or meaning.

And yet, somehow, here I was. Accidentally becoming someone who mattered to people who didn't even know me. Feeling jealous for reasons I couldn't explain.

Or didn't want to explain.

I felt disoriented in my own life, like I'd been plucked out of my body and dropped into someone else's timeline. Nothing was anchoring me. Not my job, which felt increasingly fragile now that coworkers whispered when I walked past. Not the podcast, which had ballooned into something bigger and more public than I ever signed up for. Not Eli, who was once my constant, but now felt just slightly tilted. Just enough to make me lose my balance.

There was pressure everywhere. Invisible, but palpable. Pressure to keep being sharp and funny. Pressure to hold the audience's attention. Pressure to not mess up this thing we'd accidentally built. Pressure to say the right thing, to avoid the wrong one, to make it all look effortless.

But there was another kind of pressure, too.

Quieter. Slipperier. Harder to name.

The pressure to *not* figure out what I was feeling.

To avoid the full weight of it. To sidestep the questions bubbling up at the edge of my awareness: *What do you want from Eli? What did you expect? What does this mean? Why does it matter?*

Because if I really stopped to unpack it – if I let myself stare too long at the truth of it – I was scared of what I'd find.

And now there was the kiss.

That stupid, blurry kiss.

It wasn't a betrayal in any official sense. Grace wasn't my enemy. Eli wasn't my boyfriend. Nothing had technically been broken.

And yet something inside me felt split anyway.

Like I'd been walking a tightrope I didn't even know existed until it snapped.

It wasn't just that he kissed her.

It was that he *let* himself kiss her.

That he looked at her the way I'd only recently started looking at him.

That she got the moment I didn't even know I wanted.

And now the pressure was inescapable.

It wasn't coming from anyone in particular – it was just *there*. Lingering in the air like fog. Seeping in through the cracks of my windows. Curling up in bed beside me. Whispering, *pretend you don't care. Keep the show going. Don't fall apart.*

And I didn't know how much longer I could.

And it was starting to smother me.

I felt like a shaken soda can. I'd been jostled so many times the past few weeks, I wasn't sure what would happen the moment someone tried to open me. Would I fizz over? Would I explode?

I was tired. Bone-tired. And yet my brain wouldn't stop ticking. I hadn't truly rested in weeks – not since the first episode went viral. Not since strangers started DMing me like I was a licensed therapist instead of a girl sitting in her closet talking shit about modern romance.

And Eli...

Eli had become another question mark in a world already full of them.

I couldn't figure out what bothered me more – that people thought we had chemistry, or that maybe we did. That maybe the line was already too blurry and neither of us had the guts to admit it. Or worse – maybe I was just imagining all of it, while he was off kissing girls like Grace and texting thirst traps with that casual, crooked smile that used to make *me* feel special.

I didn't even know what I wanted from him. I just knew I didn't want whatever *this* was.

Right as my spiral reached its loudest, noisiest, most chaotic peak, there it was – a knock at the door.

Of course.

I flinched like someone had set off fireworks in my living room. My heart thudded in my chest like it was trying to escape.

I already knew.

It was him.

I moved fast, suddenly self-conscious, swiping a makeup remover pad from the bathroom and aggressively scrubbing at the mascara smudges under my eyes. I jammed the wipe into my pocket and padded barefoot to the front door.

I pulled it open.

There he was.

Eli stood in front of me, wearing a hoodie that often times he let me wear, hair tousled like he hadn't bothered to tame it. He looked *slightly* wrecked, in a charming, too-cute-to-be-mad-at kind of way. In one hand he held a giant iced coffee. In the other, a pink box from Bob's Donuts. I didn't even have it in me to roll my eyes.

"Oh, shit," he blinked, stepping back half an inch as he took me in. "You look–"

"Shut up and give me the coffee." My voice came out rougher than I meant it to. Not playful. Not teasing. Just done.

He pulled the coffee back, clutching it to his chest like it was a Fabergé egg. "Hey. We're splitting this. Go take a shower, you maniac."

I didn't reply. I didn't have it in me to banter.

Instead, I turned and headed for the bathroom. The floor felt too cold under my feet. The air felt too still. I cranked the shower to scalding and stepped under it, hoping the water would melt away the tightness in my chest.

But it didn't.

Because no matter how hot the water got, or how clean I scrubbed my face, I knew something was about to break.

And I wasn't sure I'd be able to fix it after.

I came out of the bathroom in sweats and a sweatshirt that Eli had let me borrow months ago that I'd never given back. I just wanted to be comfortable. In some way, I just wanted to be comfortable.

He was on the couch, scrolling Netflix like he didn't set fire to my entire brain last night. Like he hadn't looked at me the way he did or touch my waist like I was his. Like everything was normal. Like nothing had changed. The pink box of donuts was on the coffee table. My favorite mug was in his hand, and another sat on my side of the table, waiting for me.

"Thanks." Was all I could muster as I took my spot on the floor.

He knew me too well. He could sense I wasn't myself. "You good?"

I hesitated and took a bite of a donut. "I don't know how to answer that."

"Was it last night? I thought it went pretty well. Mia knows how to throw a party, that's for sure."

"She does at that."

My mind was swimming. He leaned forward and nudged the ice coffee closer to me, but my mind was spinning. I felt like I couldn't see straight. I felt like I was cracking apart molecule by molecule. I couldn't get the image of him and Grace out of my head.

"So... you had fun? Last night?" he said, settling back,

casual but still on alert.

"Yeah," I said. "a dream."

He looked at me hard. "You okay?"

"Totally."

"You sure?"

"I'm fine, Eli."

He paused. "Okay."

Silence.

I could feel the pressure building behind my ribs, like a cork about to pop. My phone buzzed. Another notification. Another follower. Another message. Another reminder that the internet had their eyes on us. On me.

The iced coffee sat in front of me, sweating like it knew something I didn't. Eli leaned back on the couch and casually tossed his phone to the side like he wasn't holding the other half of my mental breakdown in his pocket.

I hadn't touched the coffee.

He noticed. Of course he did.

"Romy." His voice was softer now, cautious. The way someone speaks when they're scared of spooking an animal. Or maybe a bomb.

"What?"

"You're not really saying anything."

I took another bite of donut I didn't want. "I don't really have anything to say."

"That's not true." He was studying me. "You always have something to say."

I laughed – dry, humorless. "Guess I'm just tired today."

"Of what?"

I stared down at the coffee. "Everything."

He didn't say anything for a moment. Then: "Is this about Grace?"

The name hit me like a slap. My stomach coiled.

"*What*?" I asked too fast.

"I mean," He seemed to look everywhere around the room except at me. "I don't know, I thought you kept looking over last night, and she was just talking to me–"

"You looked *really* cozy for just talking."

He frowned. "Okay..."

"She was touching your arm. Like, a lot."

"And?"

"And you were smiling at her like–" I stopped myself. I could feel my eyes burn with tears.

"Like what, Romy?"

I swallowed hard. "Did you kiss her?"

The question hung in the air like a loaded gun.

Eli's face changed. He blinked, caught. "What?"

"You heard me."

He hesitated. Then– "Yeah. I did."

It knocked the breath from my lungs. Even though I already knew. Even though I'd seen the picture. Hearing it out loud made it real.

He looked at me carefully. "Romy, it wasn't–"

"No," I said, cutting him off. "don't. Just don't."

The air shifted. Eli sat up straighter.

"Are you *seriously* mad about that?"

"I'm not mad," I said sharply. "I'm just–"

"Jealous?"

That word dropped into the middle of the room like a grenade.

"I'm *not* jealous," I snapped. "I just think it's weird that we have this podcast together – this thing we built – and then you go off and flirt with the first girl who says you're funny."

"That's not fair."

"No, what's not fair is how easy this all is for you. You're the charming, lovable one, the one who gets thirst traps in your DMs and girls fawning over you at *our* party. I'm the one who's panicking every second that we've overshared or said the wrong thing or become the punchline of a thinkpiece."

He stood up. "You think I'm not freaking out too? You think I don't feel the pressure? I just don't sit here and let it eat me alive."

"Right. You're just so emotionally stable and well-adjusted," I spat. "Must be nice."

"Jesus, Ro, what is going on with you?"

"What's going on is that I feel like I'm doing this alone." My voice cracked. "I feel like I'm constantly one step away from ruining everything, and you're practically coasting."

"I'm coasting?" he repeated, laughing bitterly. "You mean the podcast I spend hours editing? The socials I run? The fucking brand pitches I've been fielding while you lie on your couch doomscrolling?"

"I didn't ask you to do that!" I shouted.

"No, you just expect me to know when you're upset and tiptoe around you like a fucking mind reader."

"Because you *used* to know!" I yelled, suddenly on my feet. "You used to just get it. You used to *see* me. And now? Now you're just this other version of you, this – this Eli 2.0 who treats women like different flavors and can't clue into the fact that I'm about to fucking fall apart!"

Silence.

Then, quieter: "I'm not your boyfriend, Romy."

"*What*?" I couldn't see him clearly from the tears in my eyes, but at this point, I didn't care if I ever saw him clearly again.

He got to his feet, nothing but the coffee table between us. "I'm not your boyfriend. I'm your friend. Don't treat me like I'm supposed to make all your problems go away when you choose to keep us in this place."

My heart was pounding. Too fast. Too hard.

"I don't–"

"Yes, you do." His words cut me. Deep. "And then you resent it. You resent that I'm not breaking down like you are. And you know what?" He stepped closer, moving the coffee table with him. "I think you hate that people think we're perfect for each other. Because deep down, *you're* the one who can't handle it."

That shattered me.

"You don't get to say that," I whispered.

"It's true."

"No," I said. "What's true is that I built walls for a reason. And you–" my voice cracked. "You made me think it was safe to take them down."

Eli opened his mouth. Closed it. Opened it again.

But I didn't want to hear it.

"I need you to leave."

"Romy–"

"I *need* you to go."

He hesitated. Just for a second.

"Get the *fuck* out, Eli."

And then he walked out.

I didn't wait for the door to click shut before I crumpled to the floor, sobbing. My chest felt like it had been hollowed out.

This was never supposed to happen.

This was supposed to be safe.

This was supposed to be *ours*.

13
SWEEPING UP THE PIECES

I came to on the cold tile of my bathroom floor, cheek pressed to the grout like it was trying to hold me together. My eyes fluttered open slowly, uselessly. I didn't need to ask why I was there. I knew.

Grief had a rhythm, and my body was moving to it.

I groaned and tried to push myself up. My curls clung to my face, damp with sweat – or maybe tears. Maybe both. I reached up to shove them back and froze. The ends were stiff, matted. Coated in something thick and sour.

Of course. Vomit.

I crawled to the tub and turned on the water, fumbling with the handle like someone reaching for a lifeline they weren't sure they deserved.

The water came on with a scream. I clambered in and stood beneath it.

It was cold. I didn't care.

The spray hit my scalp and ran in rivulets down my face, tracing the hollows beneath my eyes and the corner of my mouth. I let it. I imagined it washing the night away, the kiss away, his voice away.

It didn't.

My stomach twisted. I doubled over and threw up

again – what little was left – right onto my own feet. I didn't move. I just stood there, wet and shaking and entirely hollow.

Eventually, I turned the water off and sat on the edge of the tub wrapped in a towel, dripping, empty. The kind of empty that settles deep in your bones. Then I changed into a pair of sweats with a stain I didn't care about and wandered back to my room, freezing in the doorway to the living room.

The apartment looked untouched. Untouched and entirely wrong.

The silence wasn't peaceful. It wasn't still. It *lingered*, like it was waiting for him to walk back through the door and make it right again.

But he didn't.

The coffee table was still askew – moved during the fight. My favorite mug sat where he'd left it, half-full with cold coffee and ringed with cream, like it had been abandoned mid-sentence.

I stared at it until the tears came. Silent. Slow. I didn't try to stop them.

I cleaned. Not because I wanted to, but because it was something to do with my hands. I tossed the donuts. Poured out the coffee. Wiped the rings off the table like maybe that would erase what happened.

It didn't.

My phone buzzed once on the table. I didn't touch it. I already knew what it was: likes, comments, reposts, people tagging us in reaction videos and fan art. Asking when the next episode would drop. Asking if we were in love yet.

I pictured Grace's hands on his face. His lips on hers.

The way he looked at her like she was the only person in the room. Like he'd never looked at me.

A sob escaped my throat before I could swallow it.

I wrapped myself in the blanket from the couch and curled up on my side. The TV played some old *Gilmore Girls* episode I couldn't name. I wasn't really watching. I just needed something that didn't ask anything of me.

After a while, I reached for the notebook and pen sitting on the bottom shelf of the coffee table. A relic from my journaling phase. I flipped to a blank page and sat with the pen for a long time.

Then I wrote, *I don't know what the fuck I'm doing*, five times in a row before giving up and drawing a penis in the margin. It made me laugh, which somehow made me cry harder.

I tossed the notebook aside and opened my phone, immediately swiping away all the podcast notifications. Mia had texted about the party. She had no idea. Nothing from Grace. Nothing from him.

I opened the podcast app and stared at the audio files. The episode we recorded before the world cracked open was sitting there, untouched. Waiting.

I couldn't listen to it.

I couldn't listen to *him*.

Not now. Maybe not ever.

I let the phone slide from my fingers to the floor and curled tighter under the blanket, my chest aching in a way I didn't know how to name.

Everything we built felt like it had splintered beneath my feet.

And I was the one left sweeping up the pieces.

I missed him.

We'd never fought before. Not really. Not like this. Our worst disagreements had been over the best frozen pizza brand or whether my IKEA lamp was tacky or ironic. This? This was something else. Something that felt like it had cracked open my ribcage and left everything inside me exposed.

I hated that I missed him.

I hated that I kept replaying the argument – reordering the words in my head, wondering what I could've said instead. Wondering what I should've said. Wondering if he was doing the same.

Wondering if he was texting her.

That thought made me shoot up off the couch and start pacing the room, hands on my hips like I could physically shake the emotion loose. But it clung to me.

None of this was supposed to happen.

If we hadn't started the podcast, maybe I wouldn't have felt the pressure to be someone. I wouldn't have resented the attention he got, wouldn't have felt like I was carrying the weight of something we both created but only I was bleeding for. There wouldn't have been a launch party. There wouldn't have been Grace. Or the kiss. Or the fallout.

Or maybe there still would have been.

And maybe that's what scared me most.

Why did it hurt so much?

Why did it matter that he kissed her?

He wasn't mine. Not really.

But that flicker – that unspoken, unnamed thing – had grown into something else. A pulse. A wound. A truth I wasn't ready to name until it was already too late.

God, I was so stupid.

My eyes drifted toward my phone on the floor, lying just inches from where I dropped the salsa from the last movie night.

I didn't want to be alone.

I didn't want company either.

I didn't want a solution.

I just wanted someone to *see* me.

Before I could think twice, I reached for the phone.

My thumb hovered, then moved.

I tapped the name.

It rang.

I didn't even know what I was going to say.

But then: a voice.

"Hello?"

"Can I come over?"

14
KEEP ME FROM SHATTERING

He opened the front door, and it was like nothing had happened between us. No apology, no explanation. Just that familiar pull in his eyes – and before he could say anything, I stepped inside, dropped my bag, and kissed him like I was drowning and he was the only oxygen left in the world. It was instant, ravenous, hard, desperate.

Like I'd been holding my breath for days and this was the only way to survive.

He froze for a second, surprised – but only for a second. His hands rose to my face, cradling it like he couldn't believe I was real, like I might vanish if he blinked too long.

"Ro, what's–"

"Fuck me," I breathed, voice raw and wrecked.

Something shifted. His expression darkened, not with anger but hunger, like a fuse inside him had finally sparked. He kissed me back – ferociously, deeply, like I was the thing he'd been waiting for without even knowing it.

His fingers wove into my hair, anchoring me in place. I clung to his shoulders, broad and solid beneath my grip, and pressed every inch of my body against his like I needed to memorize it. Like I'd already forgotten what safety felt like and he was the only version of it I could find.

He lifted me as if I weighed nothing, and I wrapped my legs around him instinctively, naturally, like we'd done this a thousand times before in another life. Our mouths didn't part. We were all tangled breath and teeth and restraint snapping at the seams.

Our bodies pressed like magnets. I couldn't remember where I ended and he began.

He carried me to the couch, lowering me like something breakable. He stayed standing above me, kissing me deeply, tasting me like he'd gone without me for years. His hand slid to the base of my neck – just enough pressure to make my breath hitch. I placed my hand over his and squeezed, guiding him, grounding him, needing more.

I moaned.

He growled.

There was nothing gentle about it. Not now. Not with everything burning beneath the surface.

When our eyes met, there was something feral between us. Something unspoken and undeniable. I wasn't thinking – I couldn't. My mind had finally gone quiet. The noise, the pressure, the heartbreak – it all fell away.

All I knew was his hands, his mouth, the sound he made when I kissed his collarbone like a secret. How the tension coiled tighter every time he touched me, like we were dancing on the edge of something too big to name.

And then he stilled – just for a moment. Just long enough for our eyes to meet again, to see everything we weren't saying. All the want, all the ruin, all the complicated mess of needing someone you know might break you.

"I mean it," I breathed, voice shaking now. "I don't want soft."

He leaned down, eyes burning.

"I don't do soft."

And then we stopped pretending we could.

He pulled back, breathless, pushing the coffee table aside with one foot like it was nothing. He dropped to his knees in front of me. I shoved my sweatpants down, and he caught them halfway, yanking them the rest of the way off with frantic hands.

They didn't make it past one ankle before he was between my thighs, arms wrapped around them like vines, dragging me down the couch toward him.

We paused. Just for a second. Our eyes locked.

Then he pulled my underwear aside and buried his mouth in me.

My body jolted. My back arched. My fingers flew to his hair, tugging, tangling, trying to stay tethered to something real. He licked me like he knew me. Like he knew every spot, every rhythm, like I was the first and last thing he ever wanted.

It was electric, pure intensity, all for me. My eyes rolled back in my head and my brow furrowed as he pressed his thumbs against me, circling slowly, confidently, like he knew exactly how to make me fall apart.

I was gone. I was gone and I never wanted to come back.

I squeezed the cushions, clutched at my own breasts, trying to survive it. His tongue moved like he was unraveling me on purpose – soft at first, then rougher,

NOT IN THE MOOD

deeper, relentless.

I stopped thinking. There was only sensation – blinding and endless.

And when I came, it wasn't quiet. It felt like an exorcism.

I was entirely, irrevocably, his.

But he wasn't finished.

He pulled me even lower, one hand spreading me wider, thumbs pressing against me like I was his canvas, and he was painting pleasure onto every inch. My eyes rolled back. My hips trembled.

There was no stopping it – even if I wanted to.

The second orgasm tore through me like wildfire, and I gasped at its force.

I yanked him up by the chin and kissed him, wild and grateful. His mouth tasted like me, and I loved it – I wanted to crawl inside his skin.

I wanted him in every way. Now. Fast. Hard.

I couldn't wait any longer.

I tugged his shirt off, palms running greedily over the warm muscle beneath. His chest, his ribs, the soft line of hair I'd fantasized about tracing with my tongue. He pulled my sweater off with one quick motion and kissed me again like we'd been starved. My hands traced the slope of his chest, the tension in his shoulders, the ache between us becoming unbearable.

He cupped my breasts, thumbs brushing my nipples through my bra, and I pressed his hands in tighter until the pressure made me gasp. He growled again – deeper this time, feral – and with one swift motion, he snapped the center of my bra forward. It popped open and hit the floor.

His face was in my chest before I could exhale.

I groaned. Loud. Needful.

He pushed me back on the couch, spreading my legs and leaning into me as I fumbled with his belt, unbuckling it with shaking fingers while he hooked my knee over his shoulder, eyes never leaving mine. Once the belt dropped, I unzipped his pants and reached into the waistband of his boxers, finding him hot and impossibly hard.

I brought my hand to my mouth, spit, and slid it back down.

He hissed. I grinned.

I stroked him slowly, teasing, watching his jaw clench, his throat bob, the tension coil tighter and tighter. I needed him inside me. Now.

As if reading my mind, he lowered his jeans and boxers just enough. I reached between us, wrapped my hand around him, and guided him to me.

He pressed forward slowly, savoring it. The stretch, the connection, the gasp I let out when he filled me completely.

He stayed there for a beat, inside me, still and shaking with control.

Then I grabbed his hair, pulled his face to mine, and looked him dead in the eyes, like he was the only thing that could keep me from shattering.

"I said, *fuck me*."

15
EMOTIONAL DESTRUCTION

I woke up tangled in unfamiliar sheets, the fabric clinging to my skin like guilt. The ceiling above me was not my own. Too smooth, too beige, too impersonal. And yet – familiar.

Then it all came back.

The kiss.

Eli and Grace. The blurred photo. Her hand on his chest. His lips on hers. That sick feeling rising in my throat like something sour I hadn't finished swallowing.

The silence. The fallout. The heartbreak.

The phone call.

The goddamn phone call.

My heart thudded once – hard – like it was trying to kick me out of my own body. I sat up slowly, painfully, every muscle aching, but not from the kind of night that made you glow. This ache was shame. Regret. The heaviness of someone trying to escape herself and failing.

The blanket slipped off my chest and I froze.

Naked.

Of course I was naked.

Because why stop at emotional destruction when I could go for the full, scorched-earth package?

I scanned the room. My sweater was looped over a light fixture like a ghost had tried to hang itself. The coffee table was tipped sideways, a casualty in last night's desperate unraveling. One of the couch cushions had somehow made it into the kitchen. My bra, a delicate lilac number I'd once justified as a treat-yourself splurge, lay split at the clasp like it had simply given up halfway through the night.

I stood, limbs shaking, and dressed in silence. My sweatpants were crumpled beside the couch like they'd tried to crawl away. I shoved each leg in without looking, without thinking, like if I moved fast enough, I could outrun the memory.

I pulled the sweater off the light and slipped it on, sleeves inside out, tag scratching the back of my neck. Everything felt wrong. My skin didn't feel like mine. My hands didn't know where to go.

I grabbed my phone from the coffee table but didn't check it. Couldn't.

Not yet.

I just had to get the fuck out of this apartment, this neighborhood, immediately.

My bag was by the door, shoes kicked off with the kind of urgency that now felt humiliating in hindsight. I stepped into them, didn't bother to fix the heel that bent under my foot. Just needed to get out. Just needed air.

I opened the front door, eyes stinging from the light.

I practically flung myself down the steps of the apartment, heart thudding so loud it drowned out the sound of my shoes hitting concrete. My sweater was twisted, inside out, my bra clenched in one hand like a white flag I hadn't meant to raise. My mouth tasted sour. My thoughts were running so fast I couldn't catch a single one.

I just needed to be gone. To disappear. To make the night vanish from memory before it burned its shape into something permanent.

Then–

A voice.

"Romy?"

I stopped cold. The word hit me like a brick to the back of the skull.

Smith stood there, just at the edge of the sidewalk, holding two coffees in a cardboard tray like this was something sweet, something normal. His cheeks were pink from the cold or the run or the night we shouldn't have had. His hair was still damp from a quick shower, and his smile flickered at the corners, tentative, unguarded.

He took a step forward, scanning me. Confused. Worried.

"Are you leaving?" He asked, eyes dropping to the inside-out sweater, the mascara smudged beneath my eyes, the hickey blooming below my jawline. "What's going on?"

I couldn't speak. My throat locked around the words. All I could do was shake my head – slow, small – and raise a trembling hand like that alone might stop this moment from spinning further out of control.

"Romy," he said again, slower now, like my name alone might bring me back to the place I'd just fled. "Where are you going?"

"I can't," I choked. "I'm sorry. I'm so sorry, Smith. I

shouldn't have stayed. This – this was a mistake."

He blinked. "What?"

"I need to go." The words tumbled out, shapeless, messy. "I'm sorry. I shouldn't have called. I just – I didn't know what else to do, and then I – *God*. I can't be here."

"Romy – hey – look, it was just a hook-up, okay?" He tried to smile, but it didn't reach his eyes. "You don't have to run. Come back inside. We can figure it out. Or not. Whatever you want."

But I was already stepping back. Shaking my head again and again like it would undo it. My fingers were trembling around the strap of my bag. My eyes burned with the threat of tears. "I can't. I'm sorry. I'm so sorry."

And then–

It was like someone sliced open the sky above me.

I turned.

And there he was.

Eli.

Standing just a few yards away at the street corner, holding a small paper bag, probably filled with croissants from my favorite bakery. His coat unbuttoned, hair a little mussed, eyes squinting slightly in the morning sun.

He'd been walking toward me.

Toward us.

His expression was soft at first – almost hopeful. Like he was surprised but glad to see me. Like he'd missed me and was about to say something easy, something stupid and kind, and this would all blow over.

Then his gaze shifted.

To Smith.

To the coffee in his hands.

To the sweater twisted on my body. The raw look in my eyes. The bra still balled in my fist like a weapon I hadn't meant to carry. The hickey.

And I watched it happen.

That flicker of light in his eyes blinked out like a candle crushed between fingers. His expression didn't crumble. It cracked. Subtle and brutal, like ice under pressure. The kind of heartbreak that doesn't show itself in screams – but in stillness.

He didn't say a word.

He didn't have to.

Because everything was right there.

In the distance between us.

In the silence that hung like fog in the cold San Francisco air.

And in the look he gave me – one I would never, ever forget. Not for the rest of my life. Not even when I tried.

Pain. Betrayal. Understanding. And worst of all – resignation.

I opened my mouth. I didn't even know what I meant to say. His name. A plea. A lie.

Nothing came out.

I watched him turn away, his head bowed, shoulders slack with something heavier than confusion – something closer to heartbreak. He shook his head once, slowly, disbelieving, like he couldn't quite make the pieces of this moment fit together. Like maybe, if he walked long enough, far enough, it would all make sense. Or at least hurt less.

And then he was gone.

Around the corner.

Out of sight.

I stood there, frozen in the middle of the sidewalk, my breath catching painfully in my throat. The city moved on around me, indifferent.

I looked down at the bra in my hand.

And I started to cry.

NOT IN THE MOOD

16
KEEP GOING

I ordered a car. I couldn't walk. I couldn't be trusted with my own two legs. I was a wreck and the universe knew it. If I attempted to walk on my own, I'd probably run into someone from work, or my parents – even though they didn't live here. Or Jesus Christ himself.

I was convinced, in that moment, I was God's favorite punching bag.

I cried – quietly, bitterly – in the backseat of the rideshare. The driver didn't say much. Just glanced at me in the mirror and asked if I was okay. I nodded. That was enough for him.

I'd leave him a generous tip.

When the car pulled up to the curb, I nearly lost it at the sight of her building. Stately. Polished. Manicured hedges. An actual driveway. And there, parked just behind the gate: the Audi I knew like an old friend.

Seeing it nearly shattered me.

I climbed the steps on autopilot, rang the doorbell, and waited. Just standing there felt like a confession.

The door cracked open a moment later.

"Romy?" Mia blinked, her voice equal parts surprise and concern. "What're you–"

"I ruined everything."

I collapsed in her arms before she could say another

word. She pulled me close, shut the door, and let me sob against her shoulder while the rest of the world stayed locked outside.

We sat in what Mia called her parlor – a smaller room off the dining area that was part library, part cozy den. The walls were lined with leather-bound classics, their gold-foiled titles catching the firelight, and the air smelled like old paper and expensive nostalgia. An honest-to-God fireplace flickered in front of us, which she'd lit just for me. She'd made tea I hadn't touched and brought a tray of snacks I couldn't even look at.

I'd choked out the whole story between sobs before she shoved me into the shower and handed me a pair of cashmere pajamas. Now, clean but hollowed out, I was curled up on her couch like a ghost of myself.

"I don't even know what to say," Mia said, cradling a Pottery Barn mug and staring into the flames. Her brain was clearly running at lightning speed, trying to make sense of it all.

"That makes two of us," I murmured. My arm dangled off the edge of the couch, my head resting on it, my voice heavy and slurred from exhaustion.

"What's upsetting you the most right now? Let's talk through this."

She turned slightly toward me, and I sat up, dragging my limbs with me like they weighed twice as much.

"That I can't just fall into a coma and never wake up?" I said, pulling my legs up and crossing them.

She rolled her eyes and pulled the blanket off her lap, draping half over mine.

"Seriously, Ro."

"I am serious," I muttered, rubbing at my swollen eyes. "in the span of twenty-four hours, I singlehandedly torched everything that mattered to me."

Mia nodded, listening.

"I lost it, Mia. I really lost it. That kiss – it did something to me. I can't explain it. I just snapped."

"What do you mean?"

"I screamed at him. I told him to get the fuck out of my apartment. Like – actually screamed it. I don't even really know why. And then I went running back to the one guy who never deserved me in the first place. Just because I wanted to feel wanted. Because I wanted someone to look at me the way Eli looked at Grace. Because I was hurt. How pathetic is that?"

"You're not pathetic."

"I never even went to Smith's apartment when we were together. Not really. Twice, maybe, at the beginning. And now I go back like some walking cliché? And Mia – he lives right near Eli. Right fucking near him. I shouldn't have been so surprised to see Eli, honestly, he lives there."

Mia's lips pressed into a thin line. "And you're sure Eli picked up on what was happening?"

I nodded, pressing my hand to my face.

"Yeah. Definitely. I'd just walked out, and Smith was coming back with coffee, and we were arguing on the street, and then – there he was. Eli. Just... standing there."

She was quiet. I didn't blame her. What could she say?

"I saw his face," I whispered. "I watched the exact

moment something in him broke. And I didn't run after him. I didn't say anything. I just stood there and let him go."

Mia paused, brow furrowing as she set her mug down on the coffee table. "Why did you call Smith, anyway?" she asked softly. "Why did you call *anyone*? Why not just call me?"

I opened my mouth, but no words came. My throat was dry. "I don't know."

"Romy."

"I *don't*, Mia," I snapped, too quickly, too harsh. But then the adrenaline of that flash of anger faded, and I slumped forward, elbows on my knees, eyes on the threads of the blanket pooled around us. "I didn't want to be alone with it."

"With what?"

"The emptiness. The anger. The embarrassment." I shook my head, my teeth clenched. "It felt like everything I'd been carrying – every feeling I hadn't been naming – just cracked open. Like my body couldn't contain it anymore."

"So, you called the guy who used you and tossed you out like day old sushi?"

I flinched. "Yeah."

Mia softened, instantly regretful. "I'm sorry, I just–" she exhaled. "I don't get it."

I swallowed hard, my voice quieter now. "I thought maybe if someone else wanted me, I could forget that Eli didn't."

There was a long silence. The fire popped gently in the hearth.

"Did it work?" She asked finally, voice delicate.

"For five hours and a rug burn."

We both laughed, but it was brittle, broken at the edges.

"I didn't think it through. I wasn't thinking at all. I just wanted to drown it out," I whispered. "everything felt so loud in my head, Mia. That kiss. The image of him and Grace. The way he looked at her like – like it wasn't even a question."

She was watching me carefully now. "Okay, let's talk about that."

"What?"

"The kiss. Why it wrecked you like that."

"It didn't wreck me," I said too quickly.

Mia raised a brow.

I exhaled, frustrated. "Okay, it *wrecked* me. Happy?"

"No. I want you to tell me why."

I hesitated. "Because it was so casual. Easy. Like it had always been heading that way."

"And that made you feel what?"

I rubbed my hands over my face. "Like I'd been stupid. For missing something obvious. For thinking there was space for me in his life that wasn't just professional. Or convenient."

"You thought you had more," Mia said, not unkindly.

"I *felt* like we had more," I snapped, eyes flashing. "And then she kisses him, and he just *lets* her. And I had to sit there and pretend I didn't want to scream; pretend I didn't care that I suddenly wasn't enough."

Mia's voice dropped to a murmur. "But you did care."

I didn't respond. I just stared at the tea I still hadn't touched.

I sniffed, dragging my sleeve across my nose like a

kid, forgetting that it was a cashmere sweater I was wearing that wasn't even mine. "Things started feeling different with him. I don't know when exactly. Maybe it was gradual. Maybe it was all at once and I just didn't notice until it was too late."

Mia nodded, letting me talk.

"Like, I just feel like since we started the podcast, things shifted. We started getting to know parts of each other we didn't know were there. I felt like he started looking at me differently. Longer glances, meaningful stares."

"Meaningful?"

"Yeah, like he was trying to tell me something with his eyes without having to say it out loud."

Mia nodded. "Keep going."

"He'd say certain things or make certain jokes... We had our movie night and while he was sleeping, he spoke. He said my name. He told me not to go."

"Really? *Eli* said that?" Mia said, sarcastic, surprised.

"You don't know him like I do."

"Clearly," she laughed, and I pushed her foot with my own.

"And then at the launch party he touched me, and it was different. I felt something. Mia, he called me breathtaking."

"Okay, that's sweet." She conceded.

"Disgustingly sweet. Like, why can't he just be a pig?" I laughed weakly and stared into the orange flames dancing among the fireplace, as if all the answers were in there.

"So, things started to feel differently lately, is what you're saying."

"Because of the podcast. And who even knows what's going to happen to it now – I fucked everything up."

"Ro, you didn't fuck everything up, you're just too in it, right now, to see straight."

I turned toward her. "I saw his face, Mia. I watched it fall apart in real time. There's no unseeing that. No rewinding it."

She was quiet for a moment, then leaned in, her tone serious. "So, what are you going to do?"

I didn't know how to answer that question.

I kept replaying the last week in my head like a film I hate but can't stop watching. Every scene burns. Every line of dialogue feels louder in retrospect. Every look, every silence, every mistake – I see them all in technicolor now. I don't even recognize the girl who made those decisions. And yet, she was me. She *is* me.

I just didn't know what I was doing. I really didn't.

It started with that kiss. Grace. Eli. My friend. My *Grace*. And Eli – Eli who had always been mine in this way that wasn't romantic, or maybe it was, but I didn't have the vocabulary for it. We were partners, co-creators, teammates in this weird little corner of the internet where people loved us for being single, sarcastic, and safe from the complications of real intimacy.

We built something that mattered. Something I loved. But somewhere along the way, I think I stopped being able to separate the podcast from the person. I wasn't just performing anymore – I was *feeling*. Every time Eli looked at me while we recorded, or brought me bagels when I was hungover, or touched my arm during a stupid story – I felt something shift.

And I ignored it. Because what else was I supposed to do?

We had rules. We had boundaries.

And we'd been this way our entire friendship.

And then I saw them. In that photo. Grace's hands on his chest. Their lips *on each other*. And everything I thought I'd neatly buried inside me came roaring back like a monster breaking out of its cage. It was jealousy, yes – but it was also grief. This deep, gutting ache like I'd lost something I didn't know I had.

And I panicked.

I picked a fight. I tore open a hole in the only thing in my life that had been stable. I told him to get out of my apartment like he was the problem, when really – I was. I was the mess. The coward. The saboteur.

And then I did the worst thing I could have done.

I called Smith.

Why?

Because I wanted to be wanted. Because I thought maybe if someone else looked at me like I was special, I'd stop feeling like I was breakable. Like I was disposable. Like Eli had picked someone else and left me with nothing. But all I did was make it worse.

The sex didn't make me feel better. Not really. It made me feel numb. And then guilty. And then like I was trying to crawl out of my own skin. And when I left his apartment, barefoot in my half-on shoes, bra in hand like a fucking cliché – I ran straight into Eli.

The look on his face broke me. And it should have. I deserved it.

Because in that moment – when everything else had burned down and all I had left was the truth – I realized what I'd been running from for months. Maybe years.

It wasn't just that I wanted someone to want me.

It wasn't about validation. Or loneliness. Or Grace. Or even the kiss.

It was about *him*.

The way he looked at me when I made a bad joke.

The way he always remembered to get extra sauce, even when I didn't ask.

The way I felt safer near him than I ever had with someone I was supposed to love.

The way I missed him – not just in absence, but in silence.

The way it wrecked me to think I might've lost him.

My chest was pounding. My thoughts were moving too fast and too slow at once.

The fire crackled softly between us.

Mia sipped her tea and said nothing.

I turned to her. Slowly. Like the weight of what I was about to say needed to be handled with care.

"Mia," I whispered, my voice nearly gone.

She looked at me, expectant.

I met her eyes.

"I think I'm in love with Eli."

17
SAY IT

I called out of work for the week with 'the stomach flu'. A flimsy excuse, but no one questioned it. Maybe I sounded just pathetic enough. Let them fire me. It'd be a blessing in disguise. I could finally try stand-up. Or disappear into the woods. Either option felt equally plausible.

I took up residence on Mia's couch like a Victorian invalid. For two days, I barely moved. I rotated through her collection of overpriced pajamas and designer throw blankets, blowing through her stockpile of tissues like I was single-handedly reviving Kleenex as a company.

Etienne brought us snacks, soup, and herbal teas I didn't ask for. He didn't say much – just moved through the house like a quiet ghost who knew when to retreat and when to simply place a plate on the coffee table and walk away. I hadn't realized how nice it felt to be taken care of. Not pampered. Just... *noticed*.

That part stung. How starved I'd become for softness, for someone to read my body language and respond without being asked. I'd been single for so long that 'doing everything myself' had calcified into a personality trait. I didn't even know how to want help until someone offered it without strings.

To mention that I was thirsty and have someone hand me a drink?

Insane.

I ignored my phone the entire time I was there. Let it rot in the guest room next to my purse. I needed a full, undisturbed digital exorcism. No pings. No texts. No notifications. No reminders that I was the main character in a slow-motion trainwreck of my own making.

Fuck the podcast.

Fuck Smith.

Fuck my mistakes.

I didn't want clarity. I wanted numbness. I wanted silence. I wanted the unbearable throb in my chest to die down enough that I could fall asleep without waking up gasping.

If I didn't feel better by Friday, I told myself I'd request a leave of absence from work. Say something vague about mental health and burn out. God knows, I wouldn't be lying.

The truth was, I didn't care about anything anymore.

Except him.

Eli.

Eli fucking Reed.

Once I said it – really said it, with air and sound and conviction – something cracked open inside me. Like a dam bursting in the middle of a drought. Everything I'd buried rushed forward at once: the moments, the memories, the dumb jokes, the soft touches, the unspoken things we let hang in the air between us.

Now, I couldn't stop seeing him.

In every quiet corner of Mia's house.

In the rim of the mug I drank from.

In the way my heart did that stupid half-stumble every time I thought I heard his voice.

I wasn't just in love with him.

I was drowning in it.

If you'd told me a week ago that I'd be camped out on Mia's couch, wrapped in one of her fuzzy throw blankets, spiraling into an emotional tailspin over my best friend, I would've laughed. Like, full-body, knee-slapping laughed. I might've even said, "That's rich. Someone write the screenplay."

But none of this was funny.

My adult life had been carefully, sensibly constructed – like one of those IKEA bookshelves you only build once and then pray never collapses. I had a stable job, a rent-controlled apartment with a view of exactly one tree, and a biweekly composting routine. I volunteered. I donated to charity. I once rescued a pigeon. I was a grown-up. A put-together, independent, functioning adult.

And Eli – Eli was just *there*. A constant. Our movie nights, our brunch dates, our shared disdain for people who clapped when planes landed. We made sense. He was the peanut butter to my cynical toast. We were *good*.

And then the podcast happened.

And suddenly it was like someone aimed a spotlight directly at him. Not the kind of spotlight that flatters your cheekbones and hides your pores, either. I mean a painfully bright, blinding light that forced me to actually see him. Not just Eli-the-friend. But Eli, the person. The man.

And Jesus, once I saw it, I couldn't unsee it.

The way he looked at me – like I was something to be understood, not fixed. Like he actually saw me. Those big, soft eyes of his that gave everything away. I used to think I knew what he was thinking because we were close. Now I wondered if maybe he let me know on purpose. The way he touched me, which once felt like friendly comfort, now sent an actual chill up my spine. It wasn't overt. It never had been. But it was there – the way his hand would graze the small of my back when we crossed the street, how he'd brush my hair behind my ear when I was ranting about something, how he'd tease me in ways that made my stomach flip.

How the hell did I not see it before?

That was the thing.

I think it was always there. Waiting for me to be brave enough to name it.

And maybe I wasn't. Not until now.

I kept going back to what I told Mia that night over overpriced cocktails – the reasons, the excuses. We were never single at the same time. One of us was always recovering from a heartbreak, or trying on the wrong person for size. And besides, Eli wasn't *an option*. He was Eli. The person I called first. The one I trusted most. The only man who had never made me feel like I was too much, or not enough, or anything other than exactly who I was.

Our friendship meant everything to me. It still does. Which is what makes this so terrifying. Because what if this feeling – this aching, all-consuming, slow-burn kind of love – ruins everything?

Then again...

What if it's the truest thing I've ever felt?

I left the warmth and safety of Mia's apartment like a baby being torn from its mother – screaming on the inside, clutching the metaphorical blanket of denial. Leaving meant reentering the world. The real world. The one where I slept with men who didn't deserve me and probably ruined the only relationship with someone who did.

I wasn't ready to come out of the cocoon yet. I liked it there. It was soft, and dark, and nothing expected me to put on pants.

But adulthood doesn't have a pause button. Time, the inconsiderate bitch, moves on whether you're ready or not.

Coming home felt like returning to a war zone – except the casualties were emotional, and I was all of them. It didn't feel like mine anymore. My apartment had become a haunted house. I stood in the entryway, gripping my keys like a weapon, and scanned the scene. The kitchen. The couch. The hallway. He wasn't here, but his ghost had left a trail.

The mug he always used was still in the dish rack – chipped on one side, handle too big for normal hands. I never liked it. He loved it.

One of his hoodies – gray, soft, slightly too long in the sleeves – was crumpled on the back of the couch. The one I used to steal when I stayed over at his place during that heat wave because his apartment had A/C. He'd never asked for it back.

And there it was: an unopened box of his favorite protein bars on the counter, peanut butter-flavored and wildly overpriced. I never ate them. I didn't even like them. But I kept buying them because he'd always grab one before we recorded and say, "Gotta fuel the genius."

Each of these things was a tiny emotional landmine. Not explosive – but lingering, like smoke after a fire. I thought about throwing them all away. Torch the building. Start over. But even if I did, he'd still be here. Stitched into the fabric of the place. Of me.

I looked at the couch and saw it – me, curled into the cushions, crying over a date that ghosted me so hard I was convinced he'd entered witness protection. Eli had sat next to me, handed me tissues, and said, completely seriously, "Any man who doesn't want you is syphilis crazy. Not even regular crazy. Like Old Testament, biblical plague levels of insane."

Then the kitchen. I remembered the time we got into a full-blown food fight over whose pasta sauce was better. It escalated quickly. A spoonful of steaming noodles launched across the kitchen, hit him in the neck, and gave him an actual second-degree burn. He wore it like a badge of honor for weeks. "My best friend did this to me," he'd told strangers, smiling like an idiot.

I glanced up at the ceiling, to the top corner above the cabinets – where one rogue noodle still clung to the wall like a battle relic. Too high for me to reach. Too sentimental to remove.

I dropped my bag on the floor. The silence wrapped around me like wet wool.

He wasn't here.

But God, he'd never left.

I was just inching into hour three of *The Office* reruns

– wrapped in a blanket like a sad, emotionally unstable burrito – when I heard a knock at the door.

A soft one.

Tentative. Like the person on the other side was hoping I wouldn't answer.

For one beautiful, deranged second, I thought it was him.

"Eli?" I whispered aloud, barely breathing.

I tore myself free from the cocoon of my blanket and ran the five dramatic steps from the couch to the door. I didn't bother with the peephole. I didn't care. I was ready to throw the door open and collapse into his arms. If I could've burst through the wall like the Kool-Aid man to get to him faster, I would've.

But it wasn't Eli.

It was Smith.

He stood on my doorstep with his hands shoved in his coat pockets, his shoulders slightly hunched, and his big, infuriatingly warm brown eyes looking up at me with this dumb, innocent expression like he'd just wandered here on accident. Like he didn't blow up my life a week ago with the force of a grenade lobbed into a minefield.

I visibly deflated. The hope drained from my body so fast I thought I might collapse.

"Hey," I said.

A pause.

He gave a sheepish little shrug. "Can I come in?"

"I'm not sleeping with you," I said flatly.

His eyebrows shot up. A breath of laughter escaped him – surprised, probably a little wounded. Good.

"I promise I wasn't here for that." He held one hand

up like I was a cop and he was about to be frisked. "I come in peace."

I didn't respond. I just stepped aside and let him walk in.

As he passed me, I caught a whiff of his cologne – dark, spicy, musky. It used to make my brain go soft. Now it just made my stomach flip in the wrong direction. Not because it was a bad smell. But because I hated how easily I'd once been swayed by it. By him. By that feeling of someone wanting me – even if it wasn't real.

"Sit, if you want," I said, gesturing vaguely toward the couch.

Smith perched on the far end, like he didn't know if he was allowed to get comfortable. He tapped his fingers on his thigh – three quick beats, like he was warming up to something. I sat slowly at the opposite end, but even that felt too close. I could still remember the weight of his body against mine. His mouth on my skin. And how empty it had felt afterward. I folded my arms tightly over my chest and tried not to breathe in too deep.

You'd think one of us was about to tell the other we were pregnant.

"What's up, Smith?" I asked, just to fill the silence. "Why are you here?"

He looked nervous. "I hadn't heard from you. And when I tried to call, it went straight to voicemail. I figured your phone was dead, but still. You left so fast the other day, I wanted to check in."

"My phone *is* dead," I admitted. "And I haven't felt like charging it."

He nodded like he understood. Then paused.

"You okay?" He asked gently.

I shrugged. "Not really."

Another pause.

He looked at me for a long beat. "Are you going to tell me what all that was about? The other day, I mean. We hooked up, then I catch you escaping from my apartment like a hostage victim – and now you've gone full ghost mode. I thought we had a good time."

I couldn't sit there anymore. The couch felt too small. The room too full. Him too present. I stood up and crossed the room, planting myself behind the coffee table like it was a shield.

"I had a bad reaction," I said finally.

He blinked. "To what?"

"To sleeping with you."

He let out a short, humorless laugh. "What's that supposed to mean?"

"It means I felt like shit after."

Silence.

I wrapped my arms around myself, bracing for the confrontation I knew was coming.

"You broke up with me, Smith," I said, softer this time. "In a group text. One that, thanks to the internet and the podcast, half the world now has an opinion on. You humiliated me. Then you came crawling back with a smirk like none of it ever happened."

"I didn't know what I wanted," he said quietly.

"No," I said. "You *did*. You knew when you sent that text. You just didn't think I'd ever move on."

He looked away, jaw tightening.

And suddenly, I realized something: I wasn't angry

anymore. Not really. I was just tired. Tired of convincing myself I should care about someone who only came back when it was convenient.

"You were lonely," I said. "And I was there."

He opened his mouth to argue, then stopped. Closed it. Nodded once.

"Maybe," he said. "But that doesn't mean it didn't mean anything to me."

"It didn't mean anything to me," I said, honestly. "I wanted it to. I thought maybe I could trick myself into feeling something again. But the whole time – every second – I was thinking about someone else."

There it was. The truth.

His shoulders stiffened.

"Let me guess," he said, voice low and bitter. "The podcast guy."

I didn't flinch. I didn't deflect.

I smiled faintly. "Yeah. Eli."

Smith let out a slow breath and leaned back against the couch, staring up at the ceiling like it held the answers to life, love, and whatever the hell I was doing.

"I knew there was something there," he said after a long pause. "The way you talked about him. The way you looked when you mentioned his name. It was different."

I shrugged. "It didn't feel different at the time. Or maybe I didn't let it."

He looked over at me. "You ever think maybe you *did* let it? And that's what scared you?"

I didn't have a response to that. It was too close to true.

Smith leaned forward, elbows on his knees, running

a hand through his hair. "Look, I know I screwed up. I was selfish and stupid, and I hurt you. But I think maybe I was trying to hurt you before you could really hurt me. I think I knew, even back then when it was just us and we were exclusive, that I wasn't the one."

I looked at him – really looked. And for the first time in a long time, I didn't feel angry or small or guilty. I just felt done.

"You weren't," I said softly. "And that's not your fault. But I let myself believe maybe you could be. And that parts on me. I'm sorry."

He nodded slowly, absorbing my words, my apology. "So... does he feel the same?"

I hesitated, the silence stretching between us like a thread ready to snap.

"I don't know," I said. "Maybe. Maybe not. But I'm not going to keep sleeping with people just to figure it out."

Smith stared at me. And I saw it – the faint flicker of understanding. Not acceptance. Not peace. But understanding.

He stood. "I'm sorry, too," he said. "For everything. I was an asshole. And I hope you figure it out with him. Or with yourself. Or whatever this is."

I walked him to the door. He opened it, and for a second, the cool air pushed against my legs.

He turned back. "For what it's worth," he said, "he'd be a fucking idiot not to want you."

Then he was gone.

The door clicked shut behind him. I stood there for a long moment, staring at the spot he'd just occupied, like maybe if I focused hard enough, I could still see his outline lingering in the air.

And then I walked back into the apartment. Not because I knew what to do next, but because I had nowhere left to run.

I stood in my kitchen and exhaled.

"I'm in love with Eli fucking Reed," I said aloud.

The words tasted strange – new and raw and terrifying. But not wrong.

I walked to the sink, filled a glass of water, and drank half of it in one breath. My hands were shaking. I braced myself on the counter and stared into the reflection of the kitchen window. My face looked pale and flushed at the same time, like I'd just run a marathon in a dream I couldn't wake up from.

And that's when I heard it.

The knock.

Just three taps. Quiet. Hesitant.

I froze.

No one knocked like that unless they were carrying emotional baggage and a deep sense of regret.

I walked slowly to the door, my heart already thudding like a drumline. This time, I looked through the peephole.

And there he was.

Eli.

He looked... different. Or maybe it was me. His hair was damp from the rain, his hoodie clinging to his frame, and there was something in his eyes that hadn't been there before.

Not softness.

Not regret.

Something more fragile. Like he wasn't sure he had a

right to be standing here, but he was going to do it anyway.

I didn't open the door right away. I needed the seconds.

I needed to remember the pain. The silence. The goodbye that wasn't really a goodbye.

Then I opened it.

He looked up.

"Hi," he said. His voice was small. Not broken. But breakable.

I didn't say anything. Just stared.

"I'm sorry," he continued, hands shoved in his pockets like if he let them hang loose, they'd shake. "I didn't know where else to go."

I didn't move. Didn't blink. Didn't breathe.

"I just needed to see you," he added. "And I know that's selfish. And I don't expect anything. I just needed to say something."

My pulse roared in my ears.

Not yet, I thought. This moment's not for him yet. It's still mine.

I stepped back. Just a few inches.

And then I nodded.

"Okay," I said. "Say it."

18
NOISE

Eli stepped inside like he wasn't sure he was allowed to be here.

He didn't reach for me. Didn't speak at first. Just stood in the middle of my apartment like it belonged to someone else now. And maybe it did. Maybe I wasn't the same girl he used to joke with over coffee and editing software and snack runs.

I didn't move either. My body was humming, alert, a mess of nerves I didn't have a name for. I had just said the thing – out loud – only minutes before. I was still vibrating from the aftershock.

"I saw Smith leave," Eli said, voice quiet.

Of course he did.

I looked at him sharply. "I didn't sleep with him."

He tilted his head, one brow raised. "Last time or this time?"

Oof. "This time," I muttered, sheepish.

He nodded, slow and unreadable. "Cool. Cool cool cool."

I crossed my arms. "You're not here to be snide, right? Because I already have that covered internally."

He shook his head. "No. That's not why I'm here."

"Then why *are* you here?"

A pause. He swallowed.

"Because I couldn't stop thinking about you."

"That doesn't narrow it down," I snapped. "You think about me when I mispronounce words and when I forget to mute myself during Zoom calls while I'm eating chips."

He half-laughed. It was hollow. "Yeah. But this was different."

I waited. Let the silence stretch so tight it could snap.

"I needed to see my best friend," he said.

"Why?"

"I messed up," he said. "That night at the launch party. I was overwhelmed. I didn't know what I felt, or what you felt, or what we were. I thought... maybe I was imagining it. I told myself it wasn't real," he said. "I tried to bury it in jokes. I flirted with Grace to prove a point that didn't need proving."

"You hurt me," I said.

"I know."

There was a beat of stillness. Then another.

"Why does it even matter to you if I slept with Smith?" I asked, arms still crossed, my voice sharper than I intended. "We weren't together. We weren't anything."

His expression twisted. A long pause stretched before us. His voice came out in barely a whisper. "Because I hated thinking about it."

"Thinking about what?"

He hesitated. "You. With him. Like that. After everything. After how we look at each other," His voice became more confident, crueler. "After the way you laughed at my jokes that night and then disappeared. And then I find out you'd slept with *him*. Literally, on the street, outside of his place. The guy who sent you a group text breakup, you went back to him like it was nothing."

I flinched. "Wow, you really went for the jugular there."

He wandered around the room, rubbing his facial hair and deeply lost in thought. He sat on the armrest of the couch like he needed to perch on something solid. His leg bounced anxiously.

"I was jealous," he admitted.

"Good."

He blinked.

"I'm glad," I said, stepping further into the room. "Because you think kissing *Grace* felt like nothing?"

"It didn't mean anything."

"It didn't look like nothing."

"I was trying to forget how I felt."

"By making out with someone *in front of me*? That's a new strategy."

"I didn't mean for you to see."

"Oh, so if I hadn't seen it, it wouldn't have counted?"

He winced. "That's not what I'm saying."

I took a deep breath, grounding myself. "You're not the only one who didn't know what the hell was happening that night. You think I wasn't confused? That I didn't feel the shift and completely freak out inside?"

"I think you handled it better than me."

I gave a laugh so sharp it could cut glass. "You mean by sleeping with someone else? Yeah. I'm a picture of grace under pressure."

"You were trying to move on," he said softly. "So was

I."

I stared at him. "Did it work?"

He didn't answer.

So, I did. "No. It didn't. I was still thinking about you the entire time, Eli. That's the worst part. He was – fine. Kind, even. But he wasn't *you*. He doesn't know me. Not the way you do."

He was looking at the floor, biting the inside of his cheek.

"And the whole time you were kissing Grace, what were you thinking?" I asked.

Silence.

"Tell me."

"I was thinking about you."

We both stilled. The tension rose in the space like heat from a sidewalk.

"I was thinking about you," he said again, barely louder than before. "And how stupid I was for kissing someone else just to make the noise in my head stop."

I sat down on the couch, not next to him, but close enough that he'd have to feel it.

"This isn't easy," I said.

"No."

"I'm angry with you."

"I know."

"You hurt me."

"I know."

"But I still want you here."

His eyes met mine – shaky, uncertain, and entirely vulnerable. "I want to be here."

I nodded, slow. "Okay."

We didn't touch. We didn't reach for each other. We

just sat there, like two people slowly thawing in the same room after a long, frozen silence.

"So," I said, clearing my throat. "You want some tea? I think I have a bag of something citrusy and deeply disappointing."

He smiled, and it was almost the old smile. "Only if you join me."

"I'm not letting you near my kettle unsupervised, so, yes."

I got up, walked to the kitchen, and for the first time in weeks, I didn't feel like I was pretending to be okay.

He was here. And we still had so much to say.

But at least we were finally saying something.

19
PICK A COLOR

Eli stayed for the rest of the day.

It wasn't seamless – not even close. There were pauses that stretched too long and jokes that didn't land quite the way they used to. But still, the air between us felt breathable again. Fragile, maybe. But real.

Even with the awkwardness lingering at the edges, I'd rather have him beside me like that – quiet, a little uncertain, a little too careful – than not at all. It was like trying to reattach a limb after you've already started grieving it. Clumsy. Necessary. Beautiful in the weirdest way.

And the truth was: being around him felt like being home. I hated how cliché that sounded, even in my own head. Like something a wine mom would monogram on a throw pillow. *But it was true.* He was familiar and grounding in a way no one else had ever been. Now that I had finally admitted to myself how I felt – *really* felt – it was like the entire atmosphere between us had changed.

Every glance. Every shared silence. Every casual graze of his arm against mine was dialed up to eleven.

By the time I got around to charging my phone, the screen lit up like a slot machine – buzzing, blinking, vibrating with an overwhelming backlog of texts, missed calls, calendar reminders, and social notifications.

Apparently, three days of emotional avoidance was equivalent to a month in internet time.

Fortunately, no one had noticed the hiccup between Eli and me. Not publicly, anyway. Our backlog of episodes had kept things looking seamless. Eli had even scheduled a few solo clips to tide people over, ones he'd edited and posted without saying a word to me about them. A small gesture that spoke volumes. Even in the middle of our tension, he was still thinking about the podcast. About *us.*

The next morning, after a blurry night of tossing and turning and overthinking every single word we'd exchanged, we decided to record again.

Together we dragged the couch cushions into my closet – our original makeshift setup from the early days of *Not in the Mood*. Back when we didn't know what the podcast was, or who we were to each other. Just two friends with too many opinions and not enough healthy outlets.

Eli stacked the cushions while I adjusted the mic stands. The space was cramped, full of shoes and half-folded laundry, but somehow still our version of sacred. At least it smelled like fresh laundry.

By the time we got everything settled, we were sitting cross-legged on the floor. The cushions propped behind our backs, headphones on, the mics angled just right.

And our knees were touching.

Barely. Just a little pressure. But it was there.

I told myself it was because the closet was small.

NOT IN THE MOOD

That physics was the culprit, not emotion.

But the second I noticed it; I couldn't stop thinking about it. The warmth of his leg against mine. The familiarity of it. The fact that neither of us shifted to make space.

I loved that our knees were touching.

Wait.

I *loved* that our knees were touching?

Who was I? And what had I done with Romy Becker?

"Hello and welcome back to this episode of *Not in the Mood*." Eli's voice radiated in my ears like velvet thunder.

"To *this* episode?" I laughed. "We can't be more specific?"

"I think we're at six?" Eli pursed his lips and rubbed his chin, turning to his laptop and clicking away.

"Eli's not sure because he actually can't count that high."

"I also can't read."

"He's a catch, lady-listeners."

There was a beat. Normally, we'd both crack up here. But instead, Eli just smiled faintly and looked down at his keyboard.

I cleared my throat. "Anyway. I thought we should talk about flags, today."

"*Excuse* me?" Eli choked.

"*Flags*, Eli, with an 'L'."

"Oh, God, okay, much better. So, like, parades?"

I rolled my eyes. "Pick a color to dissect, red or green?"

A pause. "Green."

"Green it is."

"You know green flags, listener. Those things we should be looking for in people but actively ignore because we're drawn to chaos and emotionally unavailable musicians."

"Speak for yourself," I said. "I'm exclusively attracted to people who ghost me and then send a meme six months later like nothing happened."

"That's growth," Eli nodded solemnly.

The tension bubbled beneath our words like a pot left too long on the stove. Still boiling, still threatening to overflow.

I made a face. "Okay, but hot take? I don't think green flags are real."

He blinked. "How can you possibly think that?"

"I mean they're just red flags with better lighting. Like, congrats, you texted me back within an appropriate timeframe – do you want a cookie or a co-dependent relationship?"

He laughed, but I didn't.

"I'm serious," I said. "People talk about green flags like they're these magical signs that someone's emotionally available and secure and drinks enough water. But the second you decide they're safe, that's when they drop the bomb. Green flags are just red flags that haven't matured yet."

"Okay, that's wildly depressing," Eli said, eyebrows raised.

"Sorry, is this *Not in the Mood* or *Live, Laugh, Love*? I thought we were still doing honesty here."

"No, I get it," he said, thoughtful now. "But don't you think that's a little cynical? Like, maybe some people actually mean it when they show up on time and remember your dog's name."

I shrugged. "Maybe. But I've dated enough people who seemed perfect on paper. The kind who ask about your day and open car doors and text good morning. You know what they all had in common?"

Eli tilted his head. "They ghosted you anyway?"

"No," I said. "They had podcasts."

He burst out laughing.

I grinned. "But yes. Also, that."

We sat in the rhythm of it for a second – me on a roll, him recovering. Then he said, more gently, "So what would it take for something to actually feel like a green flag to you?"

The question caught me off guard.

I stared at my mic for a beat.

"I don't know," I said slowly. "Maybe if it didn't feel like effort. If I didn't have to convince myself that it was good. Like, I don't want to be love-bombed. I don't want some big declaration. I just want to feel... safe. Comfortable. Like I can be around them and not feel like I'm auditioning to be their girlfriend."

Eli was quiet. The kind of quiet that said he was listening, not avoiding.

I cleared my throat. "Anyway, sorry, I derailed. What's your green flag?"

He looked at me, a smile ghosting at the edges of his mouth.

"Someone who laughs at my bad jokes."

I raised a brow. "So, you're just in love with yourself?"

He didn't flinch. "Maybe."

I was not blushing. I was *absolutely not blushing*.

"Okay, so you're telling me," I said, shifting against the pillow jammed into my lower back. The cushion deflated dramatically, like it was tired of my emotional weight. I resettled, inching just slightly closer to Eli's knee. He didn't move away. "If someone remembers how you take your coffee, that's a green flag?" I asked.

"Absolutely," Eli said, not missing a beat. "I've been a walking green flag this whole time."

I blinked. Slowly. Repetitively. Into the middle distance. Into the void.

"Okay, but I just feel like that's complete bullshit."

"How many curse words is that I'm going to have to edit out?" he asked, sighing dramatically. "Three?"

"Four. Bullshit," I deadpanned, enunciating it again just to double my impact.

He grinned. "Romy, you're too much of a cynic. I could say literally anything right now and you'd find a way to fight it. You could have the perfect person sitting right in front of you, and you'd swat it away like it was a sticky-handed toddler trying to hug you."

My stomach clenched instinctively.

I laughed, too loud, too sharp. "I have my perspective because the world gave it to me. Don't blame the messenger."

"Here we go," he groaned, throwing his hands up and collapsing dramatically into the couch cushions like he was auditioning for a community theater production of *Woe Is Me.* "'the world is a meanie,'" he said, mocking my voice, "'and it bullied me and now I wear detachment like a badge of honor.'"

"That is *not* what I sound like!"

"Pretty close."

"I don't take pride in not being able to love," I snapped, only half-joking now.

"Then prove it."

I narrowed my eyes. "Excuse me?"

"Who's the last person you loved?"

The question hit me sideways. I stared at him, my mouth dry.

"You," I said, my voice a whisper.

A pause so long I could've written a novel in the silence.

He blinked. "Shut up."

"I'm serious," I said, heart thudding against my ribs like a fist on a locked door. "You mean a lot to me. I missed you, Eli. Those few days we weren't talking? It was – honestly, it was unbearable. I hated it. I hated not hearing from you. I hated not seeing you. I hated being without you."

He was looking at me now, really looking. Quiet and still.

"I love you," I said, softer. "you're my best friend. My ride or die. My end of the world plan. This is it, man. Forever."

The space between us buzzed like it had a pulse.

He didn't speak right away. Just stared at me with something unnamable behind his eyes.

"Should I not have said that?" I added quickly, the panic rising. "I – I didn't mean to make it weird, I just–"

"No," he said, shaking his head slowly. "No, I've never heard you say you love anything before. Not a song. Not a person. Not even bagels."

"I love bagels."

"You tolerate bagels."

"That's a strong foundation for love."

He laughed and rubbed at the stubble on his jaw, and for a second I wanted to reach over and run my thumb along it. For research purposes.

"Add it to the list of things I need to work on," I muttered.

"Damn, that list is getting long."

We both laughed, the tension giving way to something warmer.

Then:

"Ro?" he said quietly.

"Yeah?"

His hand reached out and rested just above my knee. He squeezed gently.

"I love you, too."

My brain short-circuited.

My eyes immediately welled up. Hot tears, out of nowhere, as if my body had been storing them for just this exact moment.

I didn't think. I didn't pause. I launched myself across our tiny makeshift closet studio and practically tackled him, arms flung around his neck, face buried into his shoulder like it was a flotation device in an emotional shipwreck.

"And I love you! And we love each other!" I said, muffled into his collarbone.

Eli laughed and hugged me back tightly, not even reacting when one of the mic stands collapsed with a tragic clang beside us. We stayed tangled like that for several seconds, maybe longer, until I pulled back, wiped my eyes, and smacked him lightly on the head.

"Your fault for saying something nice," I said,

sniffling.

He grinned. "Worth it."

I scrambled back to my corner of the closet, re-fluffing my cushion and trying to pretend I hadn't just experienced a full-blown romantic meltdown next to my pile of shoes. Eli adjusted the mic stand that had eaten it during the hug.

We both looked at each other. Grinning. Idiots.

"So," I said, breathless, my cheeks hurting from smiling too much.

"So," he echoed.

"We're not going to put this episode out, are we?"

"Absolutely not."

"Cool. Just making sure we're both committed to pretending this didn't happen."

We laughed.

And for once, it didn't feel like pretending at all.

20
EMOTIONALLY CONSTIPATED DISASTERS

The rest of the evening with Eli moved along with unsettling ease. We ordered takeout – Thai, like always – because neither of us could make a decision and pad see ew is our shared middle ground. We fought over the spring rolls, watched a dumb movie we didn't really pay attention to, and debated whether my living room would benefit from a floating shelf or whether, as Eli put it, I'd just "clutter it with depression candles and unread mail."

For a few brief hours, it was like nothing had ever gone wrong. Like the podcast hadn't become an emotional battleground. Like he hadn't kissed Grace, and I hadn't self-destructed into Smith's bed. We were just us again. The version of us that knew which takeout places gave you extra rice without asking. That knew how to laugh at the same joke without needing to explain it. That didn't have to try so hard.

But of course, the second the door clicked behind him, and I was alone again, my brain lit up like a casino. Jackpot: anxiety.

By midnight, I was lying in bed like a corpse propped up for emotional autopsy – flat on my back, covers pulled to my chin like armor, eyes pinned to the ceiling like if I stared hard enough, the drywall might open up and deliver some kind of cosmic answer. A whisper. A sign. A PowerPoint presentation titled *What the Hell Just Happened Between You and Eli Reed.*

None arrived.

Instead, I gripped the comforter like a seatbelt during turbulence, chest tight, stomach churning with every passing second.

What did it mean?

What did *any* of it mean?

He had walked back into my life like a ghost who remembered his past life – and then stood in the middle of my living room like it hurt to be in the same space again. And then he told me – he *said* – he couldn't stop thinking about me. That I made noise in his head. That he kissed Grace to drown it out.

And the closet? Oh my God, the *closet.*

That claustrophobic, over-insulated recording studio I used to associate with audio levels and snack crumbs was now permanently seared into my brain as the site of a major emotional event. That was the space where Eli Reed – my best friend, my co-host, the man who haunts my 2 AM thoughts like an unpaid intern in my subconscious – *told me he loved me.*

Sort of.

Technically.

In a very 'ride or die, you're my person, forever platonic soul mate' kind of way.

But still.

It counted.

How was I supposed to sleep after that?

And the worst part was that I believed him. I really

did. When he looked at me with those gentle, devastatingly soft eyes and said, "I love you, too," it didn't feel like a joke or a pity throw. It felt like something real. Something terrifying.

But now he was gone again, and the echo of it all was ricocheting around in my skull with nowhere to go.

What did he *mean*?

Was that a confession or just a glitch in the system? A moment of emotional static disguised as clarity?

Because if it *was* a confession... why didn't he stay?

Why didn't he kiss me?

Why didn't I kiss *him*?

Maybe I'm the coward.

Or maybe he is.

I don't know. I don't know. I don't know.

I rolled over, curled into myself like a snail retreating from touch, the weight of my thoughts pressing against my ribs like they wanted out. I pulled the blanket tighter, as if it could hold me together.

The truth was: my body had already decided.

My chest knew it. My hands knew it. My eyes, my spine, even the softest parts of me. I was in love with Eli Reed.

And the worst part?

I didn't know if he was in love with me back.

He said the words, yes, but with different meaning.

But so do people on reality TV. So do people when they're scared, or tired, or full of Thai food and nostalgia.

And besides, my ears couldn't be trusted.

My ears were hopeless romantics with poor judgment. They once convinced me a guy who brought me gas station flowers was emotionally attuned.

So, no. I wouldn't trust the sound of his voice.

I needed action. Something real. Something unspoken but undeniable.

And until then, I would lie awake. Counting cracks in the ceiling. Tracing every second we spent together. Replaying the way he said, "I love you" and wondering what he meant.

Wondering if, maybe, tomorrow... he'd say it again. And this time, mean it in a way I couldn't misunderstand.

"Girl, are you still asleep?"

A voice pierced my dream like a dagger, and I shot upright like someone had thrown a grenade into the room. I blinked wildly, hair in my face, limbs tangled in the comforter like I'd lost a fight with it.

"What?" I croaked, the word barely coherent.

A loud slap against the comforter beside my leg. "Get up. I brought coffee."

Through the blur of sleep, I saw her: Mia. All five-foot-four of her, hair tucked behind her ears with the neat precision of a ballet dancer-slash-warlord. She wore a headband and a Lululemon tracksuit that practically screamed 'upper-middle-class menace'. The woman didn't just look like a lifestyle influencer – she was one, in another life, probably.

I flopped back onto the pillow. "Mia. What in the name of all that is holy are you doing here at–" I fumbled for my phone; fingers numb with sleep. "Seven in the morning. It's seven in the *morning*."

She rolled her eyes and shook a large plastic cup with the kind of rhythmic confidence usually reserved for dog trainers and bartenders. The coffee inside was a perfect caramel-brown, full of ice, and probably the only reason I didn't throw her out my window.

"So, it's one hour past six and one hour before eight. Big deal." She jiggled the cup again. "Come on, up and at 'em. You look like the beginning of a depression medication commercial."

She turned on her heel and sashayed out of my bedroom like she owned it.

Ten minutes later, I emerged from my room freshly brushed, questionably alive, and already annoyed.

"Just because you like waking up before the sun doesn't mean the rest of the world does." I squinted at her like she'd personally stolen my REM cycle.

"We really need to get you some cuter pajamas."

"We really need to get you out of my apartment."

"You gave me a key."

"For emergencies!"

"It *was* an emergency."

I paused, suddenly suspicious. "Wait. It is?"

She shrugged. "Yeah. I wanted to see you."

"Fair." I sighed, slumped down on the couch – and instinctively moved to the far cushion. Eli's cushion. His invisible outline still felt etched into the fabric. A faint indent where he used to sit, where he'd laugh at me, or roll his eyes, or hand me a snack without asking if I was hungry.

It made my chest tighten like someone had tied a string around it and was slowly pulling.

I brought Mia up to speed. Eli's surprise return. The awkward not-quite-fight. The apology. The declaration that he wanted to be here. His admission about the kiss with Grace. By the end of it, Mia's eyes were doing this very specific thing where one of them twitched and the other blinked too much.

"Speaking of Grace, have you heard from her?"

"She texted me a few times – just checking in, asking if I was okay. Since I said I had the stomach flu. But no actual contact." I used air quotes around the words 'stomach flu'.

"What are you going to say when you *do* talk to her?"

"I don't know. I mean... she didn't do anything wrong." I shrugged. "She had no idea I was starting to like Eli. She's just as innocent as the rest of us."

"I still say she's a bitch."

"Mia!"

"I'm sorry, but no. You don't *accidentally* kiss someone's best friend. That's the kind of thing you clear with a girl first. Group chat rules."

"Maybe she was drunk."

"Maybe she's a whore."

"You cannot just call people whores because they kissed someone!"

"Okay, maybe not a whore, but like... an emotionally tone-deaf dum-dum."

"I'll cross that bridge when I get to it. Right now, I can't get Eli out of my head."

Mia set her coffee down so hard the ice rattled. "Wait. You still haven't told him?"

I froze. "Mia. Told him *what*?"

She stared at me like I'd just told her I was joining a cult.

"That you're in love with him!"

"What is there to tell!?"

"Oh my God, I hate both of you." She grabbed a throw pillow and smacked herself in the face with it. "I mean it. I hate you. I hate him. I hate this slow-burn nonsense you're doing. This is like watching paint dry while crying."

"Yeah, okay, sure, we maybe said we loved each other during the podcast closet recording, but I don't even know if he meant it like *that*. He could've just been feeling nostalgic or performative or–"

She slapped me.

On the leg.

Hard.

"OW! WHAT THE FUCK!"

"WHAT THE FUCK IS *RIGHT*!" She slapped me again, lighter this time.

"Stop hitting me!"

"YOU TOLD EACH OTHER YOU LOVE EACH OTHER?!"

"Did I not mention that?"

"Are you fucking kidding me? Romy Tallulah Becker."

"My middle name is not Tallulah."

"It is now."

I rolled my eyes and pulled out my phone. Opened the app where Eli and I stored all our podcast files. Found the one labeled *closet confessionals*. Hit play. Set it gently on my knee.

Mia's eyes didn't blink once.

She listened like she was studying surveillance footage.

Her expression morphed from amused to shocked to confused to concerned to utterly *giddy* in about thirty seconds flat. Her hand flew to her mouth. She let out a squeak.

When the episode ended, she sat in stunned silence.

"So," I crossed my arms. "Thoughts?"

She blinked slowly. "You're both emotionally constipated disasters."

"That's not a thought, that's a diagnosis."

She leaned in, her voice suddenly gentler. "Romy. He meant it. The way he said it? That was real. He *loves* you. He just doesn't know if he's allowed to want you because you haven't told him."

I swallowed. Hard. Like her words had caught in my throat.

"I don't know if I'm ready to risk everything."

"You already are. Every time you don't tell him. Every time you lie to yourself. That's the risk."

I looked away, cozying myself into the dent on the couch cushion where Eli always sat. Where he might sit again.

Maybe.

If I got brave enough.

"Anyway," I said, way too casually, "I have a date this morning."

Mia blinked. "A *what*?"

"A date," I repeated, slower this time, as if she didn't speak English as a first language.

Her hand flew up like she was ready to smack me again, but I caught it mid-air and scowled. "No more violence! I'm emotionally fragile."

"You're emotionally stupid," she shot back, yanking her hand away. "What are you doing? A date? You, literally, make no sense to me."

"It's multi-faceted. Complex. Nuanced. You wouldn't understand."

"Try me, Tallulah."

I sighed and took a long, dramatic sip of iced coffee, like that would help the words form. "I just... I need to feel like I can still play the part. Slip back into a role I know. I want to flirt and joke and pretend I'm unaffected. If I can go on a date and it doesn't kill me, maybe I'm not as wrecked as I think I am."

Mia squinted. "So, what I'm hearing is: self-preservation through denial."

"Exactly. Thank you for validating my coping strategy."

She raised an eyebrow.

"And look, I also just need a distraction. Sitting around all day picturing what Eli's penis looks like isn't helping anyone."

"I *knew* you thought about it!"

"I can't help it, the man's got emotionally intelligent big dick energy. But that's not the point."

I stood up and started pacing in a circle, half talking to myself now.

"It's just coffee. One hour. Maybe two. Nothing major. Casual, classic, low stakes. I'll probably forget his name before the almond milk's finished frothing."

Mia narrowed her eyes. "Let me see the profile."

I sighed, pulled out my phone, and tapped around until I found Mr. Distraction. I handed her the screen.

She took one look and groaned. "*Beau Draper*? Romy. *Beau Draper*? He sounds like the kind of guy who puts 'entrepreneur' in his bio, but lives in a WeWork."

I snorted. "He's a founder. Of something."

"Oh my God, of course he is. 'Beau Draper, founder of a wellness-based therapy app for men.'"

"He said it's in stealth mode."

"They *always* say it's in stealth mode, Romy! That's bro-code for 'has no product, just a Slack channel and a dream.'"

I took my phone back and looked down at his profile again. His bio said: *Sapiosexual. Coffee snob. Disrupting the latte space.*

I groaned. "Okay, yeah, he might be awful."

"He *will* be awful. But fine. Go. Be insane. Just don't come home in love with a man who thinks servers have feelings."

"No promises," I muttered.

"Romy? It is Romy, right?"

I glanced up slowly, already bracing myself.

Beau Draper. Slightly disheveled in a curated way, dressed like he just left a Barry's Bootcamp class. And – no surprise – not six foot one. Maybe five foot eleven on a good hair day, with the kind of confidence that tried to close the gap. I didn't care about height. I cared about the lie. Why add two inches? Why lie about something so easy to disprove the moment you stood next to someone?

But fine. He was cute.

Wavy brown hair that flopped a little too perfectly over his forehead. Glasses that made his eyes look slightly owl-like – but in a charming, startup-founder-who-reads-Mark Manson kind of way. Strong nose. Smile lines that made his whole face move when he smiled. The kind of guy you'd expect to be in a wellness podcast commercial talking about 'intentional living'. Basically: textbook San Francisco attractive.

"Beau, hi!" I stood and leaned in for a polite hug. He held it just a second too long. Not offensively so – just enough to register.

Whatever. I looked good today.

"Yeah, same! I'm glad we're finally doing this," he said, laughing nervously as he took a step back. It was the kind of laugh that said *I don't do this a lot,* even though I was pretty sure he did this all the time.

I gave a practiced smile. *Dating app champion, dead inside since 2019.* I was pretty sure that exact phrase was somewhere on my profile.

"Same, same. Should we grab a coffee or...?"

"How about you hang here, and I'll go grab the drinks?" He offered, scanning the crowded café like it was a tactical field map. "It's packed, and I don't want us to lose this table."

"My thoughts exactly," I said, gesturing toward the cracked wooden table between us that wobbled every time I breathed near it. I was already counting the seconds until this ended.

"What can I get you?"

"Just a regular coffee. With cream."

He gave a single, crisp nod. "Sweet. Be right back."

I sat down slowly, letting the conversation slip away, and dropped my face into my hands. He seemed *fine.* He really did. Clean-cut. Good posture. Friendly smile.

But he wasn't Eli.

Eli was cuter. Warmer. A little dorkier, in a way that somehow only made him more devastating. He had that cozy-but-hot look. Grace said he looked like a cardigan that made a wish to become a real boy, and honestly, that was still the most accurate description anyone had ever given.

He was just soft. I mean, he worked out, sure – but not in an aggressive, gym-bro way. He just liked being outside. He liked moving. He liked *doing*. And if I had a dollar for every time he tried to get me to go running with him, I could finally quit my job and start my true dream of yelling at birds full-time.

He was the kind of guy who'd caress your face when he kissed you. The kind of guy who'd actually look at you during sex, and not in a weird, serial killer way – but in a *you matter* kind of way. Like you weren't just a body. You were *you*.

Jesus, Romy.

You're on a date.

Get it together.

Beau returned a minute later, balancing two drinks and smiling like he was such a good guy for buying our coffees. He slid a small white paper cup in front of me – piping hot coffee, no lid, steam curling gently upward.

Hot.

I forgot to specify iced. I always drink iced.

I forced a smile anyway. "Thanks."

He sat across from me and sipped his own coffee with a dramatic, appreciative sigh.

"So, how's your morning been?" He asked.

"Not bad. Not great, but not bad," I said truthfully.

His forehead creased. "Oh, no. Why not great?"

"Oh, you know," I said, waving a hand. "My best friend broke into my apartment this morning. Classic Thursday."

He blinked. "Wait – are you sure they're your friend, or should we be calling the cops right now?"

I laughed, a little too loud. "No, no, she just has a key. For emergencies. Which she interpreted as 'I wanted to see you and also brought coffee.'"

Beau smiled politely. "Sounds like a good friend."

"She is. Too good, sometimes." I wrapped my hands around the coffee cup like I was trying to warm my fingers and *not* think about how much I missed iced coffee. Or how Eli always remembered that I liked it cold, even in December.

Beau nodded, then took another long sip of his drink. The pause between us started to stretch.

"So, what do you do again?" I asked, trying to keep things moving.

"I'm a founder," he said immediately, his voice lifting slightly, like he expected a gold star.

Of course you are, Beau.

"Very cool." I said, because I'm polite and we live in a society. "What kind of company?"

"It's in stealth mode right now."

Please say something that isn't already listed on your profile.

I smiled tightly. "So, it doesn't exist yet?"

He laughed like I'd made a good one. "No, no – it exists. We're just building it out right now and refining our market fit."

I blinked slowly. "Okay. And what's the... product?"

"It's a therapy app."

"Oh," I said, already tensing. "Like BetterHelp?"

"Kind of, but better. It's specifically designed for men who've never done therapy before and think they don't need it."

"Ah."

He nodded eagerly. "We're targeting under thirty-five millennial males in tech who are dealing with burnout, emotional detachment, or identity crises."

"Are those real words?"

"We're normalizing emotional expression through push notification journaling prompts and advice breaks disguised as memes. Plus, it integrates with Discord."

Of course it does.

"Right now, we're still shaping the pitch, but think Headspace meets Joe Rogan, but emotionally evolved."

I stared at him like he'd just tried to sell me a weighted blanket made of toxic masculinity.

"Catchy," I said.

He grinned. "We're calling it *Processing*."

I nearly blacked out.

"What do you like to do for fun?" I asked, feigning interest as I stirred the too-hot coffee I didn't even want. "I remember when we were chatting, you said you were really into waterboarding?"

Beau choked on a sip of his cold brew, ran a hand through his hair. "Wind surfing."

"Same thing."

He grinned like I was hilarious. I wasn't. "Yeah, it's amazing, especially out here in the Bay."

"Are you a local?"

"Basically."

"Basically?" I echoed, raising a brow.

"I grew up in Modesto."

I blinked. "That's not the Bay Area."

"It's Bay Area adjacent."

"Sure, it is," I said, smiling into my mug as I took a sip of hot, bitter regret. My taste buds screamed. "So," I leaned forward, giving him my best polite date-face, "what brought you to the dating apps?"

He paused, like I'd just asked about his blood type and his stance on euthanasia. "Whoa. That's kind of a heavy question, don't you think?"

"Is it?" I tilted my head.

He laughed nervously and ran a hand through his hair. "I mean – for a first date it is. It's intense."

"Oh, sorry," I said, not sorry. "I thought it was a pretty standard question."

He shifted in his seat and glanced around the café like someone might be taking pictures of him. His eyes landed on a blonde woman in the corner for about five seconds too long. Noted.

"I just think," he continued, "stuff like that is better left for, like, the third date. You know, once there's a connection."

"So," I said slowly, "you want me to spend three separate hours of my life with you before I'm allowed to know if we're even remotely aligned?"

"I mean – I'm not in a rush," he said, smiling like that was supposed to be charming.

"How old are you again?"

"Thirty-nine."

"Right. Right." I nodded slowly, sipping my awful coffee like it was whiskey. "You've got all the time in the world."

He chuckled, oblivious. "Exactly. I think dating should be fun, you know? Light. Easy." He ran another hand through his hair.

I stared at him and briefly considered setting the table on fire just to make something happen. The urge passed, but the irritation remained.

I hated the way he kept running his fingers through his hair like he was in a boy band audition no one asked for.

I hated that he didn't know how I took my coffee.

I hated that he hadn't made me truly laugh – not once.

I hated that he hadn't asked a single question about me.

I hated that he was thirty-nine and still casually floating through life like growth was optional.

But mostly?

I hated that he wasn't Eli.

Because that's who I wanted to be sitting across from.

That's who would've known how I took my coffee, down to the brand of oat milk.

That's who would've teased me until I spit it out laughing.

That's who would've noticed the look on my face and asked what was wrong.

This guy was fine.

But fine wasn't enough anymore.

"You know what, Beau?" I said, reaching for the tote bag slung over the back of my chair, my fingers fumbling slightly. "I don't think this is going to work."

Beau blinked like I'd just slapped him with a packet of Splenda. "Oh, wow." He raised his hands in mock surrender. "Okay."

"I'm really sorry, but it was great meeting you."

"Wait, what's going on? I thought we were having a good time."

"No, yeah – we were. Kind of. It's just..." I stood, looping the bag over my shoulder. "I don't think it's going to work."

"But why?" He looked genuinely bewildered. "I mean, we talked on the app, we seemed to click. We come here, I buy you coffee – you're welcome, by the way – and now you're just leaving?"

I stopped and turned back to him. "Yeah, Beau, thank you so much for the three-dollar coffee." I smiled tightly. "Really generous of you."

As I pivoted toward the door, he reached out and lightly tugged my sleeve. Not hard – just enough to make me pause. "Seriously, Romy. What gives?"

I froze.

What was I supposed to say? That he wasn't the right kind of warm? That he didn't ask about me, didn't even try to understand what made me laugh or tick or spiral? That his version of emotional depth was being 'not in a rush' at thirty-nine?

I opened my mouth and, instead of anything rational, I said, "I don't have a vagina, Beau."

Beau's jaw dropped. "You *what*?"

"I lost it," I said, somehow doubling down on the insanity. "In the war."

"The *war*?" He echoed, voice rising.

"The one... for women's rights." I gave him a solemn nod. "It got ugly. Lots of casualties."

He stared at me like I'd started speaking Elvish.

"It was great meeting you," I said quickly. "Truly. Best of luck."

I turned and made my escape, walking straight out the door without looking back.

The cool air outside smacked me in the face, and I kept walking until I hit the corner, my pulse buzzing like I'd just committed a crime. I paused, leaned against a light post, and laughed – loud and unhinged. A laugh with no punchline. Just the relief of finally being done with something I never should have started.

And then, almost instinctively, I pulled out my phone.

There was a text.

From Eli.

Hey, I bought that documentary u've been pretending to want to watch. Come over?

I was already on my way.

21
NOT EVEN A LITTLE

I didn't want to go.

That was the first thing I told Eli when he forwarded me the flyer three weeks earlier with the subject line *Let's Be Fake Extroverts Together.*

It was a networking mixer hosted by some podcasting collective I'd never heard of but pretended to know, just in case it was one of those things everyone secretly knew and judged you for not knowing. There was a logo I didn't understand, three sponsor names I didn't care about, and the promise of *free drinks and meaningful connections* – two things I had learned were almost always lies.

But Eli was excited. And Eli being excited was dangerous. It meant I couldn't say no.

"It'll be fun," he said, standing in my kitchen the night before, popping a grape into his mouth like we were discussing brunch, not impending social doom. "Free wine, a name tag with your pronouns, and a room full of people pretending they're not desperate for download spikes."

He wasn't wrong. But still.

"I just feel like mixers are for people who say the word 'content' too much and wear ironic eyeglasses," I said.

"Exactly. We'll fit right in."

So, here I was. Friday night. Wearing my one good blazer and my one bad attitude, standing outside an event space in the Mission that smelled like freshly varnished wood and ambition.

The sign on the door read: *PodBrew Collective Presents: Creators Unmuted.*

Kill me.

I never thought starting a podcast would mean I'd be required to *network*. And I definitely didn't anticipate it would mean brushing elbows with people who called themselves 'audiopreneurs' without irony. But Eli insisted showing up to these things would boost visibility – and be good for the brand, great for potential sponsors. "Enthusiasm gets engagement," he said. "And engagement gets checks."

He wasn't wrong. We were in negotiation talks with a few companies. Real ones. With websites and money and interns named after flowers. The idea that I might get paid to talk about my many, many failed relationships and general disdain for modern dating? Wild. Beautiful. Terrifying. The dream.

The venue was dimly lit with Edison bulbs and exposed brick walls. The ceilings were high, and the air buzzed with voices that mingled into one insufferable hum, like a swarm of bees that had earned marketing degrees.

As we checked in, I took stock of the crowd. A sea of startup-chic men and aggressively cool women, all in cropped jackets and circular glasses, circling each other like Bluetooth-enabled vultures. Nearly everyone held a glass of wine or champagne, and there was an invisible fog of networking tension – like everyone was on their third espresso and second self-introduction.

Words floated around me like verbal static:

"Listener conversion."

"Affiliate partnerships."

"Cross-promo visibility metrics."

I understood none of it, and I had no intention of trying. That was Eli's domain. I was here to look good, drink wine, and try not to spiral.

We slipped around the perimeter of the room, me subtly guiding us toward the bar like I was magnetized. I had no interest in talking to anyone unless a drink was buffering me. Eli must've known. He didn't say a word, just moved in sync with me, one step behind and to the left, like always.

As we waited in line, I could feel eyes. Not in a paranoid way – *actual* eyes. People whispering. People looking.

Was it... us?

We weren't influencers. We didn't get free clothes or hawk probiotics on Instagram. But we *were* a top trending podcast on Apple and Spotify. And apparently, that meant something here.

By the time we each had a drink in hand – mine a glass of white wine I didn't even pretend to know the name of, his a whiskey neat – I was already regretting the too hot blazer I'd decided to wear.

I turned toward the crowd to say something when I felt it. Eli's hand slipped gently into mine. No fanfare. No performance. Just a quiet, grounding gesture.

I looked down at our hands, then up at him.

"You ready?" He asked, voice low, his breath warm

near my ear.

God, he smelled like bergamot and clean laundry. Like comfort. Like danger.

"Now I am." I smiled, even though my heart was beating like a trapped animal.

We walked in together. Two podcast hosts pretending not to be codependent.

Clusters of creators stood in trendy formation, sipping and posturing. We drifted past them, and one by one, they clocked us. The double take. The realization. The flash of recognition.

"You're *the* Romy and Eli?" One woman asked, her voice coated in both admiration and disbelief.

"In the flesh," I said, managing an easy laugh, even though my stomach was doing an anxiety samba.

This one wasn't bad. She wore a leather jacket and a bold lip, and had a voice made for late-night radio. Her show, she explained, was about dating solo – each episode a recap of a recent date and her reflections, as though her audience doubled as her group chat and therapist. It somehow worked.

"Honestly, I don't know how you two do it," she said mid-sip, giving me a once-over like I was a puzzle she couldn't solve.

"What do you mean?" Eli asked, curious but casual.

"The chemistry," she said, pointing between us with her glass. "it's insane. Like, are you sure you're not together?"

That sentence hit me like a slow, rolling wave. I glanced up at Eli just as my cheeks went warm. I hoped the wine was enough of a cover.

Eli smiled. "No, we're not together. We don't want to

mess up what we have."

I laughed. Light. Easy. Like it didn't carve a tiny hole in my chest to hear him say it so definitively.

Mess up what we have.

Is that what he really thought? That *this* – whatever it was – was a delicate machine that couldn't be touched too hard, or it'd break?

I took a longer drink of my wine and blinked toward the room, tuning out whatever polite conversation came next. The mixer was a blur of lights and movement after that. Every conversation felt like it had one foot in our podcast and the other in our personal lives, like we were always performing – even here.

The room itself was sensory overload: soft jazz looping under a thrum of clinking glasses and nonstop chatter. Everywhere I looked, someone was pitching something. Podcasts about murder, podcasts about motherhood, podcasts about mushrooms and crypto and healing your inner child through tarot and tax deductions. It was a podcast buffet, and everyone here thought their dish was Michelin-starred.

"Romy?" A voice piped up from my left. A woman in neon heels and a graphic tee that said *This Mic is My Therapist* beamed at me. "Oh my God. I *love Not in the Mood.* You and Eli have such great tension – like, professionally. The banter? So real."

I blinked. "Thanks?"

"No, seriously, we've used your format as inspo in our brainstorm meetings. I run *Please Recycle This Relationship.* It's a sustainability-meets-breakups pod. Like, what's compostable about heartbreak, y'know?"

I didn't know. I smiled anyway.

We traded business cards – hers was translucent and biodegradable, of course – and she promised to DM me about doing a "collab minisode." I made a mental note to immediately forget.

Eli, meanwhile, was a social machine. He moved through clusters of people like a charming virus, infecting everyone with chuckles and head nods. He had a way of making people feel important when they talked, like he was giving them the cure to loneliness.

We met a couple from L.A. who ran a podcast about polyamory and French cinema. A man with a waxed mustache pitched us on his wellness pod for male influencers called *Bro, Do You Even Breathe?* We picked up swag as we went: four stickers, two mugs, and six unsolicited story pitch decks in our inboxes.

By the time I finished my second glass of wine, I couldn't tell if the room was spinning or if I was just that tired.

I needed air.

"Be right back," I muttered to Eli, not waiting for a response.

Somewhere between the networking, the wine, and the not-together declaration, the room started to shrink. I made an excuse and slipped out the side door of the venue into the alley behind it.

The cool night air slapped my cheeks. San Francisco in fall. Always flirting with fog, never committing. I leaned against the brick wall and closed my eyes, trying to inhale something that wasn't mingled body spray and tech-bro ambition.

The door creaked open behind me. Footsteps. I didn't have to turn to know who it was.

"You okay?" Eli asked.

I opened my eyes and looked straight ahead at the flickering streetlamp casting a slow dance of shadows on the asphalt. "Yeah. Just needed a break from the words."

Eli stepped beside me. Not too close. But not far, either. Just enough space for tension to breathe.

"I shouldn't have said that back there," he said, voice low.

"Which part?" I asked, turning to him.

"That we're not together. That we don't want to mess up what we have." He rubbed the back of his neck. "I just... I didn't know what else to say. I panicked."

"Oh," I said, because that was all I could manage. I wanted to ask why it was so easy for him to say something that broke me in half. I wanted to ask what we were doing. Why we kept orbiting like this – so close we burned, so far we froze.

Eli looked down at his hands, then up at the sky, like maybe the constellations had advice for people who fell for their best friends. "This used to be so easy."

"It's not easy anymore?"

"No," he said softly. "Not even a little."

We stood in silence. Street sounds echoing from blocks away. A door slammed. Someone laughed. A car drove past with music vibrating from the trunk like a heartbeat.

I crossed my arms over my chest. "Do you regret it?"

"Regret what?"

"Telling me you love me."

His face tensed. "No. God, no."

"But you're scared."

"Terrified."

I nodded. "Me too."

He turned to me. "But I'm more scared of not trying. Of being too scared to try."

A breeze caught the hem of my blazer and made me shiver. Eli noticed. He shrugged out of his coat and placed it around my shoulders with a gentleness that made my stomach ache.

We didn't say anything else. We just stood there in the alley behind a room full of people who thought they knew us. Who listened to us every week like we were a finished story. Like we weren't still trying to figure out the next chapter.

Eventually, we went back inside.

But I knew, without knowing how I knew, that something had shifted.

And the next chapter?

It was already starting to write itself.

22
WELCOME TO THE CLUB

I returned to work the following Monday – reluctantly. My body was there, sure, slouched in an ergonomic chair that had lost its will to support about the same time I did. But my heart was somewhere else entirely, still stuck in that quiet place between what I felt and what I couldn't say.

Still, being back helped. The constant ping of Slack, the ritual of emails, the mindless spreadsheets – it gave me something to do that wasn't *feel*. And then, just as I was almost successfully distracting myself, a Slack notification popped up in the lower corner of my screen.

"Hey. Grab a coffee later? My treat."

It was from Grace.

I exhaled, leaning back in my chair like the message had physically pushed me. I'd been dodging her texts all week. Watched them go from "Hey! Need soup?" to "Did you die?" with the slow desperation of someone trying to be respectful and still hoping you'll show up.

And now here she was, asking the thing I'd been low-key dreading.

I knew this was coming. I just didn't know why I'd been avoiding it so hard. Grace hadn't done anything wrong. Objectively. She kissed a guy at a party. That was it. That was the whole crime.

And if I could surgically remove my own feelings from the equation, I'd probably agree. But it wasn't just some guy. It was *Eli.* My best friend. My not-boyfriend. My confusing, infuriating, possibly heartbreaking co-host.

And Grace?

Grace was sweet. Smart. Funny. Confident in that effortless way I had to rehearse in a mirror. She was also oblivious. She hadn't known how I felt. She couldn't have.

Still, my mind – traitorous, insecure thing that it was – did what it always did. Jumped straight to the most dramatic, soap opera-adjacent possibilities.

What if she was really into him?

What if he was texting her?

What if they'd been on dates?

What if they were... together?

What if she was pregnant with his child?

A fresh wave of nausea rolled through me, and I glanced at the trash can under my desk. Just in case.

But underneath all of it, I missed her. She was my friend. And deep down, I knew the thing I was really avoiding wasn't the conversation. It was the *confirmation* – that Eli was moving on, and that maybe I wasn't as important as I thought.

It was time to rip off the Band-Aid.

"After lunch – 1PM?"

She liked the message immediately.

We met at the bougie café down the street from the office – the kind of place that probably had a CBD latte on the secret menu and considered oat milk the default.

Inside, it looked like someone had Googled 'millennial Pinterest dreams' and said yes to everything. Leather couches. Edison bulbs. Coffee tables made of reclaimed wood. Neon signs on the walls declared things like 'It's a good day for coffee' and 'Coffee now, stress later.' Inspirational lies, basically.

Bookshelves lined the walls, filled with color-coordinated hardcovers that I was pretty sure were just there for aesthetics. Plants trailed from hanging pots and perched on shelves like they'd been strategically feng shui'd. It was simultaneously too much and somehow perfect.

The place was mostly empty, probably because it was a gray Monday in the Financial District and no one had the emotional capacity to pretend to be thriving.

I snagged a seat on one of the leather couches and kept my eyes on the front door. A few minutes later, Grace walked in.

She looked... well, like Grace. Effortlessly put-together, even in a slouchy sweater and jeans. She had that innocent I-just-learned-how-to-make-sourdough-during-lockdown kind of charm that made you want to both hug her and knock over her tote bag. If she weren't half my size, I would've already raided her closet by now.

She spotted me, smiled, and gave a small wave before heading to the counter to order. I pretended to be extremely busy on my phone, rereading an email I'd written three hours ago and still hadn't sent.

When she finally sat beside me on the couch, the cushion shifted under her weight, and I felt the conversation stretch out like a tightrope between us.

"Hey," she said softly.

"Hey."

Silence.

I looked at my coffee like it might save me.

It didn't.

"What the fuck is going on?" Grace asked gently, a slight laugh in her voice, though her eyes were full of concern. "Did the flu actually kill you, or...?"

I glanced up at her and tried to smile, but it didn't stick. The awkwardness hit me like a slow wave, rising steadily until it coated every inch of my skin. I didn't want to have this conversation. I also didn't want to keep avoiding it. A paradox of dread and necessity.

"What do you mean?" I asked, already knowing.

"There's a vibe," she said. "you're not being yourself. I mean, Romy – you didn't text me for a week. I was genuinely worried."

I looked down at my coffee cup like it might hold the script for what to say next.

Now was the time. Just say it.

"I'm in love with Eli."

Grace blinked. Once. Twice. A few more times for good measure. Then she carefully set her coffee down, like she was defusing a bomb.

"Okay," she said slowly, with the same tone someone might use after being told the building was on fire.

"I didn't realize it," I rushed on. "Not fully. Not until we started doing the podcast. Until the launch party. Until the morning after when I looked at my phone and saw..."

I trailed off, staring into the swirl of cream in my coffee like it might hypnotize me into courage.

"The picture of you two kissing," I finished.

Her face shifted like I'd slapped her.

"Oh, God. Oh, no. Romy." Her hand darted across the table and grabbed mine like I was her last hope at survival. "That didn't mean anything, I swear. I – I had no idea. I *never* would've – oh my God, I'm so sorry."

Her voice cracked. I swore I saw tears pooling in the corners of her eyes.

"Grace, you did nothing wrong," I said, squeezing her hand. "You didn't know."

"No, but still – I totally crossed a line–"

"You didn't."

"How could I be so *stupid*?"

"Hey," I deadpanned, catching her hand between both of mine. "Grace. Seriously. You did nothing wrong."

She blinked rapidly and glanced up at the ceiling, trying to compose herself.

"But why didn't you *tell* me?" She asked finally.

"Tell you what?"

"That you liked him! That I hurt you! *Anything!*"

I sighed. "I'm not the best communicator, okay? You know this."

She let out a teary laugh and wiped one eye. "You've got that right."

"I didn't even know I felt that way about him until it was too late," I admitted. "And when I did, everything felt messy. Complicated. You didn't do anything. I'm the one who made it weird. I should've said something, but I didn't. That's on me."

She sniffled and gave me a tight smile.

"I *know* that if you knew how I felt about him, you

wouldn't have kissed him that night."

"Absolutely not. I mean, I've never claimed to be a good friend, but I'm at least a *decent human being.*"

"You're a great person, Grace," I said, and meant it. "I've just been... confused. Since we started this podcast, it's like I started seeing him differently. More clearly. And then seeing that photo – it just hit me in this place I didn't even know existed. I was already dealing with the pressure of the podcast, trying to keep up appearances, and suddenly I had feelings for my *best friend* and there he was kissing someone else – *you.*"

I paused, the memory still raw, like pressing a bruise. "We had this huge fight. Didn't speak for days. But he came back. He apologized. We talked. And now... things are good again. I think. It feels normal. Or close enough to normal that I don't want to break it."

Grace studied me carefully. "Does he know?"

"Know what?"

"Oh, I don't know. That you want his babies and all?"

I laughed, grateful for the levity. "No. He has no idea."

She gave me a long look over the rim of her cup. "Ro, what are you waiting for?"

I hesitated. "It's not clear how he feels. And I can't be the one to make that jump unless I know where he stands. What if I say something and ruin everything? What if we can't come back from it?"

"So, you're just going to keep this whole slow burning yearning-across-the co-host-table vibe going until one of you explodes?"

"Pretty much."

She sighed dramatically and shook her head. "You're killing me."

"Welcome to the club," I muttered.

Grace softened. "Well, whatever happens, I'm rooting for you. Both of you. And also slightly terrified I'm going to end up officiating your wedding."

I raised a brow. "Only if you promise to call him Eli-fucking-Reed in the vows."

"Deal," she said, raising her coffee.

We clinked cups in solemn, chaotic friendship.

23
VAMPIRE

I hadn't been to Eli's apartment in weeks. Not since before the fight. Before Grace. Before the closet confessions and the almost-something between us that still buzzed in the silence like a dying lightbulb – faint, flickering, impossible to ignore. That apartment used to feel like a second home. A place where I could exhale fully and toss off the weight of the day with my shoes. A place where Eli and I lounged in the kind of silence that wasn't empty, just easy. Where movie nights weren't emotional landmines. Where I didn't have to be careful about how long I looked at his mouth.

But now? Now I stood in the doorway like a guest in a life I used to live. Shoes still on, jacket still clutched in my hands, trying to act casual even as my heart pounded out Morse code against my ribcage. I glanced around like something might jump out at me – a memory, a feeling, a confession we didn't mean to say out loud. The room hadn't changed, but I had. We had.

Eli looked up from the kitchen, gave me that small, familiar smile – the one that had once felt like mine. And suddenly it hit me, sharp and stupid: I didn't know how to do this anymore. I didn't know how to be around him without wanting things I wasn't sure I was allowed to want.

I wondered if it was too late to back out. To say I'd forgotten I had plans. That I'd come down with something infectious and emotionally inconvenient. Maybe I could fake an allergy – to popcorn, to dim lighting, to slow-burn unresolved sexual tension.

Or commitment.

God, commitment. Just the word made my skin feel too tight.

But I was already here. And he was already smiling. And the part of me that missed him – that always missed him, even when he was close – walked through the threshold anyway.

"You gonna actually come in, or are you waiting for a formal invitation?"

"Formal invitation," I replied, still hovering in the doorway like a skittish houseguest.

"Vampire," Eli muttered with a smirk.

"Be nice or I'll make you watch *New Moon*."

He groaned. "Those movies make me feel bad about my hair. Everyone's so... coiffed."

I dropped my coat on the entryway bench and made a face. "Coiffed?"

"You know. Perfectly windblown at all times."

I snorted. "You have wonderful hair. What are you talking about?"

Eli paused mid-step in the kitchen, a brow raised. "I do?"

"It's like butterscotch," I said before I could stop myself.

And there it was. A traitorous little thought that had slipped past the heavily guarded gates of my mouth and made itself known to the world.

I froze. Time froze. Even the microwave seemed to hold its hum, waiting to see what would happen next.

Eli's hand hovered on the microwave handle as he turned to look at me, one eyebrow arched, a slow grin curling at the corners of his mouth. "Someone's given this a lot of thought."

My brain flatlined. Then restarted in a full sprint. "I'm bored at work a lot, okay? Mia's hair reminds me of a chocolate truffle, don't read into it."

He laughed, but softly – the kind of laugh that settled in my chest and made everything inside me stir uncomfortably. Longingly.

I kicked off my shoes a little too aggressively and sank into the corner of his couch, curling up like a human burrito of defensiveness. The loveseat – God, that word – was approximately the size of a generous napkin, which meant personal space was not an option. I wedged myself into the farthest corner as if physical distance could create emotional insulation.

Eli joined me a moment later, holding a bowl of popcorn like a peace offering. He sat down without ceremony, his thigh brushing against mine for a millisecond too long. I pretended I didn't notice. Pretended I wasn't already cataloging every brush of contact like I was prepping for a final exam in Unspoken Feelings.

I stared at the screen, anywhere but at him. My heart was a caged thing, rattling against its ribs, desperate and dumb.

The worst part?

I wasn't afraid he'd pull away if I told him how I felt.

I was afraid he wouldn't.

It was Eli's turn to pick the movie – something with explosions, car chases, and a suspicious amount of leather. He claimed it had "more emotional depth than *The Way We Were* which was an absurd thing to say, and I told him so.

"You'll see," he'd said smugly, queueing it up. "This one's practically Shakespeare with guns."

We settled in – or rather, I tried to settle in. My body was stiff as a board, limbs too long, too obvious. I curled one leg under myself, then changed my mind and crossed my ankles like a dignified Victorian widow. Meanwhile, Eli reclined next to me, loose-limbed and unbothered, his fingers disappearing into a bowl of popcorn with an ease that infuriated me.

My eyes were technically on the screen, but my mind was entirely on him. Every shift of his body, every smirk at a poorly delivered line, every time he brought a snack to his lips – it was like someone flicked a light switch inside me. I could feel my pulse in the base of my throat. My heart was playing double-dutch with itself.

I was genuinely worried I might develop an arrhythmia.

Still, I tried. I made jokes. I did my best to mock the movie, which was our tradition – if one of us picked something dumb, it was the other's sworn duty to make them feel bad about it. Eli, of course, took it in stride. He laughed at my commentary, lobbed back dry retorts, and somewhere between the bad guy's dramatic monologue and the hero's motorcycle montage, things felt almost normal again.

Almost.

And then *she* walked in.

Cue the gorgeous woman in a slinky, red satin dress – slit practically up to her ribcage, legs for days, a pout like a weapon. She strode across the screen with the kind of confidence you only see in perfume commercials and dreams. Opposite her stood our action hero, suddenly soft-eyed and brooding. Their banter died off. The violins swelled.

Oh, no.

No, no, no, no.

I knew what was coming. I could smell it. Like a storm rolling in. My internal monologue launched into prayer mode.

Please don't kiss. Please don't have chemistry. Please don't do the thing where you breathe near each other and then slowly melt together like horny popsicles.

But the universe had no mercy tonight.

They kissed.

Not just kissed – *kissed*. The kind of kiss that's slow and breathy and full of unbearable tension finally collapsing into something inevitable. A kiss that says *I've been in love with you this whole time, but I didn't know how to say it until now.* The kind of kiss I'd thought about having with Eli more times than I cared to admit. In the shower. In meetings. In traffic.

I stared at the screen, my entire body tense, not daring to move. Next to me, Eli had gone still too. Too still.

He wasn't reaching for the popcorn. He wasn't making a joke. He wasn't even breathing, as far as I could tell.

The tension swelled around us like rising water. I glanced sideways, just enough to catch the edge of his jaw – clenched. Focused. His gaze glued to the scene in front of us. I didn't know if I wanted to scream or crawl inside the couch cushions and disappear forever.

My brain flailed for a joke. A snarky comment. *Anything* to cut through the silence. But I was blank. Dry. Every sarcastic thought I'd ever had had apparently fled the premises and left me here, stranded and awkward.

And then Eli spoke.

"It never works out well when this kind of shit happens," Eli muttered.

I turned my head slightly, eyes now on the screen but attention fully on him. "What?"

He exhaled, slow and heavy, like he'd been thinking about it long before the scene even started. "You know. This. The moment. The kiss. The build-up. It's always so dramatic. They give in to the tension and everything changes. Never for the better."

I looked at the screen again – the two characters now tangled in each other, kissing like the world was ending – and then back at him. "You're saying what, exactly? That they should've just ignored it?"

"I'm saying they had a good thing," he said, his voice quieter now, almost reflective. "They were a team. Two badass loners making it work together. And now? Now it's going to get weird."

I tilted my head, studying him. "It doesn't have to be weird."

He laughed softly under his breath, still watching the screen. "Come on, Ro. You know it always gets weird."

His words hung between us, too pointed to be casual, too abstract to be direct. I felt my throat tighten, like something inside me was trying to rise and speak but couldn't find the air.

I shifted slightly, pretending to readjust the blanket over my lap, but really I was grounding myself. The space between us on the couch had never felt smaller. Or louder.

"Maybe," I said slowly, cautiously, "it only gets weird when no one says what they actually want."

He glanced at me, and for a split second, I saw something flicker behind his eyes – hesitation, maybe, or hope, or panic.

"Or," he said finally, "maybe they say it and it just... ruins everything."

My stomach dropped. Not in a dramatic, cinematic way – in a sick, quiet way. A slow-motion sort of ache. But I forced a smile, because if I didn't, something real might happen. And real was dangerous. Real was irreversible.

"Now who's the romantic pessimist?" I said, my voice light, teasing, betraying none of the tremble I felt just beneath the surface.

He glanced at me, briefly, then back at the screen. "Maybe you're rubbing off on me."

And just like that, we were back behind our carefully drawn lines. Pretending like nothing had shifted. Like our hearts hadn't both just flinched.

But the thing about pretending is that it never really holds.

It just buys you time.

"I disagree."

Eli turned on the couch, shifting toward me. His expression was relaxed, amused, but there was something curious in the way he looked at me now – like he was tuning in a little closer than before.

"Is Romy Becker having a change of heart?" He asked.

I nudged him with my foot, a laugh escaping before I could catch it. "I'm just saying, it doesn't always have to play out the way you think it's going to."

Eli tilted his head slightly. "You mean it doesn't always end in disaster?"

I shrugged, trying to sound breezy while my heart tapped SOS against my ribs. "Maybe. Maybe sometimes the risk is worth it."

"Look, I'm not saying the tension always ruins things," he said, voice lower now, more thoughtful. "I just mean that sometimes it changes things. And you can't go back to what it was before."

He said it like he was talking about the movie.

But I wasn't sure he was talking about the movie anymore.

And I knew I wasn't.

Both of our eyes flicked to the screen where our main characters were making love rather passionately.

I didn't say anything for a moment. I couldn't. I was too aware of the way the lamplight softened the edges of his face, the way my brain had started to auto-scroll through all the ways this could go wrong – and all the ways I desperately wanted it to go right.

Finally, I swallowed. "Maybe that's not always a bad thing."

His eyes met mine.

And held.

"It's just..." He started, then paused, searching the ceiling for words. "It's risky."

He threw a kernel of popcorn in the air and caught it in his mouth, a flash of his usual self returning, but it didn't erase the weight of what had just passed between us.

"Isn't love supposed to be?" I asked, my voice quieter this time. I pulled my legs out from under me and planted my feet on the floor, needing to feel grounded, tethered.

He didn't respond.

Instead, he stood up abruptly and headed for the kitchen.

"I need a beer," he muttered.

"If you have to be drunk to be around me, that's generally not a good sign," I called after him, trying to hide the tremble behind a joke.

From the kitchen, I heard the fridge door open and close. Bottles clinked. Silence stretched. A beat too long.

Then he returned – one beer in each hand. He handed me one and sat down close, maybe even closer than before. Our knees touched again. Not by accident.

We tapped the tops of our beers together with a soft *clink* and took a sip in sync.

"Romy Becker," he said, glancing over at me with that lopsided grin, "instigating alcoholism since nineteen-ninety-three."

"Wow," I said. "You remembered my birth year. I didn't think I made enough of an impression."

His gaze lingered. "You made an impression."

The room went impossibly still. Not quiet – still. Like the air had thickened, like time had decided to wait and see what would happen next.

Eli sat beside me – *right* beside me – our entire sides

pressed together, shoulder to knee. I could feel the heat of him through his jeans and my leggings. I wondered, not-so-casually, if his mid-movie beer run had just been a strategic excuse to sit closer. God, I *hoped* it was.

Everything else disappeared. The sound of the TV, the popcorn bowl on the coffee table, the ambient noise of the city bleeding through the open window – it all fell away. It was just him. Him, and the impossibly loud thud of my heartbeat in my ears.

His eyes locked onto mine – those big, thoughtful eyes I knew better than my own. There was something tight in his brow, something unspoken working its way through him. His jaw flexed, like he was trying not to say something.

I couldn't stop myself – my gaze dropped to his mouth. Full. Familiar. And suddenly devastating. A quiet ache unfurled low in my stomach. I wanted so badly to kiss him. To feel the softness of his lips against mine, the tentative beginning of something we'd spent months ignoring.

First soft. Then greedy.

He leaned in – just a breath.

I mirrored him. A slow, steady tilt toward danger.

His scent hit me first – something warm and clean, and the faintest trace of hops from the beer. My breath hitched. My lips parted. He was so close now I could feel it – that magnetic pull between two people on the edge of an irreversible choice.

And then –

A deafening *boom.*

The TV erupted in a cinematic fireball – orange and yellow swallowing the screen in chaos. An action sequence. A building on fire. A character screaming.

Eli jolted upright like he'd been shot.

"Oh my *God*," he gasped, grabbing at the cushions. "I sat on the fucking remote."

I blinked, dazed, heart racing. He fumbled to pause the movie, finally hitting the right button as the screen froze mid-explosion.

He laughed – a short, startled thing. "Jesus, I thought that was real for a second."

And for a beat, I just stared at him.

That did it.

I lost it.

I laughed, too. Not because it was funny – but because the alternative was either crying or confessing my undying love and launching myself at his face like a horny raccoon. Which, I was *this* close to doing.

A full-body, belly-deep laugh erupted from my chest, and Eli joined in instantly. We laughed so hard we couldn't breathe – the kind of laughter that left you clutching your stomach and wiping tears from your eyes. I doubled over on the couch, wheezing. Eli practically folded in half; his forehead pressed to the cushion.

"We almost had a *moment* and you Michael Bay'd the shit out of it." I choked out between gasps.

"I panicked! My ass betrayed me." He shouted, voice cracking as he laughed harder.

"Your butt set off a literal explosion."

It went on like that for a solid two minutes, both of us breaking into fresh fits of laughter every time we tried to calm down. When it finally subsided, and we were both just lying there catching our breath, I wiped a tear from my cheek and exhaled.

That was close.

Too close.

And, if I was being honest... not nearly close enough.

24
OH, SHIT

To say I was useless at work the next day would've been a gift to the concept of understatement. I was dressed in my business casual uniform, perched in my business casual chair, doing my business casual thing on the twenty-fourth floor of a skyscraper smack in the middle of the Financial District. But mentally? I was miles away. Galaxies away.

I wasn't thinking about policies or PTO requests. I was thinking about *the moment.*

The build-up. The banter. The slow, glacial leaning in. The shared breath and barely-there space between us. That unbearable pause just before a kiss, like the whole universe holds its breath and waits to see who moves first.

We *were* going to kiss. I'm not crazy. It was right there.

And then? Boom. Literal explosion. TV flared up with a fireball the size of my emotional repression. Eli panicked, leapt off the couch, scrambled for the remote like it was a bomb, and we both collapsed into a fit of manic laughter.

But what if the TV *hadn't* gone off?

What if we'd kept leaning?

What if we'd kissed?

What if we hadn't stopped?

I was gently grazing my bottom lip – just *wondering*, okay – when Grace's head popped into the doorway of my office.

"What are you doing?" She said, pointing a suspicious finger in my direction.

I snapped my hand down like she'd just caught me with a cigarette behind the school gym.

"Romy *Tallulah* Becker."

"Oh my God, where are you people even getting *Tallulah* from–?"

Grace gasped and covered her mouth with one hand. "You guys *hooked up!*"

"Shut up!" I hissed, drawing out the "shhh" like it could smother her entire personality. I got up, closed the door behind her, and shoved her into the chair across from my desk. "We did *no such thing*."

"Then why the innocent little lip-play I just walked in on?"

"I was *thinking*, Grace."

"Uh-huh. Thinking with your lips."

I groaned and flopped back into my chair, tugging my cardigan tight around me like it could protect me from her laser-focused girl gossip energy.

"Something happened!" She whispered in a way that felt louder than shouting. "You are so *not* being a girls' girl right now."

"I *am* a girls' girl. Don't start."

"You're being cagey! Spill!"

I folded my arms, debated the merits of telling her, but I was losing steam. My heart was still in recovery. I exhaled.

"There... may have been a moment."

"A *moment!?*" Grace shrieked.

"If you don't calm down I'm going to tell HR you keep touching me in the breakroom."

She rolled her eyes. "You *are* HR."

"It wasn't a hookup," I said, almost annoyed at how disappointed she looked. "It was – I don't know. A moment. An almost."

Naturally, she needed a play-by-play. The popcorn. The flirting. The TV glowing in the background like a third wheel. Eli getting up for a beer, coming back and sitting even closer. The shared drink. The silence. The lean-in. The breathless beat before everything combusted.

Grace listened with her mouth half-open like I was reading aloud from a fanfic she'd secretly written.

"And then the TV exploded?" she asked.

"Basically."

"Oh my God. Oh my God. This is *so hot*. You're living a slow-burn, friends-to-lovers rom-com and I'm over here trying to decide if my Bumble date ghosted me or just forgot how phones work."

I smiled, but it didn't quite reach my eyes. Because beneath all the popcorn and sparks, there was still that lingering ache in my chest. We'd nearly kissed. But we hadn't. And that was the part killing me.

"I just wish I could know what he was thinking." I sighed, letting my head fall back against the mesh of my office chair like maybe it could hold up the weight of all my over-analysis.

Grace didn't miss a beat. "He's wondering what it

would sound like to clap those cheeks."

"*GRACE!*" I half-shrieked, half-choked on my overpriced oat milk latte, and that was it – game over. We both collapsed into a fit of full-body laughter, limbs slack, breath stolen, eyes wet.

It took us several minutes to recover, gasping like we'd just come out of a spinning class taught by Satan himself.

Grace wiped under her eyes with a tissue she produced from the bottomless pit of her bag. "Sorry, but someone had to break the tension. You were spiral-core, babe."

I shook my head, still grinning despite myself. "I just – ugh, I hate this. I hate *feeling* like this. Vulnerable and exposed and like I'm waiting for a verdict."

"Welcome to literally being alive."

"I liked it better when we were just friends," I muttered.

Grace raised a single skeptical eyebrow. "Did you? Or did you just like *pretending* you didn't want him?"

I didn't answer. Mostly because she was right, and I wasn't in the mood to admit it.

A quiet moment passed between us. The kind where the weight of everything unsaid settles into the room like dusk. I glanced out the window beside me, watching as the sky over the Bay shifted from pale blue to bruised lavender. The city was winding down, but my brain was still revving like it had missed the off-ramp.

"You should go home," Grace said gently. "Get out of here, take a hot shower, eat something that didn't come from a break room, and maybe – just maybe – don't replay the moment on his couch another eighty-seven times tonight."

"Easier said than done."

"True, but try anyway."

I exhaled deeply, gathering my things as she stood to leave. Grace reached for the door, then turned around and wagged a finger at me. "If he texts you tonight and you *don't* tell me, I swear to God, I'll swap your shampoo with Nair."

"Noted." I smirked, slinging my bag over my shoulder.

"Now go. Be mysterious. Elusive. Let him wonder what *you're* thinking for once."

And with that, she was gone.

I stepped into the elevator and pressed the button for the lobby. The ride down was silent, except for the thrum of my pulse in my ears.

Outside, the air smelled like fog and jasmine and bus exhaust. My heels clicked against the sidewalk as I made my way home, the weight of the day – and of everything left unsaid between Eli and me – pressing in on all sides.

I kept my promise to Grace and didn't text Eli.

He sent a few messages – one about the podcast, something dry and logistical, another about an upcoming interview a publication wanted to do with us, and a follow-up from that one girl at the mixer who apparently 'couldn't stop thinking about our chemistry' and wanted me on her show.

But not a word about movie night.

Not a single syllable about what nearly happened.

Which was fine. Totally fine. It's not like I expected him to say anything. Why would he? It's not like we'd almost kissed or anything. It's not like our mouths hovered so close together I could taste the hops from his breath. Definitely not.

I left him on read.

A night without texting him would be good for me. A little emotional detox. A palate cleanser. Like a lemon sorbet for my heart.

I clambered up the steps to my apartment, arms full, keys slipping, grocery tote smacking against my hip – and the moment I stepped inside, I dropped everything on the floor like I was in a dramatic breakup scene and someone had died.

I didn't feel like cooking, but I also didn't feel like ordering delivery and spending $30 for someone to bring me a single taco.

So, I defaulted to my signature lazy girl standby: scrambled eggs.

I cracked them into a bowl with a flourish, pretending I was on my own personal cooking show. I whisked aggressively, like the eggs were responsible for my feelings. I added a questionable amount of salt, then poured them into the pan, listening to the sizzle like it was applause for keeping my life together for one more day.

As I stirred, my mind wandered.

I thought about Smith – sweet, stupid Smith – and hoped he was doing okay. I wished he wasn't so good at going down on me. That level of skill complicated things. It made it harder to write him off entirely. And yet, here I was, writing him off anyway.

I thought about Mia and Etienne. I hadn't checked in since my brief post-flu-couch-crash, and I missed their weird little domestic haven. I made a mental note to text her later. Maybe tomorrow.

I thought about Grace and how grateful I was that things between us felt normal again. Like we'd never skipped a beat. Like she hadn't accidentally detonated my emotional landmine with a single kiss.

And, of course, I thought about Eli.

The couch.

The beers.

The *moment.*

The almost-kiss that still felt like it was hovering between us, ghost-like and weightless and full of so many things we didn't say.

I padded into the living room, eggs in a bowl, and flopped onto the couch. I flicked on *Downton Abbey* because sometimes it feels better to watch other people's emotional trainwrecks – preferably with corsets and orchestral strings.

As Lady Mary delivered some icy one-liner about love and duty, I took a bite of my eggs and tried not to imagine what Eli's mouth would've felt like on mine.

Tried, and failed.

And then, as I shifted to grab a blanket and tuck it around my legs, I felt a strange tightness in my lower belly. A small discomfort. Nothing major – just a soft reminder. A whisper from my body.

I froze.

And did a quick mental scan.

Wait.

When was my last period?

Oh, shit.

25
I'M HERE

The air outside was unnervingly still – the kind of still that made everything feel suspended, like the world was holding its breath right alongside me. Even the breeze had vanished. The only sound was the soft hum of a streetlamp buzzing faintly overhead, casting a pale orange glow across the quiet sidewalk.

It was just past 11 PM on a weeknight. The kind of hour where even the houseless people have called it a night. All the windows on the street were dark, curtains drawn, sidewalks empty. San Francisco had never felt so silent. So still. So indifferent to the unraveling happening inside me.

The car eased up to the curb and I didn't wait for it to stop. I threw the door open before the tires had fully stilled, half-leaping from the backseat and landing with an uneven step on the sidewalk.

"Thanks!" I called over my shoulder, voice breathless, as I slammed the car door shut and bolted for the house.

I was running. Not in a cute, flirty rom-com jog. No, I was full-on sprinting, clutching the fabric of my hoodie around me, heart hammering, adrenaline a thick syrup in my bloodstream.

The porch steps blurred beneath my feet. I took them

two at a time and skidded slightly on the landing. My fingers fumbled for the doorbell and jabbed it like it owed me money. The chime echoed inside, and I bounced from foot to foot, nerves bouncing inside me like rubber balls.

My stomach twisted sharply, threatening revolt. I pressed the back of my hand to my mouth, trying to will it down.

Please, please open the door.

Because if I stood here any longer, I was either going to pass out... or confess everything I'd been holding in.

Or both.

Etienne's face appeared in the doorway; his brow instantly creased in concern. "Oh – Romy? Is everything okay?"

He stepped aside without hesitation, scanning me from head to toe like he was checking for a visible wound – a knife in the side, blood running down my legs, anything that might justify showing up at their house just before midnight on a Wednesday.

"It's–" My voice cracked. "It's an emergency. Is Mia here?"

He nodded quickly, his eyes softening. "Of course. She's here. Come in." His French accent, usually like warm honey, felt especially comforting now. He motioned for me to come into the living room.

I shook my head, breath catching in my throat. "No – I'll be in the bathroom. Can you... can you please get her?"

Etienne didn't hesitate. "Yes. Of course." He disappeared up the stairs without another question, and I turned toward the hallway, heart pounding in my ears.

I barely made it to the bathroom off the kitchen before collapsing over the toilet and vomiting. It was violent and ungraceful, an exorcism of everything: anxiety, regret, scrambled eggs, and the weight of possibility.

The door clicked open quietly. I heard slippered feet pad across the tile, and before I could register much else, a hand gently swept my curls from my face and gathered them into a bun. A drawer opened. A hair tie snapped softly. Then, a damp towel touched the back of my neck, cool and steady.

"Hey," Mia whispered, crouching beside me. "you're okay. You're okay."

"No," I croaked between dry heaves. "I am very much not okay."

She flushed the toilet and reached into a closet, pulling down another washcloth, running it under warm water, dabbing at the sweat on my hairline with motherly precision.

"What happened, babe?" She asked softly, sitting cross-legged beside me on the bathroom floor. "Is it Eli?"

Eli.

Oh God, I hadn't even thought about Eli yet.

Not really.

What this might mean for us, for our friendship, our podcast, our entire existence. My mind swirled, frantic and directionless.

I didn't speak. I couldn't. Instead, I reached into my hoodie pocket and pulled out the thin rectangular box. I held it out to her with shaking hands.

An unopened pregnancy test.

Her expression shifted – eyebrows pinched in confusion, then lifted in realization. She reached out and took it gently from my hand.

"You haven't taken it yet?"

I shook my head.

"So, you don't know?"

Another shake.

"How late are you?"

I swallowed, then croaked: "A week."

The nausea returned instantly, and I bent forward, dry heaving into the toilet. Mia pulled my hair back again and rubbed circles into my spine. We stayed like that for a long time. Eventually, when the worst passed, I slid to the floor and curled up, head in her lap, tears streaming quietly down my cheeks.

She didn't ask questions. She didn't press. She just held me.

We sat in silence for what could've been minutes or hours. Only the sound of her fingers gently combing through my curls, and my soft sniffles breaking the stillness.

"Romy," she said at last, voice delicate but firm. "You have to take it."

I sat up, bleary-eyed. And that's when I saw it.

Her eyes.

Wet with tears.

"Mia?" My voice dropped to a whisper. "What's wrong?"

"It's nothing," she said quickly, laughing too loudly as she wiped at her cheek. "It's – it's really nothing. I'm fine."

I blinked at her, confused. "Did I come at a bad time? God, Mia, I didn't even think – was I interrupting something? I'm such an asshole, I didn't even–"

She cut me off with a squeeze of my hand. "No. Stop. You are always, always welcome here. Any time. Day or night."

I opened my mouth to protest again, to apologize harder, when I followed her gaze down to the floor.

The box.

The test.

And suddenly, I understood.

My stomach dropped. Ice-cold.

"Mia..."

She looked away.

"I didn't think. I – I didn't even think–"

"It's okay," she whispered. "You don't have to think about me right now."

But I couldn't let it go. "You've been *trying*."

Mia nodded, eyes cast upward toward the ceiling. "For months."

Tears filled my eyes again, but for a different reason now. "I'm so, so sorry."

"You don't have to be sorry."

"I barge into your house crying over something you'd give anything to experience. I didn't even consider–"

"Romy." Her hand covered mine, her voice strong despite the wetness in her eyes. "You're allowed to be scared. I'm allowed to be sad. Both things can be true."

We sat in the tension of that truth. In the overlapping ache of what I didn't want, and what she couldn't have.

She pulled me into a hug, and I melted into her arms,

sobbing softly. We held each other for a long time. The bathroom light hummed above us. Somewhere in the distance, Etienne moved about quietly, giving us space.

Eventually, she pulled back, her hands on my shoulders, her voice steady.

"But you have to take that test."

I stared at her, eyes wide and glassy. "Mia, what if it's positive?"

She held my gaze, even as her own eyes filled again. "Then we figure it out. Together."

"I didn't want this," I whispered. "I just wanted to feel wanted. I didn't want to think about Eli. I wanted to make one stupid decision. And now I might be..."

I couldn't finish the sentence.

"You're not alone," she said. "No matter what that test says. You're not alone."

"What about Eli? What about the podcast? What–"

The words tangled in my throat, stacking on top of each other, faster than I could breathe them out. My chest tightened, vision tunneling. I was spiraling fast, headed straight into full-blown panic.

"Okay, okay, hey," Mia said quickly but gently, slipping an arm around my shoulders and guiding me upright. "Come on. Stand up."

She walked me to the sink, flipped the faucet handle all the way to cold, and stuck my trembling hands underneath the stream.

"Keep them there," she instructed, her voice low and even. "Ice cold. It'll help. Just breathe, Ro. In through the nose."

I bent forward, my forehead pressed against the cool counter, the sound of running water loud in my ears.

NOT IN THE MOOD

My palms stung from the temperature, but the chill grounded me, tethered me to something real.

She rubbed slow circles into my back with the flat of her palm, and I tried to follow the rhythm of her breathing. In. Out. In. Out.

My thoughts still chased each other like a stampede. *What if I'm pregnant? What if I have to tell Eli I'm pregnant with someone else's baby? What if he never talks to me again? What if the podcast implodes? What if my whole life changes from one dumb night I barely even remember?*

More than that, I didn't even know what I wanted.

Would I keep it?

I'd always been on the fence about having kids – figuring that decision belonged to some future version of me, the one who had her life together and made green smoothies and paid for dental insurance. But now the question was clawing at the door like something feral.

And I didn't have an answer.

I pressed harder into the counter, desperate to keep the thoughts from devouring me whole.

"That's enough," Mia murmured after a few minutes, her hand never leaving my back. "Look at me."

I did. Her face was steady. Warm. Kind.

"None of that matters right now. Eli doesn't fucking matter. The podcast – forget about it. All that stuff can wait."

Her eyes didn't waver. "Right now, all that matters is *you*. What *you* want. What *you* need. Not what anyone else thinks. But sitting here running circles in your head won't help. In three minutes, we can know. And knowing is always better than not knowing."

I wanted to believe her. I wanted so badly to believe

that no matter what happened in the next three minutes, I wouldn't unravel completely.

The faucet sputtered as she turned off the water. My hands were bright pink from the cold, shaking slightly as I dried them on a nearby towel.

Then I heard it – a soft rustle beside me.

I turned.

Mia stood there holding the test, already unwrapped, already prepared. Like she'd done it a dozen times before. Because she had.

My heart cracked just a little more.

She didn't say anything. Just held it out to me, eyes calm but glistening.

I stared at it for a long second. Then reached out and took it from her fingers, my own feeling too clumsy, too unsure.

"I'm here," she said simply.

I gave a weak nod and shuffled over to the toilet.

The plastic test felt heavy in my hand. Heavy with possibility. Heavy with consequence.

I sat down slowly, the bathroom quiet but full of so much unsaid.

Mia didn't leave.

She leaned against the counter next to me, waiting.

So, I closed my eyes.

And I went for it.

26
RED FLAG WITH LEGS

The pregnancy test lay on the bathroom counter like a cursed object. Just... sitting there. Small. Harmless. Plastic. And yet somehow heavier than any object I'd ever held.

I couldn't look at it.

I couldn't even look in its direction.

I stood frozen a few feet away, arms wrapped tight around me, my stomach twisting so hard I felt like I might vomit again.

"I can't do this," I whispered.

Mia, quiet as a ghost, stood nearby. "You can."

"I really, really can't."

"You already did the hard part." She gestured to the toilet, to the test, to the space between us. "This is just the knowing."

That was the problem. The knowing.

I wasn't ready for the knowing.

For hours, my brain had been a carousel of extreme worst-case scenarios. I'd spent every free second Googling things like 'false positive pregnancy test' and 'can stress delay your period' and 'how fast can scrambled eggs kill you if undercooked'. Now here I was. No more distractions. No more delay.

Just this.

Just maybe.

I turned away from the counter and stared at the towel rack like it might offer guidance. "What if it's positive?"

Mia didn't answer. She didn't need to. I could hear her breathing shift – slower, heavier – like she knew her role now was just to anchor me.

I sat down on the closed toilet lid and pressed my hands to my face. My fingers were cold. My cheeks were hot.

"I can't raise a baby," I mumbled.

"You don't have to decide anything right now."

"I can't tell Eli."

"You don't even know if you need to."

I looked up at her through my fingers. "He's going to think I'm reckless. That I don't take things seriously. He's going to look at me and see a red flag with legs."

Mia sat down on the edge of the bathtub, facing me. "Eli would never think that."

I didn't answer. I couldn't. Because part of me wasn't so sure.

Part of me thought about how close we'd come to kissing. How warm his hand felt against mine. How his eyes had lingered too long, and how mine had followed his mouth like it might explain everything I didn't know how to say.

The night of the almost-kiss now seemed light years away.

And now...

Now there was this.

This test. This possibility.

This seismic shift of what if.

What if I was pregnant?

What do I tell Smith?

What if everything with Eli was ruined before it even began?

What if I was about to be thrust into a version of adulthood I never signed up for?

I squeezed my eyes shut and tried to slow my breathing. I thought of stupid things: My favorite hoodie I left at Grace's house. The fact that I'd forgotten to water my one remaining plant. That I had laundry in the dryer I'd probably need to re-fluff for the third time. Ordinary things. Safe things.

Because the moment I opened my eyes and looked at that test, my life might not be ordinary anymore.

And I wasn't ready.

"Time's up," Mia said gently, after a long stretch of silence.

I blinked. "Already?"

She gave me a tight smile. "Three minutes. That's all it takes."

Three minutes.

Three minutes that felt like they'd stretched across a lifetime.

I still didn't move.

Mia stood. Walked over to the counter. Picked up the test without ceremony. She didn't look at me right away. Just stared down at the tiny plastic stick in her hand, her brows pulled together, lips pressed into a thin line.

"Mia?" I asked, my voice cracking like a sheet of ice.

She still didn't speak.

And that silence – that tiny, torturous pocket of time

between her knowing and me knowing – stretched longer than anything I'd ever felt.

I stood slowly. My knees wobbled beneath me.

"Mia, please. I need you to tell me."

She finally lifted her head.

And her eyes met mine.

"It's negative."

The words barely registered at first. Like a foreign language I'd once studied and forgotten. My brain tried to grasp their meaning while my body surged ahead of comprehension.

"What?" I croaked; eyes locked on Mia's.

"It's negative, babe." She turned the test to show me, her voice soft but steady, like she knew I wouldn't believe it until I saw it.

One pink line.

Just one.

The single greatest image I'd ever seen in my entire life.

My heart collapsed in on itself, like a dying star – imploding with a force of overwhelming relief. My knees buckled and I let out a sound I couldn't name – part sob, part laugh, part scream. A whole mess of emotion that punched its way out of me without my permission.

I hit the side of my face on the bathroom counter as I dropped, but I didn't care. Couldn't care. Not even a little bit. The impact barely registered – just a dull thud in a body suddenly light as air.

I was sobbing now. Ugly, full-body sobs. Not from grief, not from fear, but from something more primal. A release so total it left me boneless on the tile floor.

Mia laughed softly and folded down beside me, wrapping her arms around me like she was trying to hold all my loose pieces together. I clung to her like she was a lifeboat, and I'd just survived a shipwreck.

"Holy shit," I whispered, voice cracking.

"I know." She tucked a loose curl behind my ear. "I know."

I felt everything and nothing at once. The bathroom was too warm and too cold, the overhead light too bright, the silence between our breaths too loud. It was like the world had shifted a few inches and I hadn't caught up yet.

"I really thought I was."

"I know," Mia said again, and the way she said it made me believe she'd carried some of that fear for me.

I couldn't stop shaking. Not from cold, but from sheer adrenaline as it drained from my system all at once. My hands tingled. My limbs felt weightless. I was floating and falling at the same time.

"I don't think I've ever been so relieved in my life," I said.

Mia smiled. "I could tell. You just dropped like a fainting goat in a thunderstorm."

We laughed then, real laughter, the kind that bubbles up from somewhere deep. I wiped my face on my sleeve and leaned back against the cabinets, breathing like I'd just run a marathon through all my worst fears.

"You're safe," Mia said gently.

I nodded, my chin wobbling. "For now."

"But it's enough. It's enough for tonight."

And it was. It didn't fix everything. It didn't solve

how I felt about Eli or erase the consequences of my recklessness. But for tonight – for this moment – I wasn't pregnant. I wasn't trapped. I wasn't about to break everything I'd just started to build.

I was just Romy again.

And that was enough.

27
SOULFUL EYES AND A MOURNFUL PRESCENCE

I spent the night in Mia's guest room, curled up beneath the gauzy white duvet like a child hiding from a storm. I didn't cry. I didn't even think. I just stared at the ceiling, listening to the low hum of the house around me until everything blurred at the edges. At some point, without realizing it, I slipped under – into something heavier than rest, softer than sleep. When I woke up, I couldn't remember closing my eyes.

The next morning, I called out of work for the rest of the week. I didn't bother with excuses. Just a quick message sent into the corporate void. No one asked questions. Sometimes, not mattering is a strangely beautiful thing.

Later, I stood in Mia's shower for what felt like hours, letting the hot water beat down on me like an absolution. I imagined it washing away the past twelve hours – scrubbing off the panic, the tears, the vomit, the what-ifs, the ghost of a pink line that never appeared. I breathed in the steam like it might rewire my brain. Like it might dissolve the parts of me that had spiraled into chaos just a day before.

Needless to say, it had been a ride. An emotional roller coaster from hell. And I'd barely buckled in.

Once the adrenaline had worn off, once the panic had drained from my bones, I was as useful as a soggy tissue. My limbs had gone slack. My mind, even slacker.

But now, in the quiet aftermath, a few thoughts remained. Sharp. Clear. Inarguable.

First: I had absolutely zero interest in having a baby anytime soon. I could barely commit to a skincare routine, let alone keep a whole human alive.

Second: I also had zero interest in sleeping with anyone again anytime soon. The thrill, the distraction, the self-sabotage of it – it all felt paper-thin now. Reckless. Fragile.

Third – and this one took root in my chest like a stone dropped into a pond – I needed to tell Eli. Not just about the scare. About everything. About what I felt. About what I had come to realize.

No more hiding behind sarcastic quips and popcorn bowls. No more almosts. No more pretending.

I had to tell him.

God, help me, I had to tell him.

Outside of the shower, sitting on Mia's guest bed in nothing but a towel, I texted Eli.

When are you off today?

A few moments later, he replied: *I called out. Super sick. Probably the plague.*

I responded: *Can I come over in a bit?*

He wrote back: *Only if u also want to feel like death. Also, bring crackers.*

I hearted the message.

I reached for the handle to Eli's apartment door and froze.

When I left this apartment – whenever that would be – there was a real chance I wouldn't be able to take any of it back. Whatever I said tonight could alter us forever. The words I was about to say, the truth I'd been holding in like a dam about to break, might splinter the one constant in my life that I never wanted to lose.

And yet... I realized I didn't care.

Mia was right.

Knowing was better than not knowing. Even if it hurt. Even if everything ended.

I pushed the door open.

And immediately let out a laugh I hadn't expected.

Eli was curled on the couch, wrapped entirely in a fleece blanket like a... well, like a man who was sick. Over the top. Dramatic as hell. Only his face peeked out, flushed and blotchy. His eyes were glassy, his nose red and raw, and his lips were dry and a little cracked – like a tragic French poet with seasonal allergies. Recording equipment had been half-set-up around him like a fever dream podcast séance.

He stuck out his bottom lip in a pout. "I can't breathe through my nose."

"You look like an old dying woman."

"I *am* an old dying woman."

I held up a grocery bag like I was presenting a gift to royalty. "Don't worry. I brought crackers. And apple juice."

"I won't be able to taste them," he mumbled, already reaching for the juice like it was holy.

I padded into the kitchen and grabbed a cup, filling it while trying not to think too hard about what I was doing here. This wasn't how I planned it. Nothing about this was how I planned it.

Back in the living room, I handed him the cup, and he peeked one arm out from the blanket like a withered oracle accepting an offering. He took a long sip.

I pointed to the microphones set up across from each other. "What's up with the mics?"

He looked at me like I'd just asked what a podcast was. "What do you mean *what's up with the mics*? We have a podcast."

"Yeah, but we don't need to record right now."

He sniffed dramatically. "We always need to record, Ro."

I rolled my eyes and sat beside him, slipping the headphones over my ears and reaching over to place his on as well.

But he suddenly pulled away. "Wait. No. I can't do this."

"Do what?" I asked, confused – until my breath caught.

He stood.

And just like that, Eli fucking Reed was shirtless.

I'd never seen him shirtless before. Not once.

And it was... much worse than I imagined.

Worse, as in I was immediately rendered speechless and borderline savage.

His shoulders were broad and taut, sculpted like someone who did pushups not for vanity, but out of boredom. His chest was firm, lightly dusted with hair, and when he reached to adjust the blanket slipping off his shoulders, his biceps flexed in a way that made me reconsider every moral boundary I had set for myself in the last 48 hours.

Then there was the V. *The* V. The sharp line that dipped into the waistband of his sweatpants and made me want to call God directly.

Before I could form a coherent thought – or throw myself out the nearest window – he casually tilted to pull his pants back up, like he hadn't just set my entire nervous system on fire.

I blinked hard and cleared my throat.

So, this was how I died.

"I can't record topless," Eli called from his room.

"Topless?" I echoed, trying (and failing) to keep my tone neutral.

"I feel too exposed," he said, his voice muffled by the wall. I heard the telltale squeak of wood on wood as dresser drawers opened and shut. He emerged a moment later in a faded band tee and pajama pants, wobbling back into the living room like an oversized toddler.

"I preferred it with the shirt off," I teased, toeing the line like it owed me money.

"I'll take mine off if you take off yours," he said as he flopped onto the couch and plopped his headphones on. Without missing a beat, he leaned over, tapped a key on his laptop, and the soft red light on the mic lit up. We were recording.

I ignored him, though I couldn't stop the dumb little smile that tugged at my lips. I was still stuck on the image of him helping me out of my top – slowly, carefully, reverently. So, naturally, he noticed.

"Stop having dirty thoughts and talk, Ro."

I snapped back to reality, coughing out a laugh. "Hello, friends, and welcome to *Not in the Mood* with your hosts, Eli Becker and Romy Reed."

There was a pause.

"What?" Eli said.

"What?" I echoed.

"You got our names wrong. You called me Eli *Becker*."

"No, I didn't."

"Do you want me to show you the tape?" He asked, grinning, already queuing it up like the gremlin he is.

I shrugged. "For this episode, we *are* Eli Becker and Romy Reed. We're living new lives now."

"Are you feeling okay?"

"Says the sick one."

"No, seriously. Did you hit your head recently? Have a minor stroke?"

My hand instinctively flew to my temple. "Actually, I did hit my head." I pushed my curls aside and leaned toward him to show the faint bruise near my hairline.

His face sobered immediately. He leaned in, brow furrowed, his hand hovering near my cheek like he wasn't sure if he could touch me. "Whoa. That's a bruise, Romy. What happened?"

"I had a small emotional manic episode. No big deal."

"Does this have to do with why you ghosted me for two days?"

"No comment."

He didn't look convinced, but he moved on. "Anyway. For those tuning in for the first time, around these parts I'm known as Eli *fucking* Reed."

"And I'm his slightly concussed co-host, Romy Becker."

In sync, we said, "And together, we are *Not in the Mood*."

"I was thinking," I said, settling back into the couch, "we should talk about something we both have way too much experience with."

"Oh, dear. What could this be?"

"Things we thought were romantic – but actually weren't."

Eli practically did a wiggle in his seat. "Oh, hell yes. I've been waiting for this one."

"Because unfortunately," I continued, "we've all been teenagers before. We've all had our deeply delusional moments."

"Like the time you made a handmade midterms care package for that guy you were seeing?"

"You're supposed to talk about things *you* did."

"And then his roommate texted you asking if you could make him one too, because they thought you were selling them?" He laughed so hard he almost choked on his tea.

I glared at him. "I'm hiding the DayQuil."

"Please don't. That bottle's the most action I've had in weeks."

"Okay, what about that girl who wrote you a poem and said you reminded her of her dead cat?"

Eli's laughter cut off abruptly. He looked out the window like he was remembering a war.

"I still think about her on rainy days."

I clutched my stomach laughing. "You're so dramatic."

"She said I had the same soulful eyes and mournful presence."

"She was onto something."

He took a beat. "She also said I shed a lot. I didn't

know how to take that."

"What about the guy who tried to be poetic and told me my freckles reminded him of mold on strawberries."

"Didn't you keep seeing him after that?"

"I still can't eat strawberries."

"Did I ever tell you–" Eli was already laughing, his voice breaking on the inhale, "oh, God, this one's good." He leaned toward the mic and sniffled dramatically, adjusting the stand like he was about to deliver a TED Talk. I took a cautious sip of apple juice, already bracing for impact.

"Did I ever tell you about the time I told a girl I wanted to grow old with her?"

I blinked. "No? Wait – how old were you?"

"Seventeen."

I choked back a laugh. "Already planning retirement?"

"She was very cute. And I was very hormonal."

I bit my lip to contain the grin. "And how'd that go over?"

He grinned. "She said, 'That's a lot of pressure. We've only been to Chipotle once.'"

I snorted. Then, without warning, full-on sprayed a mouthful of juice straight across the couch and directly onto Eli.

"OH MY GOD!" Eli shrieked, jerking back like he'd been shot.

I doubled over. "I'M SO SORRY! I'M SO–" I couldn't even finish. I was laughing too hard to breathe.

"YOU JUST PEARL-HARBOR'D ME WITH JUICE. I'VE BEEN HIT. THIS IS WHAT WAR FEELS LIKE."

I staggered off the couch, holding my stomach, tears

leaking from the corners of my eyes. "My mouth betrayed me."

"My *face* betrayed me," he called out behind me. "I knew I shouldn't have moisturized."

Still howling, I waddled into the bathroom, grabbed a hand towel, and returned to find him sprawled dramatically on the couch. His cheeks were speckled with juice and his shirt had taken the brunt of the hit.

"I have to file a workplace harassment claim," he muttered.

"You're not an employee. You're an unpaid intern at best."

I dabbed gently at his face, still laughing. "It's just apple juice. You'll survive."

"I'll never be the same," he said solemnly, eyes closed. "This shirt was my podcast shirt."

"I think it adds character."

He opened one eye and smiled at me. "Remind me to tell you about the girl who tried to kiss me after feeding me salmon jerky."

"Oh, we're *so* doing a part two of this episode."

We didn't hit stop on the recording for a while. At some point, the episode dissolved into tangents and inside jokes and long, winding stories we both kept remembering mid-sentence. We laughed until our stomachs hurt, until his voice gave out completely and mine wasn't far behind.

Eventually, after the headphones had been removed and the mic stands put away, Eli tugged a blanket up to his chin and let his head tip back against the couch. "God, I'm so tired," he murmured, half a breath.

"You sound like a haunted house," I said gently.

He cracked one eye open and gave me a sleepy grin. "Tell my ghost I went out happy. Because of you."

I smiled and shifted to sit cross-legged, folding one leg under the other. I reached for my phone and was mindlessly swiping through notifications when, without a word, he curled sideways and rested his head in my lap.

My breath caught.

He didn't say anything. He didn't ask if it was okay. He just... trusted me to hold him.

And I did.

I stayed perfectly still, my hand resting lightly in his hair. He fell asleep almost instantly, the tension in his shoulders melting beneath the weight of exhaustion – or maybe comfort. His breathing evened out. His fingers curled slightly near my knee like he didn't want to drift too far.

I didn't move. Not once.

I didn't check my phone, didn't shift to get more comfortable, didn't think about how awkward my hips would feel in an hour. I just sat there, watching his eyelashes flicker in sleep, letting the quiet wrap around us like a second blanket.

Because if this was all I could have – just this small, stolen moment – then I would hold it for as long as I possibly could.

28
HETEROSEXUAL TENSION CAVE

Some mornings don't feel like mornings.

They feel like echoes. Like leftover feelings stretched thin across your consciousness, lingering long after the sun's come up.

That's how I felt the next day – or was it two days later? Time had gone a little slushy on me, like the world was playing in half-speed and I was just watching. The sunrise that cracked through my apartment window didn't feel golden. It felt sepia-toned. Washed out. Like a memory I wasn't ready to file away.

I stayed in bed longer than usual, curled around a pillow that still smelled like my hair, clutching it like it could rewind time. The quiet of the room was oppressive – not lonely, exactly, but loud in the way silence sometimes is. Every creak of the radiator, every chirp from the street below, felt like it was asking me: *So, what now, Romy?*

I kept thinking about the sound Eli made when he shifted in his sleep – soft, breathy. Like a page turning. I'd never had someone fall asleep on me like that before. Not out of exhaustion. Not out of trust. Not like *that*.

And the strangest part?

I hadn't moved. Not once. I sat there, perfectly still,

for nearly two hours with his head heavy in my lap, just listening to him breathe and trying not to think about how much I loved him. Trying not to imagine what would've happened if I'd let my fingers trail across his jaw. If I'd bent down and kissed the top of his head. If I'd whispered something too soft, too dangerous, into the crown of his hair and ruined everything.

But I didn't do any of those things.

I sat there. Quiet and reverent. Like I was holding something sacred. And maybe I was.

Because loving Eli felt like that – like this quiet, solemn thing I wasn't supposed to name out loud.

Eventually, he stirred. Sat up groggy-eyed and flushed, blinking like he forgot where he was. And that's when it hit me.

God, help me – sleepy Eli was *sexy*.

Not in a try-hard, cologne commercial way. Not in the 'just rolled out of bed for a Vogue shoot' kind of way, either. He looked like a real person, stripped of his usual charm and sarcasm. Vulnerable. Warm.

His hair was mashed down on one side and sticking up on the other, like a crooked halo. His eyelids were heavy and pink at the corners, his voice deeper – huskier – coated in sleep. He had a small crease on his forehead and a faint flush across his cheeks, and when he ran his hand through his hair, groaning just slightly as he stretched, I had to look away.

Because I wanted to climb him like a tree.

There was something impossibly tender about that version of him. Like I'd been given a glimpse into something private. Something not even Grace or the rest of the world had ever seen.

I watched as he yawned and blinked toward me like a bear coming out of hibernation. Then, without thinking, he patted my knee – all casual, all sleepy and soft – like it was second nature. Like he did it every morning.

Like I was his.

And for one stupid, aching moment, I let myself believe I could be.

"Did I drool on you?"

I shook my head. "Not enough to press charges."

And then I left. Walked home just after midnight, air cold on my cheeks, something unspeakable and fragile fluttering behind my ribs the whole way.

Now, in the morning stillness of my apartment, two days later, I wondered what any of it meant. And worse – if it meant nothing to him.

I finally dragged myself out of bed and into the kitchen, where the egg carton sat sideways and the coffee grounds stared at me like they knew I didn't have the energy to make anything. I grabbed a granola bar instead, sat cross-legged on my couch, and scrolled aimlessly through my texts, avoiding the one thread that really mattered.

No new messages from Eli.

Of course not.

He was probably asleep still, or editing a reel for the podcast, or brushing his teeth with some stupidly charming toothpaste like *Cinnamon Rush*.

I turned on music – something low and ambient and a little too emotional – and got dressed slowly, like each item of clothing was a decision I wasn't quite ready to make. Black jeans. Gray sweater. Low effort but moody.

Perfect for pretending you've got it together when you're actively falling apart inside your chest cavity.

I had nowhere to be, no obligations, no looming podcast deadlines. But my body felt like it needed to move. To go outside. To *do* something before the day folded in on itself.

I slipped on my shoes, tied on my coat, and left my apartment, not really knowing where I was going.

But hoping, maybe, I'd run into someone who could help me figure it out.

It was one of those fall mornings where the air had a bit of a bite, but the sun was doing its best to convince you otherwise. I stepped out of my apartment, throwing on a pair of sunglasses too dramatic for the occasion. They were giant, round, and vaguely tinted rose – which felt appropriate given my current state of emotional delusion.

I hadn't seen or spoken to Eli since he fell asleep on my lap two nights ago. He slept like he trusted me. Like I was safe. Like I wasn't the one holding in a thousand unsaid things just under my skin. I stayed frozen the entire time – didn't shift, didn't breathe too loudly, didn't even let myself think too hard. I just existed beneath him like a human pillow with a heartbeat.

And when he finally stirred awake, rubbing his face with the back of his hand and mumbling something incoherent and painfully adorable, I couldn't look at him. I faked a yawn, said I had to go, and practically fled my own feelings like they were on fire.

I wasn't ready to unpack it alone. But I also wasn't ready to unpack it with him.

So, naturally, I texted Grace.

We decided to meet at her favorite coffee spot a few blocks away, the one with overpriced cold brew and cashmere-sweater energy. It was the kind of place that played Bon Iver unironically and sold tote bags with phrases like 'Books & Feelings' for $32. I ordered an iced lavender oat milk latte and found Grace already seated in a sun-drenched corner outside, looking aggressively chic in vintage Levi's and a rust-colored cardigan I knew for a fact she stole from an ex.

She looked up over the rim of her glasses and smirked like a cartoon villain who had just cornered their prey.

"Well, well, well," she purred. "Look who finally emerged from the heterosexual tension cave."

I slid into the chair across from her and pulled my sunglasses off with a sigh. "Please be normal."

She cackled. "I am! I'm being so normal right now. It's not my fault you keep giving me the juiciest rom-com plotlines to work with."

I sipped my latte. "He fell asleep on my lap."

Grace blinked. "Sorry, what?"

I nodded solemnly. "Out cold. Just... curled up like a Victorian child dying of consumption. On my lap."

Her face twisted with glee. "You're fucking joking."

"I'm not."

"Oh my God. That's not even a metaphor; that's just foreplay with better lighting."

I covered my face. "I hate you."

She leaned forward. "No, you *love* me. Because I'm going to say what you're too scared to say."

"Don't."

"You're in love with him."

"Grace."

"And he loves you back."

"Please–"

"And you two are so close to kissing that if I stood between you for longer than five seconds, I'd probably catch fire."

I sank deeper into my chair, trying to disappear into the upholstery.

She grinned and poked at her croissant. "So, what's the plan? When are you going to tell him?"

"I don't know. I'm still figuring it out."

Grace shrugged, suddenly gentler. "Okay. Then let's not talk about it anymore. Let's talk about literally anything else. Like, I don't know–"

She stopped abruptly.

I turned to follow her gaze.

And there he was.

Smith.

Holding a green juice in one hand, sunglasses propped on his head, looking very... *fine.* In the neutral way. The way you look at an ex-hookup and go, "Yeah, I see why I did that. And I also see why I stopped."

"Oh, no," I muttered.

Grace's eyes were saucers. "Wow, okay, he's hot?"

I sighed heavily and sipped my iced coffee.

"What?" She asked, unable to take her eyes off of him.

"That's Smith."

"*What?*"

"Yup."

"He's *gorgeous.*"

"Unfortunately."

"He looks like a walking CrossFit ad."

I hissed. "Stop talking."

But it was too late. Smith had spotted me.

He did that chin-tilt thing guys do when they think they've been missed. Like they're the main character returning for a surprise third act cameo.

"Romy?" He called out.

I turned back to Grace and whispered, "If I die right now, tell Mia she can have my hair products."

Smith jogged over and I pasted on my best neutral face.

"Hey," he said, all teeth and cologne. "Didn't expect to see you around here."

"Hey, Smith." I stood awkwardly. "This is Grace, my friend."

He gave her a little nod. "Nice to meet you."

She nodded slowly, like she was reading the nutritional label on a questionable snack.

He turned back to me. "How've you been?"

"Oh, you know. Busy. Life. Podcasting."

"Yeah, I've been keeping up. That one episode about toxic masculinity? Bold."

"Bold is my middle name," I deadpanned.

Grace snorted into her coffee.

Smith smiled, oblivious. "Well, listen – maybe we could catch up sometime. Grab a drink?"

My stomach turned. I didn't need to say no. My entire body was saying it for me.

But before I could answer, Grace leaned in sweetly.

"She's kinda seeing someone, actually."

Smith blinked. "Oh. Yeah, sure. No problem."

He waved and walked away, the back of his shirt

sticking slightly to his muscles like he was contractually obligated to be sweaty.

I turned to Grace. "Kinda seeing someone?"

She shrugged. "He didn't need to know it's only in your dreams."

We both burst out laughing.

And just like that, the morning felt lighter.

29
NEW MOON

The next week passed with surprising ease – like my life had finally exhaled after holding its breath for too long. Work at LumenLoop was mercifully uneventful. I filed expense reports, skimmed decks for the upcoming summit, made a few too many coffee runs, and spent most of the week hiding behind noise-canceling headphones and pretending to be Very Busy. It was the kind of mental white space I didn't realize I needed. No drama, no explosive fights or pregnancy scares or almost-kisses. Just the soft hum of fluorescent lights and the occasional Slack ping pulling me back into a routine I could wrap around myself like a weighted blanket.

Grace and I got lunch twice – something spicy and comforting the first time, something green and penance-like the second. We didn't talk about Eli much, but she gave me a look once when I zoned out mid-story and sighed into my soup. I think that said enough.

I also called Mia, just to hear her voice. She answered with a cheerful, "You alive?" and I laughed for the first time that day. She didn't push me, didn't bring up That Night or The Test or The Conversation I Still Hadn't Had. We just talked about her work schedule, her new shampoo, the dog she saw on the train. It was the kind of friendship that asked nothing and gave everything. I hung up feeling lighter.

Still, despite the quiet, the buzz in my chest hadn't gone away. If anything, it had settled in like background music – low, constant, impossible to ignore. Eli hadn't texted me about That Night, and I hadn't texted him either. We were circling something, and both of us knew it. I just didn't know which one of us would make the first move.

Until he did.

Movie night tonight?

I should've been more nervous. That's what surprised me most.

My legs carried me towards his house like I was on my way to pick up dry cleaning, not to potentially detonate the entire emotional infrastructure of my most important friendship. A normal person would be sweating through their clothes, second-guessing their outfit, their breath, their life choices. I was oddly... calm. Or maybe I'd just moved past fear and straight into inevitability. Like a woman marching confidently into her own execution, knowing the gallows were waiting but still choosing the heels that made her ankles look good.

I said yes before I had the chance to think too hard about it. Before Grace could talk me out of it. Before Mia could remind me for the hundredth time that honesty doesn't always come with a happy ending.

But tonight wasn't about a happy ending. It was about relief. About saying the thing that had lived in my chest for far too long, gnawing at my ribs every time he smiled at me or leaned just a little too close. I was tired of pretending I didn't care. Of pretending he didn't mean more to me than he should.

I rounded the corner onto his street and forced myself to slow down. The sun was setting in that golden, cinematic kind of way that made even cracked sidewalks look beautiful. My heart beat steadily, but my palms were slick. The closer I got, the more I imagined it. Saying it. Just saying it.

I love you. I'm in love with you. I don't know when it started. But it's here, and it's real, and I can't keep pretending it's not.

I imagined his face. His silence. The way he might shift uncomfortably, or worse – reach out with a pitying smile and call me "sweet." I imagined him saying it back. I imagined him saying nothing at all.

No. No, that wasn't what tonight was for.

Tonight was for the truth. And whatever came after, I'd handle it.

I reached his front door and stood there for a moment, my hand hovering just above the frame. The porchlight flicked on automatically. I caught my reflection in the glass – a little flushed, a little wide-eyed. But ready.

I was going to tell him.

I knocked.

"Why the hell are you knocking?" He called out before the door even opened.

I blinked. "I don't know. Lost in thought." I laughed weakly, cheeks already flushing, and stepped inside – into the warm familiarity of his space, and possibly, into the most defining moment of my entire life.

The apartment smelled like something criminally good – greasy, indulgent, and American in a way that made my stomach growl. Burgers. Fries. Two chocolate milkshakes sweating on the coffee table. The cushions on the couch were slightly dented, and a book lay open spine-down like it had been abandoned mid-sentence. I recognized the title – some weird, poetic memoir he'd been reading for months and refused to finish because, according to him, it made him "feel things".

There were two glasses on the sideboard – one clean, one used. His sneakers were kicked off near the wall, haphazardly, like he'd just gotten home and barely had time to pretend he wasn't living like a boy. The whole place was stupidly, irrevocably him. I swallowed.

He stepped past me and grabbed the remote off the coffee table. "Okay, so I know it's your turn to pick the movie tonight."

"It is," I said, slowly. Something about the way he was smiling made me suspicious.

"But I have a request."

I raised an eyebrow, setting my coat and bag in a neat pile on the floor. "A request, huh?"

"Yeah," he said, leaning in with a conspiratorial grin, eyes gleaming with barely contained mischief. "I was thinking... maybe we could watch *New Moon*."

I froze.

I stared at him like he'd just confessed to eating my entire extended family.

"What?" I whispered.

"I know, I know what you're thinking," he said quickly, still not looking at me. "Why would a guy like me voluntarily want to watch a hormonal supernatural love triangle?"

"Uh huh," I managed, though my voice sounded far away.

"But the truth is... I think I'm in. I think I'm invested now. I might even be Team Jacob. I need to see this saga through to the end, Ro."

"Eli," I said.

He finally looked at me. "Yeah?"

I stared at him. At the stupid smile on his face. At the way he tried to cover his nervous energy with jokes. At the way he ordered food without asking because he already knew what I liked. At the way he made me feel safe without ever trying to.

"I'm in love with you."

A beat.

His smile faltered – just slightly at first, like a record skipping. "What?"

I looked at him. Really looked at him. The wrinkle between his brows. The cautious, hesitant way he searched my face. The way his lips parted like he was afraid to breathe, afraid to ruin something fragile and floating in the air between us.

"I'm in love with you," I said again, softer this time. Like a confession. Like a prayer.

Another pause. This one longer. He blinked slowly, like he couldn't tell if I was joking or having a breakdown.

"Romy..." he said carefully.

"I'm in love with you," I repeated, firmer now, because it was true and I couldn't keep swallowing it. "And I have been. For a while. And I know this might be the worst timing in the history of the universe, and I know telling you this might totally ruin everything, but I physically can't keep it in anymore. I'm going to explode. Like, actually combust. Every time you do something sweet or thoughtful or weird or perfectly *you*, I feel like I'm going to word-vomit all over the room."

I laughed a little, breathless, unhinged.

"When you bring me bagels. Or when you say something sarcastic under your breath that only I hear. Or when you make some dumb joke about me being topless. Or brush my hair out of my face like it's nothing. Or sit way too close to me on the couch like it doesn't make me lose my goddamn mind."

I took a step towards him, slow and unsteady. Like I was approaching a wild animal. Or maybe the rest of my life.

"I can't do it anymore," I said, voice catching. "I can't keep pretending this isn't happening. I love you. I'm in love with you. *I'm in love with you, Eli fucking Reed.*"

Another pause.

And for a second – just one fragile, infinite second – it was like my life hung in the balance. The whole world stilled. The sound in the room drained to nothing. Just me and him. Just this moment.

Then he dropped the remote.

It clattered to the floor with a thud that barely registered, because before I could breathe, before I could second guess a single word that had left my mouth–

He was in front of me.

He *ran* to me.

And then–

He grabbed my face like he'd been waiting a

thousand lifetimes to do it. Like he was afraid I'd disappear if he didn't hold on tight enough. And then–

He kissed me.

And it was not gentle.

It was desperate.

It was every repressed feeling, every late-night movie, every near miss and almost-something and loaded silence bursting like a firework between us.

His lips crashed into mine, hot and hungry, and I swear I *melted*. His hands slid from my cheeks to the back of my neck, pulling me in like I was the only thing tethering him to the earth. My body folded into his like we were made to fit, and God, the way he *held* me – like he'd been starving, and I was the only thing that could feed him.

My hands gripped the collar of his shirt, clawing at the fabric like it was all that was keeping me from floating away. I wanted more – I wanted all of him. I pulled him closer and still it wasn't close enough. Nothing could be.

His lips parted, tongue sliding into my mouth with the kind of passion that should've been illegal. And holy hell – he kissed like he meant it. Like he'd felt every single second we'd spent apart. Like he'd been holding it back just as long as I had.

I gasped, caught off guard by the heat between us, and let out a soft, involuntary moan. His breath hitched. One of his hands moved to the small of my back, fingers curling into me. Possessive. Desperate. So *fucking real*.

Every inch of him against me. Every nerve in my body lit up.

And somewhere in the back of my mind, one single

thought sang like gospel:

Eli. Fucking. Reed. Was a good kisser.

No – he was a *devastatingly* good kisser.

The kind you never recover from.

My hands found the hem of his shirt like they were drawn there by instinct, by hunger, by something older than logic. I tugged it up and my fingertips skimmed across the skin of his stomach – hot, hard, perfect – like it held the secrets to the entire universe. He let out the softest breath, a stutter of air, and helped me pull the shirt over his head in one smooth motion, glasses and all. His hair was mussed, disheveled, chaotic – and *Jesus*, he looked like a fallen angel.

And then he grabbed me.

Pulled me into him so fiercely I nearly lost my footing, but I didn't care. I pushed back, and our mouths met again with an even deeper urgency – no longer asking, no longer teasing. It was happening. *We* were happening.

Somehow, in a tangle of limbs and breathless laughter and whispered curses, we found the bedroom.

He reached for the bottom of my shirt and didn't hesitate. There was reverence in the way he touched me, but also hunger – like he needed me now, like his hands were burning and I was the only thing that could cool them. The fabric lifted, slow and searing, and then it was gone. My arms looped around his neck and his hands found my back, strong and possessive, squeezing like he couldn't get enough of me.

Then – the click.

The quiet, perfect sound of my bra clasp unfastening, and my breath hitched.

I stepped back just far enough for it to fall away. And in that moment, everything felt so exposed, so intimate, so real – but he looked at me like I was the only thing he'd ever seen. Like he was memorizing me in candlelight.

Without a word, I took his hand and guided it to my chest.

He didn't hesitate. His palm closed around me with such aching tenderness and desperate need that I thought I might shatter from it. I could feel him – *every* part of him – pressing hard into my hip, and something primal lit up inside me.

My fingers found the button of his jeans and popped it open with confidence I didn't know I had. At the same time, he hooked his fingers into the waistband of my leggings and pushed them down like he'd been waiting for years for this moment.

And then – like gravity gave up – we collapsed onto the bed in a beautiful, perfect tangle.

Clothes half-off, hearts all-in. Lips never leaving lips. Hands learning new languages on skin. Bodies speaking truths words never could.

We didn't just fall into bed.

We fell into *everything*.

He climbed on top of me like a lion – strong, assured, all sinew and slow-burning fire. The weight of him above me sent a pulse straight through my core. His eyes locked onto mine for a fleeting second, asking a silent question I answered by parting my lips in a breathless yes.

Then he moved.

His hand traced the line of my face with a type of

devotion that stole my breath. He turned my head gently, and his mouth followed – hot kisses pressed against my cheek, then lower, trailing along my jaw, down the fragile curve of my neck, until I was nothing but pulse and shiver. He lingered at my collarbone, then lower still, as if worshipping each inch of me with lips and tongue, slowly kissing across my chest until he took one breast into his mouth with an aching, swirling enthusiasm.

And he didn't stop.

Every part of me felt aflame – electric and tender, all at once.

But even in the heat of it, something inside me caught – a flicker of hesitation, of nervousness. Suddenly I became aware of every part of my body, every softness, every flaw. I felt exposed, bare in a way that wasn't just physical.

Without saying a word, I tried to close my legs, knees drawing up instinctively.

And then, God, *Eli*.

He was impossibly tender. He kissed the inside of my thigh, a soft whisper of a kiss that felt like reassurance. Then the other. His hands moved to gently part me again, reverent and slow, like I was something sacred.

He made me feel wanted. No – *devoured*.

His mouth trailed lower, and my breath caught in my throat. His lips found the softest, most secret part of me and I gasped, arching against him. One hand reached up, finding my breast again, kneading gently, anchoring me to the bed, to this moment, while the other gripped my hip as he pulled me impossibly closer.

And then–

"Fuck, Eli." The words tore from me, wild and involuntary, my body a live wire under his tongue.

I wasn't just unraveling.

I was *reborn*.

He took his time with me – *really* took his time – in a way that felt both new and ageless, like he knew this wasn't just about sex, but about discovery. It felt like worship. He moved with such focused intent it made my heart ache, like I was the first and last thing he ever wanted to touch. Every kiss, every slow stroke of his tongue, was a question he already knew the answer to. He was learning me by heart.

He started slow, his mouth working in gentle, rhythmic swells, then deeper, firmer, more insistent. His hands never left me – one gripping my hip with a quiet possessiveness, the other cradling my thigh open, fingers stroking gently in time with his mouth. I was held there. Open. Bare. Safe.

And it was all-consuming.

He wasn't rushing to the finish – he was *memorizing* me. Finding every flutter, every gasp, every barely audible moan that gave me away. And each time I twitched or arched or whimpered, he adjusted – like this was some kind of holy ritual and I was the altar.

When it hit, it was like a fuse had been lit inside me and the firestorm had nowhere to go. I came fast and hard, like a dam breaking. A white-hot bloom erupted low in my belly and spread through me like lightning – blinding, ecstatic, and endless.

I sat up without meaning to, like my body couldn't stay still through the intensity. My hands flew to my own hair, gripping it tightly, helplessly, trying to anchor myself to the world. My mouth fell open in a silent cry. My breath came in short, fast gasps. I couldn't think, couldn't speak – only feel.

I felt the soaked sheets beneath me, warm and wet and real, and I still couldn't quite comprehend that it was me who did that. That *he* had done that to me. The pleasure crashed over me again in aftershocks, like waves licking a shore long after the storm had passed.

I collapsed back onto the bed, boneless, shaking, utterly wrecked. My body trembled like it was still trying to understand what had happened. My mind was blank and overflowing at the same time.

And I couldn't stop smiling.

I opened my eyes, and he was there – watching me like I was the only thing in the world worth looking at. His gaze was heavy with something between awe and hunger, like he couldn't believe I was real.

"Romy fucking Becker," he whispered, almost like a prayer.

He slid more comfortably between my legs, the heat of his body melting into mine. I felt the pressure of him, firm and ready, pressed against me, and my entire body shuddered in anticipation. When I leaned up to kiss him, he didn't meet me halfway. Instead, his hand cupped my jaw, thumb brushing my bottom lip, his eyes never leaving mine.

He pushed forward just enough to make me gasp, and pulled back again, teasing, torturing. He rubbed against me with a measured rhythm, like he was trying to coax every nerve in my body to life. His control was maddening – and deeply, darkly thrilling.

"Please," I whispered, breathless.

He bit his bottom lip, a soft sound in his throat betraying how much he wanted me too. His hand trailed lower, slipping between us to stroke me with devastating precision. Every movement was deliberate, every touch meant to unravel me, and all the while he watched – like he needed to see what he was doing to me.

"You asked for it," he murmured into my ear, voice thick and reverent.

And then – slowly, tenderly, completely – he was inside me.

He exhaled sharply against my mouth, forehead to mine, as if the moment might break him in half. I kissed him, hard, and he kissed me back like he'd been waiting years to do it. When he moved again, deeper this time, I couldn't help the sound that escaped me – a raw, vulnerable noise I didn't know I was capable of.

His gaze locked to mine, and in that instant, I knew. We weren't just doing this. We were *becoming* something.

Something more.

Something real.

Something inescapable.

30
THE CRASH

Sunlight spilled in through Eli's windows like it had been waiting all night to wrap itself around me.

I blinked slowly, waking not with a jolt or a groan, but with the hazy, heavy-limbed pleasure of someone who had just lived through the best dream of her life – and was still half inside it. My body ached, but in a way that was tender and good. Like a song I didn't want to stop playing. My mouth curled into a smile before I even opened my eyes. I stretched – catlike, slow, sore in all the right places – and reached out, blindly, instinctively, for him.

My fingers met with cool sheets.

I frowned. Eyes open now, I turned over, expecting to see him somewhere else in the room. Maybe in the bathroom. Maybe in the kitchen, pouring coffee in those stupid mugs he liked with the sayings that didn't relate to him at all like "World's Best Dad." Maybe still beside me, just out of reach.

But he wasn't.

His side of the bed was empty.

Still rumpled, but empty.

I sat up, tugging the sheet against my bare chest. The room smelled like him – like cedar and heat and the faintest trace of laundry detergent – and also faintly, like sex. Our clothes were still in a scattered mess on the floor, the shirt I'd worn last night half-tucked under the nightstand like it had tried to run away from all the emotions in here. My heart swelled for a second with the memory of it all – the way he kissed me like he'd never get another chance. The way he touched me like he already knew my body better than I did. The way I let him in, completely, fully, and for the first time, not just physically.

Emotionally, too.

I reached for my phone, heart starting to pick up a little speed now. Maybe he'd texted. Maybe he'd left a voicemail. Maybe he'd gone out to get bagels.

But there was nothing.

No missed calls.

No unread texts.

I glanced toward the bedroom door, cracked slightly. I slipped out of bed, wrapping one of Eli's hoodies around myself. My legs were still a little shaky. I padded softly into the hallway, into the living room, hoping I'd find him hunched over his laptop or nursing a mug of DayQuil like some dramatic Victorian ghost.

Instead, I found silence.

No coffee brewing.

No creak of a desk chair. No clatter of dishes. Nothing.

Except a single yellow Post-it stuck to the front door.

I don't know what I expected it to say. Something dumb and flirty. Something about breakfast.

But when I got close enough to read it, my stomach dropped.

"Went out. Needed to clear my head."

That was it.

No heart. No dash. No "back soon" or "love you" or "last night was everything."

Just: Needed to clear my head.

And just like that, the post-coital dream fog snapped out of focus.

My hands started to tremble. The silence in the apartment turned cold. A thousand thoughts screamed through my brain all at once, each louder than the last.

Why didn't he wake me?

Why did he leave?

What the hell was there to clear?

I backed up from the door like the note had burned me. My breath caught somewhere in the middle of my throat. Last night, I'd given him everything. Every part of me. And he'd kissed me like I was the only girl in the universe.

So why did I feel like I'd just been left behind?

Like a one-night stand.

Like a mistake.

Like maybe – just maybe – I'd read everything wrong.

And the worst part was: I had no idea if, or when, he'd come back.

I wasn't going to wait for it.

For the explanation. For the apology. For him.

As the enormity of what we'd done began to settle – seep into the cracks of my skin like cold air – I felt something twist violently inside me. That fizzy, glowing warmth from the night before soured in an instant, and it took everything in me not to be sick right there on the hardwood floor. I needed out. Now.

I scrambled to the bedroom, pulling my clothes on in

a frenzy – shirt inside out, bra clasped unevenly, shoes jammed on the wrong feet before I fixed them. I didn't even look back at the living room, where the remnants of our night – fries, milkshakes, the faint outline of my body against his – stood like ruins. I slammed the door behind me and choked back the panic bubbling up my chest like bile. I felt it rise past my ribs, tighten my throat, blur my vision.

I didn't remember walking home. I must have. But it was like my body moved before my brain could register it. Suddenly I was peeling off my clothes in my apartment, stepping into the shower like I'd sleepwalked there. The water was too hot, but I didn't adjust it. I stood there, letting it scorch me, hoping it would burn the memory of last night off my skin.

I tried – God, I tried – to reframe the note into something lighter, something forgivable. Maybe it was nothing. Maybe he'd just needed space. Maybe he had a migraine. Maybe he–

No. No maybes. If it wasn't meant to hurt, he wouldn't have disappeared. He wouldn't have left a note like a fucking thief in the night. He would've stayed. He would've woken up beside me. He would've kissed my cheek and told me I was beautiful in the morning light. He would've looked me in the eye.

Instead, it felt like the perfect little bubble we'd built – of safety, of want, of finally – had burst before I'd even gotten to breathe it in. I hadn't caught up to reality yet. I was still somewhere in the in-between, where last night was real and this morning was a mistake.

It reminded me of the day after a breakup, when your brain hasn't yet accepted the facts. When your heart is still reaching, stupidly, for a version of the story that might still be salvageable.

I wasn't ready to grieve it yet.

I showered slowly. Slower than slow. Washing every inch of my body like a ritual. His hands had been everywhere – my collarbone, my thighs, my lower back, the nape of my neck – and I hated that it still made my skin tingle. I hated that even in the heartbreak, part of me still wanted to go back. I hated that I felt tainted. Exposed. Used.

I pulled on a giant T-shirt I didn't remember owning and collapsed onto my bed. My phone sat beside me like a loaded weapon.

I stared at the screen. One minute. Two.

Maybe he'd call. Maybe he'd say the note was old. That it wasn't meant for me. That he didn't mean it like that. That he didn't mean any of it.

I unlocked my phone and opened my contacts. My finger hovered over Mia. Grace. Even Smith. But I couldn't bring myself to call anyone. I didn't want to explain. I didn't even want comfort. I just wanted to stop feeling like the ground had disappeared beneath me.

I was dazed. Shell-shocked.

And I had no idea what would happen when the crash finally came.

31
DAVID LETTERMAN

The next day, I had plans with Grace – reality TV and snacks at her place in Hayes Valley. It was her guilty pleasure and my absolute favorite version of her: messy bun, fuzzy socks, screaming at a screen like it owed her money. It was exactly the kind of low-stakes distraction I needed.

I still hadn't heard from Eli.

No text.

No call.

Not even a stupid meme he thought I'd like.

And that silence – God, it was *deafening*.

He didn't need to say it out loud. I'd gotten the message.

Loud and heartbreakingly clear.

It was a mistake.

He didn't love me.

He regretted everything.

What else could *"Need to clear my head"* possibly mean, after a night like that? After the way he touched me like I was sacred, like I was made of stars, like he *wanted* me – heart, soul, and skin?

I felt hollow. Used.

Like someone had wrung every drop of joy out of me and left the rind behind.

I'd spent hours – literal hours – showering in the last day, trying to scrub the memory of him off my skin. But it clung to me like a scent I couldn't shake.

His lips on my neck.

His hands on my waist.

His voice, low and reverent, saying my name like it was saving him.

No. No. I wouldn't go there.

I couldn't.

If it was that easy for him to pull away – if I was just a night of impulse, a one-time thing, a fuck-up he'd rather not face – then it could be easy for me, too.

I could move on.

I would move on.

Even if it killed me.

Grace's apartment was exactly what you'd expect from someone like her – delicate but vibrant, warm but curated, as if every object had been placed there with an exhale of aesthetic intention. It was a small one-bedroom tucked in a Hayes Valley walk-up, the kind of building with creaky wood floors, crown molding, and windows that let in just enough light to romanticize your worst moods.

The living room was anchored by a velvet rose-colored loveseat draped with a chunky knit throw and scattered with mismatched cushions in florals and gingham. Opposite it stood a mid-century credenza she'd scored for $40 off Facebook Marketplace, now home to a record player, a vase of half-wilted peonies, and a stack of unread poetry books she claimed to be working through.

A hand-painted portrait of her dog, Henri – done in shockingly good watercolor by a girl she once flirted with at a farmers market – hung above the couch like a shrine. Next to it, a gallery wall had slowly come to life over the past year: vintage art prints, framed pressed flowers, a tiny abstract landscape she'd found in a bin marked '$3 or Best Offer', and a minimalist line drawing of two people holding hands that was, in her words, "probably about codependency, but cute."

Her kitchen was equally charming, if not a little chaotic – patterned dish towels, a magnetic poetry set on the fridge that spelled out phrases like "kiss the ache", and a bowl of lemons that had long since hardened into decorative props. A candle burned on the counter: something bergamot-based and expensive-sounding, probably named after a feeling.

Everything about her apartment looked like the set of a coming-of-age movie where the protagonist has a breakdown and then gets her life together.

I sat at Grace's tiny dining table, absently nudging scrambled eggs across my plate while she chattered animatedly about her latest dating adventures. The plate smelled great – she'd made us a full spread, eggs and breakfast potatoes with rosemary, thick slabs of toast slathered in jam – but I couldn't bring myself to eat. My stomach had shrunk into a tight little knot that no amount of caffeine or forced cheer could loosen.

Grace, however, was radiant. She wore one of those gauzy linen robes that looked effortless but probably cost a hundred dollars, her hair piled into a messy bun that framed her face like an old painting. She was barefoot, twirling a fork in one hand and her phone in the other, swiping between dating apps while regaling me with the intimate horrors and triumphs of modern romance.

"I swear, if I could marry potatoes, I would," she groaned happily, shoveling a forkful into her mouth. Her words were slightly muffled, her mouth very much open. I didn't care. I loved Grace. I also had no appetite.

She tapped her phone screen and frowned. "Where is Mia? She's never this late."

I forced a smile, trying not to flinch at how easily the world was moving forward when mine felt stuck in the mud. I still hadn't heard from Eli. Not a word. Not even a crumb.

"So, wait – George is the one you have a third date with, right?" I said in attempt to stay active in our conversation.

"Yes. Yes, George. Very cute. Very clean. I want to ruin him." She said, dreamily. Then she perked up, a little wicked gleam in her eye. "Oh! Guess who liked me on one of the apps?"

"David Letterman."

"Smith."

That got a real reaction. I snorted into my iced coffee, both hands wrapped around the glass like it was a life raft. "Oh, no. Be careful with that one."

"He's so hot, though. I mean, come on." She side-eyed me carefully. "Would it be weird if I...?"

I knew she was treading lightly. Which I appreciated. I'd rather have a friend be awkwardly cautious than steamroll my feelings.

"You're fine. Really," I said, with a gentle nod. "He'll always be the guy who broke up with me via group text on my birthday, though. So, fair warning."

Grace sipped her coffee with the intensity of someone seeking divine permission. "But, like... he'd be a good hookup, right? Just a hookup?"

I leaned back slowly, raising my eyebrow. Her puppy-dog eyes made it feel like I was the bouncer at some exclusive club called 'Bad Decisions'.

"It was the only good quality about him."

Her jaw dropped. "Details. Immediately."

As I launched into the NSFW stats – girth, stamina, an alarming lack of pillow talk – the doorbell rang. Grace bounced up, buzzed Mia in, then plopped back down like she hadn't missed a beat, eyes glued to me.

"Okay, also – uncircumcised," I added, lowering my voice like I was revealing state secrets.

Mia walked in just in time to hear that.

"Wait, what did I just walk into?" She laughed, kicking off her boots and gliding into the kitchen with that windswept glamor only Mia could pull off before 10 AM.

"Grace wants to sleep with Smith," I said, deadpan.

Mia's entire demeanor changed. "Grace. No."

"Okay, but has she seen Smith?" Grace pleaded.

Mia squinted at me. "Have I?"

I shook my head. "Picture Mason Gooding, but taller and twice as cocky."

Grace whipped out her phone and thrust a photo toward Mia. "Boom. This one."

"Oh my God. *That's* Smith?" Mia gasped, grabbing the phone and zooming in. "You didn't tell me he looked like that."

"I told you he was hot."

Mia raised a single eyebrow and took her place at the table, her plate already put together by Grace, waiting for her with love. "Honey, you have to fuck him." Then she turned to me. "Wait, is that okay?"

I lifted my glass in mock cheers. "I was literally just telling her that's the only thing he's good for."

Grace squealed and clapped like we'd just granted her a Christmas wish.

Then I tilted my head. "Wait, why were you late? You're never late."

Mia paused, her fork hovering over her plate. She looked from me to Grace and back again, her face suddenly unreadable.

She set the fork down carefully and said it with a calmness that somehow made it more dramatic:

"I'm pregnant."

Grace dropped her utensil with a clatter.

I choked violently on my iced coffee.

"Wait, what?" I gasped between coughs.

Mia leapt up to get me a glass of water and a rag. Grace stood there frozen like she'd seen a ghost. Several minutes of chaotic coughing and shrieking followed until we all collapsed into stunned silence.

"Shut up," I finally managed to say.

"You are not!" Grace squealed, bouncing in place.

"I am," Mia said, a small smile twitching at the corners of her lips. "Very early days. I found out this morning. Doctor confirmed it."

And that's when the shrieking truly began. Grace and I launched out of our chairs and tackled her into a three-way group hug that she instantly tried to wiggle out of but couldn't. We were crying and laughing and yelling and shaking her like she'd just been nominated for an Oscar.

She rolled her eyes, but she was smiling.

God, it felt good to smile.

"So... are you going to name it Romy?" I asked, once we'd settled back into our seats, breathless and pink-cheeked from squealing over Mia's news.

Grace grinned, eyes wide. "Honestly? Romy Grace would be adorable. You're welcome, by the way."

Mia rolled her eyes but couldn't suppress the small smile pulling at her lips. "No idea what the gender is yet, but you two will be the first to know – well, after Etienne of course."

"Oh! How is he taking the news?" Grace gasped, practically vibrating. "Dad-to-be alert!"

Mia's face softened with a kind of reverence I hadn't seen on her before. "He's over the moon. We've... well, we've been here before. But this is the furthest along we've made it. And it feels... real this time. Like it's actually happening."

Her eyes began to glisten. Grace and I instinctively reached across the table to take her hands.

"Of course it's going to happen," I said quietly, my throat tightening.

"Nobody deserves this more than you," Grace added, squeezing Mia's hand.

Mia gave a sheepish smile, then let go and dabbed at her eyes with a napkin. The moment felt sacred. Tender. Safe.

Until the doorbell rang.

The shrill *buzz* echoed through the apartment like a starter pistol, and something in my body instantly recoiled.

I stood up to hug Mia again as Grace walked over to the intercom.

"Yes?" She called into it, cheery and distracted.

A beat.

"Hey, Grace, it's Eli."

The room tilted.

I grabbed the back of Mia's chair and the edge of the table to steady myself, as if the ground itself had just cracked open beneath me.

"Whoa, Ro, you okay?" Mia rose from her seat; concern etched into her brow. She tried to guide me down into her chair, but I couldn't sit. I couldn't think.

I couldn't hear his voice.

Not now. Not yet.

"I'm not here," I managed to whisper. My pulse was jackhammering in my ears.

Grace turned, confused. "What do you mean?"

"I'm *not here*, Grace! Okay!?" I shouted louder than I meant to. My voice broke halfway through. I stumbled to the sink, bent over, and vomited.

"Hey – hey, Eli," Grace's voice wavered as she pressed the intercom button. "What's up?"

"Oh, no," Mia sighed, yanking a decorative dish towel from the oven and rushing over to me, gently sweeping my hair back as I retched again.

"I've been trying to get a hold of Ro," Eli's voice crackled over the speaker, static and all too familiar. "She's not at home, and she's not picking up the phone. I just – can you tell her to call me? Or come by? Please. It's extremely important."

I couldn't breathe. I stared into the sink as Mia

turned on the faucet and began rinsing it out. I wished she could rinse *me* out.

Grace hesitated, then pushed the button again. "Sorry. I haven't seen her."

There was a pause – one of those weighted, heavy silences that hang in the air long after a heart drops.

"Okay. Well, just let me know, yeah?" Eli said, voice more somber now. "And please tell her if you see her."

"Of course," Grace replied.

The moment she released the button; she turned back to the room with wide eyes. "Okay, so, what the fuck was that?"

I groaned and collapsed over the edge of the sink, my forehead hitting the cool countertop. Mia pulled me gently toward the loveseat, draping a throw blanket over me as I curled into myself, shaking.

"Mia, what the fuck was that?" Grace whispered, like I couldn't hear her from three feet away.

"I have no idea," Mia said, adjusting the blanket to fully cover me.

Grace perched on the ottoman beside me. Her voice softened. "Ro, hey. You don't have to tell us anything. Not if you're not ready."

"Totally," Mia echoed. "But like – if you need us to hit him with my car or something, just blink twice."

That pulled a half-sobbed laugh out of me. And then the dam broke.

The sobs came fast and hard, shaking my entire body. I couldn't stop them, couldn't hold anything back. It was like all the pressure I'd been keeping inside had finally ruptured – a dam cracking open under the weight of weeks, months, maybe years of loneliness and longing and confusion. My chest heaved as the tears spilled down, hot and relentless, soaking the blanket Mia had pulled around me. I felt like a child. Like a broken thing. I couldn't catch my breath, couldn't string a coherent thought together.

The sound that escaped me didn't even feel like it belonged to me – it was too raw, too guttural, too vulnerable. I cried in that way you do when you're not just grieving the person, but the hope. The version of the future you'd already begun to build in your mind. The safety you thought you'd found, only to discover it had never really existed in the first place.

I curled tighter into myself, ashamed of the mess I'd become, but was powerless to stop. The grief came in waves – thick and choking, like I was being pulled under over and over again. Every time I thought maybe I could breathe, another memory would surface. His lips. His laugh. The way he'd looked at me that last night, like I was everything.

I didn't know how to reconcile that version of Eli with the one who'd left me without a word yesterday morning.

And so, I cried – not because I was weak, but because I was human. Because I had opened my heart, handed it over without condition, and was left holding the jagged remains.

Grace and Mia stayed close, quiet and steady, like anchors in the storm.

And I let it out. Because I didn't know what else to do. Because pretending I was fine would've broken me more.

Because this time, the pain was too big to contain.

"I told him I was in love him," I said finally, voice cracked and barely above a whisper.

They both gasped in tandem.

"And we kissed."

"What!?" Grace whisper-screamed, leaning closer.

"No way," Mia said under her breath, her mouth slightly open.

"And we slept together."

Mia froze mid-motion. Grace's jaw dropped.

"And... and when I woke up the next morning... he was *gone.*"

The silence was deafening.

Grace reached for my hand like she was grounding me to earth. Mia didn't say a word, but her other hand tightened the blanket around my shoulders.

I stared blankly ahead.

"I don't know if it meant something to him. I don't know if it was just some moment he needed to burn off. But it meant everything to me." My voice wavered, cracking in disbelief. "And when I woke up the next morning, I... I was alone. He'd left me there, alone, with a note on the door saying he had to go, that he needed to clear his head."

There was a beat of silence. Then–

"Oh, Romy," Grace murmured, her face crumpling. "That's terrible. I'm so sorry."

"That's fucking awful," Mia said flatly, no frills, no sugarcoating. "I hate that you went through that. I hate that he left you like that."

I felt their words land somewhere deep inside me, but they didn't soften the sharpness of what I was feeling. "I just – I keep replaying it. All of it. The way he touched me, the way he looked at me. How careful he was. How much it felt like he... like he loved me. And maybe I'm stupid for believing it, but I did."

"You're not stupid," Grace said quickly, scooting closer to take my hand. "You're not. Anyone would've thought that. I would've thought that."

"I just wish I could go back," I whispered, blinking hard. "Not because I regret it. But because I don't think I can live through the silence again."

Mia let out a slow exhale. "Look. We don't know what he's thinking right now."

"But he left," I said. "He left a note."

"I know," Mia nodded, her voice softening. "But that note doesn't mean it didn't mean something to him, too. People do weird, messed up things when they're scared. When they feel overwhelmed."

Grace nodded in agreement. "You said he looked at you like he loved you. I don't think you imagined that."

"But then why leave?" I asked, so small, so broken. "Why not just stay? Wake up next to me, talk to me – anything."

"Maybe he needed space. Maybe he freaked out. That doesn't make it okay, and it definitely doesn't make it fair to you," Mia said. "But it also doesn't mean it didn't matter to him."

Grace rubbed my shoulder gently. "Yeah. This silence might not be the end of the story, Ro. Just... don't decide how it ends before it's finished."

I nodded, but it felt like the kind of nod you give when you're too tired to fight, not when you believe anything will actually change.

Still, I let them hold me. I let their words settle

around me like gauze over a wound, even if it still stung underneath.

Because for now, this was the only version of comfort I had.

32
DOUBLE HEARTBREAK

I didn't realize Eli had called me thirty-seven times. My phone had been on Do Not Disturb for days. Every call went straight to voicemail. Every text – silent. I'd turned off the world because I couldn't stand to hear from the one person I wanted to hear from most.

When Mia dropped me off back home that afternoon, she circled the block first, just in case he was standing outside my apartment with that look on his face – that damn apologetic look that would destroy me. But the sidewalk was empty. The street was quiet. And I was still alone.

There was no way I could be expected to work, or focus, or show up as some cheerful, grounded HR rep ready to guide others through their emotional crises. I could barely remember to eat. I filed a leave-of-absence request under "family emergency," filled out the necessary forms, and gave myself a minimum of two weeks to try to get my shit together. I wasn't sure it would be enough.

The days blurred together. I moved through my apartment like a ghost, haunting the same few rooms, surviving on toast and canned soup. Sometimes I'd catch myself standing in the middle of the kitchen, unsure of what I'd gone in there for. I barely turned on the lights.

My phone remained in Do Not Disturb, but I checked it obsessively – only for texts from Grace or Mia. They were the only ones I could bear to hear from.

And Eli.

He kept calling.

Not constantly, not all at once, but with a kind of rhythm. A steady knock on the door of my silence. Like he thought if he kept reaching out, maybe eventually I'd open the door.

He only sent two texts.

We need to talk.

I can't say what I need to over text.

At first, those messages made something flutter in my chest. Hope. Longing. Something cruel and masochistic like that. But I shut it down just as quickly.

It didn't matter what he had to say.

Whatever it was, it was too late.

He'd left me in a bed we made together. With a note. A *note*.

And maybe that said more than anything else could.

So, I stopped rereading the texts.

I told myself I was done.

I was done with Eli Reed.

I said it like a prayer. Like a spell I could cast to make it true.

But spells are tricky things. And hearts have a way of misbehaving.

I sat on the couch, deliberately far from *His Side*, the worn indent where Eli always sat still taunting me from across the cushions. I tucked my legs underneath me and propped my phone against my knee, headphones in my ears. The loading screen spun for a few seconds – too long – and I stared blankly at the reflection of myself in the dark screen until it shifted.

There she was. A warm-looking woman in her late thirties, maybe early forties, sitting in a sunlit room with pale walls and a plant shelf behind her. She looked oddly familiar. Not like someone I'd met before, but like someone I could've been. Short, curly hair. Big brows. Kind eyes. I immediately relaxed a little. She waved gently into the camera like we were old friends.

"Hi there! Romy, right?"

I smiled faintly. "Hi, yes. I'm Romy."

"It's great to see you again. I'm really glad you decided to move forward with our clinic for mental health services. Just a reminder, I'm Martha, licensed marriage and family therapist."

"Yeah," I nodded. "I'm glad too."

"Last time we went through the basics – your family, medical history, why you're seeking therapy. Today is more of a proper first session. We can talk about whatever you want. Or not talk at all. I can just ramble at you for fifty minutes if that's more helpful." She chuckled, something light and musical, and I found myself smiling in return.

"I've done therapy before," I offered. "I know the drill."

"That's great. So, what made you decide to come back?"

I inhaled slowly, but the emotion caught in my throat faster than I expected. "Well..." My voice cracked, and my eyes welled up before I could stop them. "Sorry.

I don't want to cry already."

Martha's face softened, her voice patient. "Crying's good, Romy. It means you're feeling something that needs to come out."

"I'm *so* tired of crying though," I admitted, wiping my sleeve across my cheek. "Like... *bone tired.*"

She nodded. "Why do you think that is?"

"I don't know. Maybe because I feel stupid? Or like I should be over it already? I–" I hesitated, suddenly embarrassed by how much I was unraveling just a minute into the call. "I just had my heart broken. And it wasn't even a proper breakup. There wasn't a fight or a conversation. Just... silence."

Martha didn't speak. She just waited, gently, letting me fill the space.

"I took a leave of absence from work," I continued, laughing humorlessly. "I told them it was for a family thing. I mean, technically, heartbreak is kind of like losing a family member, right?"

Her expression softened further. "Absolutely. That grief is real."

"I just... I couldn't function anymore. And I didn't want to keep dumping it on my friends. They're there for me, yeah, but there's this guilt that starts to build up, like I'm being too much. Like I'm repeating the same sob story over and over and they're all too polite to say they're sick of hearing it."

"They sound like good friends."

"They are. But it's different. You know? It's not the same kind of space. I don't want them to start secretly dreading my texts."

She nodded in understanding. "So, let's make this

your space. No guilt, no shame, no audience score."

I smiled weakly, grateful. "You're going to regret saying that."

"Doubt it."

I took a breath. "So... I think I mentioned in our intake call that I co-host a podcast?"

"Yes, *Not in the Mood,* right? I actually listened to a few episodes. You're very funny."

I blinked, surprised. "You *listened*?"

"Of course. I like to get to know my clients however I can."

I swallowed hard. "Well... he's the guy."

Her face didn't change, but something in her eyes grew more alert. "Eli."

"Eli *fucking* Reed," I said, voice catching on his name. "My best friend. The guy I was always not in love with until suddenly I was."

"What happened?"

So, I told her. Not every single detail – I didn't need to revisit the way his hands felt on my body, or the way he said my name in the dark – but enough. The group text breakup. The podcast. The slow, confusing shift. The kiss. The confession. The night that felt like a dream. And the note on the fridge that brought me back to earth so violently I hadn't been able to breathe since.

Martha listened quietly, her hands folded in front of her. When I finally stopped, there was a moment of quiet.

"It sounds like you've been on a rollercoaster," she said gently. "And it also sounds like you haven't had much time to actually process any of it."

"I don't think I know *how* to process anymore," I said.

"I think my processing bone is broken. Like, genuinely. Snapped in half."

"That's okay," she said. "That's what we're here to reset."

I laughed softly, blinking tears out of my lashes. "I feel like my brain is made of mashed potatoes."

"Well then," Martha smiled, "let's scoop it back together."

"It hurt in that way only real love does. To want someone so deeply it felt cellular – like craving, but in your bones. To fall – not in some sudden, dramatic plunge – but slowly, helplessly, for someone you already knew by heart. We weren't just close. We were best friends. The kind of best friends who didn't need to fill the silence. The kind who spoke fluently in glances and half-sentences.

He knew how I liked my coffee without asking. Knew which restaurants I fake enthusiasm for, which ones I secretly love. He could read me with frightening accuracy – knew my moods based on my socks, my silences, the way I tied my hair. It was like he tuned into a frequency no one else could hear.

There were these moments – strange, almost magical – when I'd be craving something, and he'd show up with it. Or I'd be spiraling, and I'd get a text that pulled me back down to earth. Like he was tethered to some invisible thread that let him feel when I needed him. Before I even said a word. Who *does* that?"

"Sounds like he really cares for you," Martha said gently.

"Cared," I corrected, voice flat. "Past tense."

"So, what changed?"

"The podcast," I said, after a pause. "Talking to him about love, week after week – about heartbreak and attraction and bad dates and intimacy – it did something to me. I started seeing him differently. Or maybe I was seeing him clearly for the first time. And I fought it. God, did I fight it. I told myself I was imagining it, projecting. That I was lonely. But it was like trying to stop a train with my bare hands."

I gave a weak laugh and wiped my eyes again.

"He used to say these things. That he wanted to be in my life forever. That the podcast mattered more than we realized. That I created this... noise in his head that he didn't know how to shut off. And I didn't know what to do with that. It felt like he was circling something but refusing to land."

Martha waited, her expression soft and patient.

"So, I went over there. I was done. I couldn't keep it in anymore. I felt like I was going to burst open if I didn't say something. He was standing in his living room – it was movie night. We take turns picking movies. And even though it was *my* turn, he asked if we could watch *New Moon*, because the time before I made him watch *Twilight*."

Martha smiled. "A classic."

"Thank you." I managed a real laugh. "And he's standing there, going on about Jacob and vampires, and I just – blurted it out. I told him I was in love with him. That I couldn't hold it in anymore. That it was killing me to keep pretending we were just friends."

"And what happened?" She asked, even though she knew.

"He kissed me. I mean, really kissed me. Like he'd

been waiting for it too. And then... we slept together. But it didn't feel casual. It didn't feel like a one-time thing or like we got caught up in the moment. It felt like... *everything*. Like something in the universe had finally clicked into place. I felt safe. I felt seen. I felt *chosen*."

I paused and let the silence fill the space between us.

"And then you woke up."

"And then I woke up. Alone. In his apartment. To a note that said he needed to clear his head. And I just..." I swallowed. "That's not how we are together. That's never been us. We don't *leave* each other. We don't disappear without saying something. We talk. We joke. We always check in, even about the smallest things – what takeout to get, which movie to watch, if something I said came off weird. He doesn't vanish on me. Not like that."

I blinked, hard, trying to keep it together. "And it wasn't just that he left. It was *how* he left. The note was so... impersonal. Like he couldn't even bear to look at me. Like the second I fell asleep, he had to get away from me. And the worst part is, I woke up smiling. I woke up feeling warm and full and so sure that everything had changed. That we had crossed into something new. Something real. I was literally lying there, wrapped in his sheets, thinking *this is it*. This is the start of something. And instead... it was the end."

I paused, my voice a whisper now. "And I know it was just a note. I know people panic. I know sometimes silence isn't cruelty, it's fear. But it felt like abandonment. Like rejection in its most cowardly form. Because he didn't even give me the dignity of a conversation. He left me with nothing but a sentence and all my own worst thoughts to fill in the blanks."

Martha's expression softened, the kind of softness that doesn't pity but understands. She let the silence hang for a moment, like she was making room for the weight of what I'd said.

"That makes perfect sense," she said gently. "What you experienced wasn't just about the note. It was about what it *represented*. That moment – waking up alone, finding those words – it activated something deep. It wasn't just about Eli leaving. It was about being left *without answers*, left with your own fears, your own narratives. And that kind of silence can feel louder than any fight, any breakup. Because your mind rushes to fill the gaps, and it always reaches for the worst possibilities."

She paused, her voice steady.

"You're right – sometimes people do act out of fear. But that doesn't mean your pain isn't valid. It doesn't make what you felt any less real. You weren't asking for a perfect ending. You were asking to matter enough to be looked in the eye."

I paused, swallowing back the lump in my throat, trying not to look at the time ticking by on the corner of the screen. "Now I just... I miss my friend," I said, voice trembling. "I miss him so much it aches. It burns. It's this constant, gnawing hole in my chest. I just want my friend back." My words dissolved into sobs, sharp and unfiltered. "But I'm so hurt. And the timing – he picked the worst possible time to walk away. The worst."

Martha gave a soft, understanding nod, then leaned forward a bit, her voice measured. "I'm going to say something you might not agree with."

"Go for it," I said, wiping my face with the sleeve of my sweatshirt.

"You don't actually know what he meant by those words, Romy. You think you do. And that's completely understandable. Your brain is doing its job – trying to make sense of something painful. But the truth is, until you talk to him, really talk to him, you're building the story alone. You're filling in the blanks with your own pain."

I shook my head. "No. Absolutely not. I'm not talking to him."

"That's okay," she said gently. "You don't have to – not now, maybe not ever. But I want to be honest with you: the longer you keep circling the same questions without answers, the more those questions are going to hurt you. They'll start to define the whole thing. And maybe they already are."

"What else could he have meant?" I snapped, suddenly hot with anger. "What else could he possibly have meant by leaving a note on the front door like I was some casual overnight guest?"

Martha didn't flinch. She waited a beat, then said, "I don't know why he left, Romy. I wish I did. But I can tell you that fear does strange things to people. He might've been terrified – of what it meant to cross that line with you. He might've thought, 'I just ruined the best thing I had.' Maybe he felt shame. Or guilt. Or total panic. Maybe he didn't trust himself to say the right thing. Maybe he was scared he'd say something that made it worse."

I stared at her, eyes glassy. "I'm too hurt to care about

his reasons. The point is, he left. He left me right after the most vulnerable, intimate night of my life. He left when it mattered most. Because when everything changed, when we crossed that line, he couldn't handle it."

There was silence between us. Not heavy. Just honest.

Martha exhaled slowly. "And that's okay to feel. It's okay to be angry. You *should* be. But I also want to gently remind you of something: you're still in this moment. You haven't reached the end yet. This is the part where it still hurts. But it's not necessarily the end. And he might need space too. That doesn't excuse how he left you, but it might explain part of it."

I looked away, blinking rapidly.

"You don't have to forgive him," she said. "You don't even have to speak to him. But if you want to start healing, you have to let go of the idea that you already know everything that's in his head. Because right now, you're grieving what he did *and* what you've imagined he meant by doing it. And that's a double heartbreak you don't deserve."

I paused, thinking. "You're good at this."

Martha paused too and leaned back in her chair, laughing a melodic laugh. "Thank you. I think that's a good note to end on."

"Thank you for listening to me."

"It's my pleasure. See you soon?"

"Yes, soon."

I disconnected the call.

33
INTERMISSION

I sat in my closet alone. Just the one couch cushion for myself. I didn't have the fancy mic setup that Eli usually brought with him. I didn't have a high-tech recorder on my phone. But that didn't stop me from hitting the record button anyway.

"Hey everyone, it's Romy. Coming to you solo for... honestly, I don't even know what episode number this is anymore. Let's call it a bonus breakdown. A little emotional intermission. I wasn't planning on recording today. Actually, I was planning on doing literally anything *but* this. But there's something about talking to you all that feels easier than talking to myself. Or a therapist. Or my friends. Or him.

The past few weeks have been – crazy doesn't even begin to cover it. A complete, absolute mindfuck. I've felt some of the highest highs of my life. The kind of highs that make you feel like your heart grew three sizes and might just float out of your chest. And then – like clockwork – I crashed. Hard. So, yeah. To anyone keeping score at home: I'm now in therapy. We love personal growth. I don't think it'll affect the show much – if anything, maybe it'll make me more tolerable. Jury's still out.

I don't even really know what I wanted to say on

here. Just that I've been... going through it. And I can't give away too much because some of you are terrifyingly observant and have already cracked every code we've ever tried to be subtle about. But – okay. Here it is. I met someone. I met someone, and it was... it was everything. It was ecstasy. It was an orgasm. It was Christmas morning when you're still young enough to believe in magic and old enough to remember the wait. It was laughing so hard your stomach aches. It was crying in someone's arms and feeling safer for it. It was the kind of love you think only happens in indie movies. The kind that doesn't just crack you open – it hollowed me out and rebuilt me. Like love as a religion. Like a home I'd been homesick for before I even knew it existed.

And then, like all things that burn too bright, it ended. Or – it broke. Or I broke it. Or he did. Or maybe it was always going to break, because that kind of love isn't designed to last. It's designed to change you. And it did. I will never be the same person I was before him. He ruined me in the most beautiful, unfixable way.

Nobody really prepares you for what it's like to lose someone who's still alive. Someone who still walks around this world, probably brushing his teeth right now, probably making coffee, maybe even laughing. And meanwhile, you're grieving. You're mourning this invisible death that no one else can see. There's no funeral for when a relationship ends. No closure casserole. No sympathy cards. Just silence. Just space. Just you, clutching the ghost of something that was once so vividly real, you swore you could taste it.

But I'm okay. I'm getting okay. Some days still suck.

Some mornings I wake up with his name burning a hole in my throat, and some nights I almost text him just to feel something. But then I remember – I loved someone. *Really* loved someone. And even if it didn't last, even if it hurt, that love was real. That version of me was real. And for a little while, I was brave enough to feel all of it.

Anyway. I didn't mean for this to turn into a Greek tragedy. I swear I'll be back next week with more dating horror stories and bad advice. But tonight, this felt important. So, thank you for listening. Thank you for letting me fall apart in your headphones. And if you're hurting too – just know, you're not alone. You're never alone."

I pressed 'stop recording' and uploaded it immediately.

34
FOR ROMY

The video found me before I could stop it.

I was curled up on my couch, wrapped in a cardigan that smelled vaguely like lavender dryer sheets and heartache, absently scrolling through TikTok with my phone at half brightness and my expectations lower. I wasn't looking for anything in particular – maybe a cute dog, maybe a breakfast sandwich recipe I'd never make – but the second I saw my face on screen, my thumb froze mid-scroll.

It was us.

Me and Eli.

Clips from the podcast, expertly stitched together, captioned in cursive font with some unreasonably emotional Phoebe Bridgers song playing in the background. Eli's voice echoed first from an episode I didn't even remember recording: "Sometimes I think it's hard because we don't actually believe we're worthy of the thing we're looking for."

Then it was footage from the launch party – flashes of movement and light, a lingering glance, a near-touch that didn't quite happen. The kind of look you'd miss if you weren't watching for it. Then random clips from people recording us in public that I'd never seen before: us out laughing together, at an event, holding hands, gesturing wildly at each other, me winking, him trying not to smile too wide. And then – my voice, sweet, tender: "You don't scare me." And Eli's, deep, serious: "Why not?" Then me again: "Because you're safe."

The comment section was chaos.

I CAN'T DO THIS RIGHT NOW.

THE TENSION BETWEEN THEM IS LITERALLY FERAL

not me crying in traffic over these two idiots in love

Someone had tagged me.

Someone had tagged him.

I dropped the phone on the couch like it had burned me.

Because suddenly, I wasn't just some girl with a broken heart. I was the protagonist in a story that people had watched unfold. Strangers had pieced it together with more clarity than I'd allowed myself. The tension. The longing. The love.

And all I could think was:

Oh, God.

They see it, too.

I grabbed my phone again, heart pounding, scrolled through the comments, watched the video again.

Then again.

And again.

I didn't know what I was doing – what I was hoping to feel. Vindicated? Understood? Furious? All I knew was that I felt awake in a way I hadn't in days. Like someone had taken a match to the fog in my brain and lit it all on fire.

Because for the first time since everything shattered...

I didn't feel so alone.

I brought my phone back up to my face and began looking up *Not in the Mood* edits and there were hundreds, *thousands* of clips just like that first one I'd seen.

I slammed my phone down on the couch cushions.

My heart was pounding. My pulse roared in my ears like ocean waves crashing against stone. It felt like the air had been sucked out of my apartment, like everything in me had been called to attention, shaken loose from its grief.

Because it was all there. In the clips. In the edits. In the way strangers – *strangers on the internet* – had seen us more clearly than we ever let ourselves.

We'd been in love in plain sight.

And now?

I didn't know what we were.

I grabbed my phone and opened our episode archive app – the one for the podcast. I hadn't touched it in weeks. The file titles stared back like ghosts: *Ep12_FinalEdit.wav*, *Eli'sNotes.docx*, *AdReadIdeas_RomyLOL.*

I opened the folder labeled 'Unused Intros'.

There was one file, timestamped just two days ago. It was named simply:

For Romy.

I didn't remember recording it.

But I hit play.

And there it was – his voice, unpolished, uncertain.

"I've been rewriting this in my head for weeks. Hell, maybe years. Since the day we met, I've felt like I've been living in parentheses – and everything outside of you was just filler. I didn't know how to say it back then, and then when it got real, when it finally happened, I froze. Not because I didn't want you – but because I did. And I didn't trust myself not to ruin it."

He paused, sighed deeply, and continued.

"The day you told me you loved me, something cracked open inside me. Not in a bad way – like an earthquake, but the kind that breaks apart old foundations so you can finally build something stronger. But I panicked. I got scared that if I let it happen, if I let myself have you, I'd lose you. And I thought... maybe running would hurt less than staying and messing it up.

You've been in my life for so long, I forgot that the world doesn't give you people like you more than once. I was stupid enough to think I had time – time to figure it out, time to say the right thing. But time kept moving, and I kept messing up. And then I lost you. And I realized, for the first time, how quiet my life is without you in it.

You were the noise in my head, Romy. Every quiet moment, there you were – laughing, correcting my grammar, making some offhand comment about the patriarchy. You were the background music to everything. And I left. I walked away from the one person who made silence unbearable.

I didn't leave because I didn't love you. I left because I did. And I didn't know how to hold that – how to hold *you* – without dropping something. Without dropping everything. And the irony is, I dropped you anyway. So, yeah... I'm sorry. I'm sorry I was too late. I'm sorry I made you think you weren't everything to me. I just hope you can forgive me one day."

I didn't breathe while he spoke.

Not once.

It was like my body had gone completely still, like if I moved even an inch, I'd miss it – like his words were made of glass and the slightest motion would shatter them. And when he was done, when the last syllable hung in the air between us, trembling like a lit fuse, I still couldn't breathe.

Because this wasn't just an apology.

It was a confession. A reckoning. A heart cracked wide open and handed to me without armor, without pretense, without a single damned excuse.

And I'd waited for this. God, I'd waited. I'd begged the universe for a moment like this, in quiet tears on the bathroom floor, in the soft ache of my chest at night, in every second I told myself I was done with him and knew I was lying.

But hearing it – *really* hearing it – was something else entirely.

It was like watching the world tip back into alignment after months of walking sideways. Like someone had been holding their hands over my eyes and finally let go.

And I didn't know what to say.

Not yet.

Because even though my body was screaming to run into him, to kiss him until the pain dissolved, my heart was still bruised. Still tender.

Still not sure if this was *the end* of our story or the beginning of something new.

But I knew one thing.

I loved him.

I loved Eli fucking Reed so much, it broke me.

And somehow, in the middle of all that wreckage, I still wanted him to be mine.

35
BRINY LITTLE FETISH

San Francisco grew cooler as the weeks on the calendar flew by. There was something about the city in the fall that always felt like an exhale. The heat and chaos of late summer slipped out with the tides, and in its place came the fog – low and steady, curling around buildings like a protective shawl. I always loved it here during this time of year. The way the light softened, the way the chill in the air demanded something warm in your hands and something wool around your shoulders. It felt quieter, more thoughtful. Like even the city was trying to reflect.

I walked along Crissy Field, the narrow path that winds along the northern edge of the city, hugging the water and nudging you toward the Golden Gate Bridge. Eli and I used to come here all the time. Early weekend mornings, coffees in hand – his hot, mine iced, no matter the temperature – trading stories and half-formed thoughts about everything and nothing. True crime podcasts. A ceramics class he once took and immediately abandoned. The absurd but critical importance of separating your laundry.

I smiled at the memory, but it came with a pang so sharp it felt like a pulled muscle – sudden and deep and hard to stretch away. That was the thing about grief, I was learning. It didn't arrive on a schedule, and it never left politely.

Ahead of me, the Golden Gate Bridge was mostly invisible. From midway up, it disappeared into a thick layer of fog that made it look unfinished, like the heavens hadn't yet installed the rest. I stood there, squinting up into the haze, thinking about everything that bridge had seen over the years – earthquakes and protests, history unraveling in real time. And yet it stood, bold and impossible, painted like a wound that never quite closed.

If that bridge could survive all that, maybe I could survive this.

Right?

I hadn't cried in about a week. Which, if you've ever been through heartbreak, you'll know isn't always a sign of healing – it's a sign you've entered The Abyss. That muted, numb limbo that follows the white-hot pain of The Grieving. I was in it now, deep. A blank slate of nothingness, where food didn't taste like much and time bent weirdly. Days passed, but I didn't feel them.

I had officially extended my time off work to twelve weeks. And if I'm being honest, I didn't see myself going back. Not to Human Resources, not to team-building emails and awkward PowerPoint trainings about workplace empathy. I couldn't return to the version of myself who had once thought that was enough. I'd gone through something seismic. I was different now.

So, instead, I started fantasizing about what came next. Maybe I'd walk dogs. Maybe I'd apply at a bookstore or open an Etsy shop called *Romy's House of Horrors*, where I'd sell my emotional baggage alongside snarky embroidery and haunted thrift finds. All I knew was I needed something that didn't require pretending.

And yet, somehow, despite the chaos in my chest and the blur in my brain, the podcast was thriving. My confessional episode had gone viral – the good kind, the terrifying kind, the kind you don't expect when you're just talking into a mic at 2 AM in your pajamas. Suddenly, we weren't just a modest indie relationship podcast anymore. We had *followers*. Six figures and climbing. Real ones. Listeners. Fans. Strangers who felt like they knew me.

I was getting tagged in TikToks and reels. Fan edits paired my monologue with scenes from sad French movies or videos of people staring out rain-streaked windows. Florence + The Machine, Phoebe Bridgers, Taylor Swift, dominated the background music. People were grieving with me. For me.

Why is this podcast hitting harder than therapy right now?

I wasn't ready to cry in traffic today but ok.

The way she talked about love like it was a religion? Hits different.

Someone even coined the hashtag #RomyNation. Which was wildly cheesy but also kind of amazing. There were thinkpieces on BuzzFeed and Jezebel. Relationship podcasts name-dropped me in their intros. Articles came out with titles like *Why Romy's Episode on 'Not In The Mood' Is the Heartbreak Blueprint of the Year* and *We're All Romy: The Power of Vulnerability in Podcasting*. And people were speculating – hard. Who was the man I'd fallen for? Was it Eli? Was it a mystery ex? Was it some obscure tech bro I once followed on

Instagram? Anyone I'd ever been seen with in public was fair game for theories.

I watched from a distance as Eli continued uploading our pre-recorded episodes each week. We had a backlog of them – enough to keep up the illusion that everything was fine – but I could see the end approaching. We were running out. Soon, there'd be nothing left to post. Nothing left to hide behind.

I hadn't talked to him since The Morning After. We hadn't even texted. Not even a passive-aggressive link to a song or a TikTok or a meme. Just silence.

And yet, the world kept spinning. The podcast kept growing. Sponsors reached out. Brand deals arrived. Eli's accountant friend emailed to ask for my banking info so he could start splitting royalties and ad revenue between us. It wasn't a full-time income yet, but it was close. Closer than I'd ever expected.

People loved me. Or the version of me they heard on the podcast. They were fiercely protective, which was sweet, if slightly unsettling.

Romy from Not in the Mood just dropped the best breakup monologue of the year and I need her to know I'd fight for her until the end.

I don't know who hurt Romy Becker, but I need his social security number.

It was surreal. Like watching your own heartbreak get remixed into a pop culture moment. And still, I felt hollow. Grateful, yes. Touched, deeply. But underneath it all, I was just tired. Tired of being strong. Tired of being content. Tired of pretending I didn't miss him everyday.

I didn't know how long the podcast would last. Or if

it should. Maybe it had served its purpose. Maybe it was time to let go of that, too.

But not yet.

Not today.

My phone buzzed in the pocket of my coat, and even though I instinctively reached for it, I no longer expected to see Eli's name. That particular hope had burned itself out quietly – no drama, no ceremony. Just a dull ache that eventually stopped flaring up.

It was the group chat between Grace, Mia, and I.

Grace had sent a message.

Still on for coffee this AM?

Mia liked it immediately.

I sent a thumbs-up emoji, the universal symbol for *barely functioning, but present.*

In the wake of what the internet now lovingly referred to as *Romy's Episode* – which, honestly, made it sound like a scandalous e-news docuseries – Grace and Mia had become my saving, well, grace. Both of them. Consistently. Quietly. Fiercely. I'd once said Eli was my buoy in a storm, but he'd let go of the rope. Grace and Mia? They became the raft. My life had turned into an unpredictable sea of emotional swells, but they held me steady, kept me close, made sure I didn't drift too far into the dark.

We were together constantly. I spent afternoons on Grace's couch while she worked from home. We'd talk about everything and nothing – an annoying coworker, the lack of good dating apps, why men couldn't load a dishwasher properly if their life depended on it. With Mia, it was long walks, deep chats, and reorganizing the nursery-to-be in color-coded bins. She'd taken time off work to prep the house, and I offered myself up as emotional labor in return for snacks and occasional use of her bathtub.

At least once a week, the three of us would gather in someone's living room, usually with cheap wine and bad TV and no makeup, just vibes and truth. We'd yell at reality show contestants and cry over dumb commercials and talk brutally, beautifully, honestly about life and love and what it meant to be women trying not to fall apart. It was better than therapy. Or at least, complementary.

Speaking of – I was still seeing Martha. Twice a week now. I'd decided if the podcast was going to drag my mental health through the mud, it was only fair I used the podcast money to clean up the mess. Self-care, but make it reparations.

Martha was calm and wise and deeply unafraid of my chaos, which made me trust her more. She didn't try to fix me. She just helped me make sense of the wreckage. Like emotional archeology. We were still digging, still cataloging, but every session made me feel a little more like a person and a little less like an open wound.

I wasn't okay. Not even close. But I was getting better at *being* not okay. I'd started to believe that okay was out there somewhere – maybe not close, maybe not visible yet – but a possibility. Waiting. Like a distant shoreline on the other side of grief.

And for now, that was enough.

Coffee helped, too.

Grace buzzed me up, and I took the rickety elevator to her seventh-floor apartment. The hallway smelled like laundry detergent, and someone's forgotten takeout. Comforting in a weird, urban way.

When I stepped inside, I found Mia already there, dramatically draped across Grace's loveseat like a renaissance painting of a child recovering from consumption.

"Oh, no," I said, setting my tote down, "why does Mia look like a depression-era mother of twelve?"

"Fuck off," Mia groaned, one hand cradling the bump that was finally starting to show. "I'm pregnant."

"She wants pickles," Grace muttered, already sounding exasperated, "and I don't have any."

"It's ten in the morning," I said, eyeing her from across the room. "Is it pickle hour already?"

"Pickle hour is *every* hour," Mia said with all the gravitas of a constitutional law scholar.

"Wow. Baby's got quite the briny little fetish going on, huh?"

We'd taken to calling Mia's bump "Baby" like it was a nickname with a capital B. We weren't creative people, okay?

"I should just start carrying my own around with me," Mia grumbled.

"Honestly? Not the worst idea." I laughed, peeling off my Patagonia and looping it onto the hook by the door. I slid into the empty chair next to Grace at her kitchen table, where she already had mugs out and her espresso machine humming in the background. She gave me a soft, knowing smile – not pushy, just present.

"How're you feeling?" She asked, voice low and even.

"Fine. I'm fine," I said, keeping my eyes on the table. "I went for a walk this morning. Crissy Field."

"Oh, I love Crissy Field. I don't go nearly enough."

"Why on earth would you go there?" Mia called out from the couch, raising her voice just enough to carry through the apartment.

Grace glanced at me, eyebrows arching. She mouthed: *Tread carefully.*

Mia had been a little more... sharp-edged since her pregnancy announcement.

Understandable. She was, after all, building a human. If anyone had earned the right to be a little bitchy, it was her. I considered her my honorary sister-wife at this point. We were in too deep for pleasantries.

"Because it's my favorite walk in the city," I replied. "why wouldn't I go there?"

Grace stood to busy herself with the espresso machine, probably in case Mia and I started bickering like two old women at a bingo table.

"You and Eli used to go there all the time," Mia said. "That doesn't sting?"

I paused, letting the question hang. "It only stings when you bring it up, Mia."

Mia sat up straighter, tucking a pillow behind her back. "You always do this to yourself."

"Mia," Grace warned, firm.

I touched Grace's arm lightly. A signal: *I've got this. I'm not about to throw a latte.*

"I always do *what*, exactly?" I asked, looking over at Mia.

"It's like you have this need to rake yourself over the coals," Mia said, eyes narrowing. "You revisit places that hurt. You drink out of that ugly mug of his that you claim to hate – yeah, I noticed. You keep poking at the bruise just to feel it again."

Grace turned sharply. "Mia."

"What?" Mia said, unapologetic. "The girl has serious self-destructive tendencies."

"It's not like I said I was going to *text* him," I snapped.

"Good. You're not allowed to."

That got to me.

I blinked. "You know, clearly you read somewhere that being a total bitch while pregnant is charming, but I hate to break it to you – it's not."

Grace placed an iced coffee in front of me. I took it, grateful for the distraction and the caffeine.

"I'm just saying," Mia continued, sitting up now, fully invested. "it's like – you close the door on people, and then when you get bored or lonely or hurt, you set the door on fire and act shocked when you get burned."

Grace sat back down, eyes fixed on her coffee like it was telling her something important. "I know you think you're being casual," she said softly, not looking up, "but Ro, this is what you do. You throw yourself at people who can't meet you where you are. You say it's just a text, or just a hook-up, or just a walk – but it's never *just* anything. Not for you. You dig the knife in slowly and then ask why it hurts when you finally twist it."

The room went quiet.

I let the moment breathe before I said, quietly, "I just... miss him."

It was the first time I'd said it out loud to them. And it felt like dropping a small bomb in their breakfast cereal.

Mia's expression softened. "I know. But missing

someone isn't a good enough reason to keep breaking your own heart."

My throat tightened. My eyes stung, but I knew no tears would come. I'd wrung myself dry.

Mia leaned forward slightly. "You avoid anything that makes you feel secure. The podcast. Your job. Structure. You say you don't want to be tied down, but the second things start to feel *safe*, you find a way to torch it. And then you joke about it. You use sarcasm and deflection to avoid actually dealing with your shit."

"I get it," I said flatly. "I'm the problem."

"No," Grace said immediately, reaching across the table to grab my hand. Her voice was low and warm. "You're not the problem, babe."

She held my gaze.

"I don't think you're trying to hurt yourself. I think you're just trying to feel something that makes sense. And when you're hurting, sometimes the only thing that does make sense is to focus on the person who caused it. Touching that bruise again and again because it reminds you it was real. That you were real."

She squeezed my hand.

"You're not weak. You're just not healed yet."

My apartment was quiet, save for the hum of the refrigerator and the occasional creak of the building settling into itself. I didn't turn on music. Didn't light a candle. Didn't even bother to change out of the jeans I regretted putting on this morning. I just dropped my keys into the bowl by the door, shrugged out of my jacket, and collapsed onto the couch like a puppet whose strings had finally been cut.

My phone was face down on the coffee table. Taunting me.

I knew what I wanted to do. I knew what I shouldn't.

I curled my knees up beneath me, wrapping my arms around a throw pillow that still smelled faintly of his cologne – though that was probably a lie my brain made up, like a cruel party trick.

I stared at the phone. Just stared.

It would be so easy. A four-word message. *Hey, how are you?* Harmless. Friendly. Emotionally reckless in a very subtle way. I could convince myself it meant nothing. That it wasn't a plea, or a breadcrumb, or a thinly veiled I-miss-you. But we both knew it would be.

My fingers hovered over the screen, thumb trembling slightly. It was muscle memory by now. Tap. Type. Regret.

But this time... I didn't.

Instead, I pressed the side button and let the screen go black again. I leaned back against the couch and exhaled, long and slow and shaky.

Maybe he didn't want to talk. Maybe he did. But I was so tired of reaching across the distance and coming back with splinters.

I sat there in the silence, letting the ache settle somewhere deep inside me like sediment at the bottom of a river. Not gone, but not as loud.

And for the first time in weeks, I listened to what I *should* do.

I didn't even draft a message.

I just let the silence be the answer.

Maybe it was time to really let go.

36
ACCOUNTABILITY

Eli sat in the dark of his apartment, the only light coming from the blue glow of his laptop screen and the faint glint of streetlamps leaking in through the blinds. His living room – usually full of soft sounds and background noise – was dead quiet, like even the furniture was holding its breath.

In the course of just a few weeks, his life had quietly unraveled. No explosion, no dramatic confrontation – just a slow bleed. He'd watched the distance between them stretch wider and wider until there was nothing but silence at the other end.

He adjusted the mic stand with shaking fingers. Pressed record.

A moment of static. A pause.

Then–

"Hey, everyone. It's me. Eli. Of *Not in the Mood*, allegedly. I'm alone tonight. Not sure where Romy is, if I'm being perfectly honest. I wish I did. I wish a lot of things were different. But life doesn't really care about what you wish for. It gives you what it gives you, and it doesn't always feel fair. And lately, it feels like life's been trying to teach me a lesson I didn't sign up for.

Anyway. I wanted to come on here because... I owe you something. I owe her something. You've all been with us on this ride for a while now – laughing, venting, spiraling right alongside us – and I think we've done a decent job of hiding just how messy things got behind the scenes. But if Romy had the courage to be honest with you, then I don't want to be the coward who disappears into the edit. So, here it is.

I also met someone.

And then I hurt them.

Not just once. Not in one big, obvious, villainous way. But in slow, quiet ways. With silence. With distance. With avoidance dressed up as indifference. I thought if I kept things light, if I kept her laughing, if I never crossed the line, I could keep her in my life forever. But all that really did was put her in a cage made of maybes and what-ifs. And I let her sit there, wondering if I cared at all. When the truth is – I've never cared about anyone more in my life.

Accountability's a weird thing. Everyone says they want it. But when you really sit with it – when you see the ways you've failed the people who meant everything to you, it's... brutal. Like holding a mirror to the worst version of yourself and realizing *that* guy is still you. That guy said nothing when he should've said everything. That guy walked away when he should've run straight toward her.

I'm not brave. Not in the ways that matter. I used to think bravery looked like big gestures, like showing up at someone's door in the rain or yelling your love across a crowd. But maybe it's quieter than that. Maybe it's being honest before it's too late. Maybe it's letting yourself feel instead of performing the version of yourself that's easier for everyone else to love.

I loved her in the way a wave loves the shore – relentlessly, selfishly, over and over again. But I didn't realize I was pulling her under. I thought keeping my distance would protect her. That if I left the truth unspoken, it couldn't ruin anything. But silence is its own kind of violence. And mine pushed her away. I stood at the edge of something extraordinary and chose safety instead.

I think part of me believed that if I ran first, it wouldn't feel like losing her. It would just feel like leaving. And somehow, that would hurt less. But it doesn't. It doesn't hurt less. It just hurts alone. So... if you're out there listening. I'm sorry. For all of it. For not choosing you out loud. For not being brave enough to say what I felt when I had the chance. You were never hard to love. I was just too scared to let myself do it properly.

And to everyone else... thank you. For sticking with us. I don't know what happens next. I really don't. But maybe love is just showing up anyway. Even when you're late. Even when it's messy. Even when it might be too late.

That's all for now. I'll see you soon... I hope."

He reached for the mouse. Pressed 'stop'.

The room returned to silence.

37
FORT POINT

It was raining, but that didn't stop me from going to Crissy Field again. If anything, I preferred it this way – less people, less noise, less chance of running into someone jogging with too much optimism.

I held my umbrella like a shield, the rain falling in a steady, meditative pour. My boots crunched over the wet gravel of the winding path, each step a soft echo in the mist. The fog clung low, wrapping around the base of the Golden Gate like it had secrets to keep. Ahead of me: no one. Behind me: still no one. I was truly, completely alone. And for once, I didn't mind.

I listened to his episode the night it went live.

Then again.

And again.

And again.

Each time it ended, I found myself pressing play like muscle memory. Like it was a ritual I didn't remember inventing. Like some part of me still thought if I listened closely enough, the ending might change.

The first time, I sat stiff and frozen, barely breathing, hands clenched in the blanket I hadn't realized I'd dragged onto my lap. By the third listen, I was curled into a ball on the couch, letting the words wash over me like the tide – soft and steady and utterly indifferent to how much they hurt.

He sounded wrecked.

Not just sad. *Wrecked.*

Like the words cost him something. Like every syllable was a wound.

And still, I couldn't tell if that made it better or worse.

Part of me wanted to scream. *Why now?* Why say it all now, when the silence had already done its damage? When I had already bled out the version of myself that waited for him to show up?

And the other part... the quieter part...

It just wanted to crawl into the sound of his voice and stay there.

Forever.

He said he ran because staying meant being brave, and he wasn't sure he knew how to be.

He said my name – not directly, but it was there in every pause.

Every breath.

Every broken sentence that trailed off like it couldn't carry its own weight.

The internet exploded, of course. It always does.

Someone check on Romy.

I knew it was about her.

This is the most heartbreaking thing I've ever heard. Someone give them a second chance, please.

I couldn't bring myself to post anything.

Not a story. Not a tweet.

Not even a cryptic quote about timing and pain and ships passing in the night.

I just kept listening. Over and over.

The truth is – I didn't know how to feel.

Part of me wanted to believe every word. Part of me already did.

But love, once broken, doesn't just reassemble itself on command.

Even if it's still alive. Even if it's still aching.

I'd spent so long grieving him in silence.

Now it was *his* turn.

And somehow, that didn't feel satisfying.

It just felt lonely. All over again.

I wished he'd said it sooner. I wished I hadn't needed to hear it at all.

But mostly, I wished I could believe that this version of him – the brave one, the honest one – wasn't just a voice behind a mic.

Because the voice I loved most was the one that stayed.

And he never did.

Above, seagulls cried out like old ghosts. I peeked at them from under the rim of my umbrella, watching their white bodies blur into the gray sky. I wondered what it might feel like to disappear with them – to fly away, destination unknown, no plan, just instinct. To live without wondering who might be waiting. To land wherever felt soft. To shit wherever I pleased.

But I wasn't a bird. I was a girl in the rain, walking a path I'd walked before, trying not to look for him in every grain of sand.

And for once, my mind was quiet. Not empty, but quiet. The way the sea is quiet when it's tired of roaring. There was no clarity, not really. Just the dull understanding that things had calmed. The worst had already happened.

And I was still here.

Things had calmed. I wasn't healed, but I wasn't bleeding anymore. And although I had no idea where this path was taking me, I had a strange, small certainty that I would be okay.

Timing, they say, is everything. But timing had never been my friend. It came too early, or too late, or not at all. And maybe that's the cruelest part – knowing something extraordinary had to end not because it wasn't right, but because it wasn't ready.

Still, I counted myself lucky. Truly.

I got to feel something real. Not almost-love. Not performative love. Not breadcrumbed affection masquerading as romance. But the kind of love that splits you open and lets the light in.

The kind people write about.

The kind people ruin their lives for.

The kind you don't forget – even when it forgets you.

What no one tells you about that kind of love, though, is this: when it ends, the pain is bigger than the love ever was.

It doesn't just break your heart. It burns through your bones.

And I knew, without hesitation, that I never wanted to feel that kind of loss again.

If I couldn't have Eli Reed, I didn't want anyone else.

Not like that.

Would I love again? Of course.

Would it be good? Absolutely.

But it would never be *that*.

It wouldn't be *him*.

What we had was chemical.

It burned – bright, fierce, and fast.

It was love, yes, but it was also friendship. Deep, effortless, elemental friendship. And I think that's what made the ending unbearable. It wasn't just that I lost the person I loved. It's that I lost my person.

And love, for all its beauty, will never feel quite like that again.

I made my way to Fort Point, the old Civil War-era fortress tucked beneath the Golden Gate like a secret the fog was trying to keep. The stone walls were slick with rain, the air echoing with absence. I wandered its empty halls in silence, my footsteps the only sound – soft, steady, alone.

And I was. Alone. Not just here, but in the bigger sense.

I knew that. I'd known it for a while now.

But I was trying to make peace with it.

Trying to see solitude not as punishment, but possibility.

I had people who loved me. I wasn't blind to that.

Mia – sharp as ever, slicing through my excuses with that no-bullshit love that bruises a little, but always heals cleaner.

Grace – gentle and grounding, who could calm a storm in me with a single look.

And Martha, my therapist, who was slowly teaching me how to live inside my own mind without treating it like enemy territory.

They didn't ask me to be anything other than exactly what I was. Broken, beautiful, bitter, soft. They stayed. They held space. They didn't flinch.

But most of all–

I had me.

And that was the part that scared me the most.

Because I was the only one who would always stay. The only constant. The only home I could never leave.

Martha said that once, in a session.

"You're the only person you're guaranteed to have forever."

And I guess I've been trying to figure out what it means to make peace with that.

To stop waiting for someone else to save me.

To find light inside myself when everything feels swallowed by shadow.

To speak to myself with softness, to stop setting fire to my own joy before anyone else can.

I deserve tenderness.

From others, yes – but especially from me.

So, I'm trying.

Bit by bit.

Day by day.

I don't have all the pieces yet.

But I'm learning how to give them to myself.

I just have to tape up my heart first.

Then maybe, someday, I'll be ready to carry it again.

I climbed the winding stairs, each step echoing like a breath I hadn't fully taken in weeks. The staircase emptied out onto the rooftop, where the wind hit me first – sharp and salt-soaked, the kind of cold that reminds you you're alive even when you'd rather not feel anything at all.

Above me, the Golden Gate rose out of the fog like a cathedral. Immense. Eternal. A thousand tons of steel stitched together by hands that must've believed in permanence. I tilted my head back, eyes tracing every beam and rivet, every impossible piece holding it all together.

It didn't seem real – this structure, this strength, this endurance.

How could something manmade hold so much weight and never collapse?

I stood there, alone, small beneath its shadow, and wondered if I could be like that.

If I could be made of something stronger than heartbreak.

If I could carry everything I'd lost and still not fall apart.

And maybe – I already was.

I was still standing.

Still breathing.

Still here.

A single tear slipped down my cheek, carving its path without apology.

I let it fall.

It deserved to be seen.

So did I.

A rustle cut through the rain – subtle, but enough to pull me out of the fog of my thoughts.

I turned slightly, peering out from beneath the edge of my umbrella.

Ugh.

Some guy was standing at the far end of the rooftop, bracing himself against the wind like some moody, windswept poet. He was staring up at the bridge like it held all the answers. No umbrella. No hood. Not even a hat to shield him from the downpour. Just soaking in the rain like he deserved it.

What a sap, I thought.

Ruining my personal moment of poetic solitude with his soggy silhouette.

I was just about to turn back, roll my eyes and head down the stairs, when he turned too – slowly, like a movie scene I didn't know I was in.

And then–

We locked eyes.

My breath caught. My heart cracked like ice underfoot.

"Eli?" I said, barely above a whisper.

But he heard it.

Of course he did.

Somehow, even through the rain–

He looked just as wrecked as I felt.

Maybe worse.

"Romy?"

A gust of wind pushed against me, cold and biting, as if the city itself was trying to pull me back.

But I stayed rooted in place.

Eli was there across the rooftop, standing like a mirage I didn't trust. The rain fell between us in sheets, the bridge stretching above like a cathedral of steel and regret.

I could barely see his face through the blur of it all. And yet somehow, I saw everything.

"Romy?" He said again, voice raw, barely holding together. Like he was afraid I might vanish if he said my name too loudly.

We stared at each other across the rooftop battlefield – neither of us brave enough to move first.

"What are you doing here?" He called out, louder now, over the wind, over the rain, over the screaming in my chest.

I hesitated, my hand white-knuckling the umbrella. My pulse was a drumline in my ears.

"Trying to forget!" I yelled back.

His body stiffened. He took a single, shaky step closer.

"Forget what?"

And then came the word that had been living in the back of my throat for weeks. Bitter, sharp, and soaked in truth.

"You."

The rain didn't even flinch. But he did.

Eli didn't move for a long time. He just stood there, his shoulders rising and falling, his mouth parted like the words had hit harder than he expected.

And then – he laughed. Just once. A hollow, broken sound.

"That makes two of us," he said, his voice catching on the last word.

Another gust of wind tore between us, and I thought for a moment he might disappear with it.

"I didn't expect to see you," I said, quieter now. "I came here to clear my head."

"I know," he said. "That's why I came."

I blinked. "Why?"

"Because I couldn't stop hearing your voice in mine."

That stopped me.

He stepped closer.

"I've been here before," he said. "But it never felt like anything until now."

I didn't say anything. Couldn't.

"You meant it?" He asked. "That you're trying to forget me?"

I hesitated. I could feel tears burning behind my eyes, but I refused to let them fall. I didn't want to cry in front of him. I didn't want to give him that. I didn't want to give *me* that.

"Yes," I said.

He swallowed hard, a muscle in his jaw twitching.

"Well," he said, voice barely audible over the rain, "you've always been better at letting go than I have."

I laughed, bitter and breathless. "No. I just do it first, so I don't have to watch you do it."

That landed. He winced like I'd slapped him. The words sat between us, cold and unmovable.

Another long silence.

"I listened to your episode," I said. My voice trembled. "I listened to it more times than I'll ever admit. You said all the right things. Every last word. But Eli – why now? Why only after everything broke?"

He closed the distance a little more. Ten feet. Maybe less. Rain dripping from his lashes, his chest rising and falling like he was trying to breathe through years of silence.

"You were this spark. This wildfire. And I'd spent my whole life building walls to make sure nothing ever got close enough to burn me. But then there you were – loud and sharp and *alive*, and I knew. I *knew* that if I let myself fall for you, I wouldn't come back the same."

He exhaled, like the truth was clawing its way out of him.

"And I wanted to. God, I wanted to. But wanting you

felt like standing on the edge of something I couldn't name. And I didn't trust myself not to fuck it up. So, I kept you at arm's length. I smiled and stayed casual and convinced myself that if I didn't name it, it wouldn't matter."

His eyes met mine, glassy and unblinking.

"But it did. It mattered more than anything ever has. And the scariest part wasn't losing you. The scariest part was knowing I *never really had you*, because I was too much of a coward to ask you to be mine."

He swallowed hard.

"You were brave enough to love me out loud. And I hid behind half-truths and timing and convenience, because I didn't believe I deserved someone like you. I didn't believe I could survive what loving you might cost me."

"I was scared too," I whispered.

"And you showed up anyway."

I didn't respond.

Eli kept talking, voice lower now, full of gravity and regret.

"I thought that if I didn't cross the line, I wouldn't ruin the one good thing in my life. But all that did was make you feel like you weren't wanted. And Romy–" He stepped closer, inches from me now. "I will never want for anything, the way that I want you."

My chest caved.

He looked at me like I was oxygen and he'd been drowning.

"I don't know how to fix what I broke," he said. "But I'm sorry. I'm sorry for all of it. If all I can do is stand here in the rain and tell you that you were never hard to love

– not once, not even a little – then that's what I'll do. Over and over."

My voice cracked. "You think that's enough?"

"I think it's a start," he said. "I think it's the only thing I know how to offer right now, besides the truth."

"And what's the truth?"

He stepped forward, no hesitation now.

"You are the greatest thing this life has ever given me. The only place I've ever felt known – not just seen, but known. You were never just a person to me, Romy. You were home, long before I even realized I was lost."

I sucked in a breath, teetering on the edge of something I wasn't entirely sure of.

"You weren't just a chapter in my life – you are the entire story. The only place I've ever wanted to end up."

He was close enough now that I could feel the warmth of him, even through the cold.

His eyes searched mine – desperate, open, unguarded.

"I don't want to be the voice in your headphones anymore," he said. "I want to be the one who shows up. Who stays. Who holds you when the world goes quiet. I want you in the mornings, in the chaos, in the calm, in the dark. I want *you*, Romy. Not almost. Not eventually. *Now.*"

The tears finally came. Hot and silent.

"And if it's too late," he whispered, "then I'll spend the rest of my life showing you it doesn't have to be."

My heart shattered.

A beat passed.

"I love you, Romy fucking Becker. I am deeply, eternally, maddeningly, in love with you."

And then – I dropped the umbrella.

It hit the ground with a soft thud. Water soaked through my sweater. I didn't care.

Because a second later, he stepped forward and grabbed my face and kissed me like he'd been waiting his whole life to remember how.

And just like that–

It wasn't raining anymore.

Not for us.

38
ONE LAST QUESTION

San Francisco in the fall always felt like a secret the city kept to itself. The air was sharp and salt-laced, curling in from the Bay with a kind of sacred hush. Fog clung low over the streets, weaving between lamp posts and rustling tree limbs like it had someplace to be. Leaves – what few the city had – twirled in loose, uncertain spirals across the pavement, red and brittle, like they were trying to hold on just a little longer before letting go.

Outside my apartment, everything looked silver.

The buildings were washed in morning mist, the sidewalks slick with last night's rain. You could hear the whoosh of Muni buses gliding through the quiet and the low murmur of someone's dog barking three floors up. A siren moaned in the distance, soft and stretched out, like even emergencies moved slower here in the cold.

I pressed my forehead to the window, watching my breath bloom across the glass.

It was the kind of morning that made you believe in blank slates. In do-overs. In maybes.

I wasn't sure how I felt these days, but if I had to sum it up in one word: happy. Life had a way of rewriting everything when you least expected it.

I'd lost it all once – held everything in my hands and watched it slip through my fingers. I thought that was the end of the story.

But it turns out, some things don't end.

They just... pause.

And come back different.

Truer.

Eli came up behind me without a word, as if drawn by instinct, and wrapped his arms around my waist, his body fitting against me like he'd been made for it. He pressed his lips to that place just beneath my ear, like he'd kissed me there a thousand times before and planned to do it a thousand more.

I closed my eyes. Let myself feel it.

The warmth of his chest against my back.

The safety of being held by someone who knew every version of me and stayed.

The stillness that only came when the noise finally stopped.

Every second, every minute, every hour of my life had been leading here.

To this room.

To this silence.

To this love that didn't ask me to be anything but myself.

His voice was a whisper, low and steady. "You ready?"

I didn't answer right away. Just let my eyes close. Let the moment stretch.

I leaned back, resting my head against his, breathing in the smell of him – coffee, rain, something steady.

"Yes," I finally said, certain, unwavering. "I'm ready."

We padded quietly through the apartment like we might wake something. There was something sacred about the silence between us. Something full. We passed the living room, stepped over a tangle of cords, a discarded hoodie, my *Twilight* socks. The city hummed outside – foggy and slow, the kind of morning where the world felt paused.

Then we were in the bedroom. In front of the closet.

Our closet.

The place where all of it had started.

The door creaked open, and everything was exactly as we'd left it. The same tiny space where this whole thing had started – a closet turned makeshift studio, littered with couch cushions pressed against the walls, wires tangled like vines. It still smelled a little like dust and a lot like memories.

We crawled in like old versions of ourselves – like time travelers. It was cramped, intimate, nostalgic. A little ridiculous – but it was ours. It had always been ours.

Eli adjusted the mic stand with the same easy grace he always had, and I folded myself onto a cushion, pulling my knees close to my chest. We didn't speak. Just settled in. Comfortable in the silence. Comfortable in each other.

The red light blinked on.

We were recording.

I leaned into the mic, my voice a teasing purr. "Hey," I said, winking at him. "Fancy meeting you here."

Eli smiled across the narrow space between us, his eyes bright, full of life. "Well, well. If it isn't the woman who turned an existential breakdown into a business model."

"Welcome, one and all, to this episode of *Not in the Mood*."

"I'm your host, Eli Reed."

"And I'm your much better host, Romy Becker."

We let the banter breathe for a beat; our smiles audible in the silence that followed.

"Before we jump in," Eli said, slipping effortlessly into his producer voice, "a reminder that you get fifteen percent off your order at Nest Theory Furniture, when you use promo code *Not in the Mood*, all one word, all lowercase, at checkout."

"Please note," I added, "we are not legally responsible if your new couch outlasts your relationship."

We laughed together – genuinely, easily, like the sound of healing.

Then I shifted.

My hand found his, our fingers curling together like roots. And when I spoke next, my voice was different. Quieter. More certain.

"Now, we'd like to take you on a journey."

"This episode's going to be a little different," Eli said. "no listicles. No dating horror stories. No half-hearted advice we're unqualified to give."

"Just us," I said.

We looked at each other. Really looked.

"We've been doing this podcast for a while now," I said. "What started as a joke between friends turned into something... bigger. And stranger. And honestly, more vulnerable than I ever thought I'd let myself be."

"It was supposed to be simple," Eli said. "a way to

laugh through the ache. A way to make sense of all the mess."

"And somehow, somewhere along the way, it became the place where we told the truth. Even when we didn't realize we were doing it."

I swallowed, the lump in my throat sudden and sharp.

"We told you everything except the most important part."

Eli nodded slowly. "That we fell in love."

It didn't sound like a revelation. It sounded like a fact. Like gravity.

"We didn't mean to," I said. "or maybe we did. Maybe we always knew. But we buried it under banter and edits and clever captions because it was easier than saying it out loud."

"We thought if we said it, it would break everything," Eli added. "turns out, not saying it did."

Silence again. Not uncomfortable. Just true.

"We thought about ending the podcast," I said. "thought maybe it had run its course. That we'd told all the stories we had to tell. That the premise – *two people who don't believe in love* – had finally outlived itself."

"But then we realized something," Eli said, turning slightly toward me. "The premise never really mattered. What mattered was the conversation."

"And the conversation isn't over," I said.

"So," He continued, "this is the final episode of *Not in the Mood*. But not the end of us."

"We're changing things," I said. "because we've changed."

"So, we're starting fresh," Eli added, "with a new

podcast, called *In the Mood.*"

I smiled. Not the bright, performative smile I used to hide behind – but something quieter. Softer.

"It's still us. Still the same messy, honest, sometimes stupid conversations. But now we're starting from a different place."

"Not from cynicism," Eli said. "not from distance."

"From love," I said. "from trying. From choosing each other every day, even when it's hard."

"Especially when it's hard," he echoed.

We sat in that. Let the red-light blink on. Let our breathing sync. Let the silence say what words hadn't.

"Thank you," I said. "to everyone who listened, who reached out, who saw us when we were still figuring out how to see ourselves. You gave us space to grow. And we're so grateful."

Eli nodded. "This podcast saved me, more times than I'll ever admit."

"It saved us," I said.

He turned to me then, something shining in his eyes. Not a tear, exactly. But something close. Something undone.

"So," I said, softly, "what do you want to talk about today?"

He looked at me like I hung the stars.

"You."

ACKNOWLEDGEMENTS

You may have noticed I dedicated this book to heartbreak, and although we aren't friends, and I hope to never see her again, none of this would have been possible without her. Equally important, thank you to all the men who made this book possible. You know who you are. Unfortunately, I do too. Sadly, you will not be named here because you don't deserve the publicity. Still – credit where it's due. Without you, I wouldn't have met heartbreak.

Thanks for the introduction.

Writing this book brought me face-to-face with parts of myself I thought were long healed – turns out, they were just quietly waiting for the right sentence to start sobbing. I cried more than a few times while writing, which is honestly impressive considering I'm on enough antidepressants to legally qualify as a pharmacy.

Some things in life you don't bounce back from. I've made peace with that. In fact, in a strange way, I hope I never fully recover. The pain reminds me it was real. That I tried. That I was brave enough to want something.

Even if I came up empty.

This book also wouldn't exist without the perfect storm of free time, courtesy of my post-op recovery.

Thank you, Dr. Carter, for slicing me open and giving me an accidental writing sabbatical. You're a real one.

To my brilliant friends, Mia and Grace, my beta readers, my dearest friends, and to whom I probably owe royalties to. Thank you for letting me talk obsessively about this book. I didn't know what it felt like to be special until I met you.

And lastly, to myself: thank you for not quitting. You're still here. Even on the days you don't want to be. And that counts for something.

It counts for everything.

ABOUT THE AUTHOR

Ariel Henwood is a writer, reader, and unapologetic romantic with a soft spot for sarcastic banter, messy friendships, and slow-burn love stories. When she's not writing about fictional heartbreak, she's probably over-caffeinating in San Francisco, haunting local bookstores, or adding "just one more" book to her ever-growing TBR pile. *Not in the Mood* is her debut novel.

Made in the USA
Monee, IL
25 August 2025

23877215R00218